# HYPNOTIC, TREMBLINGLY ALIVE

But where was I? The room was pitch black. Perhaps there was a bedside table with a lamp on it. I reached out to see, but my hand struck the wall. It would be on the other side, then. But my hand struck a wall there too. Walls abutted the bed on both sides of me. Then I reached up and touched the ceiling—only a few inches above my head. Surely the ceiling of the room couldn't be that low, I thought. The walls and low ceiling, I discovered, were padded. This was a box that I was in—a large, cloth-lined box. I was in a—

  *"Oh, God," I murmured. "No!"*

# *If The Reaper Ride*

## ᴀ Romance of Terrifying Dimensions

*Other Avon books by*
**Elizabeth Norman**

CASTLE CLOUD                                    31583   $1.95

# IF THE REAPER RIDE

## ELIZABETH NORMAN

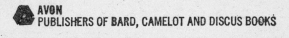

AVON
PUBLISHERS OF BARD, CAMELOT AND DISCUS BOOKS

*"for Lorana"*

IF THE REAPER RIDE is an original publication of Avon
Books. This work has never before appeared in book form.

AVON BOOKS
A division of
The Hearst Corporation
959 Eighth Avenue
New York, New York 10019

Copyright © 1978 by Elizabeth Norman
Published by arrangement with the author.
Library of Congress Catalog Card Number: 78-50881
ISBN: 0-380-01886-1

First Avon Printing, April, 1978

AVON TRADEMARK REG. U.S. PAT. OFF. AND IN
OTHER COUNTRIES, MARCA REGISTRADA,
HECHO EN U.S.A.

Printed in the U.S.A.

# Author's Note

SUZANNE DE RIOCOUR, the heroine of this book, really did exist, but her name was not Suzanne. It was, I believe, Lady Charlotte A., and I believe this story is basically her biography. The events described in it may well have been experienced by Lady Charlotte when she was a young girl. I can only guess how much of it actually occurred, but I can not believe that Lady Charlotte's life was ever in danger—at least not as Suzanne's life is threatened here.

The Warton Hall of this story existed too—though not by that name and not in Somerset—and it stands to this day. I was astonished to come across it in a picture book of English country houses looking exactly as I had described it and its gardens in *If the Reaper Ride* more than a year before. Shortly after that, I discovered that a Lady Charlotte A. had lived in the house in the 1850s and had continued to live there until her death in 1894.

I do not know if she wrote stories or novels during that time, but Lady Charlotte never had a novel published; at least I have found no book by her, nor does anyone in the family today know of any writings by the Lady Charlotte A. of ——— House.

Yet this book that you are about to read is her novel. I think it better not to attempt an explanation of this, nor even begin to describe the very odd, sometimes frightening, relationship I have had with Lady Charlotte or the things that have caused me to write her story down. But I must say that I have had to write some of it without her guidance and that it was often difficult to know when this happened. I do know, though, that this story is largely as she would have it because sometimes she would not permit what I had written to remain on the page, and then a sentence, a paragraph, or even several pages had to be destroyed.

However, the story is the important thing, and not how it came about. This one fascinates me, and I hope it will bring you pleasure. It is Lady Charlotte's story, not mine, and I am happy that it is to be published because I know she will be pleased.

E. N., New York, 1977

# ⚔ Chapter One ⚔

A CARRIAGE STOOD before the steps of the entrance front. I would find visitors at Warton Hall, then. This had not occurred to me. I had expected to meet my mother and new stepfather in private—not in front of strangers. So I willed the intruders to leave. During every moment of the long drive from the gateway to the house, I willed their carriage to move and carry them past us and away. But it did not move, and finally we swung around the battered old brougham and stopped in front of it.

Immediately my carriage door was opened for me by a footman wearing blue livery that matched the blue of our barouche and carrying an enormous umbrella of the same color. I had seen him hurry from the house and run down the stairs as we approached. Now he extended his hand to help me down, and I gathered up my skirts and stepped for the first time on the ground of my new home.

I glanced at the sky: at any moment, the storm would break. The world held its breath. The horses were quiet, the birds mute, the air still.

A heavy, heady fragrance enveloped us. Masses of roses perfumed the air but, though I looked about, I could see no roses growing. Instead, the massive stone facade of the building rose before me, stretching endlessly to my right and left.

Behind me stood the ragged, black brougham. Something made me turn and look into it. A man sat erect inside the carriage, and, before he pulled back into the shadows, our eyes met. I saw a pale, gaunt face fringed with straight, white hair. One eye was covered with a patch. A deep scar ran from beneath the patch and ended at the corner of his mouth.

In that moment, two lines from a poem that I had recited at school leapt to mind. "If the Reaper ride a carriage,/ All the world shall smell of roses." I shivered. Suddenly it seemed to have turned very cold.

Then thunder crashed, and enormous drops of rain plopped on the ground, followed by a rush of smaller ones. Followed by the footman holding the umbrella above me, I dashed up the steps and into the house through the downpour.

Once inside, I stood for a moment gasping for breath and straining my eyes in the gloom. To my astonishment, I found myself looking into another pair of eyes as startled as my own. They belonged to the most enormously fat man I had ever seen. He was out of breath. Wheezing, he pulled a handkerchief from his pocket, wiped his bald head, and laid a finger on the side of his nose.

"Who have we here?" he asked. Then he took a quivering step closer and thrust his tiny head close to mine, examining me.

I was too surprised to answer.

"A child," he said, "a visitor. The footman has your bag there. Yes. Can a flower of the spring be blooming in this winter's cave? Beware, my child. Avarice has laid its cold hand upon this place. 'Cassius, you yourself are much condemn'd to have an itching palm.' Shakespeare: *Julius Caesar*."

Without another word, he waddled slowly past me and out the entrance door into the rain, wheezing as he went. The footman followed him, holding the umbrella above his head. He had gone, I decided, to join his companion in the black carriage.

But the fat man had not left me alone: a second

2

footman stood beside the doorway. He directed me with a nod to the first landing of the grand staircase in front of me.

There in the semidarkness, where the staircase divided to flank opposite walls of the massive hall, a tall, thin man stood behind a little boy who held a large bird against his breast. The bird flapped one of its wings, which the boy was trying to hold still with his right hand.

While we stood there looking at each other, I heard the sound of wheels on the drive and the crunch of hoofs as the fat man's carriage drove away.

Well, I thought, we can't go on standing here like this. If they won't come down to me, I shall have to go up to them. And I began to walk across the marble floor and up the oak steps toward them. What fun it will be to have a little boy about. Perhaps we can—

But just then, lightning flashed outside the windows, lighting the staircase hall. I stopped, frozen by what I saw. The little boy was not a little boy at all, but an older man about four-and-a-half-feet tall with a strong-looking body and stunted legs. His right arm looked normal, but his left was baby sized and seemed fixed, at the elbow, at a right angle. It ended in a tiny, malformed hand that had only three fingers. And although he was trying to hold it still, the little arm moved up and down rapidly in uncontrolled spasms like the flapping wing of a bird.

I was so shocked by this that I could not move, nor could I stop myself from noting all the gruesome details of this grotesque little man. Then the thunder crashed and jerked me back to life.

"Come here!" snapped the dwarf.

I climbed the remaining steps and stood in front of him. I could see that he was in a fit of temper. He was so angry that he could barely speak.

"Apsley will take care of you," he said.

Then he ran down the stairs, across the hall, and

into a corridor to the right. In a moment I heard a crash from that direction. It sounded as if a large glass object had been hurled against the stone wall.

The sound did not seem to surprise the tall, thin man. In fact I saw no emotion on his face at all. He was Apsley, the butler.

"Titus," he called down to the footman who had just come in out of the rain, "would you please go and fetch Miss Clair for Miss de Riocour? She will be in the hall chamber."

And as Titus scurried away, he turned to me and said, "If you would follow me please, miss. Mrs. Danley, the housekeeper, has recently engaged a young woman whose name is Anna Clair. She is a young lady's maid with the very best character. Mrs. Danley hopes you will be completely satisfied with her. She will show you to your room and see that you have everything you require. Do not hesitate to call upon me or Mrs. Danley if there is anything you need. His lordship has most particularly stressed that everything be done to ensure your comfort at Warton Hall."

By this time we had descended the stairs to the ground floor and entered a small room off the hall.

No sooner had we stepped into it than he said, "Ah, here is Miss Clair now."

A well-scrubbed girl of about my own age, dressed in black, entered the room. When she stood before me, she gave me a very welcome and, I knew at once, a sincere smile.

"Will you want to go to your room straight away, miss?" she said. "You must be very tired and want a wash after your long trip."

"Yes, thank you," I said. "And thank you, Apsley."

Then Clair and I left the hall chamber together. Before ascending the stairs, we paused at a shelf to light candles, as it was by then quite dark.

"My bag," I thought aloud.

Clair laughed. "Don't you worry, miss. Titus will

4

be halfway to your room with it already. Why, are you feeling all right, miss?"

She had seen me put my hand to my forehead. I was very tired and almost faint with exhaustion.

"Oh, Clair," I whispered, "I just want to be sure that I am still in England—that it is still today. I feel as if we have gone back to another time."

"No, miss, you are still in England, and it is still the first of August 1856, and when you have seen the beautiful room you are to have, have washed, and had something to eat, you will be as sure of it as I am."

Then we climbed the stairs, this time all the way to the second floor, and turned to the left, beginning what was to be a long walk to my room. We walked down a straight corridor, past countless closed doors and heavily framed paintings, and then turned to the left again.

Clair said, "As you know, miss, some say Warton Hall is the grandest house in all England. I wouldn't be too sure about that because, after all, there are the palaces of the queen and the prince consort and the palaces of the dukes, but it is surely one of the largest and prettiest. . . ."

But I was not listening to Clair's patter. I could only think how hollow and empty I felt and how I should never have looked forward to coming here, never imagined arriving with my mother waving and standing by the front door with my new stepfather, the eighth earl of Trevenbury. Would he hold my hands? I had wondered. Would he kiss me on the cheek? In my fantasies, I had seen my mother smile, had heard her say how happy she was, now that we were together.

Well, they were not even here to meet me. This strange, enormous place. *Was* this to be my home from now on? And those horrible men. Who were they? And where was my mother? Why wasn't she here to greet me? And where was my stepfather? Why had they made me endure this monstrous welcome? I wished

5

I were back at school, among familiar people and familiar things.

Against my will, my eyes brimmed with tears, blurring my candle. I stumbled against a low object and would have fallen if Clair hadn't grasped my arm.

"Oh! Please, miss," she said. "I should have warned you about those steps. They jut out into this corridor whenever a cross corridor comes into it. There, are you all right? I would never have forgiven myself if you had fallen and hurt yourself. Do watch out for the steps. There are more down the way. They shouldn't have been put there for people to trip over.

"We are halfway there now. It must seem a long way the first time. You see, the house is built like a great hollow square, and those narrow cross corridors connect the four sides and form the courts. Warton Hall has six interior courts."

It could have had fifty for all I cared. I was wretchedly tired, much too tired to think, and all I wanted to do was go to bed and let this miserable evening drain away into sleep. Tomorrow, when I was rested and my head was clear, I would think.

"Here we are, miss," Clair announced at last.

She flung open a door to a large room filled with the warm light of several lamps. The curtains were drawn and the bed turned down. I was too tired to notice much else. The colors were yellows and golds, and someone had placed a large bowl of yellow roses on a table next to a white porcelain elephant.

Then, almost magically, a housemaid brought a jug of hot water. After I had washed, dinner arrived on a tray. I ate mechanically. I remember braised veal with a lemony sauce and fresh raspberries.

As I ate, Clair unpacked my bag and hung my four dresses away. I was vaguely uneasy about such a poor showing, but I didn't want to think about it then. I didn't want to think about anything: I wanted to be left alone. Clair seemed to sense my mood, and after

I had finished eating, she picked up the tray and started from the room.

"Good night," she said. "If there is anything you need, I will be in the servants' hall. Just use the bell pull there."

She was almost through the door when I remembered.

"Clair, who is the dwarf?"

"Why, Lord Trevenbury, miss, your stepfather," she said. "Didn't you know? Good night. Sleep well."

She closed the door silently behind her.


For some moments I watched the needle-thin streak of light lying across the gold flowers on their yellow ground, and then I realized what it was. A shaft of sunlight had found its way between the curtains and slashed at the wall with its brilliance. And I realized that I lay in my bed at Warton Hall.

Then every detail of my arrival the night before flew into its proper place in a vivid reality that fell heavily to the bottom of my stomach.

But this was a new day, I thought, throwing aside the covers. After pulling the curtain cords, I stood before the windows, bathed by the sun and entranced by what lay before me.

The windows reached to the floor and opened onto a balcony—actually the roof of a porch. It was edged with a stone balustrade. The balusters themselves were carved stone figures.

I pushed open one of the windows and walked out onto the balcony into a cool, scented morning. I looked down at the roses—large, full, double ones hung their heavy heads with the weight of dew, little, single ones flocked in brilliant masses, and straight, sturdy-stemmed ones stood rigid and proud. Yellow roses, white roses, pink roses, red roses abounded. Roses in bud, roses in full bloom with falling petals—thousands of them!

The roses were arranged in intricate, formal beds edged with low hedges of box; and separated by gravel walks of different widths. Beyond the rose garden lay a formal garden, surrounded by a high, beautifully clipped yew hedge. A fountain flashed a shower of crystal. Beyond this stood an orangery and then a cluster of glasshouses. More gardens stretched to the left toward a stable block and to the right toward soft lawns lying on either side of a little river. The river was spanned by a white marble bridge, its roof held up by columns and arches.

To form a background for all this, there were oaks, chestnuts, beeches, and elms, tremendous trees all planted long ago and beautifully massed to give the effect of having grown there by chance.

Beyond the trees rose a steep, grassy hill on top of which was a temple or pavilion, a lovely building with a round colonnaded portico. Its roof held something, perhaps a golden bird.

The scene was too beautiful to be real. I flung my arms wide, whirled to face my room, and then back again to the sun. It *was* real, and I was part of it now.

"Good morning, miss."

"Oh! Good morning, Clair. You startled me. Isn't it a marvelous morning, and isn't this"—I swung my arm to encompass the view—"unbelievable?"

"Yes, miss. I brought your tea tray up and put it on the little table by your bed. Did you sleep well?"

"Yes, thank you, Clair. Bring it here, please, and put it on the table by the window."

She brought the tray and set it down. The tea set on it was white, patterned with violets. I poured my tea and then took a slice of bread and butter. The bread was sliced very thin, the butter still cool and delicious.

While I sipped my tea, a housemaid, a terribly thin

woman with protruding, haunted eyes, brought hot water and tidied the washstand. Then she placed a hip-bath on its sheet and poured the water for my bath. And as I bathed, Clair began laying out my things for the day and putting away the clothes of the night before.

While she puttered about, I lay back thinking what a lovely room I had been given. It was called the yellow velvet room because of the magnificently patterned yellow velvet hangings of the four poster bed. The walls were yellow also, and covered with gold-framed engravings of the queen and Albert, as well as her uncle, William IV, the duchess of Kent, the duke of Wellington, the dukes of Cumberland and Sussex, and views of Warton Hall and its grounds. Yellow fabrics had been used on the furniture: at the foot of the bed stood a pillowed couch in pale yellow silk; and a deep arm chair, covered in yellow orange damask, stood next to one of the bedside tables. Two other chairs and the table with the roses and white elephant furnished the Alcove. But other colors had been used, too. Red and orange Turkish carpets covered the floor, and on the mantel sat two beautiful blue Chinese porcelain vases. Above them hung a portrait of the sixth earl of Trevenbury. This had been his wife, Harriet's, bedroom.

I finished my bath, and Clair brushed my hair as I sat gazing out of the open window, admiring the lovely pattern the sun made on the building on the hill.

"What is the building on top of the hill, Clair?" I asked.

"That is the Trevenbury mausoleum, miss. That is where all the earls and their families are buried."

A gong sounded as we talked, and Clair moved hurriedly toward my clothes.

"We will have to make haste," she said. "That gong is for morning prayer. That is at nine, and breakfast is at nine-thirty, and his lordship insists that everything be on time."

I finished dressing, and we hurried toward the chapel. As we went, Clair explained that a young curate, a Mr. James Bowden from Taunton—the town beyond Fawsley, where the household attended services every Sunday—rode all the way to Warton Hall every morning to say morning prayer.

"I have heard," she said, "that the rector from Fawsley used to say the service here, but it is said that the Reverend Ashley and his lordship are not on the best of terms."

By then we had arrived at the open doors of the chapel. The staff, in a single line of forty-five or fifty people arranged according to rank, was just passing through them.

"The family pew is the first one, nearest the altar," Clair whispered. "I sit in the second pew with Mr. Apsley, Mrs. Danley and Madame Mérinée, your mother's maid."

Then she drew back to allow me to enter alone.

The chapel could seat sixty or seventy people, and it wasn't quite full. As I walked down the aisle, I knew that everyone was looking at me. I glanced up at the lofty, dark, hammer-beam roof and then at the brilliant windows of painted Flemish glass and hoped I didn't look as ill at ease as I felt.

Finally I reached the blessed haven of the family pew and sat down. I sat there alone—my mother and Lord Trevenbury were not present. I was not surprised by this: Clair had said that they rarely attended morning prayer, but that they especially wished the staff to do so. I made up my mind then and there that I would never miss the service if I could help it.

It was a very short service, and when Mr. Bowden had finished, Apsley got up from the pew behind me and walked to the front of the altar.

He looked down at me and said in a loud voice,

"Miss de Riocour, on behalf of the staff, I wish to bid you welcome to Warton Hall. We all wish to extend our warmest good wishes. May your days here be happy ones. Please be assured that every one of us will do everything possible to make that wish a reality."

I was so surprised and touched by this little welcoming speech that all I could do was to stand and turn to all those beaming, expectant faces and stutter, "Thank you—thank you all *very* much."

But Mr. Bowden rescued me.

"And may I echo those fine sentiments, Miss de Riocour," he said, coming to stand beside me.

Then he accompanied me down the aisle and out of the chapel. We were followed first by Apsley, then by a twinkling little woman who I suspected was Mrs. Danley, the housekeeper, and then, one by one, by the rest of the staff.

Outside in the corridor, Mr. Bowden excused himself, saying that he had to hurry back to Taunton. Mrs. Danley introduced herself.

"Did you have a comfortable night, Miss de Riocour?" she asked with a wide smile. "I wanted to get up to see you last night, but I thought you might be too tired to want company. Is there anything you need? Is there anything that is not quite right? Please tell me about it." And after a slight pause, seeming satisfied, she went on, "Now, if you will excuse me, I must hurry away. We have a new housemaid, and I must show her just how we like things done here. And you must have your breakfast. Mr. Apsley, does Miss de Riocour know the way to the breakfast room?" And then she was gone.

Apsley showed me to the breakfast room. Coventry, the second footman, had just finished placing the hot dishes on the sideboard when we entered. There were dishes of scrambled and soft-cooked eggs, hot bacon, a side of cold bacon, ham toast, two kinds of fish,

11

porridge, little sausages, steaks, and fried cakes. And on the table stood silver pots of butter, honey, marmalade and jams of all kinds, and bowls of fruit. Coventry helped me to be seated. Apsley asked what I would like, and, when I had decided, he brought me two soft-cooked eggs, sliced ham, a hot scone, and coffee.

"Apsley, will his lordship and her ladyship be down to breakfast?" I asked.

"No, miss. His lordship rode off very early to Weymouth on business, I believe, and will probably not be returning until late afternoon. Her ladyship is not feeling well this morning and is having her breakfast in her room. Madame Mérinée told me before prayers that during the night she had one of those terrible headaches that make her very ill."

"Thank you for telling me, Apsley. Then I shall not disturb her."

"No, miss. Luncheon is at one o'clock in the dining room."

After breakfast, I found my way back to my room and changed into an old, comfortable pair of walking shoes. I would need them: I had decided to go exploring. What else could I do? Since there was no one to ask about the house and its surroundings, I would have to find out as much as I could for myself. And besides, it was a glorious morning for a walk.

But first I wanted to find my way to the porch below my balcony. This would lead me to the rose garden. Perhaps a stairway that opened off the far end of the corridor beyond the door to my room would take me to a hall below and then to the porch. I went that way. The stairway spiraled down to a landing with a door leading into a very long parlor. Beyond a wide doorway at the end of the room lay another parlor, and beyond it yet another. But at last I found the door to the porch and went out onto it.

From there I descended to the rose garden, choosing the path that led to the orangery. Beyond the orangery lay the hill that I wished to climb to see the view. But I did not wish to climb to the mausoleum, though I could see it looking down at me. No, my destination was farther along the hilltop, nearer the house.

At once, however, I was captivated by the flowers. Roses have always been my special passion, and as I walked along the path, I recognized a few late-blooming old friends: La France, Medea, Boule de Neige, Merveille de Lyon. But there were countless enormous blossoms completely new to me, and I stopped to ask a gardener about them. He knelt, digging in a bed among a mass of huge yellow blooms.

"Good morning," I said. "I've never seen roses like these before. What are they?"

"China," he replied, "come all the way from China, some of 'em. Others are mixtures. Reverend Hollingsworth—he brought 'em over hisself, he did, from the other side of the world, he did. His lordship, the late earl, was a friend of his, and he sent 'em over. As you see, miss, these bloom all summer long, not just mainly in June. Wouldn't be worth growin' roses in June when they's still all in London, you see."

Then he resumed his digging, having forgotten me, and I ambled on, admiring these new enormous flowers—stopping to drink in the particular fragrance of a blossom here and to reach out and touch another there. I felt the sun, warm on my hand. It beat down through a delicate breeze that mixed the rose fragrance with the musty, moist odor of earth. And the garden air was filled with the buzz of bees, busy at their work.

At the end of the rose garden, the walk led through an arched opening in the yew hedge, and there stood the fountain in the center of four large squares of perfect lawn that fronted the orangery. I stepped inside the building for a moment. Its glass roof had been whitewashed against the summer sun. The air was heavy with moisture and tart with the scent of orange and lemon trees. They stood in pots, covered with little green fruit that would be ripe in January.

But I did not stay long. Too many other things remained to be seen, though it would have taken a week of wandering to see all the gardens. I had reached one edge of them, however, when I came to the glasshouses behind the orangery. Beyond them, I stepped into the cool shade of a wood, and I was glad, for I had begun to feel hot and thirsty. Ahead, I could see the base of the hill and I followed the path leading up it.

The path ended near the hilltop where, to my delight, a spring poured in a stream from a hole in the rock into a marble basin near the ground. I bent and drank greedily and splashed the icy water on my face and wrists.

Then I sat down on an iron bench in the shade to examine the view. Below me, Warton Hall and its environs lay like a map come to life. The great, square stone house, three stories high, sat staunchly on its green plain. It would have been cold and austere if it were not for the ornaments and statues that stood a few feet apart all along the rooftop balustrade, and towers and turrets that rose from the interior courts and stood upon the roof, poking their round and square and hexagonal heads yet another story higher to look about, and, of course, the countless banks of chimneys. The house was like a square, flat-sided cake topped with all the fantasy peaks and pinnacles a pastry chef could imagine. And there, sure enough, were the six interior courts.

I could not see the entrance front, where I had arrived the day before. It was on the other side of the house. But I could see the long, straight drive down which I had ridden and the emerald park stretching away in front of the house, treeless and plain. Above it the sky was intensely blue and filled with cotton clouds that cast their moving shadows on the green lawns. And out beyond the gateway, beyond another mile or so of rolling fields lay the empty, blue-gray sea.

Just to the left of the house, curved the river. Beyond it, screened from the building by trees, lay the farm that supplied the house with food. To its right lay the stable block, a long, low line of one-story buildings built around an oblong yard as large in area as the house. Beyond it, a road ran through a fringe of trees and then past the ruins of what must have been a large abbey. It was set in its own park surrounded by oaks. It appeared to be very old, possibly eleventh or twelfth century. Its bleak stone skeleton, roofless and windowless, lay bleaching in the sun. And in the distance, beyond the abbey, a church spire, at the outskirts of the village, rose to the sky.

So this was what lay at the end of my journey. The day before, at about this same time, I had been wondering what my new home would look like. I had been at school then. I had been at school for the last eleven of the seventeen years of my life—most recently at Miss Busser's School for Girls in Woolwich, just outside London.

Three days before, after luncheon, Miss Busser had called me to her study and told me that my stepfather, the earl of Trevenbury, had requested that I be sent without delay to Warton Hall, Somerset. I would be expected on the train arriving in Taunton at seven-thirty in the evening on Friday, August first. I would be met at the station. I was to bring all my personal belongings with me as I would not be returning to school. And so, on the appointed day, I had kissed Miss Busser goodbye—I had become very fond of that rather mannish, big-hearted woman, whose two loves were teaching her girls and riding her magnificent horses—and waved farewell to the school as her coachman drove me through the gates and toward

London. There, from Paddington Station, the train had left on time. And I had been on it, dreaming all the way.

I had dreamed, not of the luxury I knew would be waiting for me—Warton Hall was one of the great houses of England—but of a home, a mother and father. I had expected, if not love, at least warmth and affection.

Filled with expectations, I had been met at the railway station by Martin, the coachman, and driven to the house, where Lord Trevenbury had given me the coldest possible welcome. He had been terribly angry, but that had certainly been no fault of mine. And my mother had ignored me entirely.

Why am I here at all? I wondered. Why is *this* the end of my journey? All those people, down there, have their lives to lead, their work to do, their loves to love. Where do I fit in?

A sparrow interrupted my thoughts. He fluttered to the marble basin beside me and drank, ducking his beak and then holding his head back, watching me all the time with his little glassy eyes.

"Well, little bird," I whispered to him, "I have always been able to manage, and I shall manage here."

Then the sparrow flew off, and I stood and began to descend the hill. Soon it would be time for luncheon.

# ⚔ Chapter Two ⚔

THE DINING ROOM at Warton Hall was on the north side of the house, beyond the serving pantry from the breakfast room. It was a long, formal room with the longest table I had ever seen. Eight chairs had been drawn up along each side of it with plenty of space between them.

I sat in lonely, silent splendor while Apsley carved a lovely roast and Coventry served the food. The table was set with beautiful silver and china, but as I ate, I noticed that there were no flowers on it. Wasn't it strange that there were no flowers in the room or anywhere else in the house except for the roses in my room?

The silence made me uncomfortable, so I said, "Apsley, I suppose the ruins that I saw today were an abbey at one time?"

"I wouldn't know, miss, I'm sure," he replied. "Antiquities are not of interest to me at all, you see. Mr. Bowden or, better still, the Reverend Ashley over at Fawsley would be able to tell you all about it, I am sure. You have had a long walk this morning, miss. Did you get as far as Fawsley, the village beyond? His lord and her ladyship and the staff go to services there every Sunday."

It occurred to me that my behavior would be the big topic of conversation in the servants' hall and that the servants must be nearly as curious about my future at Warton Hall as I was. Apsley, having the supreme rank of butler—there was no house steward at Warton Hall—and Mrs. Danley the housekeeper, would surely be looked to for information about me. I could afford to be generous.

"No, Apsley, I didn't walk to the ruins. I walked through the gardens to the orangery and up the hill to the spring, along the hill from the mausoleum. It is a wonderful view from there. The grounds are so beautiful. I have really fallen in love with it all."

"Is that so, miss? Well, I am very pleased, indeed, to hear you say so."

I did not continue because at that moment Coventry handed me a steaming raspberry ice. As I tasted it, I noticed that Apsley fiddled at the sideboard, obviously waiting, hoping that I would say more.

Now was the time to ask the question I had wanted to ask all during luncheon. "Apsley, I am very curious. Who was the very portly man who called on his lordship last night?"

Apsley hesitated a moment, and then he answered, "The name on the card was Martin Shark, miss. If there is nothing further you require, miss, Coventry will bring you coffee directly."

Then he hurried away into the pantry, and Coventry followed, leaving me to finish my dessert in solitude.

When I had finished my coffee, I wandered into the summer parlor, the long corner parlor that I had passed through on my way to the rose garden that morning. There I noticed from the window that wide steps led from a flagged yard down to the basement below me. The yard must be the kitchen courtyard, I thought. Yes, there beyond it was the herb garden. From the yard a wide, cobbled lane led past the herb garden directly to the stables.

I wanted to see the horses, and the cobbled lane seemed to be a simple way of getting to the stables. So, determined to find the exit to the yard, I descended

18

the stairs I had used that morning and then down yet another flight toward the distant clatter of pots banging and voices chattering. There on a landing below, a door stood open. I walked through it and climbed the steps to the yard. I stood for a moment, watching the trout and pike swimming in the fish still, an artificial pond in which fish for the table swam to cleanse themselves of their muddy river taste. But then, from behind me, wheels sounded on the paving stones, interrupting my reverie. I turned around to see a gnarled, bent old man slowly pulling a wagon toward me. It was a very large wagon, beautifully made of a pale, varnished wood with the Trevenbury crest painted on its side. It had enormous rear wheels and much smaller front ones. The wagon was filled with vegetables, freshly washed and partially covered with sacking to shield them from the sun. The man must have pulled this heavy load all the way from the farm to the stable block.

"Good afternoon," I said. "May I have one of your carrots? I am on my way to the stables, and a carrot might help me to make a friend or two there."

The man dropped the handle of the wagon, and I expected that he would straighten up, but he did not. He seemed permanently bent.

He grinned at me and cocked his head. His eyes, one more open than the other, twinkled, and he said, "Ye'll not need carrots to make friends with, miss, and that be clear for the eye to see." He chuckled. "But I'd be pleased for 'e to take the lot of 'em, miss, or as many as 'e would like."

He thrust a large bunch at me holding them by their tops, and I tore two large carrots from it.

"Thank you," I said. I couldn't help laughing. "Thank you twice."

And he laughed up at me in return.

A dozen saddle horses stood in the nearest range of

boxes, and there was room for more than a dozen more beyond. A magnificent black hunter drew my attention at once. He was a huge, intelligent-looking animal with a wide forehead and bright, prominent eyes. I walked to him quietly and offered a piece of carrot. He took it very gently from my palm, and I was about to offer him another when someone spoke from behind me.

"Don't go near him, miss."

The horse lurched away, and I turned and walked toward the groom who had just entered from the yard.

"Why shouldn't I?" I demanded. I didn't like being given orders by a groom.

"He's a killer, miss."

"Nonsense!"

"He trampled a man to death once, miss, I saw him do it. He did it on purpose. He is a killer, he is."

This man had steel in his eyes. He was not being impertinent, but he was not being friendly, either. He was simply doing what he felt he must. I liked that.

"I am sorry," I said. "You startled me. The animal seems so gentle. Will you tell me about him?"

The tension left the man's eyes then, and he relaxed a little.

"Well, miss," he began, "we had a groom here about two years ago by the name of Meagher. The Saturday after his old lordship passed away, in comes Meagher leading this big black gelding. 'Whose horse is that, Meagher?' I asked. 'Mine. Bought him in Weymouth,' he says. 'And what are you going to do with him?' I asked. 'Keep him,' he says. 'Better ask Benson about *that*,' I says. Benson was the head coachman here at the time, miss. Well, Benson says he can keep the horse here as we didn't any of us know what would happen to us when his new lordship came.

"Well, the horse took to hating Meagher from the start, and I can't say I blame him, and after a time Meagher got to hating the horse. He used to beat him and starve him and kick him, and the horse would hardly let him near. When Meagher did get on him, he either wouldn't move or would rear and buck like a mad thing.

"One of them had to win the battle, and it was the horse, miss. One morning he threw Meagher in the yard over there and turned and trampled him to death, he did, before anyone could stop him. Smashed his skull flat. We had to pull him away from the body. He went mad, the horse did."

"Horrible!"

"Yes, miss. Well, no one's rode him since. His lordship says he's a fine piece of horseflesh and we'll keep him, but we don't ride him, miss, even to exercise him. We turn him loose in the paddock, there. He's a devil, miss, and if you take my advice, you'll stay away from him."

"Thank you. I appreciate your concern for me, but I don't believe a horse is inherently bad any more than any other animal is. Any animal will respond to love and kindness and patience."

Just then someone called his name from across the stable yard.

"Excuse me, miss," he said, turning to go.

"John," I said, "thank you for telling me."

"That's quite all right, miss," he said, as he strode off across the yard.

But I was not left alone. A little boy, about eight years old, with a pink, cherubic face stood gazing up at me with something akin to rapture. He seemed to have arrived by magic. His scrutiny embarrassed and amused me at the same time.

"Hello," I said.

At once he became very serious. "I'm the 'tiger,'" he said, "and my name's Monckton. People call me Monk."

I had heard of "tigers." They were little boys who

21

sat on the boxes of aristocratic carriages, their arms folded as they sat very upright and solemn in their resplendent livery. They really *were* called "tigers." I suppose someone had given them the name in jest, and it had stuck.

"Monk, what is the name of the big black gelding?"

"Thunder, miss. He's a killer, he is."

"He is a beauty."

"Not as fine as Bourton. That's the bay gelding over there. That's his lordship's private horse. He won the Grand National in 1855, and his lordship bought him right after. His owner didn't want to sell, but he couldn't help but take two thousand guineas for him."

"How do you know that?" I asked.

"His lordship told me, he did, miss. You should see them ride. Oh, yes, miss, they go like the wind. Have you seen the carriage horses and the saddle room and the blacksmith's shop? If you'd like to see them, I'd be pleased to show them to you, miss."

And he did.

After our tour, I returned to the house. It was four o'clock by that time, and I wanted to be quiet in my room to think and perhaps to take a nap before dressing for dinner.

I was halfway to my room when I had a feeling there was someone behind me. It was not that I had seen or heard anything, but I turned my head nevertheless and saw a woman gliding slowly down the hall toward me. She carried herself like a queen—but like a queen walking in her sleep. Her heavy, dark gray muslin riding habit, cut full but plain, moved without a sound. She was very beautiful, probably in her middle thirties, with flawless, milky skin, a faint touch of rose at the cheekbones, and enormous blue eyes under heavy lids.

She was removing her gloves. The jeweled handle of her riding crop flashed from under her arm. And when she had drawn quite near, I noticed bits of grass clinging to her skirt.

She walked in a dream world of her own and was about to pass me when she became conscious that she was not alone. She paused and looked at me for a long moment with those enormous eyes, and a ghost of a smile.

"Suzanne?" she said. "My dear. So you are here. I hope you have everything you need. You won't be lonely, will you? I can not imagine why Fitz insisted that you come—you would have been so much happier staying at school with the other girls to keep you company."

"You are—" I began.

"Not now, dear." She raised an exquisite hand to her temple and shut her eyes for a moment. "I must lie down."

And she began to move once more, slowly, down the hall, away from me. Then she paused, opened a door, and disappeared.

Moments after that, I began to run. I ran down the hall to my room, opened the door, stepped inside, and slammed the door shut with all my might, glaring at it, hoping that it would fall from its hinges.

"Miss! What is it?" Clair asked. She had backed toward the table and held onto it with both hands behind her.

"I have, for the first time in my memory, met my mother," I said. "I have always wondered what she would be like—she never visited me—hardly ever wrote—"

And then all the deep, buried hurt of years seemed to come alive and swell, rushing to my eyes and throat to be let out. I crumpled into the deep yellow chair and burst into tears. Immediately, Clair was on her knees beside me, holding my hands and murmuring

23

that it was going to be all right. Finally my sobs became less frequent, and I lay back drained, wiping away the tears with Clair's handkerchief.

"I have needed to do that for years," I said. "I could see, just now, in her face, what I have been fighting not to believe all my life, and now I know it is true. She doesn't care the slightest about me."

A little while later, Clair was saying, "It is enough to make you wonder if there is any reason behind anything, miss. There was Virginia, daughter of Viscount Warburton. She was pretty and her father had given her a very good dowry, which made her very popular with the gentlemen. She was in the middle of her London season—I was her personal maid before I came here, miss. In the middle of her London season, when she was very happy, miss, she came down with cholera, and she died. It was horrible. She should have stayed alive and married and been happy.

"Now, my father was the blacksmith in Maiden Weston, near Weston House, Dorset, and he came to Weston House once a week to operate the blacksmith's shop there. That is where he met my mother, miss, who was Lady Pendrook's maid. My mother was French, and Lady Pendrook brought her to England with her when she returned from a trip to the Continent."

*"Alors, tu parles français!"*

"Oh, no, miss, I never learned to speak French. My mother and father lived in a cottage at Weston House then, but my father died when I was five years old. Why did he have to die, miss, and leave my mother all alone? There doesn't seem to be a reason for anything, does there, miss?"

"And your mother, Clair?" I asked.

"She is still in the best of health, thank you, miss. And she is still with her ladyship at Weston House, and a very fine lady she is. I like her very much.

"Mother and I write regularly, and I manage to get over to Weston House quite often to see her. She is just as interested in fashion as she always was. I received a letter from her yesterday. She said that friends of hers in Paris have seen the empress wearing the crinoline more and more, and she seems to be endorsing it. Mother said that this will make skirts even wider, and how will ladies get through a doorway?"

"I suppose, then, that doorways will just have to be widened," I said. "Oh, Clair, you make me feel much better. But no wonder you sew and are so clever with my hair, if your mother was French."

"Yes, miss, she taught me a great deal. I am very grateful for that. What will you wear to dinner tonight, miss? I have some very pretty rose ribbon. Your gray merino dress would be so pretty edged with it, and I could make bows of it for the shoulders."

"Thank you, Clair. That is very thoughtful. I know my school dresses are plain, but they are all I have. I cannot be ashamed of my poor clothes before my mother and stepfather because *they* haven't given me something better to wear. You are quite right—I shall wear the gray merino. But I shall wear it as it is, and I would like you, please, to do my hair very plainly to keep it company. We shall see if they plan for me to look differently.

"Dinner is at seven-thirty? That will give me an hour to rest. What is the name of the housemaid who brings my water?"

"Dorothy Sloanes, miss."

"Would you ask Dorothy to bring a can of hot water at six? I would like to bathe before dinner. Now, will you help me out of my dress, please."

After she had done so, I lay down on the couch, and Clair drew the curtains.

"I will leave you then, until six, miss."

"Clair, before you go, I have been meaning to

25

thank you for the roses. I love the yellow ones, and they are so pretty on the table."

"I didn't put the roses there, miss. I thought your mother did."

I was sure she had not.

I wondered who had. But then I closed my eyes, and my mind began to wander. I thought how easily I was lapsing into the luxury of being waited on. And then I wondered about dinner. How would they act during it, and what would they say? I dreaded the meal as much as I looked forward to it.

"His lordship and her ladyship are in the corner room, miss," Apsley said, as I reached the bottom of the grand staircase. "Through the hunting room and the tapestry room, there."

I could see them from the tapestry room. They stood in the corner room before a high, elaborately carved, white-marble chimney piece. The painting above it was, I felt certain, a Rembrandt. Directly beneath it, Mother faced my stepfather. The fingers of her right hand touched the chin of her tilted head. The dwarf's head reached only to the level of my mother's breasts.

She wore a very low-cut, off-the-shoulder dress of deep peach satin, which complimented her creamy skin and showed off her full bosom and blue eyes to perfection. Its skirt was elaborately flounced to the ground, and it was swathed with pale yellow tulle, embroidered with white flowers. Her wheat-colored hair was parted in the center, swept severely back, and gathered behind her head in a bouquet of flowers— tiny yellow and white silk ones. She needed no jewelry and wore none.

As I drew nearer, I heard her say, "But surely, Fitz, it couldn't have been necessary—"

Then they saw me. And as I walked into the room, I could hear the brush of my skirt on the carpet.

"Good evening, Mother and Lord Trevenbury," I said.

Mother's eyes rested on me for a moment. But then, with an almost imperceptible smile, she looked down at the carpet, seeming to withdraw into her dream world. My stepfather's eyes bore up into mine, and then over my dress and every detail of me in quick, cold appraisal.

"Sit down," he said.

A table separated two chairs in front of the hearth, facing into the room. Mother and I sat down in them, and my stepfather stood before us, silent, still, almost triumphant—his eyes not far above the level of my own. I could only think: please don't let his little arm start to flap.

"Our little girl has arrived," he said. "We hope our style of life will not be hard to get used to after the plainness of school." His eyes traveled over my dress again. "We live well. As well as anyone in England. Most people would be uncomfortable. Most people would not know enough of the etiquette important to people of our position. Most people would give a great deal simply to *see* the inside of this house. You are lucky. You will live in it. This house has 114 rooms—not counting the kitchens, etcetera." He paused and looked at me expectantly. "What do you think of that?"

"It—it is a very large house," I answered.

"Yes," he continued, watching me carefully. "We have ten carriages and thirty-four horses. Horses for carriages and horses for saddle. My gardens cover sixteen acres. I have twelve gardeners. There are fifty people in staff in the house, thirty people outside—not including the farm."

Again he paused. His eyes narrowed.

"Eh?" he questioned.

"A great number of people to superintend," I replied, being required to say something.

I was astonished by his behavior and most uncomfortable. His eyes never left mine. He never moved.

I glanced sideways, from him to my mother. She sat still, her hands beautifully posed in her lap, gazing at the carpet.

"I own 160,643 acres of land," my stepfather said. "Net income 231,322 pounds last year. I manage it. I know where every penny comes from." His red eyebrows rose, trying to reach his sparse, tufty red hair. His eyes stared into mine. Again the pause.

"You are a very wealthy man, indeed, and a very clever one," I said.

"My horse won the Grand National. I bought him that day—paid 2,000 guineas for him." He spoke loudly and actually bent toward me from the waist.

"Marvelous! You must be the envy of the countryside." Had I gone too far? I had nothing to lose by pleasing him.

He straightened up and beamed, then strutted in a little circle in front of me, inviting my admiration—rather like a pigeon strutting before its ladylove. The performance would have been horribly pathetic if there had not been a great deal of brutal strength about the little man.

Then, thank heaven, Apsley announced dinner, and we went into the dining room. Mother tucked her hand under the dwarf's arm, and I followed them.

Mother sat at one end of the long table, my stepfather at the other, and I in the middle of one side, facing the windows. The curtains had been drawn, and we dined by the light of two enormous silver candelabras standing at either end of the table. Before me, nesting in its porcelain holder, a tiny menu card indicated that dinner would be a long, formal one.

I was not hungry.

"Clear or white soup, miss?" Coventry asked.

"Clear, please," I said.

Dinner had begun. During the meal, Apsley would carve from the sideboard and pour the wines, and Coventry and Titus would pass the food.

They moved noiselessly on the deep carpet. The only sound in that hushed room was the sucking sound my stepfather made as he ate his soup.

I wanted to say something to break the silence. I began, "Lord Trevenbury—"

But he interrupted me as he wiped his mouth. He had finished his soup, drinking the last of it from the dish, which he held in his right hand.

"I have the most beautiful wife in the world. Now I have a daughter. I am your stepfather. You will call me father. I have always wanted a family. I have always wanted the love of a family—the peace and beauty of the family together in the evening. 'It is more useful to be loved than venerated. Take away love and our earth is a tomb.'" He smiled at me with exaggerated graciousness.

I was sure he had memorized that last part from Browning. But why on earth should *he* be reading Browning? I must try to find the poem, I thought.

Next came the fish, which we ate in silence. I could think of nothing to say.

"Champagne, miss?"

"No thank you, Apsley."

It was during the meat course that the interrogation began, and it lasted through the serving of game and well into the savories.

What had I been taught at school? Did I know the names of the classics? Yes, I did. Name them. I named all I could think of. My stepfather stared at me intently as I answered his questions. Had I read any of them? Yes. Which ones? I named them. Had I read anything else? No, I didn't like popular novels or magazines. Did I read the newspapers? No, I did not. Did I play the piano? Yes, I did. What did I play? I

told him. Did I sing? Yes, I sang. What did I sing?
I told him.

"We will hear you sing and play after dinner,"
he commanded.

And it went on. Did I ride? Yes. Did I hunt? I
had, twice with Miss Busser. Had I learned to em-
broider? I had. The servants would get an earful
tonight. I knew Apsley was listening with all his might.
Did I play cards? I did. Did I play whist? I did.
What other card games did I play? I told him. Did I
dance? Certainly. What dances? The quadrille, the
polka, the waltz, the galop, the lancers. . . .

Would the questions never end?

Did I play croquet? Yes, I did. Did I like to play
it? Yes. Had I learned to shoot with the bow and arrow? Yes, I had. . . . On and on it went until he
was satisfied—not only satisfied but, I could tell,
pleased.

I had never known such behavior, and I was con-
fused by it. Was he trying to decide whether to buy
me or not? Was I for sale? Yes, in a way I supposed
I was. If I was to live upon his bounty, I supposed I
should at least try to please him. I certainly had nothing to lose by doing so.

Again we fell silent, and Coventry and Titus
brushed the table clean.

"You look like a shopgirl," my stepfather said.

I was about to taste my ice when he said it. Wide-
eyed, I turned to him, but I kept my tongue.

"We will take care of that," he continued. "Mrs.
Danley has engaged a maid for you. She can sew.
She knows the fashions. Her mother was French. Mrs.
Danley has engaged three seamstresses who will come
each day from Taunton to sew. Cloth will be sent
from London. Merchants will come with samples. They
will come from Taunton. They will come from London.
You will have all the dresses you need. You will have
the jewels you need. You will have everything. You

are the daughter of the eighth earl of Trevenbury. You will have the best.

"You will be treated by everyone as my daughter. Your manners and appearance must be perfect. They must do credit to me. And your morals, also."

"My morals have always been above reproach." I spat the words at him. "And they always will be."

He smiled. A silent chuckle shook him. He was amused.

But I was not at all amused—I was furious at this personal attack. I sat there speechless and watched him peel an apple, holding it in his grotesque little three-fingered hand as the peel fell from his knife in one long piece.

Mother sat quietly through it all—she had not spoken during the meal—but now she rose and said, "Come along, my dear. Your father will join us in a few minutes, and then you will play and sing for us. Coventry, we will have coffee in the music room. Titus, bring my embroidery from the far drawing room, if you please."

After my stepfather had joined us, I stepped to the piano and said, "I will play an arrangement for piano of the nocturne from Mendelssohn's *A Midsummer Night's Dream* and then sing Cleopatra's lovely aria from Handel's *Giulio Cesare,* accompanying myself on the piano."

It was a very poor performance, but I didn't think that either Mother or my stepfather would realize it. He watched and listened intently. She worked at her embroidery with deliberate stitches. Once, during the Mendelssohn, I looked up and caught sight of what must have been Apsley's sleeve at the door.

"Good!" my stepfather said when I had finished. "Good night, I have things to do." And he hurried out of the room. Evidently it was not to be the "peace and beauty of the family together" that evening for him.

"Very pretty, my dear," said my mother, without looking up from her embroidery.

"Thank you, Mother," I said.

I went to her then and stood for a moment looking at her needlework on its frame. The pattern was of Cupid surrounded by a wreath of flowers. A small area of background was yet to be finished.

"Be careful not to hurt your eyes," I said to her. "The lamp is not very bright."

She did not reply.

"I think I will go to my room. It has been an exhausting day, and I shall go to bed early."

With that I left her.

## ᏰᎧ Chapter Three ᏸᏫ

THE NEXT MORNING I was awakened by the sound of curtains being pulled. Dorothy had already set my tea tray on the table in the window alcove where I liked to have it.

"Good morning, Dorothy," I said.

"Good morning, miss." She smiled, pleased that I had addressed her by name. "It's a wet morning for Sunday. I hope the sun will come out and dry the grass before it is time to walk to church."

As she spoke, she rearranged the flowers in the bowl on the table.

"Who put the roses there, Dorothy? Was it you?"

"Yes, miss. I'll go and get your water now, miss."

I got up, slipped on a robe, poured my tea, and stood gazing out the window. A breeze had blown in from the sea, drawing gauzy curtains of mist across the gardens, turning the distance to shades of gray, and hiding the orangery almost entirely.

Dorothy returned to prepare my bath, and I said, "Thank you for the roses, Dorothy. They are my favorite flower, especially yellow ones. That was a very thoughtful thing to do. Why did you do it?"

"Why, miss?" she said.

She looked up at me with those strangely haunted, protruding eyes. She was so thin. I hoped that carrying water wasn't too much for her.

"Yes, why did you bring the roses in for me? You

didn't *need* to do it—I mean, that wouldn't be part of your duties, would it?"

"No, miss." I thought that was all she was going to say, but then she said very slowly, "There's been so much that's bad here, miss. I want to do what I can to make some good."

Then we were interrupted by Clair, who had come to help me dress, and Dorothy ran off. She had many things to do before getting ready for church.

I had finished dressing, and Clair was doing my hair when someone knocked on the door. Clair opened it, and there stood Mrs. Danley, smiling, her eyes twinkling, and her wrinkled, spotted hands crossed in front of her.

"Oh, Mrs. Danley, please come in," I said.

"I am sorry to bother you so early in the morning, miss, but I came to be sure you have everything you need and to see if you could spare me a few minutes sometime today for a little—conference, you might say. There's so much to be done. His lordship may have told you that you are to have a complete new wardrobe—all the clothes you will need for the next few months. I already mentioned it to Miss Clair this morning. She will be in charge of the actual clothes. Well, you, of course, must decide exactly what you want, but Miss Clair is very much informed as to the styles of the day. I am sure we will both want to be guided by her opinions. So, that's what I wanted to talk to you about, sometime today. To plan it all, miss, and to consult with you and get it all arranged."

She was breathless, and Clair and I were nearly as excited as she.

"Let us get down to it," I said, "as soon as possible, then. Shall we meet here right after luncheon, at two-thirty this afternoon?"

It was agreed.

Later that morning, my mother, my stepfather, and I made our first appearance together at church in Fawsley. The church was crowded, hot, and steamy, and I wondered if the villagers had come to hear the Reverend Ashley or to see what I looked like. The rector preached a long, dull sermon. Whatever else he might have been, he was not a preacher. I decided that his flock *had* come out of curiosity and not out of piousness.

Mother was stricken with one of her headaches during the service and became nervous and impatient to get home. So, immediately after the service was over, we dashed through the mist to our carriage. The mist was heavy and cold and showed no signs of lifting. I, too, was impatient to get back to the house and to have luncheon over with, so that I could begin planning my new wardrobe with Mrs. Danley and Clair.

They arrived at my bedroom door promptly at two-thirty.

"There will be a lot of sewing to be done," Mrs. Danley said, "so with his lordship's permission, and I am sure you will agree, miss, I have engaged a dressmaker, a Mrs. Banks, and three seamstresses she knows and recommends. Mrs. Banks made dresses for Viscount Warburton's daughter, over at Hill House when Miss Clair was there with her."

"She is truly wonderful, miss," Clair said. "She can make anything from just a picture. Why, she made Lady Virginia's dress when she was presented at court, miss. Oh, I am sorry, Mrs. Danley."

"That's all right, child. Well now, I says to myself, Mrs. Banks and her three seamstresses are going to need a place to work. So, I says to myself, if the young mistress approves"—she nodded and beamed at me to emphasize the "young mistress"—"why shouldn't we use the schoolroom upstairs? There's a big table and a couple of little ones, lots of space, and there's

35

good light. And it will be out of the way of traffic, so to speak."

"I have never seen the schoolroom," I said, "but it sounds like a wonderful idea."

"I know you will like it when you see it. As a matter of fact, why don't we go up there now? I have had a fire made, and Miss Clair has taken all her magazines up there. It will be a cozy place to work."

The schoolroom could hardly be called cozy. It was too large and bare for that. It was a corner room on the third floor. Two of its walls were half window, which, indeed made it very light. But it would have been dreary on that gray afternoon without the fire. It took the chill dampness out of the air, and its flickering oranges and yellows were welcome in the midst of all that gray wall and sky. So it is here that the beggar girl is to be turned into the fairy princess, I thought.

"Yes, Mrs. Danley," I said, "this should be excellent."

"Titus will bring us a pot of tea in a bit," she said. "Let us sit down." And after we were seated at one end of the large table, Mrs. Danley continued, "Mrs. Banks is coming tomorrow afternoon, and she will stay at Warton Hall until her work is done. The girls are coming on Tuesday—they live in Taunton and will come out each day.

"Now, you will certainly need nightdresses and underwear and petticoats. Tomorrow morning we could go to Taunton and buy some cottons for these, and then while we are in London—"

"London?" I gasped.

"Well, miss, you will never get the poplins and linens and silks here that you will get in London. Also, it's the finest velvets and worsteds and the latest tartans and trimmings you will be needing."

"And I know just where to go," said Clair. "Hitchcock's for silks and poplins and Scott Adie for tartans

36

and linens and cloaks and stockings—they are appointed to Her Majesty. Then, Holmes on Regent Street for shawls—they have beautiful paisley patterns and lovely cashmere ones. Foster and Son for the most beautiful French gloves and perfumes—they are on Regent Street, too."

"While we are in London," continued Mrs. Danley, "Mrs. Banks and the girls could get started. We could leave on Tuesday morning and get back on Thursday afternoon, if you agree, miss. I am sure it would be all right with his lordship and her ladyship. Her ladyship would like to come with us, I know, but traveling makes her quite ill, so I am sure she would not be able to do so. I haven't been away from Warton Hall in years, miss, and I could do with a spot of shopping in London, myself. The jewelers and watchmakers will come down here from London—Popes and Worthenhouser most likely—and they will be pleased to do so, miss, so his lordship can be present at that time.

"We will have to go to London again, most likely, later on. We must not try to do too much in such a short time. But we will be able to do a lot, you can be sure, and we can send for a lot of things from the catalogs.

"Now, let us see how many dresses you will need and see if we can find pictures for Mrs. Banks to work from. Of course, we will want to change things, and Mrs. Banks will have some ideas herself."

Clair and her periodicals, *The World of Fashion, The Lady's Gazette of Fashion,* and *The Ladies' Monthly Magazine* were invaluable. She suggested that three riding habits, six day dresses, eight evening dresses, and three ball dresses be made to start. Her taste, I thought, was exquisite. By the end of the afternoon, we had our recommendations to present to Mrs. Banks for her comments the following afternoon.

Mrs. Banks, then, could suggest materials and tell us how much to buy.

I was not at all sleepy that night. I was too excited. Tuesday we would be in London, and Mrs. Banks would soon be working on my new clothes. This was all happening so quickly, as if something behind the scenes were saying, "Hurry, hurry."

I glanced at the table. The roses had turned pink! Dorothy had brought fresh flowers. She, poor dear, seemed almost miserable, while I felt so happy. It didn't seem right.

My stepfather owned a house on St. James's Square in London, but it had not been opened in years, so we stayed in a little hotel called the Victoria on Piccadilly, where we were treated royally. We had brought Titus with us to carry luggage and packages and take care of the cabs and run errands. We were four very busy people, and we accomplished what I thought was a miracle. But then, when one does not have to worry how much money is spent, one can buy a lot in a very short time.

We managed to buy most of the materials and trimmings I would need. We bought gloves, handkerchiefs, and perfume. We bought garters, bonnets, sashes, and two beautifully worked dressing gowns. We bought parasols, shawls, stockings, and even a waterproof cloak for bad weather.

And I bought Clair some beautiful green linen, which she had fallen in love with, for a dress for herself, and Mrs. Danley a length of deep-violet worsted for the same purpose.

We could not possibly carry it all home, so much of it was sent by the shops. How helpful everyone was when they learned I was the daughter of the earl of Trevenbury! Nothing proved too difficult, nothing too much trouble, there was nothing that could not be arranged.

Thursday afternoon arrived, and tired but in high spirits, we boarded the train for home.

"I love the pink and white and green and purple-striped poplin," I said as we sped southwards, "and the sea blue silk—it is such a gorgeous color. I am so glad we brought it with us so Mrs. Banks can get to work on it right away. I just can't wait to wear it."

"You will be beautiful in it, my dear," said Mrs. Danley. "It suits you perfectly."

She had progressed—cautiously, hesitantly—from "miss" to "my dear" and "dear child," and I loved it.

"It will be like old times now—young people again," she mused, "dances, house guests—"

But then she stopped speaking, and her face grew still. A veil of sadness, almost of hopelessness passed across it.

Something dreadful has happened to her, I thought. I wonder what it was?

In a moment, however, the mood had passed and she continued, "You see, in the old days we had as many as thirty guests staying for a week at a time, and there were meets and balls and dinners. The seventh earl entertained a great deal. There was such excitement in those days."

"You must have had a tremendous staff under you," I said.

"Just the same as now, child. When his lordship came, he gave orders that, even though there would be two years of mourning, the staff should remain."

"But no one does the flowers. There are no flowers in any of the rooms."

"The flowers are always done by the lady of the house, you see, and her ladyship doesn't like flowers very much, I am afraid. Oh, I try to do them, but I just never have the time, it seems. The rooms do look sad without them, don't they?"

"Could *I* do them?" I asked.

"That would be very appropriate, indeed, and a blessing if you would, child. Things would look more like they used to if you would."

And again I saw the sadness in her face.

We arrived back in Taunton on time, and Henderson met us with the barouche, just as he had met me at this same time, just six days before.

## Chapter Four

I HAD SLEPT WELL and woke refreshed on the morning after our return. The morning had begun sunny and cool, and, as usual, Dorothy brought my tea and then went to get the water for my bath.

But then as I stood by the open door to the terrace, sipping my tea and looking up at the hill, I heard a crash behind me. I whirled and saw that Dorothy had returned and that she had tripped and dropped the hot water can. It lay on its side spilling water onto the carpet. Dorothy had sunk to the floor beside it and sat in the puddle.

I put down my cup, ran to her, and set the can upright.

"I'm sorry, miss. I'm sorry—I'm so sorry," she murmured, looking up at me.

She was trembling.

"Dorothy!" I cried. "Get up out of the wet. Here let me help you." Then I helped her to a chair by the window. "No, don't worry about the chair. Here, let me get you some tea."

I rinsed my cup in the basin on the washstand, poured the tea, and carried it to her.

Dorothy sat, still trembling, her hands in her lap, staring wide-eyed into space. I knelt in front of her and brushed her hair away from her face.

"Dorothy! Please!" I said. "Drink some of this."

When I held the cup and saucer near her hands,

she seemed to come to herself, and she took the cup and sipped from it.

"What is it?" I asked. "You don't look well. Have you been sleeping?"

"I'm so *afraid!*" she said.

She set the cup down on the table with a rattle.

"But what is there to be afraid of, Dorothy? There is nothing to be afraid of."

"The man with the scar," she whispered.

This sent a chill down my spine.

"The man with the scar?" I asked.

"There is this man—and he has a scar down his face, and he's come back. He was looking at me through the window at the servants' dance Wednesday night."

"But why should you be afraid of him? Who is he?"

"Death, miss. That's who he is—death. He brought murder with him last time."

"Murder? Whose murder?" I asked.

Suddenly Dorothy's face crumpled. Her body convulsed with sobs. "His late lordship's," she cried, bowing her head and covering her face with her hands.

"Oh, no, Dorothy. His late lordship was not murdered. You don't know what you are saying."

"He was," she wailed.

"But what could possibly make you think such a thing?"

"He was murdered! I know he was murdered."

"Nonsense, Dorothy. No! The seventh earl of Trevenbury? My stepfather's father? He died of a heart attack. Mrs. Danley told me so. You don't know what you are saying. Finish your tea and *please* try to be calm."

She sipped from the cup, looking down into it, and after a few moments she looked up at me. "I'm all right now, miss," she said. Then she brushed the tears from her face with her fingers, looked at me with those wide, haunted eyes, and said, "Will you help me?"

"Well, of course, Dorothy, if I can. Of course I will help you. What can I do?"

Then it all came out like air rushing from a torn balloon. I had sunk to the floor beside her chair, and she gazed down into my eyes as she talked.

"Yes, everyone thinks it was his heart," she began. "I've never told anyone. They wouldn't believe me —anyway, what good would it do?

"I always took his late lordship's tea tray up to him first thing for his valet or Mr. Apsley to give to him. His lordship couldn't keep a valet for very long, so it was more likely to be Mr. Apsley helping out between times.

"Well, that morning I took his tray up as usual, but Mr. Apsley wasn't there yet, and I heard his lordship groaning like. So I went in and found his lordship lying on his bed on top of the covers. The bedclothes were in a tangle. He was in a fit, like. He had his hand around his throat and was pointing to the water bottle on the table by his bed. His glass was on the floor and overturned. I thought he wanted a drink of water and got a glass from the stand and poured water from the bottle and held it for his lordship to drink, but he let out an awful little scream like he was choking, miss, like he was saying, 'No, no,' and then he knocked the glass out of my hand, and the water spilled all over the bed.

"I didn't know what to do, miss, but then I thought I'd better go and find Mr. Apsley. It was lucky he was on his way—just down the hall—and I brought him back with me. But by the time we got to him, his lordship was dead with his eyes open, miss.

"I knew he'd been poisoned by the way he acted and the expression on his face, but I had to know for sure because of Patrick. I took away the water bottle and glasses and tidied up the room a bit and left his lordship with Mr. Apsley.

"The kitchen cat had had kittens the week before, miss. I poured the water that was left in his lordship's water bottle into a bowl and took the bowl and a kitty and put them into an empty wood box outside the still-room door. That afternoon the kitty was dead."

"Oh, no," I said. "Who was Patrick?"

"Patrick was a groom here, miss. He—he was all alone. He had no relatives or friends—he was all alone in the world, and he needed someone. . . . I was—to have—a baby by him, miss.

"Patrick was with me the night before in the kitchen. I had just got the water from the pump and was filling his lordship's bottle with the dipper—I always carried fresh water up to his room at night when I went to turn down his bed. So, Patrick comes in and starts to fuss with me a little, and I told him to stop.

"Well, after I found the kitty dead, miss, I went to find Patrick. We had an awful fight. He said his lordship wasn't poisoned. Everybody knew it was his heart. He said that if I told such stories nobody would believe me, and they would think I was crazy.

"I said I still had some of the water—that the kitty died from drinking it. He *forced* me to show him. He nearly broke my arm, and he smashed the bowl to pieces and took the dead kitty and said, 'Now where's your proof?' And he said if I knew what was good for me, I'd keep my mouth shut.

"I never said anything. I kept telling myself the kitty died natural, miss. I had the baby to think of, miss.

"That big black horse of his trampled Patrick to death ten days later."

"Patrick Meagher!" I exclaimed. "And your baby, Dorothy?"

"I had him at my sister's in Manchester. She's still taking care of him like one of her own, miss."

"The man with the scar. What does he look like?"

"Thin, with a patch on one eye and a scar from where the eye should be to his mouth."

"But what does he have to do with all this?" I asked.

"I seen him around here at the time, miss. I seen him talking to Patrick once, miss, and then I didn't see him again these two long years until Wednesday."

"But that doesn't mean he had anything to do with the murder."

"I know he did. And then there's that big horse. Where could Patrick get the money to buy a big devil of a horse like that?"

"He might have had savings."

"Miss—I'm *afraid!* I'm afraid something terrible is going to happen, miss. Don't tell anyone, miss. It's a bad place, this."

She was on the edge of hysteria again, and she knew it. She clapped a hand over her mouth and closed her eyes to ward it off. And I took her other hand in mine again and held it tightly.

Finally I said, "You were right to tell me about this, Dorothy. I won't tell anyone. There is no point, now." I spoke very slowly. "There is nothing to be afraid of. If you see that man again, come and tell me at once. Remember, you are not alone in this anymore. I am here to help you."

She stood up and said, "I'm better now. Thank you ever so much, miss. I feel much better. I'm so sorry about the carpet, miss, but it will dry, and I don't think it will show. I'll get you some more water."

"Oh, no, Dorothy, you should go and lie down."

"I'll get the water, miss, if it's all right with you. I'd rather stay busy. Thank you, miss. Thank you." There were tears in her eyes as she left the room.

I was stunned by what Dorothy had told me. I couldn't believe it, and yet I did believe it, every word of it. But it was all too fantastic—my stepfather's father murdered, my stepfather ignorant of it,

Meagher, the murderer, trampled to death by his own horse! Did the scar-faced man who traveled in Martin Shark's rented carriage have something to do with Meagher and the old seventh earl's death? What had he been doing here two years ago? What was he doing here now? Who was he?

What do I do now? I asked myself. Do I rush to my stepfather and say, "Your father was murdered by Patrick Meagher two years ago?" Hardly. It would do no good to rake up that horror. It was long past, and the proof of murder had long since been destroyed.

It had all happened two years ago. Why, then, was I getting so excited about it? Nothing alarming had happened recently. I would wait, and hope that nothing did.

After morning prayer and breakfast, I asked Apsley which of the gardeners could help me with the flowers. And I mentioned that Mrs. Danley had been pleased to hear that I would like to do the job.

"Excellent, miss," he said, obviously pleased at being consulted. "Old Benjamin helped the former Lady Trevenbury when he was a young man. He will be pleased to help you, miss, I know. The vases are kept in a large cabinet outside the summer parlor. If you could use Edward to help you carry, instead of Titus, I would appreciate it very much miss. We will ask Benjamin to come and see you whenever you wish."

"Tomorrow after breakfast, Apsley?"

"Very good, miss."

So it was settled, and I found Benjamin waiting to see me the following morning. He was the stooped gardener of the carrots, and his eyes sparkled with pleasure at the prospect of helping me. We decided to begin after breakfast on Monday. He would bring the flowers in then, from the cutting gardens.

But that is getting ahead of my story.

After Apsley had told me about Benjamin, I spent

almost all morning in the schoolroom with Mrs. Banks and Clair, and I was there for a while after luncheon, as well. I had decided that the first thing on the agenda would be a riding habit and the next, the evening dress of blue silk.

Dinners at Warton Hall were always long and formal. I rather dreaded them. At dinner that evening, we were silent during the soup. During the lamb and salad, my stepfather launched into a description of some acreage he had bought. He said that his holdings would soon be larger than the marquis of Bates', whoever that was.

We were silent again. Then suddenly my stepfather demanded a full account of our trip to London and our progress to date in wardrobe making.

So I told him about it. "And I want to thank you," I concluded, "for everything you are doing for me, Father. I am so happy and excited by it all."

He had listened intently. Then he gazed at me without speaking for a moment, opened his mouth, and belched.

"That was good," he said to Mother, as he patted his stomach. "The new chef is Pierre Chanlieu," he said to me. "He is a friend of the royal chef at Buckingham Palace. He worked for the duke of Summersfield before he came to Warton Hall. What do you think of that?" He smiled broadly and stroked his stomach.

"The dinner was delicious; this mousse is exquisite," I said.

"Did you like the lamb, Fitz?" Mother asked. "Pierre thought to do it in the marinade, which is his own recipe and very French."

Mother spoke for the first time during dinner. Apparently, then, she did take an interest in the menus.

"Very good," he said, belching again.

"Paul Ashley called this afternoon, Fitz, to say that Cecilia Osborne died in London on Tuesday and that

47

her body will arrive here tomorrow. She is to be buried in the mausoleum according to your grandfather's and your father's wishes, as you know. He said that there would already have been a church service in London today and that only a brief service would be necessary at the church in Fawsley before bringing the body here to the mausoleum."

"I do not want him in this house. He is not to come here," my stepfather said.

"I am sure that is why he suggested the service be in the church instead of the chapel here, my dear. I said that I was sure you would approve. You do, don't you? It would hardly be seemly—"

"Yes, yes. We will go to the service. It would be correct to go to the service."

"Fitz, it really couldn't be necessary to go into *mourning* again, could it? I think if I had to go into mourning again I should be ill." Her lovely hand went to her temple, and she shut her eyes.

"No, no. That would only hold things up. She is no blood relation to me."

"Who was Cecilia Osborne?" I asked my stepfather.

"Lord—my uncle's wife," he replied.

"You see, my dear," my mother explained, "your stepfather's father, the seventh earl, had a younger brother whose name was John Osborne. He married Cecilia Holm, daughter of Baron Park. John died two years ago and was buried in the mausoleum, and his wife is to lie by his side there."

"Did you know her?" I asked.

"I barely remember her. When I was just a young child, Baron Park willed to his daughter—she was an only child—his estates and Hornton Hall, just south of Chippenham. The estates bordered my father's. She was a constant visitor before she was married. Then, after her marriage, she came often with her husband. He was a very attractive man."

48

"I did not know that you knew my uncle. You didn't tell me this," my stepfather said.

"You really couldn't be interested, my dear. This was long before Suzanne was born." And turning to me, she continued, "They were forced to sell Hornton Hall. They moved to London, many years ago—and I never saw either of them again."

"Did they have any children?" I asked.

"They had only one son who was killed in the war. There are no heirs, I believe."

"They didn't have anything at the end," my stepfather said. "Only the house. Not worth anything."

"And when will the service be?" I asked. "Will I be expected to go?"

"On Sunday," Mother said, "at two in the afternoon, dear. I think it would be proper for you to attend. There won't be anyone else there unless someone in the village remembers her. I really wish it were not necessary to go. Funerals are such depressing, gloomy affairs. I do loathe the whole idea. Why can't bodies just be made to disappear after death and spare us all that time and misery?" Her fingers touched her temple.

The bleached, roofless arches of the abbey were like the breast bones of some long-dead prehistoric beast, the two glassless windows of the nave like the sockets of its eyes. We drove past it on Sunday afternoon as we followed the hearse toward Warton Park and then up the track that led to the mausoleum.

The long black box on wheels rolled slowly along ahead of us. Its gilded skulls and lacquered cherubs seemed almost to laugh at us; its black plumes, blown by the wind, pointed at us; the clopping horses' hoofs called to us, "One day, some day, one day, some day."

The four horses that pulled the hearse were old hacks and moved ever more slowly toward the top of the hill. Behind them on the box, the undertaker held his pot-hat. Its crape whipped madly in the gale. And above us, enormous gray puffs of cloud, their undersides rubbed in powdered charcoal, scudded across the lead sky toward the pewter sea.

The service at the church in Fawsley had been little more than a prayer. An undertaker from Taunton had been employed to move the coffin from the railway station to the church and from the church to the mausoleum and, though mutes and mourners had been dispensed with, to supply attendants to carry the coffin. They walked beside it. And the undertaker had supplied the two black carriages for the procession—one for my stepfather, my mother, and me; and the other for the Reverend Ashley and a stranger who had been at the service. Our own carriages had followed behind, unoccupied as was the custom, and waited for us at the bottom of the hill.

When we reached the hilltop and drew up in front of the mausoleum, now gray in the gray light, the attendants lifted the coffin from the hearse and carried it up the steps and into the building. It wore a blanket of scarlet roses, and as they carried it, the screeching puffs of wind blew the petals from the flowers and threw them into the air like red confetti.

The wind lashed at us as we followed the coffin up the steps and into the building. The undertaker shut the iron doors against the noise of the gale, and the mausoleum fell silent. How remote it seemed there, and how stale-smelling and cold it was. I was chilled and pulled my shawl snugly about me.

But I was curious as well, and surprised that I could see the interior of the mausoleum so clearly. I had expected it to be dark inside—there were no windows in its walls—but light fell from a round window in the top of the dome above, casting an eerie glow. The room was much larger than I had expected—large enough for eight tombs to stand away from the circular walls with again as much space between them. These tombs, great marble boxes, were built to hold the coffins of eight earls of Trevenbury and their wives. Four lids, with effigies of the inhabitants carved in full relief upon them, already rested in place on four of the tombs: my stepfather's great-grandfather's, who had built the mausoleums, and his wife's; my stepfather's grandfather's and his wife's; my stepfather's father's—how restless his sleep must have been—and his wife's; and my stepfather's and my mother's tomb. Its lid had already been carved with their likenesses lying as if asleep on it. How enormously heavy those lids looked. I wondered how many men it would take to lift one.

Behind the tombs the wall was honeycombed with vaults, each more than large enough to hold a coffin. These had been built to hold the earls' brothers and sisters and their wives and children who wished to be buried here. The vaults were sealed with marble slabs set flush with the wall. Most of the slabs wore carved decorations and inscriptions signifying that the vaults behind them were occupied, but some remained plain.

Now, in her vault beside her husband's, Cecilia Osborne lay in her coffin, her red blanket spilling down its side.

And those final words, "Ashes to ashes . . ." echoed in the chill as the Reverend Ashley finished the brief service.

Mother had not taken her eyes from the stranger, a tall, straight, slim man, perhaps thirty years old. His head had remained bowed, but, for one instant, he had looked up at my stepfather. Had I seen a look of disgust there? It had all happened so quickly that I had not been sure.

But then, as soon as the service was over, my stepfather grasped my arm and led me to his tomb.

"I have been sculpted in my prime for my tomb,"

he said loudly, his words crashing back at me again and again from the walls. "The sculptor is Power. He did the *Greek Slave* shown at the Great Exhibition. He worked for more than a year on these figures. They cost me five thousand pounds." He gestured proudly to the freshly carved figures, which he could not see —they lay above his eye level.

Mother and Mr. Ashley had walked to the doorway and now stood motionless, staring at us. I began to walk toward them, moving away from my stepfather, who slowly followed me.

"My dear, we have not really met," Mr. Ashley said to me as I approached. "Colonel Mark Lawson and I are returning to the rectory for some cake and wine and perhaps a hot drink, and we would be delighted if you would accompany us and accept our hospitality there." The rector did not look at my mother or stepfather. "I am sure your mother and stepfather have many important things to do, but we will insure your safe return if they will grant their permission."

"Not at all, Paul," Mother crooned, with a lavish smile at Colonel Lawson. "I should welcome your hospitality as well. After all, I could hardly let Suzanne go alone. We should be delighted."

And then we all started to talk at once.

"Well, Lawson," Mr. Ashley said, "we are to be honored, indeed. Her ladyship seldom visits abroad these days, I believe."

"Mother, I don't think I really—"

"Nonsense, my dear," she said. "You have never been to the rectory, and you really must become accustomed to visiting in the afternoon." She threw a purposeful glance at my stepfather, which I did not understand.

"I have other things to do," my stepfather said.

"Fitz, my dear," she laid her hand on the sleeve of his stunted arm, "would you ask Henderson to be at the rectory at five o'clock with the brougham? Or, if you need him, then Arthur? We will go in the rector's carriage."

But Colonel Lawson seemed impatient to be away. He had already opened the door and walked across the portico. He walked, I noticed, with a slight limp. We followed him into the fresh air, and I began to think how happy I was that the service was over. Still, I was glad to have seen the inside of the mausoleum. What sumptuousness immense wealth could provide, even in death! Yet, on the other hand, it made no difference at all.

The clip-clop of the pretty bays sounded almost merry as we sped toward the rectory. As we passed the abbey, I asked the rector about it.

"Cistercian," he said. "Dates from the twelfth century, probably between 1150 and 1250. The tower is, of course, later—sixteenth century. . . ."

Evidently I had hit upon one of his special interests, for he spoke enthusiastically. And while he related the abbey's history, I had a chance to examine him. His eyes sparkled in his pink, chubby face, and he wore a tall, black top hat at a rakish angle. He was, I guessed, in his early forties, and he looked as though life had been kind to him.

" . . . very important English monastery," he continued. "The order permitted little decoration, but the vast scale and dignity—" He gave me a delightful smile. "But you must be bored by all this."

I had had no idea, from watching him in the pulpit, that he was such a charming man.

"Oh, no. Please go on," I said. "I would like to know about it."

"Are you staying nearby, Colonel Lawson?" Mother inquired. "Or are you with us only for the day?"

"Lawson will be staying with me for a while, Lillian," the rector said.

"Are you fond of funerals, Colonel Lawson?" she said with a sumptuous smile, head slightly tilted.

"No, Lady Trevenbury. The Trevenbury mausoleum is architecturally famous, and Ashley thought I would like to see it."

"If you are interested in architecture, Colonel Lawson, you must come to see Warton Hall," she said.

"Thank you. I would be delighted," Colonel Lawson replied.

By then, we were approaching the drive of the rectory. Above it, the stone country church stood on its verdant knoll surrounded by its churchyard.

"The church is a lovely one, I think," the rector said. "Built in 1670, designed by an unknown architect, but very much like the St. Lawrence in London by Sir Christopher Wren. The same architect probably designed the original rectory, which I am told burned in '45. The seventh earl had this architectural horror, in which I now live, built the following year."

The "architectural horror" was a large stone house in the "Gothic cottage" style—a jumble of wings and porches, towers and cupolas, dormers and balconies; of square windows and arched windows, round windows of clear glass, and some of colored glass; and a forest of chimneys. Every bit of its roof line was edged with wooden lace. Ivy covered much of the house, and it cuddled happily on its little green lawn in a grassy hollow below the church. I thought it enchanting.

"At least the rooms are small, and warm in winter and cool in summer," Mr. Ashley said, as we entered the drawing room. "Ah, Mrs. Hobson, will you please bring some tired and hungry people something to eat and drink?"

A short, slightly bearded woman had been arranging the curtains. She was probably the housekeeper, I thought. She giggled at the rector and then hurried away.

When we sat down, I had a moment to study Mark Lawson. He was a lithe animal, powerfully built for all his leanness, with wide shoulders and narrow hips. His beautiful square jaw bespoke perfect teeth. His nose was short and straight, his eyes a pale, pale gray. There was fire in them, but it was a cold, icy flame. His cheeks were sunken, and the hollows around his eyes, deep and bluish, made him look very tired.

"And you, Colonel Lawson, what brings you to the peace and tranquility of Somerset?" Mother asked.

Mark Lawson must have sensed that I was watching him because he glanced at me before answering my mother. He looked in my eyes for an instant with those almost hypnotic eyes of his, but I could not meet them and looked away.

"Just that, Lady Trevenbury," he said. "Peace and tranquility. I have just returned from the Crimea."

"But the war has been over for some months," she said.

"Yes, but it takes some months for all the troops and supplies to return after the end of a war."

"Lawson was a lieutenant-colonel in the Fourth Dragoon Guards," the rector said. "His was one of the first regiments to arrive on Turkish soil and one of the last to leave it."

At that point, Mrs. Hobson interrupted the conversation. She brought a tray of raspberry tarts, pound cake, wine, and hot tea.

"You were wounded, Colonel Lawson?" Mother asked when we had all been served.

"Yes, my horse was shot from under me in the battle of Balaklava. I was shot in the left leg, hence the limp. I was in the hospital at Scutari during the winter of '54."

"That horrible winter."

"Yes, people here in England can have no idea of the cold, the snow, the mud, the hunger." He was seeing it all again with blank eyes as he sat there before

55

us. And then, with a start, he was with us again. "So I wrote to Ashley, who was a friend of my father, and asked if I might spend a little time with him to get my balance, so to speak."

"Your parents?" I asked.

"Both dead."

"You had no home to come home to?"

"I have no home. It has been—I have no family, and I have no wife. Can there be a home without either?"

"But surely you are not destitute," Mother said. "Your parents—they must have left you something—a house, property, somewhere to go."

"Perhaps the house is shut, and there is no one there," he replied.

"Open it. Nothing could be simpler."

Mark Lawson made no reply, but sat looking at Mother—examining her, appraising her.

"Where is it? Near here, perhaps?" Mother asked.

"It is in the north."

"Where in the north? I have friends—"

"Really, Lillian," the rector said. "I think that if Lawson wanted to tell you about his property he would do so without a cross-examination."

"I was not asking about his property, Paul. I was asking about his house. If there is a reason to make a secret of it, we will say no more, of course, but I really don't see—"

"Not at all, Lady Trevenbury," Mark Lawson said. "The house is in Durham."

"Oh? Does it have a name? Is it in the city or is it—more isolated?"

"It is near the city of Durham, but in the country-side. It is called Wellfield House. It is—between Durham and the sea." Then he added, "Is it of great interest to you, Lady Trevenbury?"

"How lovely," Mother said. "I have always wanted to visit the most northern counties, but I have never had the opportunity to do so. Perhaps I shall have the opportunity in the future."

She smiled enchantingly.

"And how is our little princess getting along?" the rector said to me.

"Wonderfully," I replied. "That is exactly what I feel like."

He laughed. I liked him very much.

Then he turned to Mother and said, "I understand that Warton Hall has practically turned into a clothing factory. Beware, Lillian, lest the princess outshine the queen."

It did not seem long after that that Thompson, the rector's butler, announced that Henderson had arrived with the carriage. Too soon, it was time to go.

I suppose everyone has his or her special place, a favorite place to go to for thinking or just to be alone. The Chinese pagoda had become my favorite place. I had fallen in love with it. It stood on an octagonal stone island near the shore of a lily pond beyond the hedge at the north corners of the rose and sculpture gardens. It was octagonal too, about eight feet across inside, and about two stories high, though its four tiers of roof, each gold leafed and separated by walls of red lacquered openwork, made it seem much taller. From the eight corners of each of its roofs hung little bronze bells that tinkled when a breeze blew. The pagoda and its island were connected to the shore by a Chinese bridge and hidden from the house by an enormous weeping beech tree.

The morning after the funeral, I sat on the circular rustic bench inside the pagoda, holding three carrots that Benjamin had brought me. I had been on my way to the stables to visit the horses, but there had been no hurry, and I decided to sit awhile in the pavilion's shade. I sat there looking out at the large pink and white lilies floating in the pool and thinking how much I wanted to ride again. I missed riding terribly, but since I had no habit—my school habit had been so worn that I had left it behind—I could not ride until my new one was finished.

It would be finished very soon, I told myself, and all was well. But somehow I felt that all was not well, that there was something terribly wrong here. I could not forget the horrible story that Dorothy had told me. But she had looked better this morning than I had ever seen her look before. She had actually smiled at me when I asked her how she felt.

"Better than I have for two years, miss," she had said. "I have slept for three nights in a row, thanks to you, miss. If only the man with the scar is gone. Is there *anything* you need, miss, anything I can do for you?"

And I had said that I was being taken care of to perfection and that she was not to worry.

"We probably won't see the scar-faced man again," I had said. "After all, what could he want at Warton Hall?"

What *could* he want? What was the connection between Meagher and the scar-faced man, and was there a connection between him and Martin Shark? I bit off the tip of a carrot and crunched it, wondering.

And I wondered at what a dear Benjamin was. He had come to find me after breakfast, after he had brought the flowers to the flower room, a little room off the landing near the vase cupboard.

In the flower room stood an L-shaped table, and there, on shelves beneath it, I found copper buckets for water, scissors, wire, twine, heavy pierced glass weights to hold the flower stems in place at the bottom of the vases, and baskets for clippings and discarded leaves.

On the table stood two large buckets of flowers, which Benjamin had brought. They filled the little room with perfume. He had picked pink, white, and peach carnations, and deep scarlet ones too, white and lavender stock, yellow and white snapdragons, lilies —white Madonna lilies and orange Nankeen lilies— white and yellow gladioli and a cloud of baby's-breath. I had been delighted with them all, and Benjamin glowed because I was so happy with the flowers he had chosen.

We decided on the pink, white, and peach carnations and the baby's-breath for the dining table. And when they were arranged in a white porcelain bowl, Edward had carried them there with genuine pride. They did look lovely on the table, whether my mother and stepfather would notice them or not.

Then white and orange lilies had gone to the corner room, stock, gladioli and red carnations to the summer parlor, and yellow and white snapdragons to the morning room.

It was between the snapdragons, in one of the flower buckets, that I found these three carrots. Benjamin actually blushed when I took his rough, old hands in mine to thank him for them.

As I thought about him, I got up from my seat, left the pagoda, and walked onto the bridge. I paused for a moment to watch the carp that swam lazily in the sun-clouded water, and I wondered what architectural experience Mr. Ashley had in store for Mark Lawson today.

Then I walked to the stables. As soon as I entered, Thunder saw me, tossed his head, and whinnied. I went to him at once, slowly but deliberately, and he came to the front of his box to greet me. I knew he was happy to see me. Gently he took my piece of carrot, and then I opened the door of his box and stepped inside. He pushed his great Roman nose at me with little nudges, coaxing for another piece of carrot, which I gave him.

"Hello, Thunder," I crooned to him as I reached

up and stroked his nose. "You must be lonely. Yes, I see you want a friend."

This horse is as sweet and gentle as any I have ever known, I thought, as I offered him another piece of carrot.

"Beautiful Thunder, could we ride together? Would you carry me across the fields like the wind?"

"Yes," he neighed, tossing his head and stomping his feet.

Then I left him to go to the saddle room. Several side saddles hung there, and I wanted to choose the one I would use on Thunder.

"Which one will it be, miss?"

I jumped.

"Oh, Monk, you startled me. Don't you ever make any noise? Why, you have a habit of appearing like magic," I said, laughing down at the proud little face turned up to me. "As a matter of fact, I am glad you appeared. Which of these saddles does my mother use? Do you know?"

"Her ladyship uses these two, miss, and his lordship uses this one."

"Then I think I will use the dark leather one with the tooled edge."

"Is his lordship getting you a new horse, miss?"

"I don't know, Monk, we haven't discussed it, but I hope not because I would like to ride Thunder."

Monk was horrified. "But you can't ride Thunder, miss. He's a killer, miss. He's dangerous. No, I can't let you ride *him,* miss."

"He may have been dangerous for Patrick Meagher, Monk, but that doesn't mean he will be dangerous for me, does it? Anyway, we will see. After all, I am not going to ride him today."

We left the saddle room and began to walk across the deserted stable yard together. Monk had become very serious and was lost in thought.

"Monk?"

"Yes, miss?"

"You seem so serious all of a sudden. Is anything wrong?"

"No, miss," He seemed surprised at my question. "I'm that way natural, sometimes. You see, miss, I'm all alone, and I got my future to look after, and that's serious business—very serious business, miss." He looked up at me with an exaggerated frown.

"Your parents?" I asked.

"Never had no mother. Father worked up at the farm—ran away with one of the dairymaids, they tell me, and left me behind. Mr. Henderson made me 'tiger' last year."

"Do you still live there, then?"

"At the farm? Oh, no, miss, I live right here with the coachman and the grooms. That's my room in the tower there, facing us." He pointed to the tower diagonally across the yard. "There's four towers at the four corners of the yard, as you can see, and they all have two rooms upstairs for the coachmen and the grooms. Me and Hippolyte have that one, there."

"And the room over the gateway?" I asked.

"Storeroom. Nothing much there, miss. Couple of old trunks and some old clothes and uniforms and things."

"Monk!" a voice demanded from the coach house.

"Excuse me, miss," he said. Then he ran off in that direction.

The storeroom, a square room under a domed cupola, was directly over the gateway to the yard. It was the only part of the buildings that was taller than one story besides the four corner towers where the grooms lived.

I found the stairway to the storeroom easily enough and climbed to the landing outside it. Its door was unlocked, and I pushed it open. Sun beat through its closed windows, and it was hot inside and dusty and

61

had that dry, bitter smell of closed-up rooms in the country. A hornet had gotten in, and it buzzed and knocked its head against a windowpane.

Between the windows, old uniforms hung from pegs in the wall. Magazines lay scattered about the floor, and in one corner stood three trunks, a bundle of clothes, a dozen small wooden boxes piled one on top of the other, and a log out of which someone had started to carve a head. That was all. The wooden boxes contained stones and rocks, some with fossils. Some had labels that fell off at the touch. Two of the trunks were empty, but the third contained what I thought I might find—Patrick Meagher's belongings. His trunk must have been moved here after he died so as to be available in case anyone should claim it. It contained dirty clothes—underwear, socks, a crumpled black dress suit, shoes, curled from disuse—an empty bottle of whiskey, two packs of cards, a cloth bag of shaving things, some cheap novels, and a small packet of letters tied with a string.

I took the letters, closed the lid of the trunk, left the room, and descended to the yard below. There was no one about in the yard, which was just as well, though I had not tried to make a secret of my expedition. If someone had seen me go up to the storeroom, I didn't care.

But what wonderful luck, I thought—not only finding Meagher's things but his letters as well. Would they tell me anything about him or his affairs?

I was impatient to find out, and since it was almost time for luncheon, I hurried back to the house and to my room to examine them.

Two of Patrick Meagher's letters were from his mother in Dublin. She was old and ill and wanted him to come home so that she could see him before she died. The others were from a girl named Nancy who lived in Torquay. How she pined for him! How she loved him and needed him! He must come, for she was to have a child. Patrick made a habit of begetting children, it seemed. Poor Dorothy.

The letters were of no interest to me, but I was puzzled by two different names in the addresses on the envelopes. The two letters from Patrick Meagher's mother were three years old and had been addressed to Patrick T. Meeker, 9 Mackin Street, London. The letters from Nancy, however, had been addressed to Patrick Meagher, here at Warton Hall. Apart from this inconsistency, I had gone to some trouble to learn nothing at all.

I had barely time to examine the letters before luncheon. After the meal was over, I returned to my room and sat in the alcove looking out at the gardens. I should have been in the schoolroom instead. Both my blue dress and riding habit were nearly finished, and I should have been there trying them on for one last fitting. Almost all the rest of my dresses were being worked on as well, and there would be questions about them. Clair would be there, however, and could answer most of the questions, though she was sure to be wondering what had happened to me.

I felt in no mood to talk about dresses. I was annoyed and disappointed in my morning's investigations. I don't know what I had expected to learn from Meagher's letters, but I felt terribly let down by them. They lay on the table next to me still, and as I glanced down at them, I noticed the corner of a newspaper clipping protruding from one of the envelopes: somehow I had missed it during my hurried examination before luncheon.

There were two clippings, as a matter of fact, and they were about Patrick Meagher. The headline of the first read: "Murder in the British Museum," and the article read:

At about twelve o'clock at night on Wednesday, a policeman named William Morris was passing the side entrance of the British Museum on Montague Street when the door opened and a figure dashed out. The deep moaning of a guard was heard. He had been fatally wounded and died soon after. The figure was that of Patrick Thomas Meeker, who was covered, most horribly, with blood and held in his right hand a knife, also dripping with blood, and in his left hand the diary of Nell Gwyn, which he had stolen from a glass case in the second floor exhibition hall. The case had been smashed to pieces. The policeman gave chase and was joined by Sergeant Roland Mc-Dermitt. They apprehended the murderer in the hallway of Number 39 Gower Street, a building consisting of four flats occupied by Benjamin Strong, John Stracham, Martin Shark, and Lewis Stoaks respectively. The murderer was taken to Newgate Prison to await trial. The four men who reside at Number 39 Gower Street are being questioned.

"Martin Shark!" I whispered. Patrick Meeker, alias Patrick Meagher, had been caught in the hallway leading to Martin Shark's flat. Then there was a connection between Meagher (one name would do as well as another) and Martin Shark: I had learned something after all.

Then I read the other clipping. It was short and told of the escape of Thomas Meeker from Newgate Prison and said that it was feared the escape was the result of bribery of the guards.

I put the clippings and the letters in the little wooden box in which I kept my few pieces of simple jewelry and some letters of my own—the few that my mother had sent me at school and some from Nana—my aunt as well as governess—from Africa, written shortly before she died.

Then I locked it—it would never do for Dorothy to come across the letters while cleaning my room.

I left my room and went up to the schoolroom where I tried on the blue dress first. I would be able to wear it Wednesday night to dinner. The habit would be finished Wednesday, too, if not on Tuesday afternoon.

And the striped poplin was almost finished. It was to be a morning dress in the form of a robe with a Watteau panel in the back. Another striped dress was being made. It would be an afternoon dress in moss green and pink stripes with a skirt of four flounces trimmed with pink fringe, and close-fitting sleeves flounced above the elbow.

Soon, only the green and violet tartan evening dress remained to be tried on, but my mind was not on dresses that afternoon. I couldn't get Meagher and Shark out of my mind. There must have been a connection between the two men. Wasn't it strange that Meagher should run to Shark while being chased by the police? Why did he? Did he want to implicate Shark in some way? I would probably never know.

## ⚔ Chapter Five ⚔

"GOOD EVENING, APSLEY," I said as I descended the last few steps of the grand staircase.

It was Wednesday evening, and I was wearing the blue dress at last and was properly dressed for dinner at Warton Hall for the first time.

And what a marvelous dress it was. Its neck was cut low, leaving my shoulders bare, and from the neckline fell a ruffle of white lace and blue-ribbon bows, concealing the short sleeves. It had a tiny waistline, in the fashion of the day, and from it billowed the blue silk skirt—sixteen yards of it, puffed out by eight starched petticoats underneath. From the waist floated a white tulle overskirt, and it was gathered all around, at knee length, by little bouquets of blue silk flowers in nests of white lace and blue-ribbon bows from which white lace streamers flew.

To complement the dress, Clair had arranged my hair in long curls that fell from behind my ears to my shoulders.

Apsley's "Good evening, miss," was definitely more deferential than usual.

"Are his lordship and her ladyship in the corner room, Apsley?" I said.

"I believe so, miss." Apsley had forgotten himself and was staring at me.

And I could still feel his stare as I turned from him and glided through those elegant rooms with their priceless paintings and tapestries. I looked as if I belonged there, but I wondered if I would ever *feel* as if I did. I loved my new dress, however. I loved the soft sighing of the skirt as I walked, and I loved the feeling of being enmeshed to the waist in a large, rather heavy, bell-shaped cloud.

Again as I walked through the tapestry room, as on that first evening, I saw them in the corner room. And again they saw me coming. But that evening I walked toward them with all the icy grace I could muster and stopped just inside the room—standing in profile, my face turned toward them, the end of my fan held lightly against the tip of my chin.

Silence.

"Very good. Very good. Oh, very, very good. Just what I wanted," my stepfather cried. "Just right. Oh, yes. Yes, yes, yes!"

He skipped toward me as he spoke, clapping his hands, and then he skipped in a circle around me. Round and round he went—three times, four times.

"Very good. Oh, very good."

But then he stopped still in front of me, and his eyes narrowed. "Where did you get that?" he screamed, pointing to the pink pearl I wore around my neck on a gold chain. His finger nearly touched my throat.

Instinctively I covered the pearl with my hand. "Nana gave it to me—in France, when I was a little girl," I said.

"Wear something better. It is not good enough," he cried.

Then we went into dinner, where, during the meal, I noticed Mother looking at me as if she had not seen me before.

The following morning, when Dorothy drew back the curtains in the alcove, the sun shone into the room and lay on the Turkish rug, glazing it with squares of gold.

"The sun is out," I said to Dorothy, "and I am going

riding today—across the fields to the sea. My habit is done. At last I shall see some of the countryside."

"Be very careful, miss," Dorothy replied.

"Don't worry, Dorothy, I have ridden since I was a child. Why, I am more at home in the saddle than I am on my feet. Good morning, Clair. I am going riding today."

The sun seemed to have filled us all with good spirits. We had not seen it since the funeral—four days of cloudiness and rain. But thanks to the rain, everything outside was lush, and the sun would open all the wild flowers in the fields and under the hedgerows.

So I was impatient for prayers and breakfast to be over, though at breakfast I ate rather more than usual because I did not expect to be back for luncheon, and I told Apsley so.

I could not leave, however, until after I had done the flowers. That morning, Benjamin brought fewer flowers because we had done a great deal of work the day before, and only the corner room and the drawing room needed new bouquets. But he always brought me carrots. Every morning their shorn heads peeped out of the water at the edge of one of the flower buckets. Their presence had become a symbol of the affection that had blossomed between us.

When we had finished, I ran to my room and rang for Clair. She brought my new habit and hat from the wardrobe and helped me on with them. The habit was a deep-blue barège, very simple and beautifully cut with a jacket buttoning down the front and with a collar and cuffs edged in a single thin band of scarlet braid. Clair thought it very becoming, and I agreed. When I was dressed, I thanked Clair, saying that I probably wouldn't be back until late in the afternoon. I took my old school crop from the shelf, and the carrots, picked up my skirts and ran from the room. I raced down the long corridor and down the grand staircase to the hall.

Titus opened the entrance door for me, and I stepped out onto the wide landing and looked down the long drive to the gateway. In a little while I would be traveling down it on horseback.

And as I stood there, I breathed deeply and looked up at the sky. A gull, very white against the intense blue, circled indolently. Then I ran down the steps toward the stables and Thunder.

He was happy to see me. He ate his piece of carrot and playfully nudged my shoulder for more. "Beautiful Thunder," I said, rubbing his long nose, but then he shied away from me.

"I see you haven't taken my warning very much to heart, miss," John said.

I hadn't heard him come up behind me.

"On the contrary, John," I said, turning toward him, "I gave your warning a great deal of thought. Thunder is not a mean animal. He was treated cruelly and he retaliated. Even human beings do that. But animals are simpler than humans—it is contrary to their natures to become malicious without a very good reason. You must know that. Thunder has no reason to dislike me. On the contrary, we have become friends, and I would like to get to know him better.

"Will you saddle him for me, please? I think the dark leather saddle with the tooled edge will do."

"I'm sorry, miss, I can't do that," John said. "You might get hurt or killed, and I can't take the responsibility, miss."

Those inexorable eyes of his met mine for an instant and then fell to the ground, and he stood silent before me.

"John, you have told me Thunder's history in detail. You have warned me against him, and I thank you for it. I know you want to help me, and I thank you for that, too. But surely you would not impose your will upon mine. You have no right to keep me from riding

69

Thunder, John. The responsibility is not yours—it is mine.

"Will you saddle him for me, please?"

"Yes, miss," he answered after a pause.

He strode off toward the saddle room without looking at me again.

I watched in the shade while Thunder was being saddled. He was nervous and did not want to take the bit, which was natural since he hadn't been ridden in two years. When he was ready, I walked to him, calling his name, and I stroked his neck until he quieted.

Then John helped me mount, and we adjusted the stirrup. And all the while I hoped that I was doing the right thing—that my judgment had been correct. Who really knew about horses, though? Once in a great while, there seemed to be one that was just plain bad.

First I walked Thunder around the yard, then we trotted around it, and then we did two half turns and a perfect figure eight. He had been beautifully schooled —I knew that almost at once—and he knew that I had been well schooled, too. He had understood and obeyed the slightest pressure of my hand or heel at once and without question.

John had stood watching us, and we walked over to him.

"Well done, miss," he said.

Poor John. How humiliating to have been lectured to by someone so much younger. I must try to make it up to him in the future, somehow, I thought.

"Thank you, John," I said. "Someone has taken a great deal of trouble with Thunder. He is superb. Good morning, Henderson. Good morning, Monk."

They had come out to stand beside John while I rode, and I could see, out of the corner of my eye, two of the coachmen and a groom standing in a little knot outside the open coach house doors, looking on.

Then I said to Henderson, "John told me Thunder's story, and I insisted that he be saddled for me. I think that we will get along very well together."

"I don't know, miss," Henderson said.

"Yes, we will, Henderson," I said, smiling at him.

"Very good, miss. You'll want a groom to go along, then, if you're going out, miss," he said.

"Yes, Henderson, but I am afraid it will mean his missing his luncheon."

"Don't you worry about that, miss. Monk, go and find Owen—I think he'll be in his room—and tell him to saddle Double Charlie. He's to go with Miss de Riocour."

When Owen was ready, I walked Thunder out of the stableyard gate and down the stable drive until we were parallel to the front of the house, and then straight onto the turf of the park. There we broke into a slow canter, and I murmured, "All right, Thunder," and let him go. He flew through the air like an arrow from a bow. Did Thunder's feet touch the ground? Was this a horse I rode, or did I ride a star? So smooth was his stride that it seemed we flew.

In an instant we had streaked across that mile of park, parallel to the drive and away from the house. At the gateway, we slowed, and I cantered him gently to a walk. Then we pulled up and waited for Owen.

"Don't worry, Owen," I called to him when he had caught up to us, "we won't be doing much more of that. I just wanted to see what Thunder could do."

"I'm glad to hear it, thank you, miss," he said, a smile crinkling his freckled face. "We couldn't keep up, you know."

Then we rode on. Sometimes we cantered and sometimes we walked toward the sea, with Owen and Double Charlie following obediently behind.

71

At last I was free. I could ride a mile this way or two miles that way. If I wished, I could ride up that hill and see what lay beyond, or I could take that lane to the left, along the little valley toward the ruined tower. And a whole, long, gentle English afternoon lay before me.

Ahead, the countryside rolled gently away in straight-sided, irregularly shaped fields bordered with hedges and juniper growths. Here and there a cottage nestled in its cluster of trees, and here and there an old oak cast up its huge expanse of green. Patches of woods splashed the landscape with their black-green shadows—a much darker green than the cloud shadows that swept across the fields. Yellow-centered marguerites and rock roses lay sprinkled at our feet in the grass, and a few late-blooming field poppies flecked it with flame. In a wide meadow to our left, men cut hay, perfuming the still air.

At length we stopped on a hilltop overlooking the sea, an almost navy sea fringed with a wide yoke of white-lace breakers. Below us, in a green hollow, lay a village with a tiny harbor. White cottages, crowded together, lined its only street. Narrow and curving, it led down the hillside to a stone quay. Here stood a long stone building with a swinging sign above its door that I could barely read. It said, The Red Lion. And I wondered if anyone knew how many Red Lions there were in England.

It was a lovely sight. I thought, then, that I would love to live in a village like this. There must be something here that I could do—teach the children, perhaps. What a wealth of joy living here would offer—honeysuckle vines on the walls, foxgloves and myrtle and fuchsias in the gardens, and white sails of fishing boats in the harbor flapping gently in the sun to dry.

But my home was Warton Hall where Lord Trevenbury, one of the wealthiest men in England, was gilding a stepdaughter.

At last, we turned reluctantly from the village and the sea toward the Hall, and soon I saw the spire of the church in Fawsley rise above the trees. We found a lane that became, beyond a humped, stone bridge, the main street of Fawsley. There stood the church on its green hill at the end of the street, and we walked the horses toward it, clattering on the cobbles as we went.

Beyond the church and the rectory, the road led past the abbey and back to Warton Hall. And as we approached the ruins, I decided to take the wide path that cut through the ruined abbey church and joined the road again just beyond the building. We swung into the path and rode down the turf of the roofless nave. The sun flicked our shoulders at each of the church's empty windows as we rode past. Its walls towered above on both sides, throwing us into deep, cool shadow.

I welcomed the coolness. I felt hot, tired, and thirsty. We had ridden for hours, probably far too long for Thunder's first time, and although I could never get enough of the beauties of the countryside, I wanted to postpone more until another day. I desperately wanted a glass of cold water and then a pot of tea and some bread and butter and jam.

I barely noticed the intricate patterns that the brilliant sun patches made against the deep-black afternoon shadows. And I might not have noticed the man that watched us from those shadows if I hadn't chanced to look directly at him. He sat motionless on a black horse against the wall of the apse. He wore a patch over one eye and had a long scar down the side of his face. He gave no sign of recognition, nor did he move as his hawk eye watched us pass.

We had ridden out of the ruin and into the sunlight before I fully realized what I had seen. I had seen the man who had waited in Martin Shark's carriage the night of my arrival, the man Dorothy feared so.

Immediately I urged Thunder into a canter; I

wanted to get away from there. I glanced back at Owen. He didn't seem to have seen the man. At least, he didn't seem surprised.

I didn't wish to pause to ask him about it, however, nor did I mention it when we pulled up in front of the house and Owen helped me dismount.

I thanked Thunder and ran my hand down his neck. His ears flicked. He understood.

Then I dashed up the steps, pausing outside the door to glance at the abbey tower. I shivered. Who was that frightening, scar-faced man?

Titus had heard the horses and opened the door for me, and as I entered the house, Apsley hurried toward me across the hall.

"His lordship has been asking for you all afternoon, miss," he said. "If you would care to follow me to his office, miss, I will show you where it is."

"Thank you, Apsley. Did he say what he wanted to see me about?"

"No, miss."

My stepfather's office was a little room just a few steps from the entrance doorway of the south front and opposite an interior stairway leading down to the large courtyard. The courtyard was connected by a passageway to the kitchen yard, which I often used. This would, I supposed, permit workmen and farmers to reach the office without going through the house.

When we arrived at the office door, Apsley gestured to it and then left me. I knocked.

"Come," said a voice.

I entered and found my stepfather sitting at a desk that almost filled the tiny room. He had probably been working on some bills—an open ledger and several neat piles of papers lay on the desk before him. He sat with his back to the room's only window. It was flanked by two recesses. The shelves of one of these recesses were stacked with ledgers and books, the other with bundles of papers and rows of polished wooden boxes. But apart from the two recesses, the dark, oak-paneled walls stood unbroken and unadorned, except for the chimney piece and a collection of weapons that had been arranged on the wall above it. There, crossed in the center of the arrangement, hung a broad sword, a rapier, a claymore, and what looked like a blowgun. Around these, arrows, a cutlass, some daggers, knives, hatchets and a cudgel or billy were fastened to the paneling.

"Where have you been? Where were you when I wanted you?" he asked.

"I went riding," I said. "I hope that was all right. I could hardly be expected to remain in the house all day, every day, in case you should wish to talk to me."

He sat there silently for almost a minute, his cat's eyes blazing into mine, his pen tapping a tattoo on the open ledger page. I returned his stare without flinching. And then his eyes began to smile, although there was no movement of his mouth. Suddenly he struck the top of a stack of three black velvet boxes with the end of his pen.

"These are for you. Wear them."

I was too surprised to move.

"Well, take them. Take them with you. They are good stones. Not many women have stones as good as these. Your mother has better ones. You will see them."

I picked up the boxes from the desk and opened the top one. It contained a brooch, a huge oval-shaped emerald surrounded by diamonds.

"Do not take my time while you open them here. That is not necessary. The necklace will be reset by Worthenhauser of London. They will be here on Monday. They will bring drawings and samples. You will be available."

"I—I don't know how to thank you—Father," I said.

75

"I do not want your thanks. While you are in my house, you will be an obedient daughter to me." He smiled, but the smile had no warmth in it.

Then I turned from him and left the room, closing the door quietly behind me.

"So," I said to myself, as I walked back toward the grand staircase, "the price of a home is to be obedient."

But I would see what I was required to do before I refused to do it. And after all, nothing had been asked of me yet.

I climbed the staircase and walked to my room. There I rang for Clair. She helped me off with my habit, and I bathed and put on a dressing gown.

"Clair," I said, "I saw a very strange-looking man on a horse as we rode by the abbey a while ago. He was very thin and wore a patch over one eye and had a long scar down the side of his face. Do you know who he could be?"

"No, miss," she said. "I don't think I have ever seen anyone who looked like that. Is it important?"

"No. I wondered who he was, that's all."

While we talked, I opened the jewel boxes and placed them side by side on the table in the light of the alcove.

"Oh, miss! Did you ever see the like of them?" Clair exclaimed. "They are beautiful. They must be worth a fortune, miss."

The two smaller boxes held the emerald and diamond brooch and a ruby pendant—a large ruby surrounded by pearls on a gold chain that was studded with tiny rubies and pearls—and ruby and pearl earrings to match. And on the satin lining of the large box lay a necklace of emeralds, pearls, and rubies worked in gold. I lifted it from its box, and Clair put it round my neck. It was very old—a lacy design using rows of tiny emeralds bordered with seed pearls to form the outline of connecting hearts. Bands of these stones intersected the hearts to hold large, round emeralds in their centers, and pear-shaped rubies dangled between.

"This should be in a museum, Clair," I said. "But he wants to have the stones reset. I can't let him do it."

"It is lovely, miss. It suits you perfectly," said Clair.

"Put it back now, please. I think I will read for a while, here by the window—would you open it for me? And would you ask Titus if he would bring me some fresh water to drink and tea and bread and butter or whatever he can find in the kitchen to eat? I am hungry, but I really don't want to upset things down there. I know they must be starting to prepare dinner. Will you come back in about an hour, then, and help me dress? I would like to play the piano a little before dinner."

I wore the green and violet tartan that evening. It was a simpler dress than my blue one. The neck was cut low and off the shoulders and the huge, puffed skirt was trimmed with bands of violet ribbon. Its coloring suited the elaborate emerald, ruby, and pearl necklace, and I wore it.

But I wanted to do two things before dinner, so I left my room an hour earlier than usual. First I walked down the corridor to the long gallery and stepped inside it. This was an enormous room that stretched across the entire second floor of the entrance front. Here, twelve years before, a reception had been held for Queen Victoria—an engraving of the event hung in my room.

The walls of the gallery were lined with family portraits. I was sure that all the earls of Trevenbury would be there, and they were—painted by Holbein, Hilliard, Peter Oliver, Kneller, Lely, Van Dyke and Gainsborough. I walked along the east wall of the room looking at those long-dead men and noticed that they all had two things in common: all the former earls of Trevenbury had prominent chins, and all were tall, slim men.

That is rather odd, I thought, as I crossed to one of

the window seats and sat down. Outside, the sun had gone down at the end of the drive beyond the gateway, beyond the distant trees, beyond the sea. Nothing moved in the park: the scene before me was like a painting. But my thoughts were elsewhere.

That is rather odd, I thought. My stepfather certainly doesn't resemble any of his line in looks or, I am sure, in manners, either. How crude he is, and how complex. Sometimes when he is pleased, he is almost like a little boy at play. But there is nothing childish about his mind—a too-brilliant one lurks behind those feline eyes.

Then below me, from near the house, a deer walked out onto the grass, destroying my imaginary painting. And I got up and went down to the music room.

While I played one of the Mendelssohn "Songs Without Words," I glanced to my right, and directly into the eyes of my stepfather, who peered over the top of the piano, watching me. Everyone seemed to be watching me today, I thought. I threw him my most charming smile, however, and asked, "Do you like Mendelssohn, Father?"

"I do not know music," he said, strutting around the piano to where I sat.

"Do you like my new dress?" I reached out to him with what I hoped was a pleading gesture and touched his arm with my fingertips.

"Yes, you are very good. Very good," he said, with unconcealed approval.

"And the necklace," I said, touching the lowest swinging ruby, which rested in the hollow between my breasts. "Clair says it is one of the loveliest things she has ever seen, that the design is timeless, that it is perfect for me, and that it would be a shame to break up such an exquisite setting. Must we break it up?" And I cast my most imploring expression upon him.

"As you wish. It does not matter to me," he said, as

he danced off to meet my mother who had just come into the room.

So, I had accomplished what I had set out to do that evening.

# Chapter Six

THE NEXT MORNING, after the flowers had been arranged, I went to find Mrs. Danley. One of the housemaids said that she had seen her climbing the stairs to the third floor. I wanted to talk to her about a mistake I had made at dinner the night before—I had to talk to someone about it.

Toward the end of dinner the previous evening, Mother, my stepfather, and I had been talking about the social life of the countryside when I asked why some of our titled neighbors hadn't called. Mother said that most of them were still in London, that Parliament had only adjourned on Tuesday and that, this being the end of the season in London, people would be arriving in the country in the next few days.

"I am sure there will be more callers than we care to have, and very soon, dear," she had said, glancing at my stepfather.

"But what about Mr. Shark and his friend who waited in his carriage—what was his name?" I had been waiting for just such an opportunity to ask about them.

"Do you know Shark?" my stepfather had screamed at me.

He had screamed so shrilly that the crystals in the chandelier had tinkled.

"No, I never saw him—"

"Then how do you know his name?"

His hand had grasped the table edge so hard

that his knuckles had turned white. He had leaned toward me, tense, his eyes popping until I had been able to see the whites all around the pupils.

At the same time Apsley's eyes had implored me not to say that he had told me Shark's name.

"I saw his card on the tray in the hall," I had lied, as I had nudged a piece of chicken with my fork. "It really doesn't matter."

My stepfather had stared at me, intently, derisively. I knew he hadn't believed me. I had made a humiliating blunder.

"A business associate. We do not talk about my business affairs," my stepfather had said at last.

There had been a note of hysteria in his voice, still, but at a much lower pitch.

After that, we had eaten the rest of the meal in silence.

I found Mrs. Danley in the schoolroom talking to Mrs. Banks.

"Oh, there you are, Miss de Riocour," said Mrs. Banks. She was always very businesslike, very professional. She stood fingering the tape measure around her neck. "Just in time. Now, if you will go behind the screen there, I will help you on with this."

"Could we do it a little later, Mrs. Banks?" I asked. "Is there something you could be doing in the meantime? I don't want to hold you up, but I really did want to talk to Mrs. Danley."

"Why, child, what is it?" Mrs. Danley asked. "Of course Mrs. Banks will excuse us. Surely we can talk. Come along, my dear."

We left the schoolroom as she continued, "You just come along with me. We will go to my rooms if you would care to see them, and we will not be interrupted there, and I will give you a little sherry. Why, you do look a bit concerned about something, and perhaps I can help."

Mrs. Danley's rooms were located next door to my stepfather's office. We passed his door to get to them, and then we entered her sitting room from the hall. She had a suite of two rooms, a sitting room and a small bedroom, both looking out on the main courtyard and the chapel. At one end of the sitting room, a maid was setting a round table for seven people.

Mrs. Danley motioned to an armchair by the hearth as she said to the maid, "That's all right, Nelly. You can do that later."

Nelly gave us a curtsy and then went out another door, which I could see led to a spiral stair descending to the floor below. Then she closed the door behind her.

"That's Nelly Tettle. She's the still-room maid, you see," Mrs. Danley said. "That stairway goes down to the servants' hall, where all of the servants have their meals together. At the end of the meal, as is the custom, the upper servants adjourn here, to my sitting room, for sweets and bread and cheese and tea."

As she told me this, she walked to a cupboard near the table, took out two glasses and a decanter, and poured two glasses of sherry. Then she handed me a glass of sherry and sat down in the chair opposite me.

While she did this, I had a chance to examine the room. It was a cheerful room with flowered wallpaper covering the walls and floral chintz covering the chairs in which we sat. On the table beside my chair stood a vase of white daisies. A ray of sunlight splashed the flowers and then landed on my lap in a wide band. Then something else landed on my lap as well—something cinnamon colored. It settled into a tight bundle of throbbing purr in the center of that band of sunshine.

"And that's Caramela," Mrs. Danley said as I stroked the cat. "All she ever wants is stroking and loving and attention. Now, tell me what's bothering you, my dear, and what I can do to help."

I told her, then, about the scene at dinner the night before.

"You see," I explained, "I couldn't have said that Apsley had told me Mr. Shark's name, so I had to think of a lie. I know my stepfather didn't believe me. He knew it was a lie, and I am worried about it. Do you know who Martin Shark is? He's bald and very fat. Do you know what he was doing here, and who the man with the scar is who was with him in his carriage?"

"Gracious no, child," Mrs. Danley said. "I don't ever remember seeing two men looking like that, and I would be sure to remember two like that if I had ever seen them before. But why all this fuss? After all, his lordship has an awful lot of people coming and going, as he owns a lot of property and it takes a lot of management to care for it the way it deserves. And he does give it the best he has, I must say that for him. You can't know about all the men who come here on business with his lordship, you know."

"But the man with the scar was watching me yesterday as I rode through the abbey," I said.

"More than likely, with you being as lovely a young lady as one could want to see. Anyone would stop and stare, they would. Why, he's a gamekeeper, like as not, or some other workman about the estates. I wouldn't worry about that. And his lordship does get upset and storms about and yells until you think his head's coming off. But it's just a bit of temper, and you mustn't mind it or let it upset you. Why, he's got a beautiful young stepdaughter, and I am sure he's as pleased as punch about that, and so a little falsehood won't matter if he does know it, which he may not. So I would just forget the whole thing if I were you, my dear."

"Thank you, Mrs. Danley," I said. "It is so good to have someone to talk to. Sometimes I feel so alone. My mother and I can't seem to get to know each other, somehow, and my stepfather is so—strange—so difficult. You know, I was looking at the portraits in the

long gallery last evening. Why, he doesn't look at all
like any of his ancestors."

"Oh? I can't say I ever noticed," Mrs. Danley said.

"Were any of his ancestors—dwarfs? I mean, were
they shorter than usual, do you know?"

"I wouldn't know, I'm sure."

"Oh, I am sorry. I shouldn't ask you to talk about
your employer, should I? I really do apologize. I didn't
mean to."

"Now don't fret, child. I'm just glad you came to
talk to me, and you must come and do so whenever you
want someone to talk to. And besides, I don't think it
will be long before you meet other young people your
own age and make friends now that all the other families will be coming down from London. You will soon
be so busy you won't know whether you are coming or
going. Why, Mrs. Banks was just saying that all your
new dresses will be finished in just another week, and
she will be off to do the sewing at Landon House, like
as not, same as last year."

We chatted for a while, then, about nothing very
much, or rather Mrs. Danley chatted and I listened,
basking in the friendly atmosphere and petting the cat
in my lap. It was a peaceful, contented time for me,
and I felt much better when I left her to go to
the schoolroom and Mrs. Banks.

That day was a pleasant day, all in all, and a rather
busy one in the schoolroom. Mrs. Banks was creating
a miracle in white embroidered taffeta. It was more
like the top of a fancy, iced dessert than a dinner dress.
It was delicious. And she had finished the deep yellow
silk—it had three tulle overskirts, each a shade of paler
yellow, looped up at the side with pink and yellow
roses, and trimmed with tiny pink rosebuds.

Trying on the dresses in the schoolroom occupied the
rest of the morning, and then it was time for luncheon.
During the meal, Apsley told me that my stepfather

had gone to Bath on business and would not be back until late the following night, that my mother would have dinner on a tray in her room, and that I would be alone at dinner.

"May I have a tray, too, Apsley?" I asked.

"Certainly, miss, if you wish," he said, "but Titus and I would be most pleased to serve dinner here in the dining room as usual if you wish it."

"I really would like to have it in my room for a change, thank you, Apsley."

During coffee, I chose what I would have from a menu Titus had gotten for me.

Titus brought the tray at seven-thirty and set a place for me at the table in the alcove. I asked him to leave the terrace door open to let in the breeze. He left me then, asking me to ring when I was finished so that he could clear the dinner tray away.

"Leave the coffee, Titus, please," I said when he returned. "I think I will sit awhile and enjoy the twilight. Don't worry about the china. Dorothy can return it to the kitchen in the morning."

"Very good, miss," he said.

I wished him good night. And after he had closed the door behind him, I knew that I would be undisturbed for the rest of the night. Dorothy had already turned down my bed, and Clair had helped me into my dressing gown and put out my nightdress. So I lay back in the overstuffed chair, sipping my coffee, looking out at the darkening garden below, thinking.

No one, I mused, seemed to know anything about Martin Shark or his scar-faced friend. Benjamin didn't know them, for I had asked him that morning. He had never even seen them. And I had asked Monk, after I visited Thunder. He had not seen them, either. He would have, I was sure, if the scar-faced man or Shark had been anywhere near the stables. No, only Dorothy, Patrick Meagher, and I. . . .

I woke with a start. How long had I been asleep? I

was chilly and a little stiff. It was dark outside. My lamp had gone out.

A brilliant moon had risen above the hilltop behind the mausoleum, throwing it and the hill into sharp silhouette. I could see it from where I sat, through the open door. It was a beautiful scene, in an eerie way, and I stared, fascinated. Suddenly a light flashed on the distant portico and went out immediately. Someone had entered or left the mausoleum. And then I saw a shape, silhouetted by the moonlight, limp a few steps along the hilltop and then disappear as it descended the other side of the hill.

How strange, I thought. And even after I had gone to bed, I lay sleepless, thinking how strange it was that someone should be in the mausoleum at eleven-thirty at night. Someone with a limp. Mark Lawson limped—was Mark Lawson in the mausoleum tonight? Why had that handsome stranger visited the Trevenbury mausoleum so late at night?

On Saturday the whole house seemed to sigh with relief because my stepfather would not be at home that day. Both Apsley and Titus were in thinly disguised high spirits at luncheon.

"Titus," I asked, "will you go to the stables after luncheon and ask John to saddle Thunder for me and have him ready at the entrance front at two o'clock, please? Or should you ask Henderson? Which would be proper, Apsley?"

"Her ladyship always has John saddle her horse, miss," Apsley said, always pleased when asked advice. "Henderson is in charge of the stables, miss, but I believe he has delegated complete authority over the saddle horses to John, who is the head pad-groom. He has Jenken, Owen, and Hippolyte to help him, of course, and if there should be a hunt or many guests with saddle horses, all the grooms and coachmen would be expected to help."

"Thank you, Apsley." Then I turned to Titus. "And Titus, I will need a groom to go with me. Will you tell John that, please?"

So I left the house at two o'clock and found Owen standing at the bottom of the steps of the entrance front, holding the horses and looking up with his crinkly smile. He loved horses, and he loved to ride, and he was happy to be going out—no matter where.

"Good afternoon, miss," he said.

"Good afternoon, Owen," I said, as I walked to Thunder.

He whinnied a greeting and nuzzled my shoulder for the carrot he knew I had for him. I stroked his neck and talked to him as he ate. Then Owen helped me mount, and we rode off.

We went directly to the mausoleum, and when we arrived, I sat for a moment looking at the view from the hilltop. In the far distance, a carriage sped along a lane, trailing a cloud of dust behind it. We needed rain. And the sky seemed to agree, for mare's-tail clouds had come out of the sea and lain their long feathery plumes across the sky, signaling a change in the weather.

Owen helped me down, and as I ran up the steps of the building, I called back to him, "I'll only be a minute, Owen."

Before me, the huge iron doors of the mausoleum were shut tight, and I paused before them. Someone had stood just here, I thought, and blown out his lantern last night. What could he have come to see?

The doors, though heavy, swung open easily, and I stepped inside. The room was still and cold, and the stone men and women slept peacefully. Behind the sleeping images of my mother and stepfather, Cecilia Osborne's coffin lay hidden behind a still-plain marble slab that sealed her vault. Her rose blanket had disappeared, but its petals still sprinkled the floor where the wind had blown them almost a week before. Nothing else seemed to have been disturbed, however, and the dead seemed to wish me gone—to leave their peace behind me.

So I left the building, closed the doors behind me, and walked slowly back to Owen and the horses.

We rode down the hill, past the abbey, to the rectory. And when we reached it, Owen went to the door and returned to tell me that the rector was at home.

"Help me down then, Owen," I said. "I may be thirty minutes or a little longer."

"I'll take the horses around to the stable then, miss," he said.

The Reverend Ashley's butler opened the entrance door for me, and I stepped inside the house and followed him down the hall to the drawing room.

"Miss de Riocour," he announced as he threw open the drawing room door.

The rector bounded out of his chair and hurried toward me. Behind him, Mark Lawson stood. Colonel Lawson had been sitting next to my mother on the sofa.

"My dear Miss de Riocour," the rector said, "what an enchanting surprise. Please come and sit down."

"Good afternoon, Miss de Riocour," Colonel Lawson said. His gray eyes burned into mine, and then he bowed charmingly.

"No, sit here next to me," Mr. Ashley said. "You will join us in a glass of sherry? No? Well, we were just talking about you and you appear. Sheer magic. Should a clergyman believe in magic? Probably not, but sometimes, as at this moment, I must confess I do." He laughed.

He was trying very hard to charm me. I felt that he was trying harder than I merited, but it pleased me.

"Have you really been talking about me?" I asked.

"Yes, your mother was—"

"I was saying," Mother interrupted, "that you have just come from school and that you have always led a cloistered life—especially in the convents in France—

that you are anything but worldly, that you are deeply religious and puritanical by nature, and that I hope life will not repel you. After all, we are very different here from the nuns in the convents, where you were so happy."

"You misinterpret me, Mother. How can you feel that way about me?" I asked. "I am not particularly religious, and if I were, I can't see that there would be anything wrong in that."

I glanced at Mark Lawson. Our eyes met. He had been examining me.

"You go to morning prayer every day, don't you?" she said. "But don't take it so seriously, my dear. It will sort itself out. You are free to do as you please, you know. If you should want to go into a convent, I won't try to stop you."

"A convent!" I gasped. I was too shocked to say more.

"Colonel Lawson," Mother said, getting up, "there is something I want to show you. Perhaps you can explain it to me. It is in the churchyard. You really must come along." Her hand rested on his arm, and she smiled at him. "You will excuse us, won't you, Paul."

Then she took Mark Lawson by the hand and pulled him along with her. He didn't seem to object, but he disengaged himself at the door to turn to me.

"Till later, Miss de Riocour?" he said, and then he followed Mother out of the room.

After they had gone, Mr. Ashley sat down again beside me.

"I wanted to thank you for your hospitality after the funeral last Sunday," I said to him. "I—don't know when I have enjoyed an afternoon so much."

"My dear—"

He looked at me steadily and with something like deep concern, which I found confusing. But he did not continue, and we were silent for a moment.

"Rector," I said then, "we are all repelled by life at

89

times, aren't we? But that is what makes it so necessary to find the joy, isn't it? I think that is what life is all about. But it is how we find it, and where we find it, that is so important. Don't you agree?" I smiled at him. "You don't have to worry about me."

"No, I don't think I do," he said, smiling back.

"I must be going. Will you have Owen bring the horses around?"

"But you have just arrived," he said, getting up to ring for the butler. And when the butler entered the room, he said, "Have Miss de Riocour's horse brought around, will you please, Thompson?"

"Very good, sir." And Thompson went off to find Owen.

"I meant what I said about having a lovely afternoon last Sunday," I said, as we strolled to the door.

"I enjoyed it very much, too," the rector said. "Will you come back and see us again soon? Perhaps it will be a happier time than today."

"Nothing could prevent me," I said.

This man wanted to be a friend, I felt, and I was beginning to feel that I would need all the friends I could get.

After we left the rectory, we rode into Fawsley, crossed the main street, and climbed the hill beyond. When we reached the outskirts of the town, we doubled back by less traveled lanes and returned to Warton Hall. The sky had become overcast, and I was glad the rain had held off until our return.

But I could not get the conversation at the vicarage out of my mind. I wished that I had been able to think more quickly, but it had all come as too much of a surprise for me. That transparent little speech of Mother's —she must think me an imbecile if she thought I didn't know what she was trying to do.

"Ah, but she doesn't care if *I* know what she is up to," I said to myself, "as long as Mark Lawson doesn't know, and he probably wouldn't care if he did. I don't like men who follow women around like puppy dogs. I think I dislike Colonel Lawson intensely. And if he wishes to go prowling about mausoleums in the dead of night, that is his affair. It is of no interest to me."

Mother and I dined alone that night, and dinner was the usual long, formal affair. Conversation was at first desultory, then completely nonexistent. After the entree, Mother slipped off into one of her dream worlds and rarely brought herself to reply to my questions. I wondered what Apsley and Titus thought about it, and I remember thinking how dreadful it was to have to pretend, to be careful of what one said during meals because the servants would surely be listening.

Since she did not seem to wish to talk to me, I had plenty of time to think. And I thought about her. Mother would not play a more important part in my future than she had in my past because she didn't want to. There could never be a close relationship between us. We would always be strangers, murmuring pleasantries instead of talking. There was no reason to refer to the conversation at the rectory that afternoon. What she said or did had little connection with me. If she wanted to run after Colonel Lawson, that was her affair.

## ⚔ Chapter Seven ⚔

IT BEGAN TO RAIN that night, and it rained for the next three days. It rained much too hard for anyone to go to Fawsley to church on Sunday. The little church must have been nearly empty, and I couldn't help thinking that Reverend Ashley would probably be relieved. Poor Reverend Ashley—he should never have been a rector in a country parish.

The rain, however, did not keep the two representatives of Worthenhauser in London on Monday. My stepfather's office was crowded that morning: Clair, my stepfather, and I were present, and the Messrs. Worthenhauser Jr. and Roth, two slick, obeisant men. They were disappointed that they would not be allowed to reset the sixteenth-century necklace, but they had taken the liberty of having their designer sketch several other necklaces with earrings to match. We studied the sketches, and both Clair and I liked one design very much, a necklace of small diamonds and large topazes in a simple rope design. It would go well with my yellow dress. And my stepfather thought another design would be impressive: it was an almost too grand one of large diamonds. So orders were given for these to be made up. Besides the drawings, Messrs. Worthenhauser and Roth had brought along a chest of bracelets and rings for our perusal. We bought a beautifully tooled solid gold bracelet and a filigree one worked with small diamonds, and a ring consisting of a cluster of diamonds and pearls. All of this made the rainy trip to the country a worthwhile venture for the two men.

Nor did the rain keep Lady Rutford from calling on Tuesday.

That afternoon, after luncheon, I had gone to the library, found a copy of Hugo's *Notre Dame de Paris,* had taken it to my room, and was reading in the armchair by the window. Occasionally I looked out at the raindrops shattering themselves on the terrace outside and the drenched gray gardens beyond. Then there was a knock on the door. Titus had come to tell me that Lady Rutford was in the drawing room with Mother, who hoped I would come down.

A few minutes later, as I passed through the corner room, I heard a booming voice say, "The weather is indeed inclement, but you must realize that we live in a rainy climate and that we cannot let weather interfere with social obligations." If a cannon could talk, I thought, it would sound like that. "The rain was fortuitous, Lady Trevenbury. We know how you like to ride in the afternoons and have seen you streaking magnificently through the forest on your—er—mysterious journeys. We believed the weather today would keep you at home."

Then I entered the drawing room and stood facing the source of the voice—a woman as mountainous as her voice was resonant. She sat in one of the Louis XIV chairs, and I wondered if the chair would hold her weight. She had several square chins and a sallow complexion. Her beady eyes stared at me through a lorgnette, which she held in her tiny right hand.

Deaf with heart trouble, I thought.

"Lady Rutford, this is my daughter," shouted my mother.

She *is* deaf—I had been right.

"How do you do? How nice of you to brave this dreadful weather, Lady Rutford," I shouted.

"We are not afraid of rain," boomed Lady Rutford. She examined me through her glasses as she might a slave on the block. Her eyes moved up and down my figure, and her head followed them, her jowls shaking like pudding. "We have heard of your arrival and, having just returned to the country, have hastened to discharge our obligation to call."

Her mouth was pursed. I wondered how much she would bid.

An awkward silence followed. I sat down. We looked at each other—not across a room, but across a glacier.

"The name is not Osborne," she stated at last.

"No, Lady Rutford," I said, "Lord Trevenbury is my stepfather. It is de Riocour, Suzanne de Riocour."

"Ah, yes. Your mother had married abroad, I believe, but kept her family name?" She turned to Mother, her mouth still pursed, eyebrows raised—haughty, disapproving, inquiring. "I believe it was Gorborn?" she said, as if tasting something sour.

Her eyes popped with distaste. If this was so distressing, why had she bothered to call?

"Garthorn-Hadden, Lady Rutford," Mother corrected, with a bland smile. "My father was the tenth marquis of Brancroft, a title bestowed on the first marquis by Henry VIII. My mother still lives at Sike Hall, the family's sixteenth-century manor house just beyond Bath. You may know of it. That is my father's portrait over the chimney piece."

"Ah, yes," said Lady Rutford. The taste had changed slightly.

"We lived very quietly after my father's death. My mother never quite recovered," Mother said.

"We have heard of Lord Brancroft." Her eyes had closed, but almost at once they popped open, and she continued, "You have known grief—your husband's death, so soon after the marriage, and your father's. But we survive," she cried. "We must!"

She sat, then, in silence. Her shrewd eyes examined Mother. Her index finger drummed the arm of her chair. I could almost see her mind racing, calculating, as she reviewed Mother's words.

"I believe you married abroad?" she demanded, finally.

"In Paris, Lady Rutford."

"And then to die so soon after in a foreign land. Distressing! Too distressing. But his family? Surely there was a family—to comfort—"

"He died at the Château Charmond," Mother replied, "the family estate just outside Nîmes, three months after we were married. His family was very kind, especially his brother, Count Leon de Riocour, and his brother's charming wife, who was a de Pounce before her marriage. My former husband's family was a very old one, going back to the court of Louis VII, and most compassionate and attentive."

"Such a tragedy." Lady Rutford gave Mother a frosty smile, and then she turned to me, raising her lorgnette. After another long pause she said, "Well, I have always said that blood will tell. Forgive me, my dear, but I knew as soon as you entered the room that such a lovely creature could come only from the best of families. Really quite beautiful." She chuckled with deliberate merriment. "You really must forgive the rudeness of a crotchety old woman. My handsome son Roundell—he is only twenty-three, yet a man of the world already—says that if I don't watch my tongue, we won't have any friends at all. But it doesn't seem to have had a bad effect. We are always busy. All the young ladies seem to find their way to Mendley House, and my husband is constantly having a hunt or a shoot or something. Oh, we do have good times at Mendley. Yes, good times.

"But, my dears, I must be going. Roundell will be wondering what has become of me." We stood, and she came to me and squeezed my arm, as if to test the solidity of the flesh beneath my sleeve. "I really cannot leave him unprotected for long." And she gave me a conspiratorial wink and giggle.

"My dears, it has been charming," Lady Rutford said, clapping her hands. "So charming. I have enjoyed our chat enormously. Simply divine." She punctuated this with another clap. Her lorgnette swung frantically from her huge bosom.

"Your carriage is up, please, your ladyship," Apsley announced.

"Lovely. Well then, ta-ta, ta-ta," she cried, waving her little hand as she sailed out of the room after Apsley.

"What a ridiculous woman," I said, when I was sure she was beyond hearing. "Oh, what a funny, funny, shallow woman."

"Shrewd and cruel and nasty and a dreadful bore," Mother said, her hand to her temple. "Now we are obliged to return the call tomorrow afternoon. Lord and Lady Rutford are very important socially in the neighborhood. Your stepfather will be pleased, but I hope *I* will be able to live through it all. I really must go and lie down. I have a dreadful headache coming on."

She left the room, and I went to the window to watch Lady Rutford's carriage retreat slowly up the drive through the gray curtains of pouring rain.

That evening at dinner, Mother had the pleasure of telling my stepfather about Lady Rutford's visit.

"She came in like a lion and went out like a lamb, dear," Mother said. "Really a beast of a woman, but Suzanne charmed her into a dove. She had such a charming visit, simply divine," Mother mimicked. "It was really quite exhausting. Quite successful, though, you may be sure."

"Oh, very good. Very, very good." My stepfather beamed. "You will call on her tomorrow, of course."

As I watched him, I thought of the portraits in the long gallery. And then I remembered that in the church at Fawsley there was a little portrait gallery in brass. The gallery would show the early Osbornes. I decided to go there in the morning.

As I rode up the drive to the rectory the following morning, Colonel Lawson rounded the corner of the house and walked his horse toward us. It was thrilling to see him on horseback. But then, I thought, that is what one would expect of an officer in the cavalry.

"Good morning, Miss de Riocour," Mark Lawson said. "What a pleasant surprise. It is a beautiful morning for a ride, isn't it?" His gray eyes bored into mine, I almost felt as though he could see through my clothes, and I felt a strange tingle that I had never felt before. And I noticed his broad shoulders, his thick neck and wrists, and his beautiful, big hands.

"Good morning, Colonel Lawson. Yes, it is a beautiful morning for a ride. It is nice to see the sun again, isn't it? But it is still muddy in places, I'm afraid."

If he asked me to ride with him, should I accept? I wondered. Yes, of course. Owen would come along, and it would be perfectly proper. The church could wait until another day.

"Ashley is at home," he said, "and I am sure he will be glad to see you. I wish I could join you, but I have an appointment to keep. I am afraid I am late for it already."

He gave me a courtly nod, looking deep into my eyes as he lifted his hat, and then moved his horse into a canter and was gone in the direction of the abbey.

This left me feeling strangely let down, as I walked Thunder to the door of the rectory. I am afraid the warmth of the rector's greeting did little to lift my spirits.

He held out both his hands as he walked across the drawing room toward me. "I am delighted," he said simply, placing my hands in his. "You kept your promise."

"I always do," I said, smiling up at him. "I shouldn't say so, but do you know—sometimes I can hardly believe you are actually the rector of St. James's Church. Somehow you don't seem like a clergyman at all."

"My dear, what does a clergyman seem like? Must he always be serious and glower at everyone—like this?" He made a grimace, which made me smile.

"But seriously," he continued, "perhaps I was not made for the church. Who is to say? I was the third son of a titled Englishman who settled a modest portion upon me at his untimely death. It was expected that I would go into either the army or the church. I liked the idea of the church better than the army, and here I am at Fawsley, rector of St. James's Church. I love the building *and* the people, and I flatter myself that I contribute some good to the community. And that is my story, in a nutshell." He spoke as though we had known each other always.

"I have a favor to ask," I said.

"Anything," he replied.

"The brass portrait gallery in the church. Will you show it to me?"

"With pleasure, my dear. Shall we go there now? And you shall see my roses on the way."

We walked out of the French doors of the drawing room, onto a terrace, and down to a rose garden. It consisted of four square beds of roses separated by a cross of perfectly edged green grass, in the center of which stood a bird bath.

"I have seen that large single yellow rose and that enormous double pink one before," I said, looking at him in mock accusation.

"Phillips, one of your stepfather's gardeners, gave me slips of them. But you mustn't tell your stepfather. I think he would begrudge me even the slips of his roses."

"Why does he dislike you?" I asked.

"Because I won't give up this living voluntarily. He

wants to get rid of me, but he can't force me out, and I have no intention of leaving. I suppose he has an acquaintance whom he would like to have here—I really haven't the slightest idea."

"It is a lovely garden. Each rose looks quite choice," I said, as we passed the bird bath.

The little church slumbered above us in its nest of gravestones. We climbed a path up the grassy bank to it. Blue Swiss columbine and purple sedum grew wild in clumps along the path, and, here and there, pink and blue hydrangeas blossomed.

When we reached the church porch, I picked a white clematis from a vine loaded with the fragrant blossoms, and carried it into the church with me. The church was a jewel box with walls of rubies, sapphires, and emeralds.

"Now," said the rector when we reached the gallery, "that is the tomb of John Osborne and his wife, Elizabeth, with their protraits in brass. It is Tudor. And here are two Elizabethans, John and Elaine Osborne. There is an interesting story about Elaine. She was asleep in her coffin when the sexton of the church, coveting her rings, broke it open. But he broke it open so loudly that he woke the good woman from her trance. She owed her life to a thief." He chuckled over his story and so did I.

"Those two figures, kneeling on their gilded cushions," he continued, "are two Osborne brothers, Peter and Paul. They died early in the seventeenth century."

"No resemblance," I murmured.

"My dear?" he asked.

"I was thinking that there is no resemblance between any of the Osbornes and my stepfather. There are portraits of all the earls of Trevenbury in the long gallery at the Hall. All the men seem to have small noses and prominent chins. The men sculptured here do, too. Look at the two brothers, for instance. And they all seem like tall men."

"Yes," the rector said. "He must have inherited his physical characteristics from his mother's side of the family. And she was of very common birth. Yes, there is a family resemblance here. It is rather uncanny, isn't it?"

"Common birth? Lady Trevenbury?"

"Well, she was never known as Lady Trevenbury to my knowledge. Good heavens! Not the Lady Trevenbury who lies beside the late Lord Trevenbury in the mausoleum," he exclaimed. "She was his first wife. No, I am talking about his second wife, Mary Danley."

"Mary Danley! We have a housekeeper at the Hall whose name is Danley—Ruth Danley. I don't suppose she could be any relation?"

"Her sister, as a matter of fact. Mary Danley died ten years ago," he said. "It is clear that you have not heard the story, though I expect you are the only one in England who hasn't. You didn't read about the trial or hear the sensation it caused two years ago?"

"No. I mean, yes—vaguely. There was a scandal or something about a title, but I didn't pay any attention to it. Mother hadn't married at the time, and it didn't interest me. Do you mean to tell me that Mrs. Danley at Warton Hall is my stepfather's aunt?"

"Yes, my dear. There is a bench under the oak outside. Let us go out into the air and sit there, and I will tell you the story. It is an interesting one, and you should know it.

"The seventh earl's, your stepfather's father's, first wife died about forty-five years ago," he began, after we had made ourselves comfortable. "You will notice that the marble of her figure in the mausoleum is a darker color than her husband's, and her clothes are of an earlier period. She had no children. To anyone's knowledge, his lordship had never remarried, so you can imagine the sensation it caused when, at the trial, it was announced that he had indeed remarried in June 1810. Not only had his remarriage been kept a secret, but the existence of a son and heir had been kept secret as well."

"But why had he kept it secret?" I asked.

"Probably because his wife had been a servant at Warton Hall. If he had made his marriage known and installed the unfortunate girl as Lady Trevenbury, she would never have been accepted into society. As a matter of fact, she and her husband both would have been ostracized.

"She had been Lady Trevenbury's personal maid, I believe. At any rate, shortly after her ladyship's death, Mary Danley left Warton Hall and moved to London, where she and the late Lord Trevenbury were married, as I said, in June 1810, in Berkley Church in the Holburn Hill area of London. Then, in—let me see— April 1811, your stepfather, Fitzjames, was born."

"My stepfather didn't know his father, then," I said.

"Yes, he did, as a matter of fact," the rector continued. "His parents' romance must not have lasted long. I suppose this was due to the distance of separation or the vast difference in background. Who knows? They were obviously very much in love just before and after their marriage, according to his letters—which were published whole in the newspapers during the trial, to the delight of Englishmen everywhere. Who knows what happened? Marriages go sour under the best of circumstances. But the late lord kept track of his son. They corresponded during the last years of his life. In his letters he told his son of his pride in Warton Hall and its history. And Fitzjames visited his father several times and was closeted with him for hours."

"But his existence was not *then* a secret," I interrupted.

"Oh, yes! You see, following his father's instructions, Fitzjames did not use his real name when he visited. His father did not want to create a sensation by having a grown son appear all of a sudden during the last years of his life. I suppose that is understandable.

"Fitzjames inherited everything."

"What did his father die of?" I asked, looking down at the grass.

"Heart. He died in his sleep. He was almost ninety years old, you see," said the rector.

"Then his son wasn't with him when he died?" I asked.

"Gracious, no! He was in London most probably," he said. "But then, Fitzjames's uncle, John Osborne, would not accept the legitimacy of the claim or of the will, which was sent to Fitzjames as his father had promised, shortly after his death. Consequently, the trial.

"There was no question of the validity of the claim. The evidence was overwhelming. Ruth Danley had been present at the wedding. The marriage register was produced, as were the gifts of jewelry, suitably engraved with the Trevenbury crest. And then, of course, there were the love letters. And Fitzjames had, after all, been most cordially welcomed by his father many times at Warton Hall during the last years of his father's life. No, there was no question that Fitzjames was the rightful heir to Warton Hall and the estates. It caused a sensation in the press."

"He hasn't acted like a man of breeding," I thought aloud, "and I have wondered why. He hasn't seemed right to me, but this explains it. Thank you so much for telling me all this." We had gotten up by then and began to walk down the hill toward the rectory. "You are right. I should know the story, and it is a fascinating one. From rags to riches, it must have been."

Shortly thereafter, I took my leave of the rector and rode back to Warton Hall, hoping that I would not be late for luncheon. But on the way, I stopped for a moment at the gateway to the stable block to speak to Monk.

"Did her ladyship go riding this morning, do you

know? She said she might, and I had hoped to meet her, but I didn't."

"Yes, miss," he called up to me. "I saw her ride out that way not long after you left this morning." He pointed toward the abbey.

"Well, I shall have to ask her why we didn't meet, then. Thank you, Monk."

Then I rode on to the entrance front, where I dismounted and hurried into the house.

During luncheon, Mother and I decided to leave Warton Hall at two-thirty. We would arrive at Mendley House at three, which would be quite pleasant. Orders were dispatched to Henderson about the carriage.

He was waiting for us at the entrance front at two-thirty with Monk playing "tiger" beside him. Titus came along, in livery, and rode up behind.

"Lord and Lady Rutford are very active in county society," Mother reiterated, as we drove toward Mendley House. "They entertain lavishly, I understand. He is the fifth earl of Rutford. He has, through necessity, actually gone into business in a way: he has invested heavily in railways in recent years, your stepfather tells me, and has become chairman of the London and Southwestern Railway—a dubious distinction, to say the least."

"What is Mendley House like?" I asked.

"I really couldn't say, my dear. I have never been there, though I know where it is. I had never even seen Lady Rutford, until Tuesday. You must remember that your stepfather and I have not entered into society here since we arrived. The period of mourning for his father prevented it."

Mendley House stood just beyond Taunton. And soon on that soft, misty summer afternoon, so very green and lush and comfortable, we swept through its gates and along its winding drive through a wood that was planned to provide peekaboo glimpses of the house. The house was much smaller than Warton Hall, no more than forty rooms, but of a lovely design with a portico of six two-story Corinthian columns and a long glass conservatory curving forward from one corner of the facade.

We were announced at the drawing room doorway. The room, its walls painted a vivid sky blue, was filled with light from enormous windows looking out on the drive. The blue made the room seem cold, and I was glad I had brought my shawl.

Lady Rutford rose and came to us. "My dears, how nice," she called. "I was just telling Lady Plummer and her daughter, Miss Bisham, what a lovely visit I had at Warton Hall yesterday."

Lady Plummer sat on a sofa next to her daughter. They were both thin women, and both had long noses.

"And this is my son, Roundell," explained Lady Rutford.

A thickset young man of medium height had risen when we entered and now advanced toward us. His hair was coarse and black and unmanageable. His cheeks were pitted and very pink. He wore a bushy mustache.

"Welcome to Mendley House," he said to my mother, and then he turned to me. "Dear Miss de Riocour, we have looked forward to meeting you ever since we learned of your arrival at Warton Hall."

"Thank you, Lord Easton. How very kind of you to say so," I replied.

Then we sat down. Roundell Wensley sat in the chair next to me.

"We were just saying, Lady Trevenbury, what a terribly drab season it was in London this year," cried Lady Rutford. "Really only three balls of any consequence: the marquis of Swandson's, the duke of Southland's, for his daughter, and the duke of Landsbury's. Oh, and of course your ball at Hastings House, Dorothy."

"Yes, a gloomy season, positively dull, and so much fog and damp," said Lady Plummer. "Only last evening I was saying to Cecil, that is my handsome son, Lady Trevenbury and Miss de Riocour—he is twenty-five. 'Surely, my dear,' I said, 'there must have been one young lady in all of London society to make your heart beat faster.' 'No,' he said, 'there was no one. If only there was one as lovely and accomplished as my sister, Iris, it would be quite a different story.' Really, Nancy, he was quite disconsolate."

"And how do you like Warton Hall, Miss de Riocour?" Roundell asked, leaning nearer.

"A remarkable building—so pure for the period, Lord Easton," I said, speaking in a low voice so as not to interrupt Lady Rutford.

I need not have worried, however, as she was talking very loudly.

"Ah—you are interested in architecture?" Roundell asked, as surprised as if I had expressed an interest in earthworms. "Then you will be interested in Mendley House. Will you permit me to show you around it? It was designed by ah—ah—in I believe—in eighteen—Mother!" he shouted. "Miss de Riocour is interested in architecture."

"How very extraordinary," boomed Lady Rutford, briefly focusing her lorgnette on me.

"I thought I would show her about the grounds a bit," Roundell said.

"Yes, let's," exclaimed Iris, jumping up with exaggerated excitement.

"Yes, yes, go along children." Then turning back to Mother, Lady Rutford continued, "Well, Lady Trevenbury, when we arrived, *there* was the duchess of Weatherford just getting out of her carriage, and *there* was the duke, having already arrived with. . . ."

Iris danced out of the room and into the conservatory even before Roundell and I got up. When we had joined her and had all begun to walk along the drive together, Iris looked back to see if we could be observed from the drawing room. Seeing that we could not, she slipped her arm under Roundell's, skipping a little and juggling his arm to express her delight.

"Oh, Roundee," she cooed, "do you remember that afternoon at Longlington House? It was a lovely afternoon like this one, and we walked alone in the garden among the box hedges." Her hand covered her mouth, and she snickered. "And you said that if it had been a Turkish garden—" She was lost in a paroxysm of giggles.

"Miss Bisham's and my family have known each other as long as I can remember," Roundell said to me. "Iris and I practically grew up together," he explained.

"Oh, yes, and now that we *are* quite grown up," Iris said, leaning forward so she could see me, walking on the other side of Roundell, "we see *more* of each other than ever, don't we, Roundee dear?" She laid her cheek on his shoulder, then, and assumed a look of heavenly bliss.

"Iris, please!" Roundell said, disengaging himself.

This caused Iris to sulk. She lagged a step behind, her hands clasped behind her, glancing now and then at the sky as though bored with us.

"It is such a lovely park," I said to Roundell. "I love the now-you-see-it, now-you-don't glimpses of the house from the drive. It is a beautiful plan and those—"

"The Wensleys seem to specialize in now-you-see-her, now-you-don'ts," Iris interrupted.

"Iris!" Roundell exclaimed.

"Are those the stables beyond the wall?" I asked.

Then Iris grasped Roundell's right hand and began to run ahead, trying to pull him with her. "The other side of the wall?" she cried. "Shall we show Miss de Riocour what we do on the other side of the wall, Roundee, dear? Just through this little door?" Again, she covered her mouth with her hand to suppress her mirthless laughter.

"Iris, please!" Roundell shouted, jerking his hand free of hers.

"There was a very different kind of 'Iris, please' that afternoon in Lady Risholm's conservatory." Iris stopped and whirled around to face us. To my astonishment, she had turned into a harridan. She clenched her fists and shouted at us. "Do you remember that, Roundell Wensley?

"And then we return to Somerset and find that a new young woman has come into our midst," she hissed. "The stepdaughter of a disgusting runt of a man, and daughter of a woman of questionable amusements. *They* could never be seen anywhere if it weren't for the vulgar, golden bait they cast before us." She was glaring at me with undisguised, malicious hatred. Each word was a sharply pointed dart. "A sixty-thousand-pound dowry for his *daughter*." She pronounced the word as if she had smelled something rotten.

Then she turned back to Roundell, her eyes narrowing as she looked down her long nose at him. "We have seen very little of you since we returned to the country, Roundell. Will you be spending your time prospecting for gold, now, in the hills of Somerset? Well then, I shall leave you with the bonanza."

And she flung herself about and stalked back to the house.

I was struck dumb by her performance, but then my thoughts went racing. So that was why I was here!

"I am so terribly sorry," Roundell said, "I would give anything if that hadn't happened."

"There is no apology necessary, Lord Easton," I said. "You have done nothing to apologize for. On the contrary, you have been most considerate. I suppose we should go back, too. It will soon be time to go home."

When we returned to the drawing room, we found

that Iris and her mother had departed. Lady Rutford looked like a cook who had just made her first successful soufflé and, to my relief, she launched immediately into a lecture on, as I recall, the current state of society in London.

At last our carriage was up, and I said good-bye to a very cowed Roundell Wensley. His mother waved and ta-taed us from the room.

"I suppose you want to know what happened," I said to Mother as we drove away from Mendley House.

"I know what happened, my dear," she said, gazing placidly at the trees as they flashed by.

"You know?"

"Lord Easton paid more attention to you than to Iris Bisham. It was obvious. Such a boring afternoon." Her hand went to her temple, and her eyes began their journey into her own private dream world.

I didn't mind because I had things I wanted to think about, too. So we rode along in silence, as I tried to piece together the puzzle. A sixty-thousand-pound dowry would bring every eligible young man within miles to Warton Hall, and with every young man, his parents—and with his parents, invitations and eventual social acceptance. It was a foolproof plan, I thought, especially when the stepdaughter turned out to be pretty. My stepfather must have thought she would, since she had such a beautiful mother.

I could well imagine how my stepfather must have planned his future when he learned that the inheritance was his. I could almost hear him saying, "After I receive my inheritance, the mansion house and the estates, I shall have all the wealth I desire. What else, then, do I want? I want a beautiful woman for my wife. She must come from a good family. Wealth will bring me such a woman. Yes, yes." And then, after the marriage: "What else do I want? I want to be accepted socially. I want to shoot and hunt and dine with other people of the class to which I now belong. This will be more difficult to arrange. Ah! My wife has a daughter at school. She will bring me social acceptance. Yes! Yes, yes."

"Well, 'Father,'" I said to him in my thoughts, "that is not so terrible for me. I will play the game and make it last a long, long time. I have no intention of marrying. Though if I have anything to say about it, I will have every eligible male within a radius of fifty miles eating out of my hand, and you will have so much sociality that you will be too tired to walk on those two little legs of yours."

As I pondered these things, I gazed out at the passing countryside—a saffron meadow here, an emerald pasture there, and then a stand of deep-jade hemlocks. In the dark cavern beneath them, the scar-faced man sat on his black horse, staring at us as we passed. I saw him clearly, but for an instant I couldn't believe what I was seeing. Why should that creature be here, on the other side of Taunton? And then I realized why: I was being followed by Martin Shark's associate, and he didn't care if I knew it.

I had great difficulty in falling asleep that night. Why, I kept wondering, was I being followed by that man with the scar? What *was* his connection with Martin Shark? And had Mr. Shark and Patrick Meagher known each other? They must have, though it *might* have been a coincidence that Patrick Meagher was caught in the hallway of the building where Mr. Shark lived. But suppose they did know each other, and suppose Martin Shark had paid Patrick Meagher to murder the seventh earl? Did my stepfather prevail on Mr. Shark to do this? What other motive for the murder could there have been other than my stepfather's wanting to inherit the estates? Could my stepfather be a murderer, then? But the late earl was close to ninety. He couldn't have lived very much longer. If that was the case, then why murder him? And why had my stepfather been so furious with Mr. Shark the night I arrived at Warton Hall? What had Mr. Shark meant that night when he told me to beware?

Moreover, what had all this to do with me? Was I in danger? I kept asking myself, and the answer was always *no*. No, I was in no danger. What had gone on here in connection with the death of my stepfather's father had happened long before I arrived. It had nothing to do with me. But why, then, was the scarfaced man following me?

Finally, after going over and over it, I decided that I could do nothing now—other than watch and wait. Nevertheless, I had a feeling that something terrible was going to happen, though I must be careful not to worry Dorothy because of it. And then I wondered if I should tell Clair about Martin Shark and Patrick Meagher. No, not yet, I decided. She could do nothing about it, so why risk upsetting her? At least I was not alone—I had Clair, and the rector was a friend. I could always go to him if I needed to.

With that, I must have drifted off to sleep.

# ⚔ Chapter Eight ⚔

THE FOLLOWING MORNING after breakfast, I walked in the rose garden for a few minutes before it was time to do the flowers. The morning was delicious. The sun turned the dewdrops to crystal. The bees droned their accompaniment to the bird's songs, and the air was filled with perfume. By the time I joined Benjamin in the flower room, the horrid thoughts of the night before seemed foolish.

When we had finished the flowers, I decided to take Thunder for a run. I changed into my habit and walked to the stables. Thunder came to the front of his box to greet me. As I was giving him his carrot, I heard footsteps behind me.

"I couldn't help admiring him when we met at the rectory yesterday. He is a beauty," Mark Lawson said.

"He's a killer," Monk said. Monk was usually at my side when I was in the stable, and, typically, he had materialized without my knowing it.

"Well, young man, he doesn't look like a killer to me."

"He did kill a man once," I said, as I swung around and smiled up into Mark's pearl gray eyes. "He stomped on a groom who had been torturing him."

"He did it on purpose," Monk said. "Smashed his head to a bloody pulp, he did."

"Monk!" I said. Then, to Mark, "He seems gentle, and he obeys beautifully. I have never ridden a lovelier

111

animal. We have become very good friends." I rubbed the side of Thunder's nose as he nuzzled my shoulder for more carrot. "There isn't any more, my beauty.

"John, one of the grooms, seems to think he might try the same thing again—throw a person and try to stomp on him, that is. But I don't think so. I don't believe any animal is inherently vicious, do you? I think they respond in kind. Having been in the cavalry, you must know horses well. What do you think?"

He considered the matter for a moment. "I agree with your analysis for the most part, Miss de Riocour," he said. "If you have ridden him several times and he seems obedient and gentle, he most probably is. With the exception of experiences on the battlefield, it is only when a horse has been badly broken or badly treated that you have trouble, and *that* you can tell almost at once. Yes, I think you are quite safe with Thunder."

"Thank you, Colonel Lawson. I am relieved to hear you say so. And what are you doing spying upon the occupants of the Warton stables?" I smiled at him.

"I was not spying, Miss de Riocour. I had no idea that you would be here. If I had known that, I *would* have come to spy." He was very serious. With such a courtly statement, there should have been a smile, but there was none. "Your mother and I were to go riding together this morning, but she is unwell, I find. Will you come riding with me?"

"I am afraid I would not make a good substitute, Colonel Lawson," I said.

"I did not ask you to be one, Miss de Riocour."

"Then I accept with pleasure. Monk, go and ask John to have Thunder saddled and ask if Owen may accompany us this morning, will you please?"

"Where would you like to go?" Mark asked, when we had mounted.

I had a sudden and intense desire not to go in the direction of the abbey, so I said, "Could we ride around

112

to the other side of the house and cross the river? There is a bridge there, and I have never been beyond it. We could explore together."

"Excellent," he said.

So we rode out of the stable-block gateway, Owen following discreetly behind, but it was not until we had rounded the corner of the house and were cantering across the lawn toward the bridge that I realized we were in full view of my mother's bedroom windows. I felt sure that she would look out to see who was riding below, and I longed to look up and see if she was watching.

But I did not, and then almost at once we were on the bridge and then across it. On the other side, we found a track that bordered the farm, led through the fields beyond, and swung back to follow the river. Farther on, the river surprised us by widening and flowing into a long blue inlet. Yellow Japanese irises grew wild along the bank, and water violets floated near the shore. In the distance, at the end of the inlet, a sand spit shone like snow. Here the gulls nested, white against the navy sea.

As we walked the horses slowly along the shore, I said, "Isn't it lovely? It is so much like an inlet in Brittany, near the place where we took our holidays sometimes when I was a little girl. It almost makes me feel eight years old again."

"So you spent your holidays in France," Mark said. "Do you speak French, then?"

"I lived in France until I was twelve. It was my home, so of course I speak the language. My father was French, you see."

"Your mother has not mentioned anything about living in France. Not that there would be anything unusual about that, but she seems so thoroughly English."

"And *I*, Colonel Lawson, what do I seem?"

"English, with foreign spice mixed in," he said. "But

113

one would not say you were of French blood, even partially so."

"Many Frenchmen are fair you know, Colonel Lawson, but my father's family was dark. Mother left me in France with Nana, shortly after I was born, and returned to England. I never knew her. There were a half dozen letters from her at school saying that she really must visit me, but she never came. I met her for the first time two and a half weeks ago, shortly after I arrived here.

"Dear old Nana had been Mother's governess in England. She had married young, and her husband had disappeared shortly after the ceremony and was never heard of again. She was a de Riocour. Her family's fortunes had never recovered after the Revolution, and rather than be a drain on the family, she had determined to work for her living, and so she came to England. Mother must have met my father, Madame's youngest brother, through Madame, but I don't know where.

"I grew up in the de Riocour family, but somehow, I never really felt like a de Riocour. Perhaps it was because, even in France, I was away at school most of the time. Do you know, I think I have never put that thought into words before? But this is becoming much too serious a conversation, Colonel Lawson."

"I think you are a very serious person, Miss de Riocour," he said, looking deep into my eyes.

What did he think he could learn from the depths of a person's eyes? I wondered.

"I am very serious about enjoying my life to the fullest," I shouted back at him, as I urged Thunder into a canter, "and not, you may be sure, in a convent."

Then we galloped on ahead—Thunder flew through the air—with Mark in pursuit. Thunder was too fast for Mark's horse. He couldn't overtake us. Finally we slowed and allowed him to catch up. Then we cantered along the shore of the inlet together for about

114

a mile farther before retracing our steps toward the farm. There was no way of crossing the inlet to ride home another way.

It is such a perfect afternoon for riding, I thought, as we headed back toward the farm. It was cool, with a breeze from the sea, and crisp and salty with a suggestion of autumn. We rode quietly, talking little. Sometimes I pointed out a bird or a berry or a tree, but most of the time we were content to enjoy the beauty of the day and each other's company without conversation.

"Are those willows, Colonel Lawson?" I asked at one point.

"Yes, a kind of willow, with a long Latin name that I would not even try to remember. The bark of those turns blue-white in winter. They have gone wild. They should be pruned back hard every spring," he said.

"How do you know so much about nature?" I asked.

"I was brought up in the country. My father was as fond of gardening as he was of hunting, which I always thought odd."

"Oh, yes, at Wellfield House, I suppose. Do they have those willows in Durham?" I asked.

"If someone has planted them, yes," he replied.

How handsome he was on his chestnut mount. I liked the way his chin jutted far out as I looked at him in profile. How relaxed and at ease he was. Still, I was very aware of the power and strength of that lithe body riding beside me.

"When you leave us, will you go to live at Wellfield House?"

"Who can say?" was all he answered.

"How long will you be staying with the rector?"

"I will be staying awhile yet. I am company for Ashley, and he enjoys having me here. Let us try the road to the right, there. It looks as if it goes back toward the stables, possibly from behind the house," he said.

115

"I think it does," I called, as I followed him.

The road was the one Benjamin took when he pulled his wagonload of vegetables and meat to the house each day, and it led us directly into the stable yard from the rear.

Mark accompanied me into the yard and then said, "I must be getting back to the vicarage. Ashley will be wondering where I am. Thank you for making the afternoon a delightful one."

Then he tipped his hat and rode away.

John had heard us enter and hurried toward me before Mark rode off. He helped me dismount, and then I left the yard and walked back through the gardens to my Chinese pagoda and sat down in it. It was a fantasy kind of place and made for daydreaming. I thought about Mark Lawson. How strange it was that I could talk to him as if I had known him for years. Why had I told him some things that I hardly admitted to myself? What a very *nice* person he was. And then I relived all the things that had made it such a happy afternoon.

## e҉ Chapter Nine ҉ɔ

"IT IS MOST EXTRAORDINARY," I said to Clair, who was brushing my hair that evening before I went to bed. "We have been invited to a dinner party at Winton House, Lord and Lady Plummer's house near Wolverton. After the scene with Iris Bisham yesterday at Mendley House, I scarcely thought I would be seeing much of the Bishams. My dowry must be all-powerful."

Clair knew about this. I had told her everything about the afternoon at Mendley House—everything except about seeing the scar-faced man.

"I have heard of Lord and Lady Plummer, miss," Clair said. "I believe Lord Plummer owns a large amount of property, including tin mines down in Cornwall."

"What should I wear, Clair?"

"I would suggest the white taffeta, miss. It is very rich looking and shows off your lovely skin so beautifully, and I would suggest no jewelry except the diamond earrings and the diamond and pearl ring. I think I would do your hair swept back severely, with masses of curls falling down the back of the neck."

"Yes, that sounds perfect. My stepfather will expect me to be weighted down with jewels, but I will manage him. Whatever would I do without you?" I asked, smiling up at her.

"Thank you, miss. I did wonder a little if you were satisfied with me."

"Clair! How could you wonder? But you must know

117

I couldn't get along without you. Know that, please!"

"Thank you, miss. It is just that you have seemed a bit upset these last few days."

"Perhaps just a little, but it is not important and has nothing to do with you.

"And here is a further bit of news. *We* are having a dinner party. The dinner at Lord and Lady Plummer's is next Tuesday evening, and then *we* are sending invitations to Lord and Lady Rutford, Roundell, Lord and Lady Plummer, and Cecil, their son, and, alas, Iris. There will be ten, including Mother, my stepfather, and me. It is to be next Friday, the twentyninth. Shall I wear my blue dress? It is still my favorite."

Clair agreed.

Tuesday evening finally arrived, and I stood before the mirror in my room fully dressed for dinner.

"Clair," I said, "I think you and Mrs. Banks have made me beautiful."

This had not been accomplished, however, in a few minutes. No, Clair and I had started my toilet at four-thirty. (Dinner at Winton House was to be at eight o'clock, and we would have to leave Warton Hall by seven to be on time.) First I had bathed, and then Clair had washed and dried my hair and done my nails. Then she had curled my hair, always a tedious process, heating the iron and doing a curl, heating the iron and doing another curl. But at last the curls had been made. Then she had helped me step into the eight petticoats I would need to puff out the skirt of my white taffeta dress, and then into the dress itself.

The dress might have been made by Jack Frost. Its low neckline was elaborately trimmed with folds of French lace, decorated with tiny glass beads, and its skirt consisted of seven flounces. Each of these, embroidered with designs in beads and edged with lace, rested on a row of puffed white tulle.

Clair had swept my hair tightly back and arranged the curls with ribbons of lace, which matched the lace on my dress, and little white silk flowers.

At last it was finished, and I was delighted and excited by what I saw in the mirror. Clair handed me my white cashmere shawl and gloves, and I was ready to go downstairs and join my mother and stepfather.

"Oh, Clair! My ring," I said, as I was about to go out the door.

She ran to my jewel box and got it.

I put it on and then left her. But I carried my shawl and gloves: I wanted to show my stepfather what he had bought without any wrapping on the package.

"You are late!" my stepfather said, glaring at me as I floated down the grand staircase toward him. He held his watch in his hand. "Yes! Yes, yes. That is very good. Good!" he exclaimed, as he looked me over.

I stood in front of him, then, and turned around slowly, haughtily, displaying myself. I thought, yes, little man, your plan will work. I will make it work. What harm could there be in it—in this game we play? And anyway, I have no choice but to play it.

But then he pointed at my throat and snapped, "Where are the jewels I gave you?" His eyes blazed, and his stunted arm began to pulsate.

"Father," I said, smiling down at him, "I will wear them if you wish. Nothing would give me greater pleasure, and it would take only a moment to get them. But my dress is so elaborate, so rich, that it needs few jewels. And you must know"—I touched the skin at the base of my neck—"that young men would rather look upon a woman's skin than upon her jewels. Everyone knows you are the richest and most generous man in Somerset. Your daughter's neck need not demonstrate that."

"Please yourself. It does not matter to me. We are late. Henderson is waiting for us. Come!"

119

He turned and ran out the door, and Mother and I followed him out onto the landing and down the steps to the waiting carriage.

When we were seated and had begun to roll down the drive, I thought that if I were Alice or Helena driving out from Buckingham Palace with the queen, I could not feel more like a princess. Mother sat beside me in a magnificent, blue-gray silk dress, wearing a breathtaking collar of diamonds and a large, single pear-shaped stone in each ear lobe. Titus and Coventry rode up behind us. They would help to serve dinner that evening in their blue Trevenbury livery and powdered hair. Henderson sat on the box ahead with "tiger" Monk riding proudly beside him.

So, in our splendid, new blue-lacquered barouche with my stepfather sitting opposite us, we drove through the warm evening air toward Winton House. Above us, the sun still painted the treetops orange against the cloudless, azure sky.

We had not spoken since leaving the house. Therefore, to break the silence, I said, "You are looking very spruce this evening, Father."

His sly cat's eyes looked into mine for what seemed too long a time, and then the corners of his mouth began to curl.

"Lord Plummer has tin mines in Cornwall," he said. "They are running out of tin. Some have already closed. He has sold some paintings in London. I will soon be buying some of his acreage, I think." He smiled craftily at me. Cecil Plummer would be very interested in my dowry.

Before long the tower of Winton House rose above the trees. Winton House was a large, austere, two-story brick house, built around a single courtyard in, I guessed, the early eighteen hundreds. Its only interesting feature was the central tower, which still survived from an earlier Tudor structure. Cramped in a tiny park surrounded by a thick wood, it was plain and un-imaginative.

We alighted and entered the vestibule, where we were met by the groom of the chambers, two footmen in red plush livery, and a maid. We removed our shawls and then followed the groom of the chambers down a corridor to the drawing room doors. He threw them open and announced, "Lord Trevenbury, Lady Trevenbury, and Miss de Riocour."

A hush fell instantly upon the room, and everyone turned to watch us enter.

The room was white, trimmed with gold and dominated by a Van Dyck, which almost filled an entire wall. Beneath it, Lord and Lady Plummer were standing with three of their guests.

They hurried toward us. "How nice to see you again, Lady Trevenbury and Miss de Riocour," Lady Plummer said. "Welcome to Winton House. Lord Trevenbury, have you met my husband?"

Lord Plummer took my stepfather's hand, turned to my mother and me and said, "Dear ladies, how very pleasant to see you." Then, to my stepfather, "I hear you have purchased some acreage from Lord Dunston. . . ." They began to walk away together toward the chimney piece.

They were joined by a baldheaded man who, I learned afterwards, was Lord Rutford. Lady Rutford now strode in our direction, and Mother and Lady Plummer went to meet her.

But I did not go with them because Roundell Wensley had approached me. "Good evening, Miss de Riocour."

"Good evening, Lord Easton," I said. "How nice to see you again."

I smiled and stood waiting for him to say something, but apparently he could think of nothing to say.

"Lord Aldergate, Lady Aldergate, Mr. Leighton,

and Miss Leighton," shouted the groom of the chambers from the doorway.

Roundell wet his lips and then wet them again.

Fortunately Mr. Ashley came up to us then and rescued him. "Miss de Riocour," he said, "the historian of Fawsley is at your service. Details of the leading families of the neighborhood furnished at your request and free of charge."

"Good evening, rector," I said, smiling at him. "You have furnished me with all the historical data I need at present, and I am most grateful. But I shall remember your kind offer."

"Historical information, Miss de Riocour?" a tall, straight young man with pale skin asked me. He seemed unable to believe that a woman could have an interest in history.

"Architecture, Bisham," Roundell said. "I mean, Miss de Riocour is interested in architecture."

"Achitecture, Miss de Riocour?" another young man asked. He was quite good-looking, with black, curly hair and almost black eyes. "Oh, good evening, rector," he said.

"Good evening, Mr. Leighton," Mr. Ashley said. Then he turned to me. "Excuse me, my dear, there are two young ladies present who are without gentlemen, and I must be chivalrous."

He went off to join Iris and Elizabeth Leighton, Edgar's sister. How *much* Elizabeth Leighton looked like her father, Lord Aldergate, while Edgar Leighton resembled his mother. Wasn't it interesting, then, that Iris Bisham should be a young edition of her mother, Lady Plummer, while her brother Cecil did not resemble either of their parents?

But I had little time to think about that, with three young men looking expectantly at me. "Lord Easton, Mr. Leighton, and Mr. Bisham, please!" I said. "You mustn't be mistaken about me. I love beautiful buildings, but I really don't know very much about architecture. Of course I am interested in the history of the region. This is to be my home, and I am interested in everything about it." As I said this, I swept my hand through the air in an arc, and all three pairs of male eyebrows rose as I did so.

And then I noticed that my stepfather was watching me. That all the young men in the room were clustered around me had not escaped his attention. He was beaming, actually beaming.

Now Mr. Ashley left Iris and Elizabeth and went to join Lady Rutford, Lady Aldergate, and Mark Lawson, who were clustered about Mother. Mark stood next to Mother, who smiled dreamily up at him. I wished I could walk across the room and join them.

Then I heard Iris Bisham cry, "I won't!" She had spoken crossly to her mother, who now stood between her and Elizabeth. And when I turned to look at them, I found the two girls glaring at me.

"Dinner is served, my lady," the groom of the chambers announced.

This was the signal for Lady Plummer to arrange the procession into the dining room. When it was organized, I found myself on Cecil Bisham's arm, and he took me in.

The dining room was paneled in dark oak hung with portraits by Gainsborough, Romney, and Raeburn. Eight footmen waited behind the chairs at the table to help us be seated. They wore the blue, red, pink, and green liveries of the families dining. The room was lit by two tall, silver candelabras standing at either end of the table. They held perhaps fifteen candles each, and each candle wore a pink paper shade. And between the candelabras, dozens of red carnations had been arranged in large silver bowls, and these had been scattered about the white cloth that covered the table.

I was seated between Cecil and Lord Aldergate in the middle of one side of the long table. Toward my left, at the head of the table, my stepfather sat at

Lady Plummer's right, and toward my right, at the other end of it, my mother sat at Lord Plummer's right with Mark Lawson beside her.

Before me on the table, a tiny menu card in a silver holder told me that dinner would be the long, elaborate meal I had expected. It read:

### FIRST COURSE
*Consommé with quenelles*
*Stewed sturgeon, matelote sauce*
*Filets of mackerel*

### TWO REMOVES
*Roast forequarter of lamb*
*Chicken à la Montmorency*

### ENTREES
*Filets of duckling with green beans*
*Mutton cutlets à la Wyndham*
*Blanquette of chicken with cucumbers*
*Timbale of macaroni à la Milanaise*

### SECOND COURSE
*Pigeon*
*Leveret*

### TWO REMOVES
*Flemish gaufres*
*Iced soufflé*

### ENTREMETS
*French beans stewed*
*Mayonnaise of chicken*
*Peas à la française*
*Peach jelly with noyau*
*Love's wells glacé with chocolate*
*Flave of apricots and rice*

124

As we drank our soup, Cecil told me about a shoot at a place called Swarthcote Manor.

"And this was last September?" I asked.

"Yes. So, we took our line of march for the fields to be drawn, and we arrived just as Lord Ross came up with fifteen or twenty men. There is no better pack of harriers in Somerset. . . . "

While I listened to him, I heard the familiar slurping of soup above the buzz of talk. It was my stepfather, sitting beyond Cecil and Lord Rutford.

Then china clinked on china, and I heard my step-father cry, "Never! They should never have repealed them. Ruined the English farmer."

"There now, Lord Trevenbury," said Lady Plummer, smiling handsomely, "they *were* repealed, some years ago, and there is nothing we can possibly do . . ."

And I noticed that Iris was talking heatedly to Edgar Leighton, and Elizabeth to Roundell Wensley. And on Roundell's left, Mother and Mark were lost in conversation. I heard her familiar, "It really can't be necessary. . . ."

". . . and how overjoyed you must be to have your stepdaughter home from school. Such a lovely child," Lady Plummer continued.

My stepfather smiled his most charming smile at her. He would do beautifully, I thought, if he kept his temper, but if he lost it for any reason, that would be the end of his social career.

". . . . they are all exactly the same size, thirteen inches high, and you wouldn't be able to tell one from the other . . . ." Cecil was describing the dogs to me.

But Iris had become agitated. I could imagine her fists clenched under the table. ". . . without any warning, out of the blue. No one had ever heard of her before, but with sixty thousand pounds, . . ." I heard her say to Edgar, as she glanced poisonously at me.

"Iris!" called Lady Plummer, "tell the rector about Harmony."

". . . . they work beautifully," Cecil was saying.

Then I noticed that Lord Plummer was speaking to Mother, who was still deep in conversation with Mark.

"Don't you agree, Lady Trevenbury?" I heard him say.

"Yes?" Mother asked him. "I am sorry, Lord Plummer, I didn't hear."

". . . . and then they were turned into the field and away we went," Cecil went on.

"How exciting," I replied.

"I really don't suppose so," Mother replied to Lord Plummer. "I really don't know." Then she returned her attention to Mark.

After the second course, Cecil asked if I didn't like the wine.

"Yes," I answered, "the champagne is excellent, Mr. Bisham, though I was never very fond of it."

Suddenly a husky woman's voice cried, "Deformed! The poor baby!" It was Lady Aldergate.

And as I leaned forward to glance at her, she covered her mouth with her hand and turned scarlet.

I prayed that my stepfather hadn't heard her.

"Yes, it was a happy time, a happy time," shouted Lord Aldergate, to cover up his wife's faux pas. "Did you know Barbara Denton, by the way, rector?"

After a few moments' conversation with the rector, Lord Aldergate whispered to his still red-faced wife, "Harriet, please! There is no need to mention Lady Tackham nor Durham—not here in Somerset, especially under the circumstances."

"Did you say something about Durham?" I asked Lord Aldergate. "What an enormous coincidence! Just the other day, I was talking to a friend about Durham and the countryside thereabouts. It must be lovely. Do you know of a place called Wellfield House?"

"Yes, my dear, what is left of it," he said.

"What is left of it?"

"Only a shell, you know. Wellfield House burned to the ground a hundred years ago, more or less. Ruins, only ruins left, and not many of those."

"Oh, but you must be mistaken. It is between Durham and the sea," I explained.

"Mistaken? Hardly, my dear. Wellfield House, or the ruins of it, lies in a direct line between Durham and the fishing village of Seaham, just beyond Pittington Abbey. All that acreage is owned by Lord Tackham, a great friend of mine. He and I have been shooting over every inch of that land a hundred times, and he has been shooting over every inch of mine north of Finchale Priory. Now how could I be mistaken?" he laughed. "I should know, don't you think? But why do you ask?"

"Oh, it is nothing important. I must have the wrong house in the wrong place. Do you live in Durham, then?"

"So there!" Elizabeth Leighton cried in triumph to Roundell. "Money doesn't mean everything, you know."

"Elizabeth!" Lord Aldergate called. Then turning back to me, he said, "We go there for shooting in the autumn."

As Lord Aldergate spoke, Roundell looked at me apologetically, and I smiled back at him.

And so it went on—the dinner seemed interminable. Some of Iris's and Elizabeth's remarks made me uncomfortable. I knew that I was not exclusively with friends. And there were too many tensions in the room.

Later on, as I toyed with my soufflé, I noticed Lord Plummer lay his hand on Mother's arm and whisper something in her ear. Mother gave him her lazy smile and then reached for her wine, effectively pulling away. As she did so, I glanced at Lady Plummer. She had seen. Her jaws were clenched, and her eyes glinted as she turned to Lord Rutford, who at that moment banged his knife handle on the table.

"Death to all poachers, filthy bastards!" he cried.

At this, my stepfather burst into laughter. "Hear! Hear!" he cried.

And there was general laughter all around the table.

Cecil laughed too, and then he turned to me and said, "There is to be a meet at Gray Park a week from Saturday. Perhaps you would care to come with us."

But before I could answer him, Lady Rutford shouted, "Caught him with the chambermaid! Ha! Ha, ha, ha. Caught them in bed together and set fire to the sheets, she did. Haw, haw."

Drunk, I thought.

Just then, Mark looked across the table into my eyes, and I wanted to be away from that room and those people—riding with him along the shore of the blue inlet where the yellow irises bloomed and gulls turned the distant sand white. I found it hard to tear my eyes away from his.

Finally, much later, after we had finished the dessert, Lady Plummer rose. It was time to leave the men to their brandy and coffee. We ladies departed for the drawing room.


"Where is the coffee? I need coffee!" shouted Lady Rutford as soon as she had been helped onto the sofa. It had been a precarious operation; for a moment I thought her enormous bottom would miss its mark entirely. "Cynthea, don't you serve your guests coffee after dinner any more?"

"Jameson will bring it along in a moment, Nancy," said Lady Plummer.

As she spoke, Jameson arrived, and he began serving the coffee.

"Elizabeth," cried Lady Aldergate, "Please sit down. You make me nervous standing there like that."

Elizabeth stalked to a straight chair at the other end of the room and sat down.

"No, darling, come and sit here with us," her mother said. "You are so far away. We would have to shout."

"I do not feel that I could be quite comfortable there with you," Elizabeth replied, looking maliciously at Mother and me. "I prefer to be here, thank you."

She is interested in Cecil, I thought.

"Foolish child," cried Lady Rutford. "Thank God Roundell is sensible. What we need are more sensible young people in this world."

"And fewer inebriates," hissed Iris.

"What did you say? Speak up, child," shouted Lady Rutford.

"Iris!" Lady Plummer cried.

"And fewer fortune hunters," Iris said. "I have a headache and am going to my room. Come with me, Elizabeth, and comfort me. We shall throw open the windows and breathe untainted air." And they swept from the room.

"Please forgive the girls, Lady Trevenbury and Miss de Riocour. They seem so upset. I cannot imagine what has gotten into them," said Lady Plummer.

"It may be the full moon," replied Mother.

"Yes, quite possibly," said a puzzled Lady Plummer. Then she turned to me. "My dear, I understand you play and sing beautifully. Would you give us all the pleasure of your music when the gentlemen join us? Cecil enjoys music most tremendously, my dear. We all do."

"What did you say?" cried Lady Rutford.

At this, Mother's hand found her temple, but she remained smiling.

"Certainly, Lady Plummer," I replied. "I would be happy to play and sing," I said.

"Oh, lovely," said Lady Aldergate. "Edgar is so very

fond of music. Miss de Riocour is going to *sing,*" she shouted at Lady Rutford.

"Marvelous, my dear." Lady Rutford clapped her hands at me. "Roundell is so fond of music."

It seemed an hour before Lady Plummer's "Ah, here they are now, and about time, too, you naughty men. Come along everyone. We shall adjourn to the music room where Miss de Riocour has promised to play and sing for us."

When we arrived in the music room, I went directly to the piano and stood beside it while everyone sat down. Lady Plummer had somehow managed to capture my stepfather and her husband and had placed them on either side of herself on the sofa. Lord and Lady Aldergate sat side by side as did Lord and Lady Rutford. Mark, Mother, and a rather uncomfortable-looking Mr. Ashley sat together on the other sofa, and my three admirers sat together on little straight chairs closest to the piano.

I waited until everyone was comfortable, and then I announced, "I will sing a song from Schumann's lovely song cycle, *Frauenliebe und Leben.* It is a cycle of eight songs that tell of the life and love of a woman. In this first song, 'Seit ich ihn gesenhen,' she tells of first seeing the man she loves."

Then I sat down at the piano, relaxed my hands in my lap for a moment, and then I turned and smiled at my audience and began to play.

It was a happy love song, and as I played, I decided to sing it to Mark, but after glancing at him twice and seeing that each time he was engrossed in Mother's whispered remarks, I smiled at the rector and then concentrated on the three appreciative young members of my audience.

My song was received with enthusiastic bravos and applause and loud honking from Lady Rutford—she was asleep and would not be awakened by her husband, no matter how hard he tried.

"That was the first song," I said. "Now may I sing the last for you? 'Nun hast du mir den ersten Schmerz getan.' She retires from the world to think upon earlier happiness."

This song I *did* sing for Mark, but when our eyes met, he did not seem to have gotten the message.

When I finished, there was more applause, and then Cecil jumped up and rushed to the piano.

"Please don't get up, Miss de Riocour," he said. "Do you read music?" He had taken a song book from a little table near the piano, and placed it open on the music rack. "Will you sing my favorite?"

" 'One Kindly Word Before We Part, One Word Besides Farewell,' Mr. Bisham?" I asked. "Well, here you are, then." I played the introduction and then began, "One kindly word. . . ."

After I had sung the first verse, I said, "Join me in the second verse, Mr. Bisham." And after we had sung the first few lines, I said, "Come along Lord Easton and Mr. Leighton, sing with us." We gave the rest of the song a rousing rendition and finished with a burst of laughter and applause.

"His lordship's carriage is up, please," Jameson announced.

My stepfather had asked Lady Plummer for our carriage while I was singing.

Getting up from the piano, I said to my threesome "That was marvelous!"

They wanted more, but of course there was no time. And then everyone began bidding good night to my mother, stepfather, and me. We said how lovely it had been, and how much we had enjoyed it all.

Through it all Lady Rutford hung her head and snored.

As we drove down the drive toward home, I heard

131

my stepfather murmur to himself, "Good, good. Oh, very, very good."

After that we were silent, each of us absorbed in his own thoughts.

My thoughts were of Mark. I had not been able to speak to him once during the entire evening. Mark—who had not inherited a house in Durham, who did not own and would never live in the shell of Wellfield House.

## Chapter Ten

As I SIPPED my tea on Wednesday morning, I wandered out onto the balcony to look at the gardens and the hill beyond. The view was very Japanese that pearly morning. I had seen misty hills like that in a Hokusai print—take away the western-style mausoleum, there might be Mount Fuji with its cap of snow.

Far to my left, I saw Benjamin pulling his wagon down the cobbled lane toward the farm. Every morning he pulled the wagon, filled with kitchen refuse, to the farm. And early every afternoon, he returned with baskets of meat and vegetables for the kitchen. From afternoon until the following morning, the wagon rested just outside the door to the kitchen yard. I had asked Benjamin about the wagon, and he had told me that it had been made for the seventh earl when he was a lad. He had said that one old woman at the farm remembered how the earl and three or four other children loved to coast down the hill in it from the mausoleum. It would roll all the way to the abbey.

"Excuse me, miss." Dorothy interrupted my daydreaming.

"Yes, what is it, Dorothy?" I asked.

"Mrs. Danley said that if it was all right with you, I could go up to Manchester to see my little boy and my sister. I'd only be gone a week at the most, miss, and Mrs. Danley says Daisy can easily do the water and your room for you, miss."

133

"Of course, Dorothy," I said. "You go along, and if you want to stay a little longer, stay."

"Thank you ever so much. Take care of yourself while I'm away. I won't be more than a week, I won't. Jean and Ralph have precious little room as it is without me staying very long at a time, but I do so look forward to seeing my little Timmy. I'll be leaving on the afternoon train then, miss, and God bless you."

Then she ran from the room, stopping to take the can of water, which she had left near the door. She was radiant.

I thought about her "take care of yourself while I'm away" two hours later, as I rode Thunder down the track toward the farm. I knew she was still concerned about the scar-faced man, but I felt sure that Dorothy had not seen him since the night of the servants' dance. If she had, she would have told me about it. I hadn't seen the man since the day we called on Lady Rutford. If he were following me, as I assumed, why hadn't I seen him since? I glanced around me, but there was no one in sight.

I decided to ride along the road that led from the stable yard to the farm and then along the inlet where Mark and I had ridden the Saturday before. Maybe, just maybe, he would want to relive that afternoon, and I would find him there.

As I approached the farm, I noticed that the spring calves were now nearly full grown. I brought Thunder to a walk so that I could watch them. They were grazing in a small pasture behind a large stone barn in which, I supposed, the cows were housed and milked. But then I saw the man sitting on his horse in the shadows of the barn doorway. He sat perfectly still, watching me.

This was a shock, and instinctively I brought Thunder to a halt. Then the man and horse walked out of the barn toward me, and I was able to breathe again. It was not the scar-faced man. It was my stepfather on his horse, Bourton. I had never seen him mounted before, and I was amazed at how beautifully he sat. His stirrup leathers had been shortened to suit his short legs. His right hand held the reins in the normal fashion, but his malformed left hand clutched them close to his chest. I supposed his right hand would have to do most of the work. How could he possibly manage that way? I wondered.

He walked Bourton up to me on the other side of the fence and said, "Do you know what you are riding? Why has no one told you about that horse? He killed a man."

"I know all about Thunder and Patrick Meagher," I replied, watching to see if the sound of Meagher's name had any effect. It did not. "Thunder is nervous and excitable, but obedient and perfectly safe. Patrick Meagher tortured him, and Thunder retaliated. We probably would have done the same thing in Thunder's place. Patrick Meagher must have been a beast."

And then it came out involuntarily, as though someone else had asked the question with my mouth. "What was the connection between Patrick Meagher and Martin Shark?" Immediately I would have given anything to retract the question. I could have bitten off my tongue. It seemed to mystify him.

"Meagher and Shark?" he asked. And then he began to laugh. He threw back his head and abandoned himself to it. He was helpless for some moments. Then, when he had gotten control of himself, he managed to repeat, "Meagher and Shark," but this set him laughing again. At last, however, with tears on his cheeks, he looked at me and said, "None. Meagher was a groom in the stables. How could Shark have any interest in him?

"You had never met Martin Shark before the night you arrived here." He had become deadly serious now. "Apsley told you his name, didn't he? Why are you so interested in Martin Shark? Haven't you ever seen a fat man before? I told you he is a business associate of mine. You will never see him again. Forget him. Attract the young men. You do this very well. Control your stupid imagination and don't ride that horse."

"Is that an order?"

"I do not give orders about little things," he said, sneering at me. "I pay people to do that for me. I go to Weymouth early next Tuesday. I will look for a horse that will suit you. In the meantime, take my advice about that one. Do not ride him!"

Then he swung Bourton around abruptly and cantered the horse away from me, and in a moment they rose into the air and sailed over the fence on the far side of the pasture. My stepfather seemed to be part of the animal, so smoothly did they ride together. They galloped off and vanished into a grove of trees.

"He is part horse, part cat, and part man," I said to myself, as I turned Thunder back in the direction of the stables. "I wonder where he learned to ride like that?"

My stepfather had spoiled my ride; I no longer wished to ride to the blue inlet. Instead, our conversation occupied my mind. "Beautiful Thunder, beautiful fellow," I said as I patted his neck, "Do *you* know if there was a connection between Mr. Shark and Patrick Meagher?" My stepfather had seemed genuinely surprised, I thought, when I suggested it. If there had been no connection between them, then my stepfather had not been involved in the murder of the seventh earl. But who else could have benefited from his death? Martin Shark? How? It didn't make any sense at all. But I knew there *was* a connection between Martin Shark and Patrick Meagher. I knew it!

Shortly I left Thunder with John in the stable yard, and then I returned to the house. As Titus opened the entrance door for me, he said rather too vigorously, "Did you have a good ride, miss? It was not a very long ride. We did not expect you back so soon."

And then Apsley hurried over to me and stammered, "It has turned into a pleasant day, miss, after all, hasn't it?"

"Yes, thank you Titus. Yes, it has, Apsley," I said.

But their loud, superfluous remarks did not cover up the soft laughter and giggles which came from the hall chamber. Mother and Mark Lawson were spending the morning there together.

Mother and I decided at luncheon to pay our courtesy call on Lady Plummer that very afternoon and get it over with. I had always thought it terribly strange that it was necessary to call immediately after a dinner party when one had spent hours with his host and hostess only a day or two before, but such was the custom.

At about three o'clock, then, we drove up to Wilton House. On the flat lawn beside it, Iris and Cecil Bisham and Elizabeth Leighton were playing a game of croquet. Cecil waved and shouted something as we drove by, though I could not hear what it was, but Iris and Elizabeth ignored us. The game prompted me to make a mental note to ask Mrs. Danley if there was a croquet set at Warton Hall and also if there was any archery equipment.

And then we entered the house and were shown to the drawing room where Lady Plummer received us. She was delighted with our praise for her dinner party.

"You are too kind," she said, "but it was a success, I think. If only Nancy could control herself. She had to be carried out to her carriage. Thank God we have two very strong footmen, or I suppose she would be sitting in there snoring still." She pointed in the direction of the music room.

"But my dear," she said to me, "such lovely music. I was saying to Lord Plummer last night, 'That girl is of professional quality,' and I mean just that. It was a treasured performance, treasured!"

"Why, thank you, Lady Plummer. Good afternoon, Mr. Bisham," I said to Cecil, who had just hurried in, out of breath.

"Would you care for a game of croquet, Miss de Riocour?" he asked.

"I would love it," I said, and he grinned, "but there wouldn't be time. We dropped by for only a minute and cannot stay long." His smile collapsed. "But I hope we can play at Warton Hall some afternoon." His smile returned.

Then he said how much he was looking forward to the dinner party at Warton Hall on Friday evening, and his mother said that she was looking forward to it, too. But I wondered if Iris could have said the same. She did not appear during our visit, nor did Elizabeth. As far as I was concerned, this added to the pleasantness of our call. It was, however, a very short one. We chatted for another ten minutes and then left.

I was glad we were able to get away quickly because I wanted to spend time with Mrs. Banks. She was to leave Warton Hall that evening, but one dress remained to be finished. It needed to be tried on one last time. As soon as we arrived at the Hall, I hurried to the schoolroom and changed into the dress. It was a ball dress, a magnificent creation in lavender and green tulle.

"It is a miracle, isn't it, Clair?" I said, as I stood before the mirror. "Mrs. Banks, I don't know how you do it. I can't wait to wear it. Thank you for making my new wardrobe. And thank you, Carol. And thank Edna for me," I said to one of the seamstresses.

"Mrs. Banks will be coming back in November to do some more work for your mother, and perhaps you will need her then as well," Mrs. Danley said. "My dear, you do look a picture in that dress. I was saying to Mrs. Banks before you came in, '*Now* there will be some goings-on at Warton Hall, just like there used to be. But they'll be even better because we have a young lady here now.' There was never a *young* lady here in my time, but there were parties and balls, and there will be parties and balls again. There's the dinner party coming up on Friday night, of course, and the chef has already started work on it."

"Is there a croquet set at Warton Hall?" I asked. I had stepped behind the screen, and Clair was helping me out of the dress.

"Why, yes, child," Mrs. Danley answered. "There are several, as a matter of fact, though there are some mallets and balls you wouldn't want to use any more. You know how the wood splits and the paint wears off. We were cleaning in that closet the other day, and I looked them all over. If you like, I can show you where they are."

"Would you, please?" I asked. "Let us do it now, then, while we are thinking about it."

After I had finished changing, I said good-bye to Mrs. Banks, asked Clair to come to my room at the usual hour, and left the schoolroom with Mrs. Danley.

As we walked down the corridor together, I smiled at her and said, "Why didn't you tell me that you are my stepfather's aunt, Mrs. Danley? Does that make you my aunt-in-law?"

"I thought you knew. I thought everyone knew," she said, "the way it was spread across every newspaper between Edinburgh and Land's End, and all through Ireland, too, for that matter.

"You see, my dear, I don't feel like your stepfather's aunt. Mercy no, and I don't think of myself as such either, no, not at all. It would be unbearable if I did, wouldn't it, now? You see, I am happy as housekeeper here—worked up to it after many years on the staff. I never knew Fitzjames until he came here as the eighth earl."

"But," I said, "he had visited his father off and on for some time before his father's death."

"Yes, we did meet several times then, but he came

to see his lordship, not me. It wasn't until he came into his inheritance that I really got to know him, and it just seemed natural for it to be 'Mrs. Danley' and 'my lord' between us. That suits me fine. You see, there's no feeling of family between us, and I am sure I prefer it that way."

"Here we are," Mrs. Danley said, opening a door.

She walked into the closet, and I followed. It was the size of a small room and even had an oval window in its far wall, which looked out on the large courtyard.

"There are the croquet sets," she said. "The newest one, here, is beautifully made, don't you think? And what lovely colors it's painted. Those mallets are still good, and there are plenty of wickets and balls."

"Oh, look!" I said, as I reached for a bow that hung on the wall. It seemed in good condition, though the string fell apart in my hands. "The arrows still look good, too, but those targets need to be repaired."

"Yes. Well, if you will excuse me, I must get down to the still-room," Mrs. Danley said.

"Thank you so much Mrs. D——"

I turned to thank her, but she was gone. Instead, a man stood in the doorway, barring it with his arm. Mark Lawson leaned against one side of the door jamb, resting his right hand on the other.

"What will Diana be hunting this afternoon?" he said.

"Men!" I said. "Men who startle innocent young ladies out of their wits. They should all have an arrow through their hearts."

He laughed.

"Colonel Lawson, what are you doing *here?*" I asked.

"If you called me Mark, would I have permission to call you Suzanne?" He looked deeply into my eyes in that disturbing way of his.

"Oh, no. I couldn't possibly."

"It would make a wounded soldier very unhappy if you would not allow it."

"Well—well, yes, then," I stammered, "I suppose you might."

Then I heard Mother's voice calling, "Mark, Mark."

"Suzanne," Mark said, "you have already put an arrow through my heart."

Then he was gone.

On Thursday afternoon Lady Aldergate and Edgar called. Poor Edgar was the only male in the room that day. Lady Westmore and Lady Wessex had called, too. Both Lady Westmore and Lady Wessex had "handsome sons," whom their mothers praised at great length.

But Lady Westmore seemed the slightest bit uncertain and hesitant. Finally she asked, "De Riocour is French?"

She was reassured, however, and all three ladies were fascinated, when Mother traced our family back to the courts of Henry VIII and Louis VII.

There was a pattern here, I thought. If a girl had money and family, that was all that was necessary. She might be short and ugly, fat as a cow, or have three eyes, but if she had family and money. . . . Well, they knew I had money, and now they had learned about my family. Suppose I suddenly said, "I have a most peculiar taste for blood—any kind of blood." What would happen? And I almost laughed aloud.

On Friday, Mother and I called on Lady Aldergate at Henton Place, a small, seventeenth-century Restoration house surrounded by an older moat. Elizabeth was not there, at least she did not appear, but Edgar more than made up for her absence.

And since Gome Castle was only three or four miles beyond Henton Place, we decided to stop and call on Lady Westmore. Lady Westmore was at home and so were her identical twin sons. Albert and Arthur were slim, sandy-haired young men who never talked about anything but shooting and hunting. Hadley, their younger brother, was not at home. I was relieved that they had no sisters.

Our dinner party on Friday evening was a success. And I think the decor of the dining table helped to make it so. In the center of it I had arranged a large bouquet of perfectly matched yellow and violet gladioli in a white Chinese porcelain bowl edged with purple and gold. I had placed a trail of woodbine down the center of the table on either side of it. And then, of course, Apsley had arranged, with the greatest care, the candelabras, silver, and bowls of fruit.

I had asked Mother to place Iris next to Roundell at the table, and Cecil next to me. Iris seemed mollified by having Roundell all to herself during dinner, and she even consented to sing a song at the piano afterwards.

During the meal, my stepfather suggested holding a ball at Warton Hall, and this idea was received with great enthusiasm. Lady Rutford clapped her hands and said she remembered the balls at Warton Hall very well—they had been famous.

She became rather boisterously drunk, but she was able to get to her carriage under her own power at the end of the evening. Mother remained charming through it all, the perfect hostess, cool and serene. And when Cecil talked about Cambridge, he was quite entertaining.

It was really a very pleasant party.

The following afternoon, Mother and I began to write the invitations to the ball, and I was surprised at the number of people with whom we had become acquainted. Besides the familiar acquaintances, we invited Lady Wessex, her son, Heston, and her two daughters, Mary and Esther; and also Lady Bagenot and her three daughters. We invited other new acquaintances who are not really part of my story.

I insisted that an invitation be extended to Mr. Ashley, and Mother agreed, since she was sure he would not accept it. She insisted that Mark Lawson be invited, and I certainly did not object. So, if everyone accepted our invitations, we would have forty-five guests at the ball—possibly more if aunts and uncles and grandmothers and grandfathers came, too.

My own grandmother and my Uncle Matthew would be coming. They would arrive the day before the ball and stay with us until the morning after it. Mother said that she really did not think it would be a good idea to have them, but my stepfather insisted that there should be other members of the family present. And he demanded that they be properly dressed, saying that Mother could send money if necessary. I wondered about this, but I did not ask about it.

## &#x263F; Chapter Eleven &#x263F;

ON SUNDAY we went to church in the morning, and in the afternoon Lady Bagenot called, bringing her three daughters, Silvia, Julia, and Andrea. They were intelligent, well-mannered girls of seventeen, nineteen, and twenty-one, all on the plump side, and pretty with beautiful skin and blue eyes. And Lady Wessex called with Mary and Esther, but Heston did not come with them. With six young ladies romping about the lawn playing croquet and with three older ladies gossiping on the terrace in the shade of the north front, Warton Hall must have looked like a girls' school that afternoon.

On Monday, I was not feeling quite myself. I discovered a book of translations of Chinese stories in the library, and I decided to spend the afternoon reading. I told Apsley that I would be in the garden, but that since I was not feeling well, I was not at home to callers.

I took my book and went out onto the porch of the east front and sauntered through the rose garden, admiring the blossoms and smelling some of my favorites. Fewer flowers bloomed now, and soon there would be none. But there would still be afternoons like this one, warm and lazy, with billowy white clouds floating above. One minute they let the sun shine down, and the next they cast us into shadow. This reminded me of the days when I was taking lessons in watercolor

144

painting at school, and my sketches ended torn into shreds.

When I reached the bridge to the Chinese pagoda, I noticed that an unusually deep lavender water lily had opened. I had never seen the color before, and I stopped to admire the flower's many-petaled symmetry. What a pity that such a beautiful thing should last so short a time.

I supposed I should have remained there to enjoy it longer than I did, but then I thought how transient everything is, really, and I turned away from it and entered the pagoda. The Chinese pagoda was a perfect place to read Chinese stories. These proved to be exotic and unusual, but so full of symbolism and strange customs that I could not enjoy them. One story particularly puzzled me, and as I sat there rereading part of it, I noticed, out of the corner of my eye, that a man stood at the entrance to the bridge. I looked up at him and saw that he was holding the railing with each hand, barring any escape from the island.

"The princess sits in her castle, but her mind is far away," Mark Lawson said solemnly.

"It was, until a moment ago," I said.

"If you would rather return it to wherever it was, I will leave you in peace," he retorted.

"No, of course not. But what are you doing here, Colonel Lawson? You have taken to turning up in the most unusual places at the most unexpected times."

"I was walking in the garden and saw the top of this pagoda above the hedge and decided to have a look at it. And now, I find that it is lovelier than I would have dreamed," he said, looking hard at me. "And haven't you agreed to call me Mark?"

"Thank you, M—Mark," I said. I wondered whether that look of his was insolence or just an effort to make those sad eyes seem merry.

"Now that I am permitted to stay, may I cross the

moat and enter the castle, or must I court the princess from afar?"

"The princess would be pleased to entertain the prince in her castle. The drawbridge is down, and he has but to walk across it."

Mark walked across the bridge and into the pagoda, and as he sat down next to me, he asked, "What are you reading?" My book lay open in my lap, and his big hand reached across and lifted the cover of it, so he could read the title. "Chinese stories in a Chinese pagoda? Is there Chinese blood here, too? A Chinese princess? No, the eyes don't slant. She is English, after all."

"Part English, part French." I said. "If I *were* part Chinese, would it make any difference to you?"

"Well no, certainly not—it was just something to say. . . ."

"But it would make a difference to most people, wouldn't it?"

"I suppose so. Well, of course. It is natural that it should."

"Why?"

"Well—"

"You see," I said, "there really isn't any reason except that it is the thing to do. In our society, one must be of very good English blood, or perhaps if there is some very good French blood or some very good German blood mixed in, that would do too, wouldn't it?"

"Perhaps, but—"

"Blood and money. Money comes first—it is more important than blood. Do you know why I am here at Warton Hall?" I paused. Did Mark look suddenly wary, or did I imagine it? "To attract the marriageable men of the countryside with the dowry my stepfather has put on my head," I continued. "You know that. Everybody knows it. Then, one day, I *might* inherit Warton Hall and the estates, *if* my stepfather leaves them to me. God knows if Mother will have another child. So everyone pretends to like me so that, perhaps, my money will become a part of their money. Some will pretend love, I am sure. But there is not a genuine look or action in the whole mess. And blood! What is your name? Who was your father? What was his family? Why, he was the brother of Count Leon de Riocour. Oh, yes, splendid! But suppose he wasn't? What difference could it make? They are not marrying my father, they are marrying me. Only, they are not marrying me—because I am not marrying.

"Oh, why am I telling you all this? I suppose it is because I am not feeling quite well, and I am tired, and it was all bottled up and had to come out, and I am not sorry, so there!"

"Don't be angry with me, Suzanne. I have done nothing to you," he said, "and don't be surprised if some of what you call pretense is real. After all, you are a very beautiful young woman, especially beautiful when you are angry—rather like a Norse goddess." There was just a ghost of a smile around his mouth.

"First a Chinese princess and now a Norse goddess, and I suppose I should be wearing a helmet with horns sticking out of it?" I couldn't help smiling at the thought. "Thank you for letting me get all of that out of my system. I had to explode to somebody."

"Anytime you want to explode, explode to me," he said.

"Can I? No, I don't think so," I whispered.

"Why not?" He had taken hold of my hand, and I did not withdraw it.

"Mark, when were you last at Wellfield House?" I asked. "Have you ever been there?"

He sat silently looking down at my hand in his.

"Do you know who owns Wellfield House?" I asked. He did not answer. "A friend of Lord Aldergate's—a Lord Tackham."

"How do you know that?" he said.

"Lord Aldergate told me all about it. It is a ruin, Mark. Wellfield House burned to a shell years ago. But you told us that your father left it to you and that you would be going to live there after you left the rectory. Why did you lie about it, Mark?" I took my hand from his and stood.

"Suzanne," he said, as he rose and stood beside me, "I have some things to do here—I may not like what I must do, but there is no choice. I—I do not want you to ask questions that I cannot answer."

"We are not going to be friends, then?" I asked.

"But you want us to be friends," he said. "You want that very badly, don't you? I can see it in your eyes."

"If we are going to be friends, then I should have an explanation. After all, how can one be friends with someone when that friendship has begun with a lie?"

"Does anyone else know?" He was very near me. "Have you told anyone about this?"

"No, not yet."

"Don't tell anyone."

Suddenly, without warning, he pulled me to him, wrapped his arms around me, and held my body tightly against his. And then his mouth came down upon mine.

I did not try to pull away, but when he released me, I turned and walked away from him—out of the pagoda and across the bridge.

"Suzanne," he called, "your book." And he came running after me with it.

"Thank you," I said, looking up into his eyes for a moment. "Don't pretend with me, Mark. Don't pretend."

Then I walked quickly away along the path through the rose garden. I was about to cry, and I didn't want him to see me do it.

But I refused to cry, after all. I went into the house instead and walked as fast as I could to the grand staircase hall, where I knew someone would be tending the entrance door.

"Titus," I said when I arrived there, "would you go to the stables, please, and ask John to have Thunder saddled and at the entrance front in half an hour? I will need Owen to come along. Oh, and Apsley, I shall not be down to dinner. Will you have it sent up on a tray? The chef may decide what I shall have."

"You won't be down to dinner, dear?" Mother asked. She had just come out of the hall chamber.

"No, I won't. I am not feeling as well as I might. I think I have the right to have dinner in my room occasionally if I wish?" I said, sweeping past her toward the grand staircase.

"Well, of course, my dear," she said. "Lady Rutford and Roundell called and so did Mr. Aldergate."

"So Warton Hall turns into Victoria Station for sixty thousand pounds," I shouted back at her as I dashed up the stairs.

When I got to my room, I rang for Clair.

"Clair, help me into my habit, please, the black one, I think. I am going riding for an hour or two. Then I shall want to change into my gray dress. I am having dinner here, in my room."

"Are you feeling ill, miss?" Clair asked.

"I am feeling well enough, but I would feel better if it weren't for this perpetual concern over my health," I snapped.

I apologized for that remark later, after we had finished dressing. "I am sorry, Clair. I am really not myself. I will feel better after I have gotten out of this house for a while."

Then I left the room and hurried down to Thunder.

As soon as I had mounted, I walked Thunder to the south side of the house, cantered to the bridge, crossed it, and galloped toward the farm. Benjamin walked slowly along, and I waved to him as his bent figure flashed by. When we came to the inlet, I walked Thunder where Mark and I had walked and talked on that happy afternoon.

There I said to myself, "Now understand something here and now, Suzanne de Riocour. Mark Lawson is a liar and a cheat. He lied to you and cheated you into thinking that he was a nice person. It is over! He spends entirely too much time with your mother. You do not know what he is. If anything, he is after your money like everyone else. You deserve and will have someone very much better than Mark Lawson. From now on, you do not think of him or anything connected with him."

But my lecture did not make me feel any better. Perhaps exercise would. So I rode Thunder farther than Mark and I had gone—to the end of the inlet. And I was surprised that it did not meet the sea, but was separated from it by a wide sand bar. The inlet, I found, was really a long, brackish pond.

It was on the sand bar that the gulls nested, and they flew frantically into the sky as we crossed it, filling the air with their white wings and raucous cries. Then we stood at the edge of the sea. It wore breakers that afternoon. They rolled towards us and then slammed on the beach with a crash of cream-colored foam that swished toward Thunder's hoofs. I could feel the spray on my face.

We stood for a long time watching the breakers and then, at last, started home, walking and cantering back along the shore of the pond. Here was where Mark and I turned to go back to the stables that afternoon, I thought, and there are the willows. I could hear him say, "They should be pruned back hard in the spring," and then I did cry. My tears blurred the track ahead, and for a while, I let Thunder find his own way.

That evening after having dinner in my room, I sat until quite late trying to read by the light of the lamp on the table in the alcove, and then I undressed and went to bed. But sleep would not come. I kept thinking about Mark. I wanted to be close to him and to feel his arms around me again.

Finally, I threw back the covers, got out of bed, put on a robe, and went out onto the terrace. "What actually happened this afternoon?" I asked the stars. "I demanded an explanation from Mark, and he refused to give me one. Well, that doesn't mean there isn't one, perhaps a perfectly good one—"

Then I saw the light shine again on the porch of the mausoleum. It seemed brighter than on the first night I had seen it there, probably because this night was so much darker—there was no moon. But for a moment, the same shadow limping the same way was flung upon the wall of the building. It grew bigger and bigger, and then vanished as it had before. Then everything was black again.

And it was even blacker inside my room as I groped my way to the table beside my bed. I fumbled with a match and finally lit the lamp. The clock beside it said half-past twelve. I dashed to the wardrobe for my gray dress. I must dress quickly. I must go to Mark. I knew it had been Mark up there at the mausoleum, and I was going to him. But then I realized that that was impossible. If I ran all the way to the top of the hill, it would take me more than five minutes. Add to this the time it would take to dress, and by that time he would be gone.

So I blew out the light, got into bed again, and pulled the covers up tightly around my neck. I had begun to feel very cold.

What was he doing up there late at night? I wondered. Who was he? What was he *doing* up there? It was a long time before I fell asleep.

During the hour or so after breakfast at Warton Hall, Edward and I were a common sight walking through the rooms, I leading the way and he following, carrying a bowl of flowers. Stopping in whichever room the flowers were to go, I would tell Edward what table to put them on and how to turn the bowl. Then I would put the final touches to the arrangements.

The following morning, Tuesday, was no exception. Benjamin had gone about his business, and one bowl of cornflowers and daisies remained to be carried to the corner room. I led the way, and Edward followed, carrying the flowers.

I had chosen the shortest way, toward Mrs. Danley's rooms and my stepfather's office and the library. And as we approached her door, I realized that I had hardly seen Mrs. Danley since the day Mrs. Banks left, except at morning prayer. I asked Edward if she was well. He said that she was very well and busy as usual, as far as he could tell.

But then, the door of my stepfather's office opened, and Mark Lawson stepped out of it, shutting the door behind him. He saw me at once, and in a moment we stood face to face.

"Good morning," he said.

"Good morning," I replied. "Edward, would you put the flowers on the table next to the wing chair, please?"

As he walked away, I said to Mark, "I thought my stepfather was going to Weymouth right after breakfast this morning. He said he would look for a horse for me while he was there."

"He decided to delay his departure," Mark replied. "I suppose he will leave shortly."

We began to walk toward the library together.

"I had no idea that you have business dealings with him," I said.

Mark was silent. He had clasped his hands behind him as we walked, and now he looked at the carpet, lost in thought.

"After all, you can hardly expect me to believe this was a social call."

Still he said nothing.

Then he stopped walking, and I stopped, too. "What does it matter?" he said, turning to face me. "Why do you ask? You distrust me, yet you have no real cause to do so."

He took my right hand in both of his and stood looking down into my eyes.

"Distrust you?" I said. "How can I trust you when——"

"Mark, dear," Mother interrupted.

She had appeared suddenly, almost out of nowhere. When he saw her, Mark dropped my hand.

"What are you doing here with Suzanne?" she asked. "I have been waiting for you for almost an hour. Come along and leave Suzanne to her flowers. We really must get out of this dreary house and into the fresh air. Walk to the orangery with me. I should love to see the little oranges."

Then she linked her arm through his, and they walked off toward the door to the south front. And Mother's laughter tinkled back to me as they went out the door.

So Mark Lawson has business with my stepfather, I thought. Is he in my stepfather's employ? What kind of business could they have together? I wonder, then, if Mark knows Martin Shark and his scar-faced companion? Why does Mark have to be a part of whatever is going on here?

Then I remembered Mr. Ashley saying, "Details of the leading families of the neighborhood furnished at your request." And I decided to pay a call on the rector that afternoon.

Just as Thompson opened the door for me, Mr. Ashley descended the last few steps to the entrance hall.

153

"Good afternoon, my dear," he said. "From the windows upstairs, I saw you arrive. It is always an enormous pleasure when you come to see me. Come along into the drawing room. The French doors are open, and we can look out into the garden. You look a little tired, but no less beautiful, I assure you. Have you been sleeping?"

"Perhaps not as well last night as I should have," I replied, "but I feel very well, thank you.

"We are having a ball at Warton Hall, and I wanted to bring you your invitation personally." I gave him the envelope. "It is my invitation to you, not my stepfather's, so please come as my guest, won't you?"

"That is very thoughtful and very kind of you, my dear. Sit down—no, not there, over here near me. If I came, it might cause trouble between you and your stepfather, or there might be a scene. I don't believe your stepfather would be at all happy to see me at the Hall, but we will see. I have told you he doesn't like me at all. But let me think about it."

"Colonel Lawson will be coming—at least he has been sent an invitation."

"I should think he would want to attend."

"How long will Colonel Lawson be staying with you, rector? When will he be leaving us to live at Wellfield House in Durham? But I suppose that depends on when he finishes his work for my stepfather, doesn't it?"

"Work for your stepfather? What makes you think that?"

"Colonel Lawson had a meeting with my stepfather this morning. We met outside his office when they had finished."

"Oh?"

But the rector did not say more.

"Will you visit Colonel Lawson when he returns to Wellfield House?" I asked.

"If he invites me, certainly."

"Did you visit his father at Wellfield House?" I tried to make the question sound casual.

"Why all this interest in Lawson's house in Durham, Suzanne? May I call you that since your mother and I are such old friends? Lawson is my guest. If you have any questions, perhaps you should ask him."

"But have you forgotten: 'details of the leading families of the neighborhood'?" I smiled.

"Lawson is not of the neighborhood, but the historian of Fawsley is at your service, as promised. Is there anyone else whom you would care to know about?" He smiled back at me.

"The rector of St. James's Church in Fawsley, then. Do you know him and his history?"

"I know him intimately, my dear. He would be very flattered by your interest. I am afraid his is a rather dull history, but I am happy to oblige.

"He was born perhaps fifty years ago, give or take fifteen or twenty years," his eyes sparkled, and he beamed with pleasure, "in the county of Gloucestershire, between Bath and Bristol. He is the third son of the fifth earl of Kingslake and attended Trinity College, Cambridge. He decided to enter the church, which he did, arriving at Fawsley eight years ago. He seems to have been a relatively contented man ever since. And that is the history of the Reverend Paul Ashley. Much of this I am sure you already know."

"Did you grow up, then, at your father's house between Bath and Bristol?" I asked.

"Yes, my dear. The house is called Norton Weston and is owned and occupied now by my brother, Arthur, who is the sixth earl of Kingslake. I lived there until I went off to school and then spent most of my holidays at home with my parents."

"Then you must know Sike Hall, my mother's home," I said.

"Yes, my dear," he replied.

"You said you were old friends."

"Yes."

"But you don't want to talk about her, either," I said.

"There is very little to tell, Suzanne. Her father was a great friend of my father, so of course the families visited back and forth. Your mother was always beautiful and much sought after by all the young men there. I was hardly ever at home after she returned from France, so I lost touch with her completely. It was a great surprise to me when she came to Warton Hall as Lady Trevenbury."

"You don't like her very much, do you?" I asked.

"Oh, it isn't a question of liking or disliking. We were friends when we were young, but, like so many relationships after a lapse of time, nothing is left. There is just nothing left anymore. That is all.

"What is it? You are troubled about something. Is it something I said? Is there anything I can do?" he asked.

"No, it is just lack of sleep, I suppose. I didn't get to sleep until after two this morning. I sat on the terrace looking up at the mausoleum, which is on the hill opposite my room."

I watched the rector carefully, but he showed no sign of surprise or alarm at this.

"You really have nothing to worry about, my dear," he said. "As a matter of fact, you are very fortunate. Most young ladies would give anything to be in your situation. Your stepfather is enormously wealthy, you live in beautiful surroundings, and wear beautiful clothes. You will marry well, have a family, and be happy ever after. Is that not so?" he reasoned.

Then he went to the window facing the drive. "Ah, that must be Lawson. Yes, it is—on his new horse. We went to the auction at Weymouth last Tuesday together. I thought perhaps I would find a carriage horse, which I shall need before long. There was a black stallion for sale, a beautiful animal, and Lawson bought him."

A few moments later Mark's voice sounded from the hall. "Ashley?"

"In the drawing room, Lawson."

"I am not wasting my time!" he shouted. "She does know something, I am convinced of it, but she—oh! Suzanne," he exclaimed, as he ran through the door. "I didn't know you were here."

"I was just telling Suzanne about your new acquisition, Lawson," the rector said.

"Saffron?" said Mark. "Oh, yes. Ashley and I went to the auction at Weymouth last Tuesday, and a stallion came up for sale. Would you like to go out and see him? He is a beauty."

"I must be going, Mark," I said.

"It will only take a minute. Did you come over on Thunder?"

"Yes," I replied.

"Well, you can leave from there."

He moved toward the French doors, and the rector stood as he did so.

"All right," I said.

I hadn't needed very much persuading, I thought, as I followed them out into the garden. We walked toward the rector's stables.

"He has a white star and white socks," Mark was saying, "and is the absolute image of High Point—the horse I lost in the Crimea, the one that was shot from under me when I was shot in the leg. You see, High Point wasn't just a horse, he was my friend. Several times he saved my life. He wasn't afraid of anything as long as I was there. The hardest thing I ever had to do was shoot that animal, but I wasn't about to see him suffer a second longer than I could help. Thank God I stayed conscious long enough to do it.

"I am sorry. I didn't mean to distress you," he said, glancing at me and then down at the ground.

"You didn't," I said.

"Well, when I saw Saffron," he continued, "I just had to have him. It was like having High Point back again."

We entered the stable yard then, and I saw a groom rubbing down a magnificent, bright black horse.

"He *is* beautiful," I said. "Oh, Mark, he is magnificent! Just look at that head and neck and what a beautiful pair of shoulders."

"You like him?" Mark asked.

"Of course I do. But why Saffron? Saffron is bright yellow, and he is bright black."

I looked up at Mark, and he was smiling. He was actually smiling down at me, and I was smiling back. And in some strange way, in that moment, we were one happy person together.

"I don't know, but that is his name," he answered. "Bart, give him a bucket of good cold water and an extra feed of corn when you are through, will you please?"

"Owen," I called.

Owen sprang from the bench where he sat and went to get Thunder.

As I walked Thunder slowly along the road to Warton Hall, I thought about how happy Mark was with his Saffron. He was like a little boy with his first cricket bat. His smile almost broke my heart. Why was he so sad? The war? I wondered.

And what had he meant when he rushed into the drawing room and said something about not wasting time and that she did know something. Who? My mother? Know what? No, don't, Suzanne, I admonished myself, don't make guesses about things you have no knowledge of. I knew so little, actually. I didn't even know whether the rector knew that Wellfield House was a ruin and really belonged to Lord Tackham. I should have come right out and asked him. I was sure, however, that the rector knew all about Mark.

But there was something else I wondered about, and instead of riding Thunder back to the house, I left him at the stables. I wanted to ask John if Mother had ridden out on her horse, Lady Jane. He told me that she had and that she had returned less than an hour before.

# ᏒᎡ Chapter Twelve ᏗᏊ

MY STEPFATHER RETURNED from Weymouth in time for dinner that evening. How much better it would have been if he had not.

I found him and Mother waiting in the corner room, as usual, and I asked him if he had found a horse for me. He had obviously forgotten about it completely, but he remembered in time to say that there had not been time to look. He was surly and, I thought, physically very tired——his left arm was not entirely at rest. It was a relief when Apsley announced dinner, and we went into the dining room

With my stepfather in such a mood, I dreaded the meal. But I had done a large arrangement of chrysanthemums for the dining table and would have, at least, the pleasure of looking at them.

During the soup, I could not help staring at my stepfather——I was so shocked by his behavior. He lifted his plate to his mouth and sucked noisily at the soup like an animal. Soup ran down his chin and dripped on his napkin. His eyes popped as he stared back at me over the rim of the dish.

"I revolt you?" he screamed at me. "Yes! Yes! Take that look of disgust off your face. Take it off!"

Instinctively, I began to rise from my chair. I would not stay in the room and be attacked.

"Sit! Sit! I have some things to say to you, and you will hear them," he said.

I sank back into my chair.

"You look at me with contempt. You think I am stupid. Do you think I do not know how to eat soup? I know how to eat soup—quietly, delicately. But it pleases me to eat it like *that*."

His left arm jerked up and down sluggishly, but I had a terrible feeling that the spasms would soon become more violent.

Hardly taking his blazing little eyes off me, he picked up his soup bowl, placed it upside down before him, took his heavy silver knife by the blade, and struck the soup bowl hard with the handle, smashing it. The bowl split into several pieces and collapsed onto the serving dish below.

"Bring me another plate," he said to Apsley.

Apsley brought the plate. My stepfather placed it on the serving dish upside down and smashed it to pieces, as he had the one before it.

"Clear that away," he said, still staring at me. "It pleases me to break those plates. They are Dresden china. I could break every plate here—they are my plates. Who would stop me?" He dared me with his eyes to answer him. "I could buy fifty thousand, a million plates and never feel the cost.

"I know what you think. You think, 'How awful he is.' You think, 'No one could ever like a person who acts like this.' Do you think anyone has ever liked me? You think I don't know what I look like? Once, in London, a woman looked at me and then went to the curb and was sick." He hurled these last words at me with what appeared to be triumph.

The room had fallen silent. No one moved.

"I do not need affection," he continued. "Only stupid, weak people need affection. Affection is a crutch for the weak.

"I am not stupid, but I was poor. You have been in Holborn Hill? I grew up there. You would not like it. *I* did not have a fancy education. *I* was not spoiled and coddled and cradled. It was a ragged-school for me, and not for very long, either. But I learned to read. I read very well."

"Your father—" I said.

"He did not help us. He abandoned us. Be quiet. I have not finished.

"I have read Miss Bell. I have read Miss Warren. I have read Miss Denswater. I have read all the books on etiquette. I know them by heart. You think I do not know *how* to eat soup?

"And I have read the account books. I have read the records of this estate. I am not stupid. I know where the money comes from. I know where it goes. My father was stupid. His groom of the chambers stole five thousand pounds a year out of his pocket. We have no groom of the chambers. Nobody steals anything out of my pocket. Isn't that right, Apsley? *Isn't that right, Apsley?* Answer me!" he screamed.

"Yes, my lord," Apsley said.

"The estates bring more profit than they ever did before. I am not stupid!"

I did not move. I was fascinated by the spectacle, and he was right: I was revolted.

"I have a net income of 231,322 pounds a year. My investments are worth ten times that amount. I have so much money that it would be hard to spend it all. What do you think of that? And you dare to look at me with contempt.

"I have more than eighty people here, who obey me. Apsley, go stand in front of the fireplace."

Apsley did as he was told.

"Do you think he obeys me because he loves me?" He pointed a finger at Apsley. "No. He obeys because I pay him more money than he would get anywhere else. That's why eighty people here obey me. How many farmers on my lands obey me? And you look at me with contempt.

"I have the most beautiful woman in England as my wife. She likes to live in luxury. That is why she married me. I am not stupid. I know that. But she knows the difference between a man and a woman, and she likes the thing that makes a man a man. Is that not so, my dear?" His eyes flicked viciously to Mother, who smiled and nodded placidly, and then back to me. "Do not get any foolish ideas. I shall have an heir. But if I did not, you would inherit nothing.

"I will soon be welcome in every great house in Somerset. I will soon be welcome in every great house in England. I will find out where they are weak, and I will use that knowledge. I am not stupid. Lord Aldergate talks about selling land. I will buy. The price will be low because I will wait until he *must* sell. He will almost give his land to me. Lord Rutford invites me to a hunt breakfast and a hunt on Saturday. Where is his weakness? I hear about his railway companies. I hear about manipulation of shares of stock. I hear about the juggling of accounts. I hear about paying dividends out of capital. He will need money, but at what price?

"They dare look at me with contempt. No, *I* look at *them* with contempt. I will rub their landed gentry faces into their own dirt. All of them!" He struck the table with the palm of his hand.

"As for you, you will do as I say. I will tell you when you will marry. I will tell you whom you will marry."

"You will not!" I shouted at him.

I could stand no more. I got up from my chair, and Titus rushed over to help me.

"No? What will you do?" he asked. His eyes were sadistic slits. "You will have to leave Warton Hall. You have no friends. You have no money. You have no family except your mother. Your grandmother and uncle? Ha! What will you do?" he sneered, "Become a governess? A teacher in some dirty little school? Do you think I would allow you to do that? There will be one place for you. The streets will be the place for you. Have you ever known a girl of the streets?" he shouted. "You would not like that. And you dare to look at me with contempt.

"You will do what I tell you to do. You want to leave the room? Go! Go! You have my permission."

He dismissed me with a wave of his hand and began to eat his chicken. His left arm was still.

I ran from the room.

I ran through the rooms to the east front and out the door, through the rose garden, past the fountain, to the orangery and around it, past the glasshouses—until I could not run any more. When I could not run, I walked, and when I got to the little stone pavilion at the base of the hill, I stood for a moment, leaning against a column to catch my breath. I didn't care how tired or out of breath I became as long as I got away from that house—as far away as possible. But I could not think yet: I was still too shocked.

After a moment, I stumbled on—up the hill path to the spring, and there I sat down on the bench. I didn't go to the spring, though I was thirsty, nor did I see the countryside spread out below me. My mind had begun to function again, and I thought of the sparrow that had watched me from the marble shell the last time I had been there. That had been my first day at Warton Hall. I remembered how I had thought about all the people down there and had wondered where I would fit in here. Well, now I knew.

But what, I wondered, had brought on my stepfather's tirade? In a mood like that he was dangerous. He was dangerous no matter what mood he was in. And why had he waited so long to tell me those things?

Many questions needed answering, and I needed to think clearly. I went to the spring, drank the icy water, splashed it on my face, and smoothed back my hair.

When I sat down again my mind began to race. Obey him indeed, I thought. Of course I would not marry when and whom he chose. I must get away from him—leave Warton Hall. But go where? To whom? Miss Busser? He would certainly look for me there and probably ruin her because she had helped me. To some other school? Without references? A governess, then. Without references? No. No one would employ me without references. And he was right—I had no one to help me. If only Nana were alive, she would help me. I might still be in France with her if Uncle Leon had not decided to emigrate to South Africa. But Uncle Leon could not help me now. South Africa was a long way away from England.

What about the rector? No, he was in league with Mark, who was working for my stepfather. Mrs. Danley—my stepfather's aunt? There was no one.

The grass rustled above me, and I turned to see a man's head rise above the grassy hilltop. The eye in his scarred face stared down at me. He was surprised to find me there, I think. He had been about to hold a spyglass to his eye, but his hand stopped moving when he saw me. He was so close that I could see his uncut fingernails.

"What do you want?" I called up to him. "What do you want with me? Why are you spying on me?"

He did not speak, but, almost smiling, he watched me.

Why was he looking at me like that? What was all this about? I had to know. I got up and began to run toward him, stumbling through the long grass, holding my skirt out of the way as best I could.

"Why are you following me?" I called out to him.

But I had to watch my footing as I ran, and when I looked up again, he was gone.

In a moment I stood on the hilltop where the scarfaced man had stood, but I could not see him anywhere. He must have disappeared into the clump of small pine trees below. Then I heard the clicking of hoofs on pebbles and the clomping of them as his horse cantered away beyond the trees.

There was nothing to do but go back to the house. I certainly could not remain out on that hillside all night. I met no one on the way, and when I reached my room, I rang for Clair and stood looking out of the window until she arrived.

"Oh, miss!" she said as soon as she saw me. "What happened? Your dress! It is muddy, and it is torn there. And your hair! Here, let me help you. Let us take that off. Don't worry. I will clean and mend it."

"Clair," I said, "ask Titus to bring me some tea, and I would like a glass of brandy with it."

After I had washed and Clair had helped me change and tidy my hair, Titus brought tea and brandy. Then I wished Clair good night. I knew she was concerned about me and wanted to know what had happened, but I was thankful that she had not asked.

When she had gone, I sat down by the table in the window and drank my tea and sipped the brandy. And I began to feel more composed.

"What can I do?" I said to myself. "I am in no physical danger, it seems. If the scar-faced man had wanted to harm me, tonight would have been his chance. I was alone in a remote place where he could easily have attacked me. No, he has simply been watching." Was he being paid by my stepfather to watch me? Or was he being paid by Martin Shark to watch me? Again, the riddle of Martin Shark.

"That little monster downstairs has demanded nothing of me yet that could harm me," I thought aloud. "He needs me to make friends for him. All right— I will make friends. And I will make him think that I am doing it for him, but I will be doing it for myself. I must find someone to help me—someone to help me get away from here."

# ᴄ⁊ Chapter Thirteen ⁊ᴐ

LADY RUTFORD HAD INVITED my mother, my stepfather, and me to her dinner party at Mendley House on Friday evening. And since my stepfather had also been invited to the breakfast and hunt that Lord Rutford was having the following day, he planned to stay the night at Mendley House. He would ride there on Bourton early Friday afternoon. This would give him time to bathe and rest before dinner. Montague, his valet, would follow him in a carriage, bringing his changes of clothing. Montague would stay at Mendley House with my stepfather and would return to Warton Hall with him late Saturday afternoon.

Mother and I would meet my stepfather at Mendley House before dinner, but we would not be staying overnight there.

That evening I wore my pink taffeta dress and the emerald, pearl, and ruby necklace. Before leaving the house, I threw a woolen shawl-mantle around me because it was cloudy and cool and rain threatened.

Mother and I traveled in the brougham. If it rained, we would be glad of the closed carriage. Henderson drove, and Coventry and Titus rode on the outside, behind. They would help serve that night just as they had the week before at Lady Plummer's party. I hoped it would not rain before we arrived at Lady Rutford's because Coventry's and Titus's hair had been powdered. If it did rain, there would certainly be a mess.

But the rain held off during the long ride through the

twilight. The heavy, gray twilight seemed to have started right after luncheon: all afternoon the clouds had hung low, seeming too heavy to float in the sky. Now the landscape was dark gray-green, as though painted on wet paper. Mother sat silently beside me, and I was glad to have my thoughts to myself.

Finally, however, Mendley House greeted us with a blaze of lights. Lady Rutford must have every lamp and candle in the house lit, I thought. She must have been determined to keep the weather's gloom from invading her party. "We are not afraid of the rain," I could almost hear her say.

The house was festive, indeed. Flowers and light made the inside as bright as the outside was gray. Many of the guests had arrived, and they seemed gay as well. The drawing room buzzed with talk and tinkled with laughter. As we entered the room, Lady Rutford hurried toward us, her arms outstretched.

"Ah! We are not afraid of the rain, I see," she cried. "Good evening Lady Trevenbury and Suzanne. You really must let me call you Suzanne, my dear. We are going to get to know each other *very* well, and I know we will be *very* close friends. Roundell!" she shouted, "Look what I have for you here, my dear boy."

Roundell hurried toward us. He had been talking to Iris Bisham and a handsome, black-haired young man who looked rather like the engravings I had seen of young Lord Byron.

"Good evening, Lady Trevenbury and Miss de Riocour," he said. "I hope you haven't gotten wet."

"Good evening, Lord Easton," I said. "No, it has not yet begun to rain."

As soon as we began to speak, Lady Rutford took Mother to join my stepfather, who was bouncing up and down on his toes as he talked to Lord Rutford and Lord and Lady Plummer. My stepfather glanced across at me, and I could see that he approved of my appearance. I smiled and nodded at him meekly. He *must* believe that I had capitulated.

I turned my attention again to Roundell. "Lord Easton, who is the gentleman with the black hair talking to Iris Bisham?" I asked.

"That is Raymond Taylor, my best friend at Oxford. He will be staying here with us for the next fortnight or so while his mother is having another—" He stopped, then continued, "His father is the sixth earl of Metborough, and they live in Kent, very near Canterbury."

"Lady Bagenot," the butler shouted from the doorway. "The Misses Crandon."

Lady Bagenot hurried directly to Lady Rutford and Lady Plummer. Her three daughters, Silvia, Julia, and Andrea in red, blue and yellow, descended on Roundell and me, and we all said our good evenings, interrupted by "Reverend Ashley and Colonel Lawson" from the doorway.

"Oh, there is Iris Bisham," Andrea said, hurrying off.

Only a moment before, she had been surveying Mr. Taylor. And now both Silvia and Julia were surveying Mark, who was being greeted by Lady Rutford.

"Lord Easton," they said in unison, "who is the man with the rector?"

"His name is Mark Lawson. He is staying with the rector, who is an old friend of his father's, I believe. He is just back from the Crimea."

"The Crimea?" said the sisters.

"Oh, he is coming over here," said Silvia with a giggle.

"Good evening," said Mark.

I said good evening to Mark, and as they shook hands, Roundell said, "Ah, Colonel Lawson, it is good to see you again."

"Oh, Colonel Lawson," Julia said, "I hear you have just returned from the Crimea."

"Excuse me," I said, "I do want to speak to Lady Bagenot before dinner."

But before I had moved a few steps away, Mr. Ashley intercepted me.

"Good evening, Suzanne," he said. "If it is permitted, I will tell you that you are more beautiful than I have ever seen you look before. You look as though you have been sleeping again."

"Yes, I have, thank you," I replied.

We talked for a minute, and then I asked if he would come with me to speak to Lady Bagenot. But he said that Roundell looked as if he needed rescuing, so he went to join Roundell and Silvia and Julia, and I walked on toward Lady Bagenot at the opposite end of the room. On the way, I passed Iris and Andrea, who were lost in conversation with Mr. Taylor. I did not see Mother, however, and Mark had disappeared.

"Mr. Leighton," the butler announced.

As I approached Lady Bagenot, Lady Rutford left her and Lady Plummer to go to Edgar Leighton.

"Lady Bagenot," I said, as I sat down on the sofa beside her, "I am so glad to see you. Good evening, Lady Plummer."

"Good evening, my dear," Lady Plummer said, leaning toward me. "Oh, I do hope you will sing and play for us tonight." She turned to Lady Bagenot. "Miss de Riocour has such a charming voice. It is of professional quality, professional quality. Oh, there is Edgar." She stood. "I *must* ask him if there is news of his mother." And she hurried off.

"Has Lady Aldergate gone away?" I asked Lady Bagenot.

"She and Lord Aldergate and Elizabeth went to visit her sister in Southampton. She broke her leg getting off a boat, I understand, but they will be back in time for the ball on Tuesday."

"I had such a delightful visit at Kessel Hall last

Wednesday," I said. "I wanted to thank you again."

"It was delightful having you, my dear."

At that, I glanced up and saw that Mother and Mark had appeared. She had taken him to see a painting on the wall, and they were standing before it talking.

"I was so interested in your friend, Lady Portman," I continued. "Did she really start a girls' school all by herself?"

"Yes, my dear. Her husband died. The estates, heavily in debt I understand, went to a cousin. So there she was, left with a jointure in horrible condition, one that brought in practically no income. She was almost penniless! And you can't start a girls' school on nothing, you know. One must give her credit. Fortunately she had some acreage, which she sold. This brought money enough to keep her help and hire, I believe, three resident teachers of the highest character. Of course, she had superb social connections."

"Hello, Miss de Riocour," Edgar said. He stood beside me.

"Chopped a big hole in his leg with a scythe, in Lord Granger's leg," shouted Lady Rutford, sitting down on the other side of a startled Lady Bagenot. Lady Plummer had accompanied Lady Rutford and sat in the armchair opposite us. "I was telling Cynthea," Lady Rutford continued, "they say he did it on purpose."

Roundell was approaching with Mr. Taylor. I was curious to know what he was like, so I stood and moved toward them. And I noticed that Cecil Bisham, who had been talking to the rector, was on his way toward me. Beyond him, Mark still stood in the corner with Mother.

Cecil was first to reach me. "Good evening, Miss de Riocour," he said.

"Miss de Riocour is interested in architecture," Roundell said to Mr. Taylor as they approached.

"Architecture? Houses and churches and buildings?" Raymond Taylor said. "I am sure you are mistaken, Easton."

I could not help laughing at his expression. "Not really, Mr. Taylor," I said. "I simply like pretty things, whatever they may be."

At that moment dinner was announced, and then began the usual confusion about who would take whom into the dining room. Roundell took me in: his mother had placed me next to him at the table, with the rector on my right.

And she had, of course, placed my stepfather on her own right. At the other end of the table from her, Raymond Taylor sat between Silvia Crandon and Iris Bisham. His neck must have ached from turning from side to side during the meal. And almost across from Mr. Taylor, Mother sat between Lord Rutford and Mark. How, after the dinner party at Winton House, could Lady Rutford place Mother next to Mark? She must be either very stupid or totally unobservant, I thought.

Her dinner proved even longer and more elaborate than Lady Plummer's, and I was not hungry. My stepfather did his utmost to charm Lady Rutford. She seemed enchanted by him but drank enormous quantities of wine and laughed louder and more often as the meal progressed. Lord Plummer also laughed a great deal, and he seemed to wish to say anything he could to please my stepfather, who sat across from him.

Roundell could think of very little to say during the meal, and when I asked a question, he replied with only a word or two. The rector and Lady Bagenot, on the other side of Roundell, helped all they could. But our conversation could hardly have been called scintillating. For Lord Rutford, however, there was almost no conversation at all. Iris, on his left, was fascinated by Mr. Taylor, and Mother, on his right, was engrossed in Mark. So poor Lord Rutford was left alone with his food. How could Mother ignore her host during the meal? I was furious with her.

When dinner was over, I was asked to sing and decided on some simple French folk songs of the Auvergne. I sang three of them, and I sang them in French. One song, "Pastourelle," I sang for Mark, but again he sat next to Mother and was so absorbed in her whispering that I was sure he didn't hear it.

When I had finished, it was the three sisters' turn. They had arranged much of the first act of Balfe's opera, *The Bohemian Girl,* for zither (which Silvia had brought with her), piano, and female voices. The performance was endless.

The clocks struck one o'clock shortly before it ended, and as soon as we had applauded politely, Mother woke Lady Rutford and asked for our carriage. When it was up, we said our good nights, collected our cloaks and bonnets, and walked out onto the portico where Henderson waited with the brougham. Lady Rutford had accompanied us all the way, begging us to stay the night because of the weather, but we were not prepared to stay, and Mother could not sleep in a strange bed, so we declined.

We had, however, agreed to allow Coventry and Titus to stay the night at Mendley House. We did not wish to run the risk of their becoming ill from riding outside in the rain, and we knew that they would enjoy themselves enormously. No doubt there would be plenty of ale and revelry in the servants' hall.

I wished that Henderson could have stayed, too. It was raining very hard when we got into the carriage and waved good night to Lady Rutford, and I felt very sorry that he must ride outside on the box in that downpour. The rain drummed loudly on the roof of the cab as we pulled away from Mendley House and moved out into the blackness. Soon all I could see out of the window was the rain, falling in thick silver threads through the light of the carriage lamp. When we swung from the drive to the highroad, the horses began to slide and splash in the mud, and the carriage swayed drunkenly. I wondered how Henderson could possibly see the way. If it continued like this, it would take hours to get to Warton Hall, and I wondered how I could endure being shut up with Mother in that little, swaying space for so long.

She sat silently, having drifted away into that secret place of her own. I huddled beside her, pulled my cloak more snugly about my shoulders, gazed out of the window, and thought back over the evening. And the more I thought about Mother's behavior, the angrier I became.

"How could you throw yourself so shamelessly at Mark Lawson tonight?" I asked at last. "It was disgusting."

"Oh?" she replied. "It may have been disgusting to you, my dear, but it was very enjoyable for me." I could see in the dim light of the lamps the calm, complacent smile she turned upon me.

"That is the only thing that matters—whether or not a thing is enjoyable to you?"

"But of course, my dear. What else could matter?"

"That is the attitude of a trollop."

"A trollop?" She chuckled. "What do you know about trollops? If that is so, then half the ladies in our society are trollops. Intelligent ones, however. You see, we know that life is only once and that it must be satisfied. And like all civilized beings, we have our rules of behavior—this avoids scandal, and as long as there is no scandal we are free to satisfy ourselves. Each in his own way, of course."

"And your way?" I whispered.

"Shall I tell you?" she asked. "Why not? It seems that we are going to be traveling together in this dreary conveyance for some time tonight. It will help to pass the time, and then you know so little about your mother. You should know more—it will make things so much easier for us both in the future.

"My mother, your grandmother, was my father's second wife. His first wife died giving birth to his son John, my half brother. How father loved John! He loved him to the complete exclusion of my own brother, Matthew, myself, and even my mother, I think.

"Many times when I was a little girl, I would hide in the stables waiting for my father to come riding home and rush out and throw my arms around his leg. Or I would tiptoe into his study when he was there, hoping for a kiss on the cheek or pat on the head. But all I would get would be, 'Lillian, leave me be—can't you see I am in a hurry?' or, 'Lillian, must you always be underfoot?'

"You see, I loved my father very much, and it took far too long for me to realize that he didn't love me—that I was just something that had to exist, something that had no connection with him. Matthew, on the other hand, was my mother's passion. I didn't exist for *her,* either. You will meet them both when they arrive for the ball.

"I suppose I needed love, whether I knew it or not, and whether I knew it or not, I suppose I was determined to have it. And I suppose I was determined to have it from anyone who would give it to me. First, I sought it from my drawing teacher, a Mr. Hungerton, who was dismissed for being a bad influence. Then from a new coachman and then from Gordon, the gardener. Hammin was the first man to make love to me—he was the pad-groom at Sike Hall. That was when I was sixteen. That was the day I learned the joy of being a woman. One day, perhaps you will understand that. I knew then that the only thing I would ever want was that joy and that I could never get enough of it. I knew that *that* was the way to satisfy myself, and I have done so ever since. And I shall continue to do so.

"You must forgive me for being frank, my dear, but I really do feel that, under the circumstances, it is necessary."

"By circumstances," I said, "I suppose you mean Mark? And I suppose you intend to satisfy yourself with him?"

"Certainly, my dear. Mark is an ardent lover—a man of deep passions. You had best leave him to someone more experienced than yourself. You had best leave him to me."

As she finished speaking, she laid her hand briefly on my arm. But I turned from her and stared out the window at the rain, and for a long time we were silent.

"And my father?" I said, finally turning back to her. "I never felt that he was a de Riocour. Was he? Or was he one of your fleeting passions?"

"What does it matter?" she answered. "De Riocour will do as well as any other name. It will avoid a lot of tedious questions and stupid talk."

"No wonder you abandoned me in France, then," I murmured. "No wonder you never visited me at school. I suppose I was best left forgotten."

To this, Mother made no reply.

It was almost three o'clock when we finally arrived at the Hall. My mind had gone numb during the long drive home, as though it refused to accept the final realization of what it had suspected all along.

I was also exhausted physically and glad that Clair, Apsley, and Edward, as well as Dorothy, who had returned from Manchester that afternoon, were all waiting up for us. Dorothy had put a brick into the banked coals of the kitchen stove, and as soon as she saw us coming, she wrapped it in cloths and put it in my bed. She brought hot water to my room. I barely had strength enough to splash it on my face. Clair helped me undress, and as soon as I had gotten into bed, I fell asleep.

I missed morning prayer that Saturday, and I did not wake until Dorothy drew the curtains shortly after eleven o'clock.

She brought my breakfast—tea, some lovely hot scones and jam, and a dish of fresh peaches in heavy cream.

While I ate, propped up in bed with the tray on my lap, she prepared my bath.

"I'm sorry I stayed away so long, miss," she said.

"But I told you to stay a few extra days if you wanted to, and it's only been three or four days more than a week," I replied. "Did you have a pleasant stay? How is your little boy?"

"Fine, miss. Oh, it was lovely to see Timmy again. How he's grown! He's a very healthy little boy—very big for his age."

"He must be two-and-a-half, isn't he?"

"Two years and four days, miss. I was with him on his birthday, though of course he's still too young to know about birthdays. He didn't even know who I was."

"No, of course not, Dorothy," I said. "We must see if there is a way that you and your little boy can be together."

"Oh, miss!" she exclaimed.

"Of course I can't promise anything, Dorothy, and you mustn't hope for too much. But we will think in that direction and not say any more about it."

By that time, she had brought the hip bath and had filled it. "Yes, miss. Thank you so much, miss. Do get in while it's still hot," she said. "Miss Clair is on her way and will be here in just a few minutes."

After I had bathed and Clair was helping me dress, I said, "Clair, what time was it when I finally got to bed last night—I mean this morning?"

"After half-past three, miss. You were exhausted," she said.

"Yes, it was an exhausting night, and such appalling weather. I have never seen it rain so hard."

"Did you sleep well, then?" Clair asked.

"I remember getting into bed, and then immediately, it seemed, Dorothy was opening the curtains. I don't remember another thing. And now it is almost twelve o'clock, and half the day is over. Oh, dear, I suppose Benjamin brought the flowers, and I wasn't there. I must go and see if they are in the flower room. I meant to tell him not to bring any this morning, that I might be sleeping late, but I forgot to."

When I was dressed, I left the room, calling to Clair, "Will you help me change after luncheon? I am going to call on Lady Rutford, and I will be leaving about two o'clock."

But then I heard distant voices and what sounded like a piano being tuned from the direction of the long gallery. I decided to go that way and see what was going on. Far down the corridor ahead of me, two men carried what looked like a rolled-up rug, and I watched them turn and carry it up the three steps into one of the narrow cross-corridors to my right.

They must have left it in a room there somewhere because they returned to the corridor almost at once and preceded me down it to the long gallery. As I entered the room, they were rolling up the last rug from the floor. The piano had also been moved—to the south end of the room—and was being played by a thin man with long gray hair. He held a tuning fork. Four chambermaids were already on their hands and knees with beeswax and brush, waxing the floor.

What endless work that floor must be, I thought. There are many blocks in London not as long as this room. Why should anyone create a room as enormous at this one—or a house the size of Warton Hall, for that matter? I supposed this was where the ball would be held. There would be plenty of room for it.

Then Mrs. Danley came hurrying toward me.

"Good morning, Mrs. Danley," I said. "I see you are hard at work."

"It's for the ball, of course, my dear," she said. "The balls at Warton Hall have always been held in the long gallery. Thank goodness for the smoothness of the floor. I don't think you could slip a piece of paper between the boards, it's so smooth. When it's finished being waxed it will be a dance floor fit for Her Majesty. The south end, there, will be the top of the room, so in the quadrilles the couples at that end of the room will lead the dance. That is why the piano is there, and that's where the musicians will be, too. Apsley has arranged for the orchestra to come all the way from London. They played for the marquis of Swandson's ball in London last season and also at Lady Plummer's ball at Hastings House there. Rumford, groom of the chambers at Wilton House, says they are highly regarded in London.

"Tupper, he's the head gardener here—I don't know if you know Tupper? He's a magician with flowers and plants. He said, 'Why not bring in some of the palms and big ferns from the glasshouses, the way we used to?' So I asked her ladyship about it, but she said that she knew you would enjoy seeing to the decorations, having such a way with flowers and things."

"Of course, Mrs. Danley. I would be delighted," I said. "I *would* enjoy it. Perhaps we could place an orange tree from the orangery, here and there."

"Yes, that would be very nice," she said. "Well, we won't be bringing in the plants and trees until Tuesday afternoon so that they will keep fresh, and then we will want bouquets of flowers. I will leave the number of bouquets up to you, but I will help you with them on Tuesday afternoon.

"We will have all the other work done by Monday

night. We will arrange the hall chamber as the ladies' cloak room, and Miss Clair and Grace will be on duty there, just in case any of the ladies has a mishap with her dress. The sitting room here," she pointed to a door at the north end of the room, "will be the refreshment room, and the supper will be set out on the dining room table, downstairs. The guests can sit and eat in the drawing room and the summer parlor. We will be bringing some extra chairs into those rooms, and they can overflow through the breakfast room into the corner room, if they want to. There should be plenty of room, and they won't be eating on top of one another. So if you can help us arrange the trees and plants and flowers on Tuesday afternoon, I would appreciate it so much, my dear." And she gave me one of her bright, twinkly smiles.

"Wonderful!" I said. "Benjamin and I will plan the cut flower arrangements on Monday morning, then, so he will know just what flowers to pick. Oh! I must go down to the flower room and see what he brought this morning and do them." I left her.

Benjamin had brought only a few chrysanthemums and had left them in the flower room for me. I arranged them for the dining room table and carried them there myself.

And as I arrived in the dining room with them, Apsley announced luncheon. I ate alone, and after I had finished, I asked Titus, who had returned from Mendley House early in the morning, to find my mother and tell her that I planned to call on Lady Rutford that afternoon and would be leaving at two o'clock, in case she cared to go with me. I asked him also to ask Henderson to have the cabriolet ready at the entrance front at that time.

The afternoon was one of those rare, clear, blue ones that sometimes comes after a heavy storm. The rain had turned the meadows and pastures to emerald, and a few wild flowers still bloomed there. Purple asters, thistle, and pink-white milfoil speckled the fields, and I was surprised to see a meadow anemone blooming in a shady bog as we drove toward Mendley House. But the orange bittersweet and red, poisonous bryony had not assumed their autumn colors, though the water-elder already wore its scarlet fruit at the edge of the copse.

How muddy it would be in those thickets and meadows! Otherwise, it was a perfect day for Lord Rutford's meet. But then, anyone who would ride to hounds would hardly mind a bit of mud.

I heard the hounds in full bay about a mile this side of Mendley House, and I asked Henderson to stop the carriage for a minute.

"Tallyho," someone cried.

At first they were hidden from me by a wood to my left, and then I saw the fox streak across the far end of the meadow with the hounds at its tail. The riders thundered out of the trees in pursuit. They were too far away, however, gathered in too tight a group, for me to pick out my stepfather. There must have been eighteen to twenty couples of hounds and about thirty men in the field. Then, almost as soon as they had arrived, they were gone, leaving the meadow in peace to sleep in the sun. The poor fox would soon be at peace, too. He was not long for this world, I feared.

We proceeded on to Mendley House, then, and found Lady Rutford at home.

"Such a to-do, Suzanne, my child," she shouted at me as I entered the drawing room. "All those men and dogs and horses chewing up the park and making such a racket. Why George has to have his meet the very day after my dinner party, I cannot imagine, but that is the way men are. How are you, my dear? So lovely of you to call. Where is your mother?"

"She had a headache this afternoon, Lady Rutford, but she asked me to remember her to you," I answered. "It was such a lovely party last night."

"And thank *you* for your sweet little French songs

—most appropriate and touchingly rendered. But, my dear, those Crandon girls—a whole opera! At least it seemed like a whole opera. I thought it would never end. They ruined my party. *Ruined* it!" she screeched. "I really cannot ever ask them to perform again, nor will anyone else, you can be sure. *Someone* must see to it that standards are kept in this part of Somerset. If it is all right with me, my dear, you can be sure it is all right, but never make a blunder. We cannot take our social responsibilities too seriously. We must set the example.

"Ah, here they come at last. I thought they had gotten lost or been eaten by the fox. The lawn will be full of holes for weeks. Oh, I wish we were in London. But then, when we are in London, I wish we were here."

Dogs yelped, boots and hoofs crunched on the gravel, and men laughed and shouted. Red coats and white breeches flashed by the windows.

Then Roundell and Raymond Taylor burst into the drawing room. Gainsborough should have seen Mr. Taylor in his red coat, posed against the blue walls with his black hair tousled and his cheeks aglow.

"Caught in Greves Wood at last. What a chase!" Roundell exclaimed. "The hounds were always—Miss de Riocour!"

"I am so glad to see you again, Miss de Riocour," Raymond Taylor said.

"Yes, George?" Lady Rutford cried to Lord Rutford, who motioned to her from the doorway. "Oh, all right! Just a minute. Roundell and Raymond, take care of Suzanne for a minute." Then she hurried out of the room to her husband.

Roundell followed her to the door, called a footman, and asked for a pitcher of cold water, some cake, and sherry. Then he returned and slumped in the chair opposite us.

As he did so, Mr. Taylor, sitting in the chair next to me, said, "We got off to a very late start this morning, and the animal was a clever one. The hounds kept losing him, and the covers and woods are so thick in places that we kept losing the hounds. Oh, it was a great mix-up at times, but we got him in the end."

"Lord Easton tells me your home is in Kent, Mr. Taylor," I said, "and that you will be staying with him for another week or so. Lord Easton, you must bring Mr. Taylor to the ball on Tuesday. Mr. Taylor, I do hope you will come with Lord Easton and his parents. I should be disconsolate if you didn't."

And I gave him my most enchanting smile.

"Thank you, Miss de Riocour. I shall look forward to it with the greatest pleasure," he replied.

"And when will you be returning home, Mr. Taylor? Let us hope we will have the pleasure of your company for some time to come."

"My mother is expecting another child, Miss de Riocour, her sixteenth. I am the second of twelve living brothers and sisters. I often wonder if that doesn't set some kind of record in Kent." He laughed. "I shall return sometime after the baby is born, if Easton and his mother and father will let me stay that long."

"You know you may stay as long as you like," Roundell said. And then he turned to me. "At least Armthrop House is big enough to hold them all, Miss de Riocour. It is a tremendous heap of brick and stone —you have no idea. Why, a person could get lost for weeks in the place."

"And what of the governess taking care of all the little children?" I asked.

"Governess?" Mr. Taylor asked, as if I had asked if there were vermin at Armthrop House. "Oh, they come and go. They have the best of characters when they arrive, but they either drink, steal, or flirt. There is a new one every other month. But what an extraordinary—"

"Now, that is taken care of. Men are so helpless —*helpless!*" Lady Rutford roared as she waddled into the room followed by a footman with a tray. "Put it down here, Alfred." She moved a crystal box on a low table at the far left of the couch where I was sitting. Then she waved the footman away and sat down next to me. "A beautiful idea to have some refreshment. You boys must be dying of thirst." She poured water into large goblets and handed them to Roundell and Raymond.

"Cake, my dear?" she asked. "You must taste this —it is one of Mumford's specialities."

She chuckled as she lifted a piece of pound cake onto a plate and handed it to me with a lace-edged napkin. Then she served the boys and, finally, herself.

"The ball, the ball, the ball," she cried, swallowing a mouthful of cake. "Isn't it delicious? How we are looking forward to the *ball*. I remember one ball at Warton Hall when Lady Campbell's mother was still alive." Roundell's eyes swept the ceiling. "The old lady must have been eighty-five, if she was a day, and the size of a doll, she was. Well, they didn't keep her out of the refreshment room long enough, and she finished the evening by sliding down the banister of the grand staircase with her dress up above her knees." By this time, Lady Rutford was laughing so hard that she could hardly speak, and the sofa rocked like a railway carriage does when the train starts. "Oh, it was the funniest thing you could ever want to see." She chuckled and wiped the tears from her eyes with her napkin. "But of course, she was never invited anywhere again." Her eyes turned cruel for a moment. "However, the dear soul died not long after, in her sleep. I always thought how lovely it was that she had that last fling at Warton Hall." The sofa shook a few more times and then was still.

About twenty minutes after that, I said that I must be going and asked for my carriage to be brought around.

"But, my dear, you have just arrived, and now you

are going so soon," Lady Rutford said as we walked toward the portico together.

Raymond Taylor had come with us, and he was the last to say good-bye. "It has been such a pleasure," he said. And I could tell by his eyes that he meant it.

He handed me into our carriage, and I waved good-bye. And as it rolled away from the house, I couldn't help rejoicing that I had entirely escaped seeing my stepfather.

"Mark Lawson is Mother's lover. Mark Lawson is Mother's lover," the horse's hoofs declared, as we sped along toward Warton Hall. They told me over and over what I had been unwilling to face all during that heavy, dull day—the sure knowledge that Mark Lawson was Mother's lover and that there wasn't a thing I could do about it.

But that didn't keep me from remembering how warm and protected I had felt in his arms that day in the pagoda. Nor did it keep me from feeling again the touch of his hair on my cheek as he had bent and briefly kissed my neck.

"Oh, Mark, why don't you love *me?*" I whispered. "God, make him love me." But I knew Mark wouldn't: he was in love with my mother.

What was I to do, then? Become a governess? Raymond Taylor thought a governess on the level of an insect. I wouldn't become one of them. Marry? Without my stepfather's permission? That would mean there would be no dowry for me: I would be penniless. Roundell would not want me then, nor would Cecil, nor Edgar, nor even Heston Nedeham. But what about Raymond Taylor? No! What was happening to me? I was beginning to think just like everybody else.

And all the way back to Warton Hall, those hopeless words repeated themselves over and over in my mind: "Mark Lawson is Mother's lover. Mark Lawson is Mother's lover."

# ᏋᎦᏍ Chapter Fourteen ᏍᎦᏢ

SUNDAY MORNING was a continuation of the crisp blue and green-gold day before. Morning dew sprinkled the grass in the shadows with billions of tiny crystal beads, and the sky lay bare, a blue dome arched above us. Gulls wheeled and dipped, their cries hardly audible above the clopping of the horses' hoofs as Mother, my stepfather, and I drove to church in the barouche. As we passed the abbey, I noticed that the servants from the hall were walking the shortcut path through it, the men wearing black suits and the women their good black dresses. They marched two by two, and for a moment the ancient building seemed to have come alive again: a religious procession marched down its nave once more.

They would reach the church on time; we would be a few minutes early. When we arrived, Mother and my stepfather went into the building to sit in the family pew and wait for the service to begin, but I chose to walk in the churchyard until it was time to go inside. After the service, Mother and I waited a few minutes on the flagstone terrace in front of the church, I to see the rector, who was surrounded by parishioners, and Mother to see Mark.

"Good morning, my child," the rector said to me as soon as he was free. "And how does this glorious September morning find our lovely princess?"

"Very well, thank you, rector," I said. "Yes, isn't it a lovely day?"

"Good morning, Lillian, Suzanne," Mark said.

Mark had said good morning to Mother first, I noticed, but then when he looked at me, there was something more than good morning in his eyes. But I was not interested in playing games, especially with Mark Lawson.

"Good morning," I quickly replied. Then I turned back to the rector.

"I had hoped you would be paying me a visit one afternoon," he said, smiling, "to bring a little joy into the somber life of an old man. Alas, the old soul has waited in vain. Are we no longer friends?"

"Of course we are," I smiled. "It is just that I have been so busy with the preparations for the ball. I will come soon, I promise. I do wish you would come to the ball on Tuesday. The long gallery is going to be full of plants and trees and flowers. It will be like dancing in a woodland, almost. Oh dear, I can tell by your eyes that you won't come. We *will* miss you."

"I think you really do mean that, my dear. That cheers the old man considerably," he said. Then he took a few steps to my right, stooping, tottering, and holding onto an imaginary can and grinning back at me all the while. It was an amusing impersonation, and I laughed aloud.

I like this man so very much, I thought. I wish I could trust him completely.

"Until three, then," Mother said to Mark. "It will be lovely there, my dear." Then she turned to me. "Come along, Suzanne. Your stepfather is waiting in the carriage."

She began to glide off toward the barouche, and I followed her, throwing a "good-bye for now," a smile, and a wave over my shoulder. I realized then, that Mother had not said a word to the rector, nor had he said a word to her.

Nor did we speak to each other as we drove back to Warton Hall; we were each engrossed in our own

187

thoughts. Mine were about Mark. Why had he looked at me more than casually? What has happened to me that a look from this man could affect me so? It had made me want to say to him, "Whatever it is, Mark, I will stand by you." And immediately after that he had planned a rendezvous with Mother for three o'clock. Where were they going at three o'clock, that would be "lovely"? Some woodland glade, perhaps? What would they do there? Would Mother's habit have bits of grass clinging to it when she returned to Warton Hall later in the afternoon? And what kind of game was Mark Lawson playing with me?

Well, whatever it was, the game must end. How could I find out what it was—and what he was doing here? Why had he lied to me? And what kind of work was he doing for my stepfather?

After luncheon I decided to walk to the mausoleum. Mark Lawson had been there last Monday night: I had seen him. Perhaps, if I looked the place over very carefully, I could find some clue as to what had been going on up there in the middle of the night.

So I walked to the top of the hill, but before beginning my investigations, I sat down for a few moments on one of the lower steps of the mausoleum and looked out toward the sea. How different it looked today from the gray, wind-whipped day of the funeral. Today the sun cast a warm lemon glow on the green fields below, and the sea was navy blue. Far out, the sails of a six-masted schooner showed white against the water. She wore all of her canvas unfurled to catch the same gentle breeze that stirred the grass at my feet.

"How peaceful it is here," I whispered, as I relaxed into the strange pleasure of being delightfully alone. I turned my face to the sun, and as I felt its heat on my skin, I wished I had no other mission that afternoon than to enjoy the day. But such was not the case. So, reluctantly, I got up and decided that first I would walk completely around the mausoleum through the tall grass to see if anything had fallen there.

The ground had not been disturbed, and I found nothing in the grass until I had walked completely around the building and returned to the place where the staircase met the circular foundation. There, hidden in a clump of weeds, I found a lantern filled with oil, its wick waiting only for the light of a match. Mark had hidden his lantern there in readiness for his next visit.

I left it where I had found it and then climbed the eight or ten steps to the portico and walked slowly around it looking at the stone wall and floor, but I saw nothing unusual. Then I opened one of the doors and stepped inside the building, shutting the door behind me. I did not especially care if anyone saw me enter the mausoleum, but I thought it pointless to advertise my presence there.

After the brilliance of the day outside, the mausoleum seemed to lie in gloom. But what light there was, falling as it did from that unexpected source above, glowed. It was a cold light—none of the warmth of the day outside had penetrated the thick stone walls. Was this what death was like?

In that cold stillness, the dead lay hidden in their coffins, sealed away in their vaults, indiscernible except for the carvings on their marble slabs. Many of the old slabs were cracked and broken, the mortar crumbled away. Half of one had fallen to the floor and lay against the wall in several pieces.

The finished tombs remained in good repair, however. The stone figures slept undisturbed. The unfinished ones stood empty and dusty, waiting patiently for their future tenants and their enormous, heavy carved lids.

I was drawn to the sculptured figure of the seventh earl, sleeping on the lid of his tomb. Below, carved into the side of it, the inscription ended with the usual

"May he rest in peace," and I thought how extraordinary, how horrible his death had been. He was certainly not resting in peace. Would he wish me to expose his murder? Would anyone believe me if I told them about it? And would it do any good if they did? I didn't think so.

Then, just as I noticed that Cecilia Osborne's rose petals had been swept from the floor, I heard the grinding of metal on metal. Someone was opening the mausoleum doors.

As I swung around to face the doors, they were thrown open wide, and a man stood silhouetted in the doorway, black against the brilliance of the day outside.

"Suzanne, what are you doing here?" Mark Lawson demanded. "I saw you come in from the road below."

"Looking," I answered.

"Looking for what?" he asked, walking toward me.

His limp was barely noticeable that day. In a moment he stood before me. His big hands gripped my shoulders, and his gray eyes looked intently into mine.

"Looking to see what you have been doing up here in the middle of the night," I said, returning his stare.

At this, his hands dropped to his sides, and he turned away. "I haven't been doing anything up here at night," he said. "Don't be absurd."

"Do you deny that you have been here late at night? I found your lantern hidden in the grass outside."

He faced me again, his eyes smoldering. "Suzanne, why have you become so suspicious of me—"

"Why?" I interrupted. "You lie to me, you have business with my stepfather that you tell me nothing about, you come sneaking up here in the middle of the night, and you ask me why I am suspicious of you."

"What I do during the day and during the night is my business!" He had raised his arms as though he were going to put them around me. "Suzanne, darling—"

"Very well, Mark Lawson, that is exactly so," I said, pronouncing each syllable distinctly as I looked directly at him. "What you do is your business. It is none of mine. What you do at night is no business of mine, and what you do during the day with Mother isn't, either. She is waiting for you." I pointed in the direction of the house. "Waiting to take you to a lovely place. What you do there is no business of mine, either. You had better hurry, or you will be late."

He turned from me then, and without another word walked out of the building.

I waited until I had heard the sound of his horse disappear, and then I walked through the open door and out into the sunshine. I shut the door behind me, descended the steps, and began to walk slowly down the track to the Hall. I felt ill.

"Oh yes, miss, there'll be more than enough flowers for what you'll be needing, even for a ball," said Benjamin. It was Monday morning, and we were in the flower room. "Not as much variety as a month ago, maybe, but plenty. Let's see, there's autumn roses, and some beauties, too, and of course the dahlias and chrysanthemums are at their best now. And there's the starwort, Michaelmas daisies, meadow saffron, torch lilies and lots of gladioli and the monkshood. There'll be plenty."

We did a tour of the rooms that would have flowers and decided what flowers we would use where.

After Benjamin had gone back to the farm, I had nothing to do. I could not remain idle. That would mean thinking, and I desperately wanted to keep from thinking about yesterday. If there had ever been any chance that Mark could love me, it was behind me. Yesterday had ended it. But I would not think about it, and in time it would not hurt so badly. So I went to find Mrs. Danley, to see if there was anything I could do to help her.

*Elizabeth Norman*

I found her in the hall chamber, where a carpenter was suspending a wooden pole from behind two large armoires that had been placed about five feet apart and out a bit from the wall.

"We'll put the guests' cloaks and shawls on hangers," Mrs. Danley said, when I had entered the room, "and hang them in the armoires and on the pole between them, you see. Then there are the big mirrors in the Pink and Chinese Rooms, which we'll hang here and on the wall between the windows. And then Miss Clair and Grace—"

"Is there anything I can do to help, Mrs. Danley, anything at all? I feel so useless," I said.

"Well now, that's just so good of you to ask, my child. Yes, as a matter of fact there is. We usually make little checks for the wraps and bonnets—just a little piece of paper with two numbers on it that can be torn in half, like. One half goes in the garment and the other half to the guest. It saves so much time when the guests are hurrying for their carriages and want to get along home. Now, if you could—"

"Wonderful!" I said. "I will go right along to the schoolroom and get to work. I suppose we will need nearly a hundred of them. We had better have more than enough, don't you think?"

Making the checks occupied me for what remained of the morning and for some time after luncheon. And when I had finished, I took them down to Mrs. Danley, who then wondered about the checks for the men's hats. So I returned to the schoolroom and made the men's checks. I was content to be occupied, and when I had finished, it was time to change for dinner.

# ✂ Chapter Fifteen ✂

I heard the brougham drive up at about four o'clock that afternoon and the distant voice of my mother welcoming my grandmother and Uncle Matthew. And when I came down to dinner, they were already in the corner room with Mother and my stepfather.

"Mother and Matthew, this is Suzanne," my mother said, as I entered the room.

"Suzanne, my dear," Uncle Matthew said, bowing as he accepted my hand.

"Suzanne?" my grandmother asked.

"Suzanne, my daughter, your grandchild, whom you have never met," Mother explained.

"This is not Suzanne," Grandmother said. "Suzanne is in France. You have hidden the child away in some French convent, and no wonder. Did you think you could fool your own mother? You should marry, find a husband. Matthew will give you a splendid dowry, won't you, Matthew?"

"But Mother, you know I am already married to Fitzjames," my mother said, as she slipped her arm through my stepfather's.

He was looking at his watch—impatient for his dinner.

"Yes, there are just Matthew and me at Sike Hall —now—" my grandmother said.

Then her face crumpled into such a look of grief and despair that it shocked me.

"There, there, Mother," Matthew said. "And we

193

are very happy, too, aren't we? But there is so much to do to keep up such a big house, isn't there?"

"Dinner is served, my lady," Apsley announced from the doorway.

We went in to dinner, and I had time to examine my grandmother. She was a tiny, pale woman with barely enough flesh to cover her bones. Her brown eyes, protruding from the hollows of her skull, were enormous, and her thinning hair had turned yellowish white. She wore a dress that had once been black but had faded to a dark, greenish gray.

She sat next to Matthew at the table, across from me. He looked like his mother—thin, pale, white-haired—but he was perhaps thirty years younger. His suit was the same faded color as her dress.

He and Mother talked about the ball and life at Warton Hall. My stepfather devoted his attention to his food. I said nothing. I had become curious about my grandmother and watched her closely. She played absent-mindedly with her soup.

Suddenly, she said, "Matthew, the Brussels tapestries must be taken down and cleaned." Then she looked across at me. "They are priceless, you know, woven in 1578. They are in the Blue Velvet Room. When you come to visit us at Sike Hall, you will have the Queen's Room. The carpets are sixteenth century and the chairs are Charles II and Queen Anne. We have the finest private collection of paintings in all of England, except for the queen's—Rubens and Rembrandts, Titians and Correggios, Murillos and all the English painters.

"Matthew, someone has poked a tiny hole in the corner of the Van Dyck—the portrait of Charles I. It must be repaired. All the furniture and hangings and paintings must always be perfectly maintained."

Then she paused, her eyes widening as if she had seen something that terrified her.

"Life is endless torment. I want it over. Let me die," she cried, looking at the ceiling and stretching her thin arms above her head. "Just let me die." Then her hands fell to her lap, and she stared silently down at them.

"Mother," crooned Uncle Matthew, reaching for her hands. "You are tired, and it has been a long day. Come, let me take you to your room. We will get you into a warm bed, and Simpson will get you settled and stay with you during the night."

He helped her up, and across the room. But they paused at the door. "We didn't want to come," he said. "Why couldn't you have left us alone?" And then they left us.

"I did not know she was like this," my stepfather screamed at my mother. "Why didn't you tell me she was so bad? She looks terrible. They both look terrible. They will be no credit to me." His little arm had begun to throb.

"Don't worry, Fitz," Mother said. "She has a new dress, a deep violet one, most suitable. She need only be present at the beginning of the ball—just put in an appearance, that is all. Now that they are here, what else can we do? And Matthew will be with her. She will not stay long—it will exhaust her. And then we will say she is not feeling well. It will all go very well indeed, believe me."

"It had better," my stepfather shouted, through a mouthful of cutlet.

After dinner, I wandered through the drawing room to the summer parlor and finally found myself at the door to the porch of the east front. Through the glass I saw Uncle Matthew standing with his back to me, his hands clasped behind him, motionless, looking at the gardens. I pushed the door open and walked to his side.

"Uncle Matthew?" I said.

"Ah, Suzanne," he answered. "Sike Hall could look like this." He paused while he gazed out across the roses. "The gardens were just as beautiful," he continued, "almost as elaborate as these. Now there are no flowers. The walks are choked with weeds, the pools are empty, their basins cracked, and Mother—poor Mother."

"What has happened? What was wrong at dinner?" I asked.

"She has been like that ever since my father's death. Oh, not so bad at first. She gets a little worse every year. I suppose it really started with my half brother's death."

"Your half brother?" I asked.

"Hasn't anyone told you about my half brother's death and what my father did? No? Well, it is not a very pretty story."

As we talked, we descended the steps together and began to walk along one of the paths. The air was perfumed with roses, even on that September night, and some of the brilliant blooms seemed to glow with an inner light. The dusk grew deeper.

"Lillian's and my father was the tenth marquis of Brancroft," he began. "He was a wealthy man—not as wealthy as your stepfather, but a wealthy man. His estates comprised something like sixty thousand acres, most of it productive. His net income was perhaps seventy thousand pounds a year. Sike Hall was a showplace, magnificently furnished.

"My father had a son, John, by his first wife. She died, in childbirth. My father idolized John to the extent that Lillian and I hardly existed as far as he was concerned. John, of course, being the eldest son, was to inherit the house and estates, but unhappily, fate decided that I should have them."

He stopped to pick a pink rose, held it to his nose briefly, and then handed it to me.

"Unhappily?" I prompted.

"John contracted diphtheria in January 1842. The disease became steadily worse, John had great difficulty breathing and the doctors looked grave. Mother nursed him as if he were her own: she never left him.

"My father was certain that John would recover. He loved his son too much to let him die, you see. *His* son could not possibly leave him. Toward the end, when John could barely breathe, my father left the sickroom and went to his office for an hour. It was while he was away that John died. My father went out of his mind with shock and grief. The three of us were in the room with John's body shortly after he died—I remember it as though it had happened this morning. Lillian was out somewhere. He accused my mother of smothering John to death in his absence. He said he knew she had secretly hated his son, that she had always wanted the inheritance to be mine. It was a terrible scene. The accusations were unfair, of course. Mother was blameless."

"How awful," I said.

"My father decided to punish my mother for what he thought she had done. His revenge would be to deprive my mother of the fruits of her supposed act. He would watch the growing realization, the frustration, and finally the gradual despair resulting from his actions: There would be no inheritance for me.

"My father had John's body embalmed and laid out in the great hall. It remained there for exactly one year, while he held what must be the longest and costliest wake in history. Sike Hall was constantly filled with guests. The wine flowed. Extra servants were hired. No expense was spared, and no bedroom was ever empty.

"While all this was going on, he was having the monument built on Troy Hill, very near the house. It was designed by Richard Terhune. You may have seen pictures of it. The obelisk is of every known kind of marble in the world, and it can be seen for twenty miles around. The elaborate base is really a tomb for John and my father.

"When it was nearly finished, John's body was buried there. After that, my father kept to his rooms. Hatley, his groom of the chambers, carried out all his orders. Mr. Bartholomew, his solicitor, came often. The staff was cut to eight, almost all the rooms were closed, and the grass grew waist-high in the park.

"After that, every so often, my father would enter my mother's sitting room and stand in the doorway and say, 'The lands to the east of Hanterham House have been sold to pay debts—twenty thousand acres,' or, 'The woodlands in the north sector have been sold to pay debts—ten thousand acres.' That was all he would say, and then he would turn and leave the room. It was torture for mother, and he meant it to be.

"Before the year was out, he lay beside John in the base of the obelisk. I inherited seventeen acres of land and the Hall. Almost all the rooms were empty. My father had sold everything to pay for the monument and the wake—the tapestries, the paintings, the furniture. The horses were gone and so were the carriages. Other than the almost-empty house and those few acres of land, there was nothing left.

"One day I came upon Mother in one of the empty rooms, and she said to me, 'We must have the tapestries cleaned, Matthew.' There were no tapestries, of course.

"Most of the time she believes it is all still there, and then those few times when she realizes it isn't, she wants to die. You saw her tonight. It is no wonder her mind is unhinged. She did everything she could to save her stepson, and then to have my father turn on her like that and ruin our lives—" He stood silent, looking away from me.

"And you?" I asked.

"I look after her. She has her three thousand pounds a year 'pin money.' This she would always have, according to the marriage contract. We manage to live on that. We throw the house and monument open to what little public wishes to see them, charging a small admission fee. We live.

"But you see, there could never have been a dowry of any kind for Lillian. She had to find a husband who had no need of money. Of course, she had her beauty. Well, she has found him. She is a very determined woman, my sister. She always gets what she wants.

"We had better go in now. It is getting late," he concluded.

And we went into the house.

After breakfast the following morning, Mrs. Danley, Tupper, the tall Scot who was head gardener at Warton Hall, and I went out to the glasshouses to see what plants and trees we would want to move into the house. This was my first real visit to the glasshouses, and I was surprised to find that Tupper had continued to keep some of them filled with palms and ferns and flowering plants and trees, as well as using some of them for raising plants that would be transplanted to the gardens in the spring. He obviously loved his work and took great pride in his plants, regardless of whether anyone ever saw them or not. I decided that, in the future, I would spend some time here and enjoy Tupper's handiwork. When I asked him if some of the plants could spend a day or two in the house from time to time, he was delighted.

He and some of his men began the job of moving them to the house, and I decided what should be placed where.

After luncheon, Mrs. Danley, Benjamin, and I spent more than two hours arranging flowers. By three-thirty, we had finished the decorations. They were more successful than I had imagined they would be.

At last it was time to change my dress for dinner, which was to be informal and served in the breakfast room at five-thirty. This would allow us time to rest and dress before the guests began to arrive at nine o'clock.

I was so excited that Clair had to ask me several times to be still as she helped me dress and did my hair after dinner. I wore my pink ball dress that evening. It was an off-the-shoulder gown, cut very low in front, with a skirt of row upon row of puffed net garlands from the waist to the floor. It would be like dancing in a mass of pink foam.

I loved the dress, I loved the way I looked, I loved the way I felt: this was my first ball, and I was going to enjoy it whether Mark danced with me or not, whether Mark spoke to me or not. I was going to enjoy myself.

# ᏋᏜᏥ Chapter Sixteen ᏨᎠᎦ

THE CLOCKS HAD STRUCK nine o'clock only moments before the first carriage rounded the gate and began the long drive to the house. I could see its tiny lights long before I could hear the distant crunch of hoofs. I watched it from one of the partly open bay windows in the long gallery. Then I saw the lights of another carriage and then another.

I thought how festive the house must appear from outside. The lamps on either side of the steps below me were lighted, as were every lamp and candle in every room on the entrance front. I thought how brilliant, too, the staircase hall would seem in the moonless night. Every candle in its great chandelier was lighted, and its wall sconces were lighted, too.

Though brilliantly lighted, the house was very still. It was a restless quiet, however, almost as though the building were impatient for the festivities to begin. Someone, perhaps Clair or one of the maids, ran down the staircase outside the gallery. Crystal tinkled on crystal in the refreshment room where one of the footmen was making preparations for serving. The musicians were a pianist, a cornetist, a violinist, and a cellist. They sat in their places at the end of the room, whispering to each other, their instruments tuned and ready. While he waited, the cornetist played a soft, thin melody.

The melody seemed a perfect accompaniment to the first carriage's arrival. It pulled up to the steps with the second close behind, and I leaned out of the window to see whose it was. It was one of Lord Wessex's carriages, and he and Lady Wessex and her mother, Lady Maine, and Heston were getting out. Mary and Esther and their two friends, Margaret Pale and Jane Patterson, arrived in the next carriage. They laughed and chattered as they walked to the steps. Mary looked up and waved, and I waved back. Then the third carriage stopped, and Lady Westmore's footman opened the door for her.

I did not wait to see who rode with her. I turned from the window and ran to the door. Across the landing, Apsley took his place at the top of the stairs. But where was Mother? She should be here to receive our guests and give out the dance programs. But when I looked down at the table, I saw that the programs weren't there.

"Apsley," I said, "where are the programs? We have forgotten to put them out."

"The last time I saw them, miss, Mrs. Danley had them in the hall chamber. I shouldn't be surprised if they are on a shelf in one of the armoires," he replied, beginning to descend the stairs.

"You can't go now," I cried. "The ladies are removing their things. I will go." And I ran down the stairs toward Lady Bagenot, Silvia, Julia, and Andrea, who stood in the hall below.

"Suzanne!" cried Silvia, as I descended the last few steps. Then all three surrounded me, talking and giggling at once.

"Excuse me, I must get the programs," I said, laughing. "We can't have a ball without them."

Then Lady Wessex and her daughters came out of the hall chamber, a mixture of pastels. When they saw me, they, too, all started talking at once.

"Go on up, and I will be there in a minute," I shouted.

I ran into the hall chamber. The programs were in

their box in the armoire. Across the little room, Margaret and Jane and Lady Maine were removing their things and primping before the mirrors. I stopped to welcome them and then, carrying the programs, walked out into the staircase hall. There I met Albert, Arthur, and Hadley Audley, who had come from the direction of the men's cloakroom, and we climbed the staircase together.

"Forty-three hares in one day," Arthur said. "How is that for a day's shoot?"

"Forty-four," corrected Albert.

"Can't you two ever talk about anything but hunting and horses and horses and shooting?" Hadley said. "Miss de Riocour doesn't—may I carry those for you?"

"Thank you, Mr. Audley," I said.

"The lord Wessex and the lady Wessex," Apsley announced from the top of the stairs, "and the honorable Mary Nedeham, honorable Esther Nedeham, and the honorable Heston Nedeham."

When we reached the gallery, Hadley gave me the programs, and I ran into the room and put them on their table beside Mother. I joined her in greeting Mr. and Mrs. Palmer, Lady Bagenot's brother and his wife, and their two sons, John and Richard.

"So nice of you to come," Mother said and then turned toward Lord and Lady Aldergate, who were approaching with Elizabeth and Edgar.

"You know Mary and Esther Nedeham, don't you?" I asked John and Richard. "Will you come with me while I take their programs to them?"

But as I spoke, my eyes were drawn to the doorway. It was Mark who had attracted my attention, and our eyes met briefly. I hope he asks me to dance. He must ask me to dance, he must! I thought.

But then for the next few minutes I was too occupied to think. First I gave the girls their programs, and no sooner had I done so than Lady Aldergate descended upon me.

*Elizabeth Norman*

"The earl of Rutford and the countess of Rutford," Apsley announced. "The viscount Easton and the honorable Raymond Taylor."

Lady Rutford, seeing Lady Aldergate and me together, rushed over to say good evening and how excited she was and how wonderful it was to have a ball at Warton Hall again. While we talked, I noticed Albert and Arthur asking Margaret and Jane for dances and John and Richard asking Mary and Esther. The girls were busy writing in their programs.

Suddenly Mark stood beside me. "May I have the pleasure of dancing this quadrille with you?" he asked.

"Thank you, Mark," I said, smiling up at him.

By that time, the orchestra had begun the introduction to the dance. Lady Aldergate and Lady Rutford left us, and we went to join John and Mary who were forming a set. Arthur and Jane were forming their set with Albert and Margaret and Hadley and Elizabeth. And Lord Westmore and Lady Wessex were forming a set. Already there were twenty-four dancers on the floor, and people had only begun to arrive.

Mark bowed to me and then to Esther, and the dance began.

"Do you know that this is my first ball since I embarked for the Crimea?" Mark said, as we advanced in the first figure.

I smiled at him. "Do you know that this is my first ball, ever?" I asked him in return. "We had dancing lessons at school, but I was never to a ball."

"You dance charmingly, and you are very beautiful tonight," he whispered, his gray eyes intent and solemn.

Does he ever smile? I wondered.

"That is because I am happy tonight," I said, as we returned to our places. "I may not have been happy yesterday, and I may not be happy tomorrow, but I will be happy tonight."

Then Mark asked me for the third dance, the lancers, and the sixth, a waltz.

"Oh, Mark," I said, "I shouldn't—but I will. Thank you."

When our dance was over, Raymond Taylor asked me for the second dance, a waltz. He danced beautifully. The waltz was by Strauss, and we whirled around and around among the swirling couples like a child's colored pinwheel blown by the wind.

"Ha, ha, ha," bellowed Lady Rutford, as she hurtled past us with Lord Aldergate. "You naughty man."

"The lord Plummer and the lady Plummer," Apsley shouted, "and the honorable Iris Bisham, the honorable Cecil Bisham, and the honorable Paul Lowe."

Mark danced by with Julia Crandon. Julia was giggling, but Mark did not seem amused. And we passed eighty-year-old Lady Maine waltzing with Heston Nedeham, her grandson.

Everyone who could dance had abandoned himself to it. This was not surprising, for balls were not held so often in the country, and when one was, everyone made the most of it. The atmosphere of gaiety was almost tangible.

But underneath the gaiety, intrigues festered. During the lancers, for instance, I heard Andrea Crandon say to Raymond Taylor, "Poor Iris, I am so sorry for her. At her age—her father almost ruined, I understand, and she is almost twenty-five, poor thing."

And while Raymond Taylor and I were dancing the fourth dance, I noticed Iris Bisham whispering something to her mother and looking daggers at me. If looks could kill, I would be long dead, I thought.

But then I noticed that Mark was not in the room, and for the rest of the waltz I could not help looking for him. No, he was definitely not there.

"Would you care for some refreshment?" Raymond Taylor asked, when we had finished the dance.

"Yes, I would love something to drink," I said.

So he led me into the refreshment room and brought me a glass of lemonade. Mark was not there, either.

As I sipped my drink, my stepfather came up behind us. "Suzanne!" he demanded.

"Mr. Taylor, have you met my stepfather?"

"Good evening, sir," Raymond said.

"Your grandmother has not appeared," my stepfather said. "Why has she not appeared? Go and find out. I want to know." Then he flung himself away from us and strode off into the long gallery.

"Thank you Mr. Taylor," I said, "that was delicious. Now I must go and look for my grandmother. She is coming to watch the dancing, and she should be here by now. I can't imagine what has happened to her."

He took me back through the long gallery to the hall doorway, and there I left him. As I walked away, I noticed Mother and Mark climbing the grand staircase together. Mother was not smiling. I did not wish to speak to either of them then, so I did not pause, but hurried down the corridor toward my grandmother's room, instead.

Her room was two doors away from mine. When I reached it, I knocked lightly, and the door was opened by Uncle Matthew in his new black dress coat and white tie.

"Suzanne! Come in," he said. "I am afraid Mother won't be coming to the ball." Then he turned to my grandmother and said, "See what a beautiful young lady has come to see us."

There was no response from her. She sat slumped in an armchair by the hearth, staring at her hands in her lap. She wore her new purple dress, and her hair was parted and combed smoothly into a bun at the back of her head. A tall, thin woman in black stood behind her chair, wringing her hands. This must be Simpson, her maid, I thought.

"It is such a lovely ball," I said, sinking to a stool beside my grandmother's chair. "The gallery is so pretty with all the flowers, and the music is lovely, and we have such nice friends. We are having such a good time. Won't you come?" I stood and offered her both my hands.

She looked up slowly, into my eyes. "You are a nice child, whoever you are," she said. "Oh, very well, I will come. I see I shall have no rest until I do. It couldn't possibly be any worse there than it is here. Go along and let me get ready."

Uncle Matthew looked at me with relief. Then he saw me to the door, and I slipped out of the room. As I walked back down the corridor to the long gallery, I hoped that perhaps the ball would bring a little joy into her life. I wanted my grandmother to have a happy evening, too.

When I reached the gallery, the dance floor buzzed with between-dance conversation, and men searched for their partners. As soon as I entered the room, Mark hurried toward me.

"Suzanne, have you forgotten we have this waltz? Where have you been?" he asked. "I have been looking everywhere for you."

"Miss de Riocour," Cecil Bisham said, at the same time from my left. "May I have the pleasure of dancing the next lancers with you?"

"Oh, Mr. Bisham, I shall not be dancing the lancers."

"The quadrille, then?" he asked.

"Thank you Mr. Bisham," I said, beginning to mark the eighth dance in my program.

He bowed and left us. The music began, and I put my hand in Mark's. His arm went around my waist.

But just then Mother came hurrying toward us. "Mark, darling," she crooned. Mark dropped his hands. "You have already danced two dances with Suzanne, and I haven't danced at all. I have been so busy with my duties." She pouted, her bosom heaved, her perfume engulfed us in its heady floral scent.

"Suzanne won't mind," she cooed, slipping smoothly between us and taking Mark's right hand in her left.

"I have this dance with Suzanne, Lillian," Mark snapped. His eyes and his voice were as cold as steel. "At one time a lady waited until a gentleman asked her to dance, but apparently manners have changed."

"But Mark darling—" Mother implored.

"Do not tell me what to do, Lillian. I am not your lackey." Mark spat these words at her. The steel had become white hot.

Mother gasped. Her hand went to her temple, and she stood paralyzed for a moment looking at Mark. Then her eyes narrowed cruelly for an instant. She grasped her skirt and flung herself away, stalking across the room. Mark did not look after her, nor did he give any further sign of his anger. His arm encircled me, his hand grasped mine, and he swung me into the waltz. We danced, however, in silence.

Finally I said, "I went to find my grandmother. She was to come to the ball, and when she hadn't appeared, I went to see if anything was wrong."

"Suzanne—" Mark began.

"There she is now, just coming through the door with Uncle Matthew. Could we go to her please, Mark?" I begged. "She is ill, and I am terribly worried about her."

"Of course, my dear," he said, and he steered us expertly through the dancers to them.

"Grandmother, Uncle Matthew, this is Colonel Lawson," I said. "I am so glad you came. Isn't the—"

"Lawson? Nonsense!" Grandmother interrupted. "I know you, young man. We have met. But where? What is the name? I can't think."

"I don't believe we have ever met, Lady Brancroft," Mark said, bowing to her.

Beside us, two chairs stood empty against the wall. Grandmother sank into one of them, and I sat down next to her. Lady Plummer was on a settee on the other side of Grandmother with Iris beside her. Mark and Uncle Matthew stood together to our left and began to talk.

I leaned over to Lady Plummer, who was all attention, and said, "Lady Plummer, this is my grandmother."

"Where is John and that husband of mine?" Grandmother asked a very puzzled Lady Plummer. "Have you seen them? They vanish. I have never known two men who can vanish the way they can. They are never to be found. Go and find them, dear," she said to me. "Our guests will be wondering where they are, and John should be dancing. Where is Lillian?"

I looked around the room, but I could not see Mother. Through an opening in the dancers, I caught a glimpse of my stepfather, at the entrance to the refreshment room. He was deep in conversation with Lord Plummer.

"If only father could be here to see our lovely ball," Grandmother mused to Lady Plummer and Iris. "He was Lord Talbot, you know. He died just last spring."

"You are not Winnie Malone? You *are* Winnie Malone," Lady Plummer cried. "Winnie! I thought I knew you. You don't recognize me? But of course you wouldn't remember. I was Cynthea Case, and my father was Lord Hawton. Don't you remember Marlebone House in Cavendish Square, and my sister Julia?"

"Little Cynthea Case? I don't believe it," my grandmother said. "Of course I remember Julia. Whatever happened to Mr. Davenport? That never made any difference, though, did it? That was the season of— I hate to remember—was it 1811 or 1812? Where is Julia?"

"She is in London. She lives in Marlebone House. She never married. It is a very sad story," Lady Plummer said. "Winnie, this is my daughter, Iris. Iris, this is a very old friend of your mother's."

The music stopped—the lancers was over. And in the confusion that followed it, I noticed Lady Rutford get up and walk toward us, her little bird's eyes bright with curiosity.

Off to her left, Cecil Bisham was weaving his way through the crowd toward us, too. I was to dance the coming quadrille with him. This would mean that I would have to leave Grandmother, and I glanced up at Uncle Matthew to see if that would be all right. He seemed to understand and smiled and nodded. But he stood alone now. Mark had gone, and I glanced about to see where. He had gone to speak to Silvia Crandon, who was talking with her mother and Raymond Taylor. Silvia stood as he approached. Mark was evidently to have this dance with her.

"Cecil, my dear," said Lady Plummer as he approached, "this is my old friend, Winifred Malone, now Lady Brancroft. This is my son, Winnie."

And then Lady Rutford arrived.

"Lady Rutford—" I said, as I stood.

"My dear, such a charming party," Lady Rutford shouted into my ear. "Perfectly delightful, exquisite taste, quite perfect. Perfect!" Then she gazed greedily through her lorgnette at Grandmother. "And who have we here?"

"Grandmother, this is Lady Rutford," I said.

"What did you say?" screamed Lady Rutford, as she sank into the vacant chair next to grandmother. "Speak up, child."

"This is my grandmother, my mother's mother," I shouted.

"Oh! How do you do?" she cried.

"Nancy," Lady Plummer said to Lady Rutford, "Winnie is an old friend whom I haven't seen in more than forty years."

"How perfectly divine," shouted Lady Rutford as she leaned closer.

"I married Lord Brancroft five years later," Grandmother continued, oblivious of the interruption.

Lady Rutford's eyes popped, and her head nodded with every word. But then I looked up and saw Raymond Taylor approaching. Iris composed her hands in anticipation, but Raymond walked past us and stopped in front of Jane Patterson. He had asked Jane for the quadrille.

The introductory music began, and Cecil led me out onto the floor and to the post of honor, placing me on his right. Jane and Raymond had joined us and stood to our left, and Margaret Pale, Hadley Audley, Mary Nedeham, and John Palmer completed our set. As we prepared for the dance, I glanced back at Grandmother, and then at Iris. She gave me a savage look and then turned back to her mother, my grandmother, and Lady Rutford. The dance began.

Halfway through the first figure, I glanced again toward Grandmother, and I saw Lady Rutford pressing her fingers to her lips, the whites of her eyes as large as egg cups. Iris had gotten up and was running to the south end of the room toward her father. Her mother's arm reached out toward her daughter's retreating figure, and I heard her call, "Iris!" I went through the figures of the dance mechanically, wondering what had happened.

"What is it?" Cecil asked.

"Your sister," I whispered. "Over there." And I motioned to her with my eyes.

By that time, Iris had interrupted my stepfather's conversation with her father. She stood before them, stamping her feet and talking very fast. Then, to my astonishment, she swung around, her face contorted with rage, and pointed straight at me in punctuation of something she was saying.

I desperately wished I could hear what it was and what my stepfather said then to Lord Plummer. It was a brief command, and as he gave it his little arm fluttered. Immediately, Lord Plummer seized his daughter's hand and dragged her away into the refreshment room.

"What happened?" Cecil whispered.

"Something dreadful, I am sure," I replied.

And then my heart sank: Grandmother was standing, her arms raised to heaven. "Let me die," she was surely saying. "Just let me die." Uncle Matthew put his arm around her waist and, whispering into her ear, led her from the room. I followed them with my eyes into the hall. Mother appeared from down the corridor and spoke quickly to Uncle Matthew. Then she walked to Lady Rutford and Lady Plummer, sat down with them, and spoke to them calmly. While she spoke, Lady Rutford laid her hand soothingly upon Mother's arm.

Thank heaven this happened during a dance, I thought, and thank heaven for the music. Did anyone take notice? Mark was looking in Mother's direction and so was Jane and so were Lady Aldergate and Elizabeth, but most of the guests seemed not to have noticed.

As the music stopped and the dance ended, I saw Mother leave the room. I was sure she was going to Grandmother. Outside the gallery, she walked past Iris. Iris flashed her a look of hatred and then, with icy majesty, began to descend the grand staircase. Iris's mother, meanwhile, rushed to join her husband, who had returned to the long gallery.

All this baffled me. What had happened? Perhaps Lady Rutford knew. So I asked Cecil to take me over to her.

"What happened, Lady Rutford? Please tell me," I asked, as I sat down next to her. "No, it is all right. I have not planned to dance this dance."

As I said this, I glanced up at Cecil, but he had already hurried off toward his parents. I noticed that Lady Aldergate was on her way to them, too.

"Everything will be all right, my dear," Lady Rutford said. "Just you leave everything to me. Why I feel as though you are practically a member of the family." Her little eyes peeped shrewdly out from between half-closed lids. "Your grandmother was upset. She said something about you being hidden away in a French convent when you were a little girl, something about the coincidence of your father's death so soon after—ah—an—abrupt and unexpected marriage in France, and something about your mother's partiality toward the servants. That was all. No one could possibly believe a word of it, especially a woman of the world like myself." She paused dramatically, slyly appraising my reaction through her lorgnette.

"We must keep up the standards, you know," she continued, "and you can be sure that I would never believe a breath of scandal of a child that I had practically welcomed into the very bosom of my family. Dearest Suzanne, rely upon me," she murmured, as she took one of my hands in one of hers and patted the top of it with the other.

"But Lady Rutford—" I began, taking my hand away.

"And then that foolish child went running to her father with heaven-only-knows-what story, but put your trust in me—all will be well. After all, we must stick together, you and I," she said with a giggle.

"Well, while Iris was creating her unnecessary little scene," Lady Rutford continued, "I realized, all of a sudden, who your grandmother is. She is the widow of the Lord Brancroft of the famous monument. Well, there are some things I have always wanted to know about *that*. So I asked her. But when I mentioned Lord Brancroft, your grandmother seemed to lose control. It was nothing I *said*. She simply lost control and began asking God to kill her. Really! But of course she must have been exhausted, poor thing."

It was now my turn to want to die. I wished a hole would open in the floor and swallow me up.

"Come along my dear," Lady Rutford said, heaving herself from her chair. "I must have some refreshment. My throat is as dry as the desert, and you look as though you could stand something, too."

I followed her, welcoming the relative privacy of the refreshment room. There I sipped lemonade while she quaffed two glasses of champagne and I tried frantically to evaluate what she had told me. As we returned to the gallery, my stepfather pushed his way through the dancers toward us.

"Where is your mother?" he demanded of me.

"I don't know," I answered. "I suppose she went to see if Grandmother is all right. Oh—there she is now."

As Mother entered the gallery, the waltz ended, and the gentlemen began to escort their partners back to their seats along the walls or to the refreshment room. Mother had seen Mark in the center of the room with Mary Nedeham, and she walked toward them. My stepfather hurried to intercept her.

"I have the next quadrille with Lord Easton," I said to Lady Rutford. "Do you see him anywhere?"

"Yes, there he is, my—"

"Who is it?" my stepfather shrieked at Mother.

All movement in the room stopped. All eyes rested on my stepfather and my mother. They stood alone in the center of the floor. My stepfather's left arm flapped wildly. He tried to hold it still with his right hand as he shouted up at Mother. She smiled calmly down at him, tilting her head as she answered him in a low murmur. Mark and Mary were nowhere near them now—Roundell was closest. He had started toward us from the bay opposite but had frozen a few feet away from them.

"His name! I want his name!" my stepfather screamed.

Mother smiled at him again and shrugged her shoulders. Then she answered—parrying his question, I was sure. How could she be such a fool as to play with him in this mood?

"Answer me, damn you!" he cried.

Her answer was short. I could tell it was a name. It seemed to stun my stepfather. He stood there trying to control his arm and looking up at her in astonishment. Then he said something to her in a low voice, and she answered. As she did so, an unmistakable expression of triumph spread across her face.

Then, to my horror, my stepfather stood on his toes and struck Mother across the face. All the strength of his right arm and body launched the blow, and she fell on her side on the floor from the force of it.

"You bitch, you filthy bitch," he screamed down at her.

He spun around, then, and ran from the room, his little arm flapping like the wing of a bird. From behind, he seemed almost to be flying, grotesquely, two feet above the floor. The guests fell back out of his path, and there was not a sound except for the scuffing of his feet as he disappeared down the grand staircase.

When he had vanished, all eyes turned back to Mother. For a moment, no one moved. And then everyone rushed to help her. Roundell reached her first and helped her up. It seemed like minutes before I could make myself move, but it was only a second before I ran to her, too.

"Mother, are you hurt?" I asked.

"Thank you, Lord Easton," she said, and then she turned to me. "On the contrary, I am superb, my dear —better than I have been in some time."

Her expression was one of triumph, as nearly as I can describe it, and there was something else there that I could not read. She was smiling and was strangely exultant.

I watched her closely. She looked into the faces of all the people surrounding us—slowly, from one to another—all the time holding her eyes wide until they teared. Then she smiled again and extended her arms dramatically in supplication.

"Forgive him," she cooed. "I do." She paused. "He has been working so—terribly hard, and he is so—terribly exhausted and upset. He has so—many terrible problems. They are such a strain. His life has—not been an easy—"

"Of course, my dear," shouted Lady Rutford, as she marched to Mother's side. "We understand. We stand behind our men. Their lot is not an easy one. They are the very backbone of England. We are proud of them! Of course we forgive! We hope your dear husband will find an ease to his tribulations. Indeed, we shall pray for him.

"Let us go on with the ball!" she shouted to the pianist, as she flung her arm high into the air. "Music, please!"

At her command, the introduction to the quadrille began, and, miraculously, the ball continued almost as if nothing had happened.

Lady Plummer, who had followed Lady Rutford to our side, said to Mother, "You poor dear. Of *course* we forgive. You are so understanding, so superb. Superb!"

I did not miss the cunning look that appeared in Lady Rutford's little black eyes as she gazed at Lady Plummer.

"Have a lovely dance, children," Lady Rutford said, turning almost immediately to Roundell and me.

And Roundell took me away to secure us a place in the quadrille.

"Lord Easton," I said, as we danced, "you were nearest them. What did Mother say? Who was my stepfather asking about? Who was it, could you hear?"

"I couldn't hear anything she said, she spoke so

softly," Roundell replied. "I am sorry. I thought you might know what they had been talking about. The only thing I could hear her say was the very last thing. Your stepfather asked if there was any proof, and your mother answered, 'There are letters.' And then your stepfather struck her."

"Oh, Lord Easton, what am I to do?" I said.

"Go on with the ball as if nothing happened," he answered. "What else can you do? If you need any help, just remember that I am here."

The dance that followed this, the eleventh, was a waltz, and I was to have it with Mark.

As we began it, Mark asked, "Suzanne, what has been going on? What was that scene between Miss Bisham and her father all about? And just now, your stepfather—what did he want?"

"I don't want to talk about it," I said. "Could we just dance, please?"

"Certainly," he replied.

We whirled around and around the room, and I watched the other dancers as we moved past them. They were smiling and laughing as if nothing had happened. They don't really care about me or my mother or my stepfather, I thought. Their own lives are more than they can handle, most of them. They have their own problems, their own intrigues. Oh, they will gossip and wonder and watch, I suppose, but there isn't room to *care* about anyone but themselves. See how Elizabeth Leighton is flirting with Raymond Taylor, for instance. Why, she just met him tonight. She doesn't even have time to think of her best friend, Iris, let alone any of us.

But then my mind demanded a respite, and I tried not to think any more, to lose myself, instead, in the whirling kaleidoscope of color and sound.

Mark brought me back to reality, however, toward the end of the waltz, by simply saying, "Suzanne."

"My first ball," I replied. "How I looked forward

to it. It was going to be a happy evening with no connection to yesterday or tomorrow—just one wonderful, joyous evening."

"Suzanne, darling," he said.

"But I can't pretend. It does have a connection," I continued. "Do you think I didn't see you and Mother coming up the stairs together earlier? What were you doing with her downstairs in one of the parlors? Do you think I don't know what has been going on? Do *you* want my dowry? You, too? Since Mother is already married, might *you* just as well have it? Well, Colonel Lawson, there are other people who have a much more powerful claim on it. *You* don't stand a chance."

A moment later the music stopped, and I said, "Please take me to the hall doorway. I must go down to the ladies' cloakroom."

He led me to the staircase landing, and I left him there. He had not said another word.

I was grateful to be able to get away from him—I wanted to be alone. And I could be, since I had decided not to dance the lancers, which was the next dance. It was the twelfth dance of the evening and would be the last one before supper. As soon as it was over, everyone would come trooping down the stairs to the dining room to eat, and I thought I would be better able to cope with supper if I could sit quietly alone in the music room or corner room for a few minutes. After supper, six more dances would have to be gotten through before the ball ended.

But when I had descended the stairs and reached the hall below, I glanced into the hall chamber and saw Iris Bisham sitting motionless on a little chair in the corner. Her hands were clasped on her lap. She held her chin high and her eyes closed.

Clair stood there looking at Iris, puzzled. She saw me and walked toward me.

"She has been sitting there like that for I don't know

how long," Clair whispered. "She hasn't said a word to anybody."

I walked over to Iris and said, "Miss Bisham? You can't stay here all evening. Is there anything I can do?"

Iris opened her eyes and looked directly at me without any visible sign of emotion and without moving.

"I shall sit here until I am permitted by my father to leave this house," she said. "There *is* something you can do: you can go back to wherever you came from and leave us all alone. If you hadn't come here, I would have married Roundell. There is not a chance of that now. And, because of you, Mr. Taylor will not look at me.

"Oh, I know your secret. Your grandmother knows it, my mother knows it, Lady Rutford knows it, and my father knows it. I told him tonight. Your stepfather knows it. I told him, too! Everyone knows it. You are a bastard. Your mother is such a whore that she doesn't know whether your father was a groom or a gardener. A French count indeed!

"It won't make any difference, though. Your money has seen to that. The men will do anything to get your dowry. They will even accept a common bastard. I have been threatened to silence. You have no need to worry—your money has taken care of that, too. Now, just go away and leave me alone." And she closed her eyes again.

"What can we do?" Clair asked.

"Carry on as if nothing had happened, Clair, thank you," I said.

And then I left them and walked through the empty rooms until I found myself at the doors to the rose garden. I opened them and walked out onto the porch and stood, for a while, cloaked in the blessed solitude of the night. And by the time I could bring myself to go back through the summer parlor to the drawing room where most of the guests were seated having supper, they had been there for some time and had almost finished eating.

As soon as I entered the drawing room, I was captured by Lady Rutford.

"Suzanne, my dear child," she cried, as she bolted from her chair and rushed toward me. "You are all alone." She took my hand. "Have you had supper? No? Come and have supper with us, then. Roundell, look whom I have brought you. Sit down here, my dear, next to me, and Roundell will get you something to eat and drink. Roundell, go and get Suzanne some cold chicken and ham and turkey and some of the tipsy cake."

So, I thought, here I am, imprisoned in the very bosom of her family. Take care, Suzanne, lest it last forever.

But I said, "Thank you, Lady Rutford. You are so kind. I hope I haven't driven Miss Leighton away."

"Not at all, my dear," she answered, turning to glance at Elizabeth Leighton, who was leaving the room. "Roundell had the last dance with Elizabeth before supper. I cannot imagine why—such a tiresome creature. So naturally he was obliged to see that she was fed. She is now going to play Florence Nightingale to Iris, who is hiding in the ladies' cloakroom. She is going to take her dear friend some food. Curiosity has temporarily weaned her mind away from the charms of Raymond Taylor. I hope Iris has the sense to keep her mouth shut."

And then Roundell returned, carrying a huge plate of food and a separate plate of cake.

"Oh, Lord Easton, thank you so much," I said, "but I really don't think I could. I am not hungry at all."

"My dear, I am so sorry," Lady Rutford said, reaching for the tipsy cake. "Waste not, want not." She chuckled as she took a mouthful. "Delicious! Simply delicious. Your chef is superb—a lovely supper.

Which reminds me. Roundell, while you were at Oxford, Lord Hinterham held the last ball at Atley House before the fire. Did I tell you? Well, his chef, an Indian, gave notice that very day. He couldn't stand it any longer, and I can't say I blame him. The supper was mostly curries. Imagine! Hot? You have no idea what hot *means*. Our mouths were sore for weeks. It was a nasty trick. Well, Lord Hinterham set out to find the chef and. . . ."

During the story, my attention began to wander, and I noticed that, beyond the doorway to the drawing room, the door to the game closet stood ajar. The movement of a face withdrawing into the darkness inside it attracted my eye.

"Excuse me for just a moment," I said to Lady Rutford and left her to continue her story.

Quickly, I walked into the semigloom of the little hallway, carrying my plate of food, pushed open the door, and stepped inside.

"What are you doing here?" I said.

There was no sound. I waited for a moment for my eyes to become accustomed to the darkness and then looked around the tiny room.

"Come out from behind that target," I whispered. "You should be in bed, Monk. Come out! I know you are there."

Monk crept out from his hiding place and stood before me, his hands held behind his back, his head bowed. But his eyes looked up into mine.

"I wasn't doing anything, miss. I just wanted to see the ball, that's all, miss."

"But you should have been in bed hours ago," I said.

"Oh, no, miss! We're all very busy taking care of the horses and carriages. And the coachmen and the maids and all are having a time in the servants' hall, miss. Oh, no, I couldn't be sleeping, miss, and I ain't doing no harm."

"Well, all right, Monk. Here, I brought you some ham and chicken. Stay out of sight and don't neglect your duties in the stables."

I left him, and as I walked back toward Lord and Lady Rutford and Roundell, I saw Lady Rutford lean forward in her chair, look intently at her son, and shake a warning finger at him. Judging from her expression, whatever she said to him must have concerned a very serious matter, indeed. Lord Rutford nodded his head in agreement, and Roundell looked terrified.

I noticed that Elizabeth had returned and now stood beside Raymond Taylor's chair. He was talking to Andrea Crandon and her mother. Elizabeth looked as if she would burst with impatience.

I was relieved when I heard the orchestra begin to play. It was time to go back to the long gallery.

"Come along, Suzanne," called Lady Rutford, extending her hand to me.

We began to follow the crowd toward the staircase hall. Ahead of us, Mother was on Mark's arm. Andrea Crandon and her mother followed them. But where was Raymond Taylor? I glanced back into the drawing room to see if they had left him behind and saw him standing there alone with Elizabeth. She had finally gotten her chance to speak with him. She spoke rapidly, and Raymond Taylor listened wide-eyed. I knew what she was telling him.

Later, when we entered the gallery, Roundell asked, "May I have the pleasure of dancing this waltz with you?"

"Thank you, Lord Easton," I answered.

"Miss de Riocour—Suzanne," he said, after we had danced awhile without speaking, "I—" He hesitated. "I know you—I know we haven't known each other for very long. I mean—well, is there any hope for me?"

"Lord Easton!" I said. "Your mother told you to do this, didn't she?"

"Yes," he said, looking away.

"Do you really want to ask me?"

"It is so sudden—yes—yes, of course I do. I—"

"Thank you, Lord Easton. I am enormously pleased and terribly flattered. But there is plenty of time, and you must be sure. Tell your mother that I said my stepfather will decide—which, I am afraid, he will. Meanwhile, let us continue to be just as close friends as ever."

Roundell looked into my eyes and smiled with relief. I smiled back.

We spoke little after that. Roundell never had very much to say anyway, and I had become preoccupied watching Elizabeth and her mother, Lady Aldergate. They had been arguing heatedly, and the argument had developed into a quarrel. As we whirled by them, I heard Lady Aldergate say, "Don't say anything! Wait till I tell your father. . . ." Then she saw me watching her, and she gave me a grin and a little wave.

She and Edgar came hurrying over to me as soon as Roundell and I had finished dancing. I don't know what she had done with Elizabeth—I didn't see her anywhere.

"Miss de Riocour—Suzanne, my dear girl," Lady Aldergate said, "such a lovely party. Simply lovely! I was just saying to Edgar how proud your mother must be of such a success. And how proud she must be to have a daughter like Suzanne. *I know I would be.*"

As she said this, she leaned close to me, opening her eyes very wide in emphasis. In the short silence that followed, she glared at Edgar.

"I agreed with my mother," he said, almost at once. "I mean, we are proud to have you here with us. Ah— may I have the pleasure of dancing this quadrille with you?"

Then I explained to them that I had promised the quadrille to Hadley Audley, who appeared at that moment and took me away from them. When the dance was over, Lady Plummer hurried toward me with Cecil in tow.

Hurry, hurry, I thought, as they approached. Come one, come all. Strike while the iron is hot. Hurry, lest the Rutfords win the race.

"Suzanne, dearest—you must let me call you Suzanne," Lady Plummer began. "Now, I am going to be quite frank, and you mustn't mind. Iris has been behaving like a hysterical schoolgirl tonight. She has always had a vivid imagination, but *this* behavior, *these* wild imaginings, *this* nonsensical talk—we cannot imagine what has gotten into her. Her father will punish her severely, and then she will see how mistaken she has been—how foolish, how utterly foolish. Oh, but I know you will forgive her, as one forgives a sister."

Then she turned to face Cecil, and her head jerked perceptibly in my direction.

"May I have the pleasure of this—" Cecil began.

"If I had a sister like Iris, I would smash her brains in," Lady Rutford bellowed from behind me. "Forgive? Really, Cynthea, I don't know if I can. We have never witnessed such behavior." Lady Rutford's eyes were slits. "How could a member of your family make such a spectacle of herself? I thought there was refinement, *breeding.* . . ."

I stepped away on Cecil's arm, thankful to leave the ladies to do battle undisturbed. I knew who the victor would be: there would be no further problems with Lady Plummer.

"Please don't say anything, Mr. Bisham," I pleaded. "Let us just dance, may we? I can't think any more —my mind simply won't work."

"I was supposed to," Cecil said, grinning down at me, "but I won't."

After that, the last three dances of the evening stretched before me. I danced all three and got through them somehow. Two of the dances I had promised to John Palmer and Albert Audley. And the last I had saved for Mark until my quarrel with him, hoping he would ask for it. This I danced with a young man whose name was Adam Dore. I don't remember a thing about any of those dances.

At last it was over, and the hubbub and confusion of departure began. Through the open windows, the carriages sounded on the gravel of the drive as they were brought around, and I could hear the coachmen calling to one another and shouting commands to their horses. As the guests, tired but pretending vivacity, flowed through the gallery doorway toward the stairs, I stood next to it beside Mother and accepted everyone's thank yous and good nights.

Finally, only Lord and Lady Plummer and Cecil, and Lord and Lady Rutford with Roundell and Raymond Taylor remained. The two families stood quite apart. It seemed they were no longer speaking to one another.

First, we said good night to Cecil and his parents, and in answer to Cecil's very warm smile, I gave him both my hands.

"Thank you. Good night," Raymond Taylor said.

"As close friends as always," Roundell whispered.

"A perfect party," roared Lady Rutford, swaying slightly. "Simply superb, in perfect taste, divine. You poor things, you must be exhausted. Sweet Suzanne, I shall pop over tomorrow to see that you are all right. We have much to discuss," she concluded, herding her family down the stairs. "Ta-ta, ta-ta," she cried, waving her fingers at us from the landing before she disappeared.

Mother and I were left alone.

"Thank you, Father," I heard Iris's haughty voice

proclaim from below, "for permitting your daughter to leave this house of iniquity at last."

"Shut your mouth," Lord Plummer ordered.

So, my first ball was over. Without another word, I picked up a candle from the table and walked down the long corridor to my room.

# Chapter Seventeen

". . . . So you see, Clair," I continued, "if Grandmother hadn't come to Warton Hall for the ball, it wouldn't have happened. I certainly don't blame her for saying what she did. She is ill—I don't believe she knew whether she was thinking or speaking aloud. She didn't know that she was here last night—she thought she was at Sike Hall and that it was fifteen or twenty years ago. Certainly, if Raymond Taylor had asked Iris to dance instead of Jane Patterson, there wouldn't have been the scene, and Iris wouldn't have told my stepfather, and my stepfather wouldn't have struck my mother. What a dreadful night. I suppose the servants' hall is buzzing with it this morning.

"You were so good to come rushing up here last night and help me to bed without asking questions. Is it morning, or is it after twelve?" I went over to the clock on the bedside table. "Half-past twelve," I thought aloud. Then I walked to the windows. "How dark and foreboding and evil the fog makes everything seem. I don't like fog. Mist can be lovely, but I never did like fog—especially when it is heavy and close like this. It frightens me a little."

I shivered involuntarily as I looked at the dripping stone knights standing along the balustrade of the terrace. Just beyond them hung the dense, impenetrable gray curtain.

"At least there won't be anyone calling this afternoon, which is a blessing," I said, pouring the last of my tea. "Thank you for my yellow roses, Dorothy," I called across to her. She was carrying the water cans and towels towards the door. "You are both so good to me.

"But now I must go down to see Grandmother and Uncle Matthew off. They will be leaving for the station at about one o'clock, I should imagine. It will take much longer to get there in this weather."

So I finished my tea and left the room.

In the corridor, I saw two men carrying a rug toward the long gallery, and for a moment, time seemed to have turned back, even though the silhouetted figures of Saturday morning were receding instead of approaching. How wonderful it would be, I thought, if Lady Rutford's dinner party could begin at its finish and then time regress to the funeral and finally to my being back in school again.

But it could not. And I found the house in chaos. The rugs were being put down in the long gallery, furniture was being moved into and out of the room, and orange trees and ferns were being carried out of the gallery and down the staircase.

Titus and Edward walked out of the long gallery toward me, each holding a bouquet from some vanished table that had stood in the room during the ball.

"You may as well dispose of all the cut flowers, except the chrysanthemums on the dining table downstairs," I said to them, "and the flowers in the drawing room and summer parlor."

I wished that I hadn't started to do the flowers at Warton Hall. I didn't feel like doing them any more. And I wouldn't, I thought as I began to walk down the stairs, if it weren't necessary for everything to seem placid and for me to seem happy and completely obedient to my stepfather.

When I reached the hall, I found Mother and Grandmother—bundled in a heavy, shabby cloak—

Uncle Matthew, and Simpson. Coventry climbed the stairs from the drive, clutching one of his big blue umbrellas. "The carriage is up, my lady," he announced.

"Excuse me, miss," said a man from behind me. He carried a tree fern past me and out of the doorway, followed by another man carrying small orange trees.

Then, from beyond them, a loud, deep voice called, "My dears!" And Lady Rutford materialized out of the fog, making room for the men to pass. "Such a day, but we are not afraid of the fog. Ah, Lady Brancroft is leaving." She rushed through the doorway toward us. "What a pity. What a pity you could not have stayed with us a little longer, Lady Brancroft. We have so enjoyed meeting you.

"Oh, Lord Trevenbury!" Seeing my stepfather, who was crossing the hall behind us at that moment, she threw out an arm and stalked forward to intercept him. "Lord Trevenbury, I had hoped to see you this afternoon. Could we chat? Could we have a little talk together, just you and I—ah—privately? I have some very interesting things to say to you, my dear, dear man."

"Business or social?" my stepfather demanded.

"Well—I—"

"You don't know? Then it's business. Come to my office. I have ten minutes to spare."

"So good of you. So good," she cried, hurrying after him. "Ta-ta, ta-ta, Lady Brancroft." She waved at us as she disappeared in my stepfather's wake.

Meanwhile, Coventry had opened the umbrella and was standing just outside the door.

"Good-bye, Grandmother," I said. I bent and placed a little kiss on her waxy cheek. "Have a safe journey. And Uncle Matthew—"

"Can you forgive us, my dear?" he asked.

"There is nothing to forgive," I replied. "Please write and tell us you have gotten home safely."

Mother gave Grandmother a swift kiss and said, "It is all right, Mamma. It is all right."

"When you come to Sike Hall, you will have the Queen's Room," Grandmother said to me.

"Yes, yes, come along now, we must go home now," Uncle Matthew said, shepherding her out the door and under the umbrella. "Good-bye," he turned to say, and then they descended the steps, their figures growning lighter and grayer and finally vanishing altogether.

Then Mother turned toward the staircase.

"Apsley," she said, "Please tell Lady Rutford that I have a headache and was forced to lie down."

"Very well, my lady," he said.

"And Apsley," I said, "I will be in the library."

The library contained religious books by the hundreds, volume after volume, shelf after shelf of sermons and religious essays, and a tremendous section of books on history, another on travel, and countless books on architecture—English and French and Roman and Greek. But there were only a few novels. These were grouped on shelves near the windows, and there I found Le Sage's *Gil Blas de Santillane* in the original French. And I decided that it might help me to stop thinking and take my mind away from England for the rest of the afternoon.

I needed to escape from myself. I had been thinking for days about what I could do and how I could get away from Warton Hall and my stepfather and the threat of, at the very least, a forced marriage to a man I did not love. But the more I thought, the more certain I had become that I was trapped.

So I took the book with me and walked back to the staircase hall. By that time, the flowers and trees and plants had all been carried away, and the maids were busy cleaning the stairs. Apsley and Coventry tended the door.

"Apsley, where is Lady Rutford?" I asked. "Is she still with my stepfather?"

"Oh, no, miss," he replied. "Her ladyship left at least twenty minutes ago. She asked me not to disturb you. She said she was feeling very unwell and must return to Mendley House at once. It was most extraordinary, miss. She almost ran out of the door—Coventry barely had time to open the umbrella and catch up to her. I suppose her carriage was waiting just below in the drive. They drove off in great haste, miss."

"How odd," I exclaimed. "Apsley, I will not be down to dinner, but will have a tray in my room. Something simple, perhaps some soup, an omelet, salad, a roll and butter, and some fruit and coffee."

"Very well, miss," Apsley replied. "I will have it sent up at about seven?" he suggested.

I nodded my approval, and then I walked to my room and rang for Clair.

"Please help me out of this dress, Clair," I asked, when she arrived. "I think I shall wear the wine-colored robe. I am going to sit here and read for the rest of the afternoon and evening, and I want to be comfortable. Will you light the fire, please? It will take the chill off. And light some lamps to make it more cheerful."

"Certainly, miss," she said. Then she began to help me with my dress. "That was quite a warm meeting between his lordship and Lady Rutford in his lordship's office this afternoon, miss."

"What do you mean by 'warm,' and how do you know about it?"

"Because I was there, miss," Clair said with a giggle. "That is, I was just outside the door."

"Clair!" I cried, in mock disapproval. "What happened? What did she say?"

"Well, just as I got to the door I heard Lady Rutford

say that it was a very serious scandal but that it could be overlooked *if* the two *dear* young people were to marry. 'Marry, my foot,' said your stepfather, 'I am saving her for a lot better than a Wensley.' Then Lady Rutford said that you have to be accepted socially before there is any question of marriage and that she could see to it that Lord and Lady Trevenbury didn't go anywhere. Then your stepfather said that he has been buying a lot of stock in certain railroad companies lately—that at the snap of his fingers the Wensleys might as well be living in a shanty in St. Giles, and her husband might as well be selling potatoes on the street. 'You go home,' he said to her, in a voice that gave me the shivers, 'and ask your husband what happens when the directors ask for restitution, and ask him who the directors are.' Then he tells her to get out of his house and not to come back until she is told to. Well, you should have seen her leave. I wouldn't have thought she could move so fast, and about two minutes later her carriage was roaring away down the drive.

"Well, miss, I just thought you would want to know."

"Thank you, Clair," I said. "Yes, I did want to know, very much."

Shortly after Clair had lit the fire and the lamps, she left me, and I spent the rest of the afternoon reading, escaping quite successfully from Warton Hall through Gil Blas's adventures.

At seven o'clock I was interrupted by Titus, who had brought my dinner. I asked him to draw the curtains and then to set the table in the alcove so that I would face into the room with my back to the terrace and watch the fire while I ate. After this was done, he left me to my meal, saying that he would return later to clear away.

Mine was a pleasant solitude that evening: the room was cheerful in the lamplight, and I ate slowly, watching the flames dance on the coals in their blue and yellow and orange dresses. I imagined a ballet with brilliant blue and yellow and orange costumes, and I began to create a fantasy world far removed from my real one.

But the click of the latch behind me and the breath of cold air on the back of my neck jerked me back to reality. I looked around. The scar-faced man stood behind my chair, staring down at me.

His white hair was plastered to his white skin by the wetness of the fog. His black woolen suit smelled of damp. Some wisteria leaves, I noticed, clung to the sleeve of his coat. He was winded—his breath foul. And from his open mouth stretched that horrible scar, deep and angry looking at that close range.

Slowly then, without taking his eye from mine, he reached into his coat pocket, drew out an envelope, and dropped it into my lap. As he did so, he tried to speak, but no sound came from his mouth.

The scream came from the other side of the room. It was Dorothy. The man gaped at her in surprise and then slipped quickly back between the curtains and out onto the terrace. Dorothy screamed again for as long as her breath lasted. I leapt from my chair, ran to her, and slapped her face. This stopped her screaming, but she continued to stare at the place where the man had stood, pointing to it with a rigid arm.

"What is it? What's happened?" called Mrs. Danley from the open doorway behind us.

"The man, the man with the scar!" Dorothy screamed hysterically. "That was the man with the scar!" She had gripped both my arms with her strong, thin hands and was shaking me. "That was the man with the scar! That was the man with the scar!"

"Dorothy!" I shouted, wrenching myself free of her. "I know it was. Control yourself. I know it was."

"What is it, miss?" asked Titus, who had appeared behind Mrs. Danley.

Two maids had also materialized. They stood behind Titus, gaping over his shoulders.

"It's all right now, Dorothy," said Mrs. Danley. "Titus, would you be so good as to fetch some brandy quickly? There's a bottle in the room Lady Brancroft used." As she spoke, she strode across the room to the alcove, where a breeze stirred the curtains, and closed the terrace door. "Nora and Charlene, don't stand there staring when there's nothing to stare at. You may go back to your work, and please close the door behind you.

"Dorothy, sit down in that chair. There is nothing to be afraid of. Calm yourself," she said. Then Titus knocked, and Mrs. Danley opened the door and took a bottle and a glass from him. "Thank you, Titus, everything is under control." Then she closed the door, poured brandy into the glass, and gave it to Dorothy, who drank it.

"Now, what's all this about?" Mrs. Danley asked me.

Dorothy stared up at me questioningly, too. She seemed to have regained some of her composure.

"There is a suspicious man whom Dorothy and I have seen lurking about the grounds," I explained. "He came through the terrace door into my room. He must have climbed the wisteria vines, and suddenly there he was. Dorothy came in to fix the fire and turn down the bed, and she screamed when she saw him. Isn't that so, Dorothy? And then the man fled."

"That's right, miss," Dorothy said.

I prayed that Dorothy had not seen the man drop the letter. It had slipped down between the cushion and the upholstered arm of the chair: I could see the corner of the envelope sticking up. But if Dorothy hadn't seen it, I was sure that it would not be noticed.

"What did he look like? Can you describe him?" Mrs. Danley asked.

"He is tall and very thin, with white hair," Dorothy said, mechanically describing the man who had haunted her dreams for years. "He has only one eye, and there is a deep scar that goes from where his other eye used to be to the corner of his mouth. When I came into the room, he was standing behind the miss's chair, and they were having a conversation."

"Hardly a conversation," I said. "There wasn't time."

"I don't remember ever seeing a man of that description," Mrs. Danley said. "If I had, I certainly would have remembered it. One thing's certain: his lordship must be told. I will go and tell him at once. A search must be made, and the man must be found and dealt with. I am sure that his lordship will take the matter in hand and deal with it as it must be dealt with. Now don't you worry, Dorothy, there is nothing to worry about.

"And Suzanne, my dear child," she came to me and took both my hands in her own, "you must have a glass of brandy too, and you are not to worry. The man, whoever he is, will be found and sent to prison for trespassing and attempted robbery, like as not, and I don't know what all. But in the meantime, lock the door to the terrace—not that you have anything to worry about, but just as a precaution. It will make you feel better if you do.

"Let Dorothy stay here with you for a few minutes until you are both calmer, and I will go and find his lordship and tell him about this extraordinary thing. He will take care of it. We will leave it in his most capable hands, and we can consider the matter closed, you may be sure." Then she hurried away to find my stepfather.

But Dorothy sat staring at me, as if she expected some sort of further explanation.

At last she said, "I'm afraid, miss. I'm afraid something terrible is going to happen. What is it, miss? What were you and that man talking about?"

"Dorothy!" I cried. "We weren't talking about anything. We had nothing to talk *about*. I don't even know who he is. He tried to say something, but somehow he couldn't. He had just burst in here when you screamed. There wasn't time for him to say anything, really.

"I have seen him watching me two or three times," I continued. "For a while I thought he was following me, but now I think he has been watching me only from time to time. I didn't say anything because I didn't want to worry you. I am sure it has nothing to do with you, anyway. I don't know what he wants. He has never spoken to me—he has never gotten near enough to speak. But whatever it is, it has to do with me, Dorothy—with me, not with you. There is nothing for you to worry about. Do you understand that?"

"I'm sorry, miss," she said. "I understand, miss. I didn't mean to make it sound as if you and him was doing something together. It's just that I was so frightened when I saw him here. I'm so afraid of that man, miss. He's death, miss." She looked at me, wide-eyed with terror. "Wherever he goes, death goes right behind. I know it." Her hands went to her mouth. "Whatever are we to do? Whatever are we to do?" She moaned through her fingers.

"Dorothy, stop it! You are hysterical," I shouted at her. Then I began to walk up and down before her chair, speaking as soothingly as I could. "Now, listen to me. This is a very fortunate thing. This is very fortunate. You see, before tonight we could not have gone to my stepfather and said that we have seen a strange man wandering about doing nothing. He would have laughed. But by now, Mrs. Danley has told him that this man has broken into his house—has broken into his stepdaughter's room and frightened her.

"Listen!"

Men were shouting in the rose garden. Joseph and Titus and Coventry called to each other, and then I heard my stepfather's voice and sounds of running. Dorothy and I ran to the window, but it was too foggy to see anything except lanterns, haloed by the mist, moving to and fro. The servants still called back and forth. One of them shouted, "This way," and then, "Look at this!" And after a bit, horses' hoofs clattered on the cobbled kitchen yard, and more voices shouted.

"You see?" I said to Dorothy. "The hunt is on. They will find him, and he will be put in jail, as Mrs. Danley said. Now let us go on with what we were doing. Tomorrow we will hear that he has been captured, and even if he should get away, he won't be coming back, you can be sure of that." Changing the subject I said, "The fire can stand a little coal, I think. Don't you?"

"Oh, I hope so, miss," Dorothy said. "Yes, I'm sure you're right. I'll attend to it right away." After she had fixed the fire and turned down the bed, she asked, "Will there be anything else, miss? Please let me know if you hear anything, won't you, miss? If there's nothing else, then, I'll say good night."

I wonder if my stepfather knows who the scar-faced man is, I thought a moment later, as I held the envelope in my hand. After all, he accompanied Mr. Shark to Warton Hall in his carriage, and Martin Shark and my stepfather are business associates.

I tore open the envelope. The writing was in an astonishingly beautiful hand and read as follows:

London, September 29, 1856
Dear Miss de Riocour,
   Please forgive the manner of delivery of this epistle, but it is a matter of some delicacy and secrecy, as you shall learn.

I hope this finds you happy and in the most excellent health.

I shall be taking the sea air for a day or two in Somerset and should consider it a great pleasure if you would call upon me at the Red Lion Inn, in Wattle, on the afternoon of October 2nd at three o'clock. The innkeeper there will provide a private room for us to converse in, undisturbed.

It will be of inestimable value to you to keep our appointment, but alas, I am afraid, a matter of great peril if you do not.

"I could a tale unfold whose lightest word would harrow up thy soul." Shakespeare: *Hamlet*.

Tell no one of this message and destroy it immediately. I beg you to come alone. Do not fear for your safety, as that will be my chief concern.

Believe me, dear Miss de Riocour,

Yours ever truly,

Martin S. Shark

I had asked for Thunder to be brought around to the entrance front at two-thirty the following afternoon.

"Owen," I said, after we were mounted, "one day, not long after I arrived at Warton Hall, we rode out and came across a small fishing village on the coast. I believe it is called Wattle. Do you remember it?"

"Oh, yes, miss, the village with the stone inn on the quay," he replied.

"Yes, it is such a lovely view from the hilltop above the village—I should like to see it again. What is the most direct way from here by road? Do you know?" I asked.

"Yes, miss. My father took me fishing there when I was a boy. The road to Wattle goes directly from the old abbey, miss. I suppose it was once the way the monks traveled—by the sea from Wattle. We can either go to the abbey by way of the road from the stable block or straight to the gateway and turn to the right and strike the road that way."

"Excellent," I said. "We will go out through the gateway and turn to the right and perhaps return by way of the abbey."

We walked the horses down the drive to the gateway, and as we went, I thought again for perhaps the hundredth time how "considerate" it was of Mr. Shark to have given me all of one day's notice. I would keep our appointment tomorrow. I didn't like the "great peril if you don't" of his letter, but, I reasoned, he wanted something from me, and he certainly wouldn't get it if I came to any harm. I would be safe enough, tomorrow, and I wanted very much to know what he had to say to me.

He and Scarface were associates: I had been right about that, at least. More than likely Scarface was employed by Mr. Shark as spy, messenger, and heaven knows what else. I looked to see if he was anywhere about, watching. But no, I didn't see him.

As we turned right at the gateway, I held out the watch that I had pinned to the lapel of my habit. It was two-thirty. The time was important: I must know how long it would take me to get to the village the following day, as well as the most direct way there.

From the crossroads, the road to the village was direct indeed: it ran as straight as a taut string from there to the top of Wattle's single street. It took us exactly thirty minutes to ride that distance, and we had not hurried. So, at three o'clock we stood on the hilltop looking down at the tiny harbor. Below me on the quay stood the inn, its sign swinging, and I half expected to see a very fat little figure come out of the inn door and perhaps strut off toward the village. But the quay was deserted and so was the village, except for a woman hanging out clothes behind her house, halfway down the village street.

It will take another five minutes to ride down there,

I thought, and then I can tie Thunder to the post next to the steps to the quay until the innkeeper can put him up. Heaven knows what he will think of my riding in alone, but it can't be helped. And heaven knows what he will think if he sees me dismount alone, but there will surely be a groom or someone to help me mount again when it is all over. I was apprehensive about it all, but at least I had learned that I would be safe in allowing forty minutes for the ride from the Hall.

We rode back to the Hall by way of the abbey, and I timed myself again. I found that it took about as long one way as the other, so I decided to ride to the abbey tomorrow and then to Wattle. That way, I would probably not be seen riding alone.

When we arrived back at the stable yard, John came out to meet us. "Everything all right, miss?" he asked, taking the reins and helping me down.

"With Thunder, do you mean?" I asked. "Of course. You still don't trust him, do you, John? He is a superb animal—one of the finest, gentlest horses in the county, I am sure. Beautiful Thunder." I stroked his neck. "Thank you for a lovely ride." Thunder blew and snorted in reply. "See that he gets something extra tonight, will you John?" I said, as I started toward the gardens.

I sat in my pagoda, having pulled my chair into a patch of sunshine and nearer a large yellow water lily that had replaced the purple one. As I watched it float, I wondered if my stepfather would be at dinner. I hadn't spoken to him since he had struck Mother at the ball.

I was determined to look my best at dinner that evening to remind my stepfather that I could be of use to him. And I was determined to behave very submissively. I wore a pale pink silk dress trimmed with fawn-colored lace and deeper pink and peach bows. Clair arranged my hair in long curls over one shoulder, tied with pink and peach ribbons.

My trouble had not been wasted: my stepfather noticed my appearance at once, giving me a long look as I entered the corner room where he and Mother waited.

But he said nothing, and when we began dinner, he ate in silence. He was preoccupied—his mind, no doubt, deep in some cunning scheme.

During the entree, however, he looked up at me and actually smiled.

"You look good," he said. "You look very good tonight. Beautiful! Yes! Doesn't your daughter look beautiful tonight, Lillian? Yes, yes. She is a credit to me. She will be very useful to me, very useful indeed. Did you see how the young men flocked around her at the ball?"

"Certainly, Fitz," Mother replied.

She seemed to have lost some of her languor. She watched him carefully.

"Thank you, Father," I replied. "I haven't seen you, actually, since the ball. I hope you have been well?"

"Yes, yes, yes. Very well, indeed. You want to know what Lady Rutford wanted? She wanted *you* for that worthless son of hers. I told her to get out. Not to come back till I told her to. I have Lord Rutford here." He held out his open right hand, palm up, as if weighing an invisible object. "I have Lord Plummer here, too. No, we are saving you for more important things."

"I hope they will be lovely things," I said, smiling at him. "Oh, I must tell you—I was so frightened last night, father. A strange man broke into my room. Did Mrs. Danley tell you about the scar-faced man?"

"She told me. No one would want to harm you. Why would anyone want to harm you? No, no, no. A scar-faced man? Yes, we looked for him. We hunted him in the house and stable."

"Do you know who he is, Father?" I asked, as casually as I could.

"No, no, no, I do not know him. I have never seen him. He is a poacher, a robber. We have driven him away. He will not come back. You will not see him again. We will see to *that!*"

"Shall I play for you after dinner, Father?" I asked, after a pause.

He looked at me in surprise. Then his eyes narrowed, and he smiled briefly. "I have things to do," he answered.

There was no further conversation during the meal.

And when it was over, I said to Apsley, "I shall have my coffee in the music room, please."

I played and sang there, alone, for almost an hour, as if practicing for some future performance, and then wandered slowly through the rooms, looking at a painting here and examining a figurine or a carved box there. At last Titus lit my candle for me, and I climbed the grand staircase and walked to my room. No one would have guessed how excited I was. No one would have imagined that tomorrow I would be galloping to a secret meeting with Martin Shark!

"No, Clair, it was a pleasant enough dinner, as our dinners here go," I replied to Clair's question. It was later that evening, and Clair was helping me into a robe. "Conversation is not one of the memorable aspects of dinner here—most of the time there is none. It was as usual. My stepfather seemed pleased with me. He actually complimented me, if you can believe it, and he seemed pleased with things in—" suddenly I heard shouting.

"What is that? Something is happening out there."

We ran to the windows at once and saw men running from the house toward the stable block, shouting to each other as they ran. And beyond the northeast corner of the stable buildings, the sky glowed red.

242

I unlocked the alcove door, and we stepped out onto the terrace. "It will be all right, Clair," I said, "I don't think we need fear an unannounced visitor while so many people are about, and besides, we can easily see him coming if he should choose to appear. Oh, look!"

A much more brilliant glow lit the sky then. Flames reflected on a pillar of smoke, turning it red orange. The fire silhouetted the roof of the stable block, and showers of sparks shot intermittently into the air.

"You can smell the smoke from here," Clair said. "Listen to the shouts. Every man on the estate must be there fighting the fire. What is it? It is not the stable block itself."

"No, it must be a building just beyond," I said. "It is two stories high, and I think it is a kind of auxiliary storehouse for feed and hay. Look at those sparks! They are like fireworks. It would be beautiful if fire like that were not so terrifying. I would like to go over there and see if I could help, but I know I would only be in the way. I hope the stables don't catch fire."

"Oh, no, miss," she said. "Look, you can see some men on the stable roof there, see? It looks as if they have pails—filled with water or sand, don't you suppose? It is fortunate that the roof is flat so they can walk on it. And there is a man on the tower roof, see him? If any sparks should land on the roof, they will put them out."

We watched for a half-hour. By then the flames had died, the fire was burning itself out, and the shouting had ceased. We went back inside, and I went to bed and tossed and turned for a long while before finally falling asleep.

At a little after two o'clock the following afternoon, I walked into the stable yard. As I entered it, John came out of a door at the base of a corner tower, and when he saw me, he came hurrying across the yard toward me.

"Good afternoon, John," I said. "I think I will give Thunder a little exercise. Would you have him saddled for me, please? I will only be riding around the park, so I won't need Owen."

"Certainly, miss," he replied. "I will do it myself, with pleasure." He went off toward the saddle room. "Jenken, Jenken," he shouted as he went. Jenken appeared with a pitchfork in his hand. "Bring out Thunder," John ordered.

In a moment Jenken brought Thunder out into the yard, and John appeared with the saddle. Shortly, Thunder was ready for me. I gave him his carrot and stroked his neck, and then John helped me to mount.

"What an awful fire that was last night," I said, looking down at him.

"Yes, miss. It was the hay barn out back," he said. "Burned to the ground, it did. It took every man on the place to keep the fire from spreading—that was the main thing."

"Well, I am glad you did and that the horses are all safe. Thank you, John," I called back, as I walked Thunder out of the yard.

Outside the yard, we turned left, away from the house, and trotted through the grove of trees beyond the stables to the Abbey Road and down it. And after five minutes at a trot, I urged Thunder into a canter, which brought us to the abbey ruins.

Thunder had become nervous and excited—not at all like himself—and I wondered if some of my excitement over the forthcoming meeting with Martin Shark had communicated itself to him. I slowed him to a walk, and we entered the hole in the wall of the apse, to follow the short path through the ruined church.

"Easy Thunder, beautiful Thunder," I crooned to him, reaching forward and stroking his neck. But he did not respond. Instead, he became even more agitated. He began to walk jerkily, now straight, now at a diagonal. Then he stopped and backed, trembling. I couldn't understand what had gotten into him. He pivoted, paying no attention to my leg or the feel of the reins, and then he gave one terrific kick and reared, coming down into a gallop straight toward the doorway at the far end of the church nave. I put more pressure on the reins and cried, "Thunder," but I couldn't hold him. We galloped full tilt toward the distant square of light. God, get us through the doorway, I prayed—don't let him smash us against the wall. And then we flew through the opening and out into the sunlight, and Thunder skidded to an abrupt halt, trembling, sweating, and snorting.

"Thunder, what is it? Easy boy, easy," I whispered to him. He kicked and reared in answer and, veering to the left, bolted down the road toward the sea. I could do nothing with him but hold in on the reins and stay in the saddle. Then suddenly, Thunder stopped short and reared and plunged and kicked in a mad frenzy. He bucked, twisting in midair and landing on the ground with a slam, and bucked again, raising me out of the saddle and slamming me down on his back. He was trying to throw me. Again and again he jumped until my foot was out of the stirrup, my leg out of the pommel, my knee out from under the horn, and I was flying through the air toward the ground.

It was very quiet. I opened my eyes and looked at a blue sky. Leaves fluttered in the breeze against it, and all about me tall grass swayed. I realized that I lay in a hollow beside the road. My head hurt, and then I felt something warm running down the side of my face. I knew it was blood even before I remembered that Thunder had just thrown me into the ditch where I lay. But I was able to pull myself to a sitting position and then lean back against the bank. As I did so, the world swirled about me, but in a moment it righted itself, and I took a handkerchief from my sleeve and dabbed at the blood. Then, embedded in the ground near my left hand, I noticed a round rock smeared with blood.

I must have struck my head on the rock after Thunder threw me. He had gone mad, but he had not, thank God, trampled me to death as he had Meagher. I was lucky. But what had gone wrong with him? What had set him off like that for no apparent reason? I realized, then, that I had been wrong about him, that there was a wild, crazy streak in him.

"Damn Thunder!" I whispered aloud, as I remembered that I had been on my way to meet Martin Shark. I had to know what Martin Shark wanted, and tears of frustration came to my eyes as I realized that I would not be able to keep the appointment.

How could I? I could not get to Wattle without a horse. Where had Thunder gone? I wondered. How can I get back to the Hall? And then I looked up and saw Mark Lawson sitting on his horse on the other side of the road, gazing down at me.

"Suzanne," he called. He jumped down out of the saddle, ran to me, and squatted in front of me, looking into my eyes. "Are you all right?"

"Where did you come from?" I asked. "How long have you been watching me?"

"Through the woods. I only just saw you sitting here. What happened? Here, let me look at that cut."

"Thunder threw me and ran off," I said. "I—I must have hit my head. We were wrong about Thunder—he threw me on purpose. I am lucky he didn't stomp on me—he might have killed me."

"Now hold still," Mark said, reaching to take the handkerchief out of my hand.

"Let go of me!" I snapped. "No doubt you're on your way to pay a social call at Warton Hall. Well, aren't you?"

"Yes. What if I am?"

"Because, then, if you would be so kind as to ask Henderson to come and get me in a carriage, I would appreciate it very much. I don't think I can walk to the Hall, and I am sure I could not ride a horse."

"But I can't leave you here alone," he said.

"What would you propose, that we sit here indefinitely together? Go and tell Henderson to come for me. I shall be perfectly safe here until he does. Go! Go, I don't want to talk any more."

So, without another word, Mark got to his feet, walked to his horse, mounted, and rode off. In ten minutes he returned with Henderson and Clair in the Victoria, and after they had helped me into the carriage, Mark rode off in the direction of the rectory.

Henderson drove me home very slowly. When we pulled up in front of the Hall, Titus ran out of the house and down the steps and opened the carriage door for me. Just then, my stepfather rode around the corner of the house from the direction of the stables.

"What has happened?" he demanded, as he approached the carriage.

"Miss de Riocour's horse threw her, my lord, and we went to fetch her," Henderson said.

"I told you not to ride him," my stepfather screamed at me. "You fool!" Then he said to Henderson, "Tell John to find that horse, but not to harm him. He is good horseflesh. No one is to ride him. I will be in my office. I want to know when he is found. No, I will go to the stables myself." Then he turned Bourton around and rode back the way he had come.

Clair and Titus helped me to my room, and Clair cleaned the cut on my forehead.

"Do you hurt anywhere?" Clair asked, helping me out of my habit. "Can you move your legs and arms and hands and feet and fingers and toes?"

"Yes, Clair," I answered, moving everything. "My head is pounding, but otherwise I think I am all right."

I looked closely in the glass at the cut. It was a gash near the hairline, but it did not seem very deep, although it was red and the area had begun to swell.

"I think you should lie down now, miss. I will close the curtains and make a cold compress for that cut."

Then she sat on the bed next to me, having brought a basin of water and set it on the bedside table. She dipped a small linen towel into the water, wrung it out, folded it, and laid it across my forehead.

"What is your name?" she asked. "Answer my question so we will know your memory is all right."

"Suzanne de Riocour. Oh, that feels so cool and good, Clair."

"Where do you live?"

"Warton Hall, Somerset."

"How old are you?"

"Seventeen—" and I fell asleep.

I slept for the rest of the afternoon, waking about seven o'clock to a knock on the door.

"Yes, Mrs. Danley? She is sleeping now," I heard Clair whisper.

"Clair," I called, "ask Mrs. Danley to come in. I am awake."

"My dear child," Mrs. Danley said, coming over to my bedside. "Is there anything I can do? Is there anything you want, anything you need? Shall I light the lamp, or would you rather be in the dark?"

"Yes, light the lamp, please," I answered.

"Why do people ride horses?" she asked, lighting the lamp by my bed. "They are big, dangerous brutes—anyone can see that. They would throw you to the ground as soon as look at you, they would. I have always been afraid of them: and everyone else would be too, if they knew what was good for them.

"Oh, my dear," she continued, sitting on the edge of the bed and taking my hand in hers, "if anything should happen to you, I don't know what I would do. You have brought such sweet joy into our lives here, and we have all come to love you so much, we have." Tears welled in her eyes, and she dabbed at them with her handkerchief. "And here I sit making a proper fool of myself. Shall I light the other lamps, or is this one enough for you? And what about dinner?" She turned to Clair. "Should she have something sent up, do you think, Miss Clair?"

"Yes, light the lamps," I said. "And of course I will have something to eat. Anybody would think I am dying. I have only been thrown from a horse, and it isn't the first time, either. Dear Mrs. Danley, it is sweet of you to be so concerned, but I am feeling much better, really and truly. Don't look so worried.

"If you could ask the chef to send me some soup and two soft-boiled eggs and toast, that would be magnificent."

So I had my tray in bed, and after I had eaten, I was sleepy again—I felt quite exhausted. I asked Clair to blow out the lamps and leave me for the night. I slept deeply and dreamlessly.

I didn't wake up until, nearer the window than it had been the first morning almost two months before, the sun had thrown its yellow streak across the wallpaper. Almost at once, I slipped out of bed, threw on a robe, and walked over to the alcove. I felt quite well and steady on my feet. It had probably been shock that had made me feel so ill the day before. My head still throbbed a bit and was sore when I touched it, but I felt well enough to ride to Wattle.

"Oh, miss. I don't know if you should be up," Dorothy said. She stood in the doorway gripping her hands together into a tight fist. Poor, thin, gaunt Dorothy. "Should you be out of bed? You could have been killed. I'm frightened! It's that man—the one with the scar. I knew it as soon as I saw him in your room,

249

and it's not over yet. Something terrible is going to happen. I know it."

"Nonsense, Dorothy," I replied. "I was merely thrown from a horse. There is nothing remarkable about that, is there?"

"The same horse that killed my Patrick when that man was here last time," she said, her wide, bulging eyes filled with fear.

"Well, he didn't kill *me*. I am very much alive, as you can see, and in need of a refreshing bath. Don't worry, Dorothy. It is all over. My stepfather didn't catch the man, but he assures me he won't be back, and I am not going to ride Thunder again, even if they have found him."

"Miss, should you be up?" asked Clair, who had just come into the room. "Wouldn't it be better to stay in bed today, or at least this morning? Let me have a look at your head. Yes, it looks very good—bruised, but clean. I think it will heal nicely."

"I am really feeling quite well, Clair, and we will have to hurry if I am to be on time for morning prayer and breakfast."

After breakfast, I went to the morning room, took a crested piece of writing paper out of the desk, sat down, and wrote a note to Martin Shark. If he was not at the inn in Wattle, I would leave it there for him.

I wrote:

October 3, 1856

Dear Mr. Shark,

I could not keep our appointment of yesterday because my horse threw me as I rode toward Wattle, and I was forced to return to Warton Hall because of an injury to my head.

It was the same horse that threw and killed Patrick Meagher, whom you may have known.

I should be most interested in talking with you

and hope this can be arranged in the near future.

Believe me, dear sir,

Yours very truly,
Suzanne de Riocour

I put the note in an envelope, but then I took it out and reread it. No, I thought, it is not wise to say anything about Patrick Meagher at this point. I copied the note again, leaving out the second paragraph, and then burned the first copy on the hearth and smashed the ashes to dust.

Then I went to my room and changed into my gray wool habit and its matching gray, ostrich-plumed hat. The hat would keep my hair in place. Clair had arranged my hair so that it fell over the bandage on my forehead.

After I had finished dressing, I put the note to Martin Shark into the pocket of my jacket and, taking my crop, crept out of the house and walked through the rose garden to the stables.

Monk ran out of the carriage house and into the stable yard to greet me.

"How are you feeling, miss?" he asked, standing in front of me, his hands behind his back, rising up and down on his toes—as he had seen my stepfather do, no doubt—and looking very concerned. "He's a killer, miss. I told you he's a killer."

"And you were right, Monk. I should have listened to you, shouldn't I? Did they find Thunder?" I asked.

"Yes, miss, John found him, miss, over by Fawsley —in a terrible sweat he was. Jenken and Owen and Hippolyte was out looking, the rest of us was at supper, miss. Did you want to see Thunder, miss?" he asked.

"Thank you, no, Monk, not right now, but I do want to go for a ride. Is John about?" I asked.

"No, miss. He and Owen went over to the farm, and Jenken is out in the far paddock, but Hippolyte is inside, miss."

"Is there anything that goes on here that you don't know about, Monk?" I asked. "Would you run and get him for me? No, just ask him to saddle one of the other horses for me. Would Thistle do, do you think?"

"Yes, miss, very good, I should think," he called back, as he ran toward the saddle room.

Hippolyte saddled Thistle and helped me mount. Then Thistle and I took the same route that I had taken the day before on Thunder, but we did not take the shortcut through the ruined church: we went around it. I did my best not to think about Thunder's throwing me as we passed the spot where it had happened.

I especially wished to avoid thinking about it because I was not feeling myself. My head had begun to ache again, but I was confident that I could make it to Wattle and back on Thistle. She was a most docile animal, and she behaved beautifully.

Nevertheless, it seemed a long time before we came out of the wood above the harbor and began walking down the cobbled main street of the village. The street was so steep, as it wound down the hill, that it had been laid in long sloping steps, and we walked rather slowly down it between the rows of whitewashed cottages that huddled so closely together on either side of us. They seemed deserted, as they had two days before.

When we emerged from between them at the harbor side, we found ourselves in a small cobbled square edged on one side with a sea wall that fell to a pebbly beach where small boats had been drawn up beyond the reach of the tide. To the left, the gray stone quay extended its long curved arm to form one side of the tiny harbor. It was really a jetty standing three steps higher than the cobbles of the square and was wide enough near the shore for the Red Lion to have been built on it and still leave space for a wide walk in front of the building.

I rode Thistle to the steps, where she stood obediently until I had dismounted, and then I tied her reins around a wooden lamppost and walked toward the inn, looking about as I went. I felt conspicuous, walking alone like that, and I felt sure that all the townspeople would come out of their houses to stare at me. But there seemed to be no one about except a little boy chasing a little dog and crying, "Towser, Towser," as he hopped from the wall to the beach in pursuit of it. And there was a wrinkled old man sitting in one of the open boats below me, smoking his pipe and mending fishing gear. He looked up, tipped his hat as I walked by, and then went back to work. Otherwise, Wattle was deserted and quiet, except for several gulls that whirled above me, screaming to one another, and little wavelets that swished on the pebbles along the shore.

Before me stood the inn, a long building, two stories high, with four doors and more than twice as many windows facing the quay. I chose the door under the Red Lion sign. It led into a gloomy staircase hall with a closed door to my right and an open one to my left. The open door led into a large room that I supposed was the travelers' room. The establishment smelled of stale beer and tobacco smoke and was deserted, except for a maid in apron and dust cap cleaning out the ashes from the fireplace.

"Excuse me," I called to her, "is the landlord in?"

She looked around without getting up from her knees and said, "He's in the taproom there," motioning to the closed door. "You can go in if you like." Then she turned back to her work.

I knocked on the door and opened it. A baldheaded little man in his shirt sleeves, and wearing gold-rimmed glasses, was writing in a ledger at a table near the window. The landlord I supposed. He seemed to be making entries from a pile of bills, one of which he held in his left hand.

"I beg your pardon," I said. "Can you tell me if Mr. Shark is in?"

He looked up. His eyebrows leaped toward the top of his forehead, his eyes popped, and he jumped up from the table and hurried toward me.

"I beg *your* pardon, miss, I didn't hear anyone come in. Sebastian Stallard, proprietor of the Red Lion, at your service," he said, pulling down his waistcoat. "You're looking for a gentleman, then, by what name?"

"Mr. Shark. Mr. Martin Shark. Is he in?"

"You're sure of the name, miss? Wouldn't care to spell it for me, then?"

"Shark. S-H-A-R-K."

"And when would this Mr. Shark have arrived at the Red Lion, miss?"

"Why, I don't know," I replied. "Perhaps Wednesday or Thursday. I am Miss de Riocour. You were to have arranged a private room for my interview with Mr. Shark, yesterday, but I was unable to come so I came today instead, hoping to find him in. If he is not, would it be possible to leave him a note?"

"What does this Mr. Shark look like, miss?" the landlord asked.

"He is a short, very heavy man—an extremely corpulent man."

"If he wasn't in, you could leave a note, then, miss. But he ain't in. He never was in. Never heard the name, and I remember names particularly well, miss. Never had a fat man staying here, not during this year—last year, maybe. We ain't had no one staying at the Red Lion for the last six months or more, miss. We don't get strangers staying in Wattle much anymore, miss. It's the taproom here that keeps us going, and a lively place it is at night, miss. But there ain't no Mr. Shark staying here, you can be sure of it."

"But I don't understand," I said. "He sent me a letter asking me to meet him here."

"No, miss, it ain't the Red Lion in Wattle," the land-lord replied. "We've no Mr. Shark here and never had." He peered up at me through his glasses with curiosity. "Perhaps it's another Red Lion, somewhere, then, but I couldn't say where."

"I see," I said, turning toward the door. "It must be an error of some sort. I am so sorry to have troubled you like this, Mr. Stallard. It is really not terribly important."

Mr. Stallard followed me into the hall and opened the outside door for me.

"Thank you and good-bye," I said, hurrying out. I almost ran back to Thistle. I am not used to mounting a horse alone, so I was not very graceful at it, I am afraid, but somehow I managed to scramble up on her, and we rode away, back up the hill. But before we turned the bend in the road, I glanced back. The proprietor of the Red Lion stood on his doorstep looking after me, and even when we came out from between the houses at the top of the hill, he was still standing there.

We walked down the road toward the abbey, and I began to feel very tired. I want to lie down, I thought. I just want to lie down and close my eyes and be quiet.

Feeling exhausted like that, it seemed like a terribly long ride. I thought we would never arrive at the crossroad, which would mean that we were nearly home. Finally we did, however, and I was about to turn Thistle toward the gateway to the drive when a carriage approached from that direction. It was one of my stepfather's broughams, and it stopped in front of me, barring my way.

"Where have you been?" shouted my stepfather, leaning out of the window. "So you are in the saddle again. So soon? You should be resting. You are a fool to ride again so soon."

"Yes, Father," I said, reining up beside the carriage.

"I am going away," he said. "I will return on Monday after luncheon. Guests will arrive on Monday. You will be at dinner on Monday night. You will look your best. Drive on, Henderson," he shouted.

And they sped down the dry, dusty road away from me.

Oh, how I loathe that little man, I thought, as I watched them go. He orders me about like a chambermaid. I must do something to get away from here, and soon. But I couldn't think about it then: my head throbbed, and all I could think of was getting to my room. I turned to the right, then left through the gateway, walked Thistle down the drive, and stopped at the entrance front. Titus must have seen me coming because he ran out the door and down the steps and helped me dismount.

"Thank you, Titus," I said, climbing the steps. "Take care of Thistle."

And after I had passed through the open door into the hall, I called, "Apsley, send for Clair, please, and ask her to come to me upstairs. I am not feeling well, and I need her."

Then I dragged myself up the stairs and down that long, dreary corridor to my room.

# Chapter Eighteen

"YOU ARE LOOKING ever so much better tonight, miss,"
Clair said, putting down the curling iron. "I was really
quite worried. There, that is done. I thought I would
gather the curls in back like this. Can you see? And
then make a sort of little nosegay of the blue ribbon
bows and little silk flowers, with some white French
lace to hold them there, and attach two lace streamers to fall down behind. They will match the ones
on your dress."

It was Monday night, and Clair was helping me
dress for my stepfather's dinner party.

"That would be lovely. What a pretty idea, Clair,"
I replied. She helped me into the bodice of my blue
dress. "Do you never run out of ideas?"

"I try not to, miss," Clair said with a giggle.

"Yes, I am feeling better—my old self again, really
and completely. Just resting these last two-and-a-half
days has restored me absolutely."

And after a pause, while I watched her in the mirror, I continued. "Mr. Clarkson, being my stepfather's
solicitor, would appreciate my wearing a diamond
necklace, but what about Lord and Lady Milne? The
way Joseph announced that the marquis and mar-
chioness of Milne were coming, one would think they
were as important as the queen and Prince Albert.
Who are they? Do you know anything about them?"

"I would say diamond necklace, definitely," said
Clair. "Tremendously wealthy! Lord Milne owns

257

practically all of Devon and Dorset, I understand. The title was his, but the money and much of the land, hers. As a matter of fact, he was working as a tradesman when they met—a shopman, I believe. Of course, since the marriage, he has increased the estates enormously. I understand he is very clever, though common in manner."

"Well, diamond necklace it will be, then," I said. "They are bringing their son, Gerald, who I hope is *not* looking for a wife, and a daughter, Eulalia—such a strange, exotic-sounding name. So, with Mr. and Mrs. Clarkson and Mother, my stepfather, and me, that makes nine at dinner. But Apsley said there would be ten. I wonder who the tenth person will be? And I wonder where Lord and Lady Milne *are?* They had better arrive soon, or they will not be at dinner at all."

"They arrived a half-hour ago, miss," Dorothy said. She had come in only a moment before and was beginning to clear away the bath things. "I'm sorry I didn't get back for these sooner, but there was a little mix-up as to who would be taking care of the Clarksons. I took Mrs. Clarkson some water, but then it turns out that Elsie Tate is going to look after them. She told me Lord and Lady Milne and their son and daughter arrived and are now settled in their rooms and are getting ready for dinner. They're leaving tomorrow after luncheon. She said that if a little breeze came up, the daughter would blow right away," Dorothy concluded with a giggle. But then, as if realizing she had said too much, she busied herself with her work.

"And I suppose you know how old she is and what color her hair is," I said.

"She's seventeen, and she has blond hair," Dorothy replied.

I couldn't help laughing, and Dorothy laughed in return.

"How do I look?" I asked, after I had finished dressing.

"Never lovelier, truly," Clair replied.

"The credit is entirely yours. Yes, I will do," I said, examining myself in the mirror. "A trifle vulgar, perhaps, but I will do very nicely, thank you. Well, now we shall see what heavenly things this evening has in store."

If I had only known how near the truth my sarcasm hit, I would never have gone down to dinner.

"Thank you, Clair. I will try to come up to bed by eleven, as usual. I will see you then. In the meantime, enjoy yourself."

I lit my candle from the one on the washstand, left the room, and walked toward the grand staircase. As I walked down the corridor, a little breeze buffeted my candle flame, and I shielded it with my hand. This reminded me of that first night when I had followed Clair to my room and how endless the journey had seemed. Sometimes long distances seem to grow shorter with familiarity, I thought, but tonight, this one seems as long as ever.

In comparison to the blackness of the corridor above, however, the staircase hall was brilliant. This, evidently, was a grand enough occasion for the great chandelier to be lighted.

"Good evening, miss," Apsley said, as I reached the bottom of the stairs. "The party has gathered in the corner room."

"Thank you, Apsley," I replied, handing my candle to Titus. "Has everyone come down?"

"Everyone except Lady Eulalia, Lord Milne's daughter, miss."

I left him and walked through the tapestry room and the hunting room, but at the entrance to the corner room, I stopped, surprised to see Mark Lawson there. So Mark is the tenth member of my stepfather's dinner party, I thought. I might have known.

He stood behind Mother's chair. Mother sat on one side of the chimney piece, separated by the little marble-topped table from Lady Milne. She was a thin, bony woman with a long stringy neck, a beaked nose, and a froth of carrot-colored hair, which clashed with the yellow-green of her dress.

Across the room from them, at the entrance to the drawing room, my stepfather stood next to an elderly, white-haired man, whose complexion was a curious gray color, making him look carved from stone. He could be no one but my stepfather's solicitor, Mr. Clarkson. With them stood a man in his early fifties, perhaps, with side whiskers. He would have been attractive if his shrewd little eyes and his nose and mouth had not been compressed into a small area in the center of his square face. He must be Lord Milne, I decided. And on the sofa lounged Gerald, Lord Gorm, a young replica of his father. His square face was flushed, and his hands were clasped over a bulging belly.

Between Gerald and the doorway to my left, a tiny elderly lady in a gray muslin dress sat in the gray damask-covered chair, staring at the carpet. This, then, was Mrs. Clarkson.

"Miss de Riocour! Do you believe in God Almighty?" shrieked Lady Milne. She had seen me approach, and as I walked into the room, she jumped up from her chair and came charging to meet me, her right arm and hand reaching out toward me as if to save me from drowning. "Do you keep his commandments and love and follow the blessed teachings of his only son, our Lord Jesus Christ?" The last two words reached a crescendo that must have been heard in the servants' hall.

"Yes—yes, of course," I replied. "We attend church in Fawsley every Sunday, and we have morning prayer in the chapel here every day."

"But that is not enough, as I was explaining to your

mother," she squawked, in a harsh, raucous voice, rather like a chicken's. Her long neck, I noticed, was covered with tiny pimples, heavily plastered with white powder. "There are no prayer meetings at Warton Hall? No? I see there are not. A prayer meeting should be held for the staff each and every evening after their supper, to bring God's ray of hope to them in this vale of tears. I will see that you receive the Lord's book for each of them as well as instruction on bringing God's word—"

"Oh, for heaven's *sake,* Effie," shouted Lord Milne, without looking away from my stepfather.

"It was such an exhausting journey," piped a reedy voice from behind me.

I looked around and saw a frail young woman with a long neck and beaked nose posing in the doorway. She stood in half profile looking at the floor. Her long, dark-orange curls hugged her pale face, and an open fan hid the décolletage of her fawn-colored dress. This was Eulalia. She stood motionless for a moment, and then, flashing a provocative look at Mark, she whisked away the fan revealing a very bony chest above a mere suggestion of breasts.

"I must be seated," she said, fanning herself rapidly. "Such a tiring day," she whispered, as she walked by me and collapsed in the chair opposite Mother. But she continued fanning herself energetically, staring at Mark all the while.

"I say, it's deuced cold in here," the prone figure on the couch observed. "Why can't somebody light the fire?"

"Dinner is served, my lady," Apsley announced from the doorway.

My stepfather, of course, led the procession into dinner with Lady Milne on his arm. Gerald and I followed them, and Mark followed us with Eulalia. Mark and I had not spoken. It was just as well, I thought, that he had decided to avoid me.

261

After we had all begun our soup, Gerald said to me, "Quite nice sherry, really. A bit off in its age, perhaps, but not at all bad." He took another sip of it, swishing the liquid around in his mouth. "Not at all bad. Jack!" he called to one of the footmen his father had brought along to help serve, "Fetch a little more of this sherry like a good fellow. Don't you think this quite passable?" he asked Mrs. Clarkson on his right, as he held his glass to the candlelight.

"I don't know, I really don't know," she whispered, looking down at her lap.

"But I *know,* if it had been *you,* Colonel Lawson," Eulalia said, leaning close to Mark and tilting her head as she gazed up at him with rapture, *"you* would have picked her up in those great, strong arms of yours and carried her away to your *den."* She giggled as her right index finger, resting on her breastbone at the neck of her dress, slid down inside it.

"No, there was no problem there, none whatsoever," Lord Milne replied to something Mr. Clarkson had said. "As I was saying earlier, Lord Trevenbury," he turned to my stepfather, "with all the families now living together in the cottages I had built for them at eighteen pence per week, it was possible to organize tremendous work forces of women during spring planting, for instance, at nine pence per head, or a force of children at four pence per head for picking berries or beans—just as an example. A tremendous economy in labor as against the old individual farm family system. Extremely lucrative, an enormously lucrative experiment. You were interested in something of the kind here in Somerset? You would not be disappointed, I can promise you."

"And we have arranged the prayer meetings," proclaimed Lady Milne, "for all those poor lost souls, each and every day after dinner. All are obliged to attend, as none will be hired for a day's work who do not. And *He* said, 'Go thou into all the world—' "

"Oh, for heaven's *sake*, Effie," cried Lord Milne.

"Very similar to the gang system. There are already demands for some kind of gangs act in Parliament, but such an act, even if passed, could be circumvented. It could be circumvented," observed Mr. Clarkson.

Later, while Apsley carved the joint, I saw Eulalia lean forward and throw out her chest and, with clenched fists, proclaim to Mark, "Oh, I wish I were as strong as a man—how I would adore to *feel* the strength of a man." At the word feel, she cupped her almost nonexistent breasts in her hands.

At this, Mark glanced at Mother, who answered with a barely perceptible shrug and raise of eyebrows.

"An excellent roast, truly," observed Gerald. "And this sauce—very good, indeed. Made with port, no doubt, though I should have preferred it with Madeira. Don't you agree, Mrs. Clarkson?"

"I don't know, I really don't know," she replied.

". . . my new daughter, Suzanne?" my stepfather said, addressing everyone at the table. " 'Take away love, and our earth is a tomb.' She is a beautiful child. She has charmed everyone. She has made us many friends. She is very valuable to me. You know," he pointed a finger at Lord Milne, "she has a dowry of sixty thousand pounds."

Though everyone at the table was his guest, my stepfather was nervous—his stunted arm was not still —and I wondered why.

" 'The *Lord* giveth, and the *Lord* taketh away,' " cried Lady Milne, pointing at the ceiling.

"Oh, for heaven's sake, Effie. Shut your mouth!" Lord Milne cried.

Without warning, Lady Milne shrieked at me, "And once he gets your money, that will be the end of that! I speak from experience. Just look at that man there," she pointed at her husband, "a common tradesman, a common shopman when I met him, with not a penny to his name. His clothes were cheap, and his shoes had holes in them." She continued to point at her husband across the table, an expression of distaste raising the corners of her nose. "And he would still be a common, dirty, little tradesman if it hadn't been for me and my money."

The room had fallen silent. All eyes were riveted on Lady Milne. Everyone expected a continuation of the humiliating attack. But none came—she had finished.

Her husband looked back at her with undisguised loathing. Then he turned to my stepfather and said, "Women should be made to work and bear children. They work well and cheaply. Only a fool would underestimate the value of women and children as a work force. . . ." And he became lost in the explanation of his new farming experiments.

Later, while I was eating my pineapple cream, my stepfather claimed the attention of everyone. "We are proud to have Colonel Lawson of the Fourth Dragoon Guards dining with us tonight. Colonel Lawson was at Balaklava." He said the last sentence with great pride.

"How romantic!" exclaimed Eulalia.

"Not the Fourth Royal Irish—I wouldn't have thought you were Irish, Colonel Lawson," Mr. Clarkson said.

"Well, you see, sir," Mark said, "the Fourth, though nominally Irish, is composed almost entirely of Englishmen. The Fifth, nominally English, is, interestingly enough, composed principally of Irishmen."

"Odd indeed," said Lord Milne. "But the slaughter —you were there. Tell us about it. You were one of the lucky ones. How could it have happened?"

"I was in the heavy brigade, Lord Milne," said Mark. "We covered the retreat of the light, of all the miserable one hundred ninety-eight of them who returned.

"There is nothing to tell that you don't know, unless

you want details of blood and maimed bodies. The brigade of six to eight hundred men was ordered to charge the entire Russian army. It was almost completely annihilated by the Russian artillery."

"But why such a stupid order? Why?" my stepfather asked.

"It was not stupid. It was an error, a horrible human error," Mark replied, looking at my stepfather with aversion. The employee does not like his employer, I thought, but that is not unusual. "Lord Raglan," Mark continued, "sent Captain Nolan to Lord Lucan with a written order. It said, and I quote almost word for word, to storm the Russian guns with his light cavalry *if practicable*. Captain Nolan was wounded carrying the dispatch, and in his mental confusion forgot to deliver the paper; instead he delivered the order verbally, omitting the all-important words, if practicable."

Abruptly, Mark turned to Mother and said, "You mentioned a Vivaldi sonata, Lady Trevenbury, before dinner. Will you play it for us tonight?" he asked.

"Suzanne will play and sing for us after dinner," my stepfather said. "Play and sing the things you did the first night, my dear." It was the first time he had called me "my dear," and I didn't like it.

So, when the gentlemen joined us in the drawing room after dinner, we adjourned to the music room, and as soon as we had entered, Mother went to the piano.

"Since Colonel Lawson has asked for the Vivaldi sonata, I will play it for him, but only the first short movement," she announced. She stood next to the piano until we were seated. "Then perhaps Lady Eulalia would honor us with a song. I am told she has an enchanting voice."

"Thank you, but I am much too fatigued to perform. I really could not," Eulalia said, shrinking back into her chair and flashing a smile at Mark, who was sitting next to her.

"How unfortunate for us all," Mother crooned. "Then, Suzanne will play and sing for us according to her father's wishes."

She sat down at the piano and began to play the Vivaldi. During it, my stepfather tiptoed from the room, but he returned just as it was ending and stood against the wall next to one of the windows.

When Mother had finished playing, everyone applauded, and Gerald said, "Charming, most charming, Lady Trevenbury."

"We must go up shortly," Lady Milne cried. Then glaring at her husband, "The *Lord* said, 'He who loveth pleasure shall not prosper.'"

"Go, then," Lord Milne replied.

It was my turn to perform. I walked to the piano, announced the Mendelssohn, sat down, and began to play, glancing from time to time at my audience as I did so. Mother had placed one of the spindly, gilded chairs next to Mark and was sitting on it and whispering to him. Eulalia dabbed her nose with a heavily scented handkerchief, which I could smell even from the piano. Lady Milne gazed at the clock, and Lord Milne traced the pattern in the carpet with the toe of his shoe.

Suddenly, without warning, my stepfather shouted, "Stop! You! Stay where you are!"

He had flung open one of the casement windows and stood with his chest pressed against the sill and his head thrust out into the night, partly covered by the curtain.

"Stop! Come back!" he cried.

I had stopped playing, of course, and we all looked at him in stunned silence. His head popped back into the room, and he swung around to face us, slamming the window shut at the same time.

"I heard footsteps on the drive," he said. "It was the man with the scar on his face. I saw him clearly."

My stepfather hurried across the room, then, toward the hunting room—in the direction of the staircase hall. "A prowler, a poacher, a thief! He broke into my daughter's room a few nights ago. I want him caught and in jail!" He screamed the last sentence, as he tried to hold his little arm still. He paused before leaving the room and said, "Go on as usual. Do not change anything and do not worry. Lillian, after the others have gone to bed, wait in the hall chamber for me until I return. Colonel Lawson, will you come with me and help?"

"Of course," Mark said. He bounded from his chair and followed my stepfather from the room.

At that moment the clock on the mantel said ten-fifteen.

"I don't understand this," Mother said, breaking the silence. "What could he possibly want? I had better go and see what is happening." Then she left the room.

"Have you had this fellow about for very long? Shouldn't you get the nearest constable?" inquired Mr. Clarkson, who had gone to the window to look out.

"Fawsley is the nearest town," I said, "and it would take three-quarters of an hour to ride there and back. Listen!"

Running footsteps sounded on the drive outside. "I will get the horses saddled, my lord," a voice called. It sounded like Titus.

Then Mother glided back into the room. "Apsley assures me that every man on the estate will soon be out searching the grounds," she said. "The man is only a poacher and will be caught or frightened away. There is really no need to be concerned. It is merely a nuisance. Go on playing, my dear."

"I am sure Mother is right," I said. "There is nothing to worry about. I am so sorry that our evening has been interrupted like this."

But I was not as confident as I sounded. I wondered if the scar-faced man had left another note from Martin Shark, and I shuddered as I remembered the words, "a matter of great peril if you don't."

"Devilishly annoying, I would say. Miss de Riocour, play and sing something soothing to restore us," Gerald said.

"A hymn to God," demanded Lady Milne.

"I am afraid I don't know any hymns, but the people of the Auvergne are very religious. Let me play and sing 'Brezairola,' a lovely lullaby, and then 'Lo Fiolaine,' a spinning song."

I played and sang mechanically, thinking of the scar-faced man being chased through the night by my stepfather. Would they catch him? *Should* they catch him? I wondered. As I finished the spinning song, horses' hoofs clattered on the drive outside the windows and my stepfather's voice shouted, "Apsley, Apsley!" Some instructions followed, but I couldn't understand them.

After that I played and sang two more songs and then asked, "Is there anything else you would like? You must be anxious to go up, Lady Milne. And I am sure we are all exhausted. I know Lady Eulalia is. But there might be time for just one more selection."

"If you can't play a hymn, I can," cried Lady Milne, getting up and stalking toward me.

"Oh, for heaven's sake!" groaned Lord Milne. "I want my cigar."

But Lady Milne paid no attention to him. She took her place at the piano and announced, " 'Lord, Cast Thy Love Upon These Troubled Waters." And she sang all five verses, ending just as the clock began to strike eleven.

After we had risen, Mother said, "I will come with you to the staircase hall. Gentlemen, the billiard room is through the drawing room and to the right into the little hall, the first door to the left."

We said our good nights to the men and then trooped to the staircase hall where Apsley assisted us with our candles, and when they were lighted, we proceeded up the grand staircase.

"Can you find your way? Shall I show you?" I asked, when we reached the landing above.

"The *Lord* will show us the way," cried Lady Milne. "Come along, Eulalia, and don't try to fool your mother. You are as strong as a horse and nowhere near as tired as I am."

They turned to the right and proceeded down the corridor toward their rooms in the north front, followed by a silent Mrs. Clarkson. Then I turned to the left.

"Good night," I called back to them, as I shielded my candle. "Sleep well." And in a few moments I had turned the corner to the south corridor and proceeded toward the blessed haven of my room, where Clair would be waiting for me.

It happened when I had gotten halfway there. Something brushed my forehead and the tip of my nose and fell around my shoulders. I remember thinking it was a cobweb and reached up to brush it away, but it wasn't a cobweb—it was a rope or cord, and it encircled my throat tightly. Then it was jerked from above with enormous power, pulling me backward. I began to fall, and I dropped my candle and dug the fingers of both hands into the flesh of my neck, trying to get them under the rope to pull it away, but I could not—it had been pulled too tight. At the same time, I vaguely remember hearing someone scream. I do not remember falling to the floor.

Then I heard Clair calling from far away, "Miss de Riocour, Miss de Riocour. . . ." Her voice came closer and closer, and as I opened my eyes, she stopped slapping my wrists and held something under my nose. "Take a deep breath," she said.

I breathed, and a searing odor shot through my head and cleared my brain with a jolt.

"Thank you, Mrs. Danley," Clair said, handing her the smelling salts.

"Oh, my God," Mrs. Danley sobbed. "Oh, my dear God!"

"It hurts! Take this away," I said, putting my hand to my throat and then clawing at the rope around my neck.

I lay on the floor with my head in Clair's lap. Mrs. Danley stood next to us, her hands shaking as she held them to her cheeks.

As I pulled at the rope, Clair said, "Here, let me help you." And she removed it from around my neck.

"Someone tried to strangle me, didn't they?" I said. "Someone tried to kill me, Clair. Right here! I was walking down the corridor when I felt something fall over my head, and then they pulled it tight, and I couldn't get it away, and it hurt. Oh, Clair, help me!" I knew I must not become hysterical, however, and I tried to calm myself.

"It is all right," Clair said. "It is all over. You are safe here with us, now. You are safe, and there is nothing to be afraid of."

Then I noticed that Coventry had appeared out of the darkness.

"Coventry, would you get a lamp from Miss de Riocour's room so that we can have some more light?" Clair asked. "Here, Mrs. Danley, hold this candle for us. Now, can you stand up, miss? We will get you back to your room."

"I—I will try. I can!" I said as Clair helped me to my feet.

"What is it?" Dorothy cried, hurrying down the corridor toward us. "Oh!" she gasped. "I knew something terrible was going to happen. I knew it! Can I help? Can I help you, miss?"

"Dorothy," Clair said, "go to Miss de Riocour's

room, pour some water into the basin on the stand, and get two of the little linen hand towels ready."

Coventry returned with a lamp, and Clair said, "Thank you, Coventry. Will you give the lamp to Mrs. Danley and then go and fetch Mr. Apsley? Mrs. Danley, will you light our way?"

Lady Milne and Eulalia must also have heard the commotion, for they arrived and stood gawking at me.

"Oh, Lady Milne and Lady Eulalia," Clair said, "I am afraid someone has attacked Miss de Riocour, but she has not been seriously hurt. I suggest you go to your rooms, remain together, and lock your doors until his lordship is notified of what was happened.

"Come along now, you must lie down," she said to me.

With Clair's help, I was able to walk to my room, where I lay down on the couch at the foot of the bed.

"Did Lady Milne and Eulalia go back to their rooms?" I asked. "Oh, Clair, it was *awful*. My neck is so sore, and it hurts."

Clair sat on the edge of the couch next to me. "Dorothy," she said, "bring that stool and put it here next to the couch, would you please, and then put the basin on it. Thank you. And hand me the towels." She wet one of the towels and sponged my neck. I could see blood on it. Then she wet another one and laid it across my throat. "Doesn't that feel better?" she asked.

"Yes," I replied. "There is no key for my door. Ask Apsley to get one."

"I have all the keys to the house," Mrs. Danley said. "I will go and get it at once." She sat on the edge of the bed beside me. Tears had left two wet streaks down her cheeks. "Are you sure you are all right?"

"I will be in just a bit," I said. "Dear Mrs. Danley, please don't cry. I am all *right!*"

"Mrs. Danley saved your life," Clair said. "She screamed, and whoever it was fled."

"I will go and get your key," said Mrs. Danley. "You will be safe with the door locked, and I will be right back. Ah, there's Mr. Apsley and Coventry and Maggie and Dolly Paget—come to see what is going on, no doubt. Girls, you come with me." She strode out of the room and down the hall with the maids at her heels.

"What is it, miss?" Apsley asked, hurrying over to me. "Coventry said you had been attacked, but that is not possible."

"It is quite possible, Apsley, and that is exactly what did happen," I said, looking up at him. My throat hurt terribly, and I couldn't help putting my hand to it. "Is my stepfather back yet?"

"No, miss. He and the men are still out searching for the poacher, miss."

" 'The poacher,' as you call him, may be in this very house," I said. "Send someone to find my stepfather, and when he comes in, ask if I may see him here at once, please. Clair and Dorothy, please don't leave me. I shall stay right here where I am for a while."

In a few minutes, Mrs. Danley returned and put the key in the lock in my door and tried it to be sure that it worked.

"There now, you can be locked in safe and snug whenever you want it," she said, "and I have been thinking that it would be best if Clair stayed right here with you tonight. She can sleep on the couch there, and with the door locked, you will be perfectly safe until the sun is shining and we all know where we are."

"Mrs. Danley, please sit down here on the bed by me," I said, "and tell me exactly what happened."

"Of course I will, my dear, though there's not much to tell," she said, and she sat down on the bed. "Being in charge of a house like this one—all the servants and the like—requires constant inspection and supervision, you see. A big part of my job is being sure that they do what they are supposed to do—that the beds are turned down, that the lamps are lit, and that water is in the jugs and such. I was just coming from the north side of the house, where Lord and Lady Milne and the Clarksons are, thinking I would stop in your stepfather's and your mother's rooms and your room.

"Well, I had just come out of one of the cross corridors—the one that forms the west courtyard—when I see what looks like a struggle down the hall, and I hear a kind of groan. Then, I see what turns out to be you throw your candle to the ground. You start to fall over, like, and your candle goes out. I knew something was wrong, so I screamed as hard as I could, thinking someone would hear it and come running—which is what Clair did, and Coventry did from down below—and then I went and got the smelling salts."

"You see," Clair said, "I was waiting for you in your room when I heard Mrs. Danley scream. I ran out into the corridor and saw you lying there. So I got right down on the floor with you and asked Mrs. Danley to get the smelling salts. And then Coventry came running up the south stairway. He must have heard Mrs. Danley's scream from downstairs. And the rest you know."

"Could you see who it was—who did it?" I asked Mrs. Danley. "What did he look like? Would you recognize him again?"

"Or her, perhaps," said Clair.

"No, it was a man, Clair," I said. "I am sure of it."

"I couldn't rightly say I saw him," Mrs. Danley said. "It all happened so quick, and there was just your little candle for light, which was mostly on the other side of him so he was just a shape. Anyway it all happened so quick. It was more an impression, like.

A tall man. I couldn't tell you anything about him. A tall man, that's all."

Then my bedroom door was flung open with a crash. "What has been going on?" my stepfather cried, running through the doorway.

He was followed by Apsley, who stopped just inside the door. But my stepfather did not pause until he stood in front of my couch, his legs spread wide apart, his left arm bobbing.

"What has been going on?" he screamed. "What has happened?"

"Someone tried to strangle Miss de Riocour," Clair said.

"She can tell me," he said.

"Someone tried to strangle me," I spat the words at him. "I have the key to my door. It will remain locked, and Clair will always stay with me. I demand you call the police."

"You demand?" he shrieked. "Demand? You do not *demand* anything. It is I who give the orders. It is I who demand. It is you who obey."

He pointed at my face—his index finger only an inch away from my nose. I wanted to bite it off.

"The police?" he continued. "What do you suppose Constable Williams would do? He is stupid! He would come out here. He would smell about. He would *hope* it would not happen again. He would talk. He would talk, talk, talk. That's all your precious Constable Williams would do—talk! Call police from London? Tell them someone tried to strangle my daughter in *my* house? By the time they got here, there would be no clue left. It would all be cold. Cold clues and hot scandal. Is that what you want?

"I go out half the night chasing that man. When I get back you give me orders. You give me stupid orders! Police, my ass!"

"While you are outside chasing him, he is in here trying to strangle me. Very smart!" I sneered.

Then my stepfather reached out his right hand and struck me hard across the face, twisting my head, wrenching my neck, and knocking the wet towel to the floor.

"Stop it!" Mrs. Danley cried.

"That will teach you to insult me," he snarled. "Bring me that chair," he said to Dorothy. Then he sat down before me. "You will tell me what happened. You will tell me every detail."

I told him everything I could remember, or rather, I flung it at him. I was furious with him, humiliated, and revolted by his behavior.

"Exactly where did this happen?" he asked.

"About two-thirds of the way down the corridor towards my room," I answered.

"Just where the cross corridor that forms the east side of the southwest courtyard comes into the main south corridor," Clair explained.

"Did you see him?" he asked me.

"No, Mrs. Danley did," I answered.

"Did you see him?" he demanded of Mrs. Danley.

"No—I—it was just an impression," she answered. "A tall man. It was too quick, too dark."

"A tall man. Is that all? You can't tell us anything else? What did he look like?"

"I—don't know. It was too dark. Too quick," Mrs. Danley said. "I didn't really see him—I didn't see him." Her hands covered her mouth, then, and she shut her eyes as a tear rolled down her cheek.

No one spoke after that. My stepfather sat deep in thought, his feet swinging clear of the floor, the heels of his boots tapping the legs of his chair. Then he bounced down onto the floor and stood glaring at us.

He shrieked, "I will not permit this to happen in my house. Nothing will happen to this girl." He pointed at me. "She is necessary to me. Everybody take note of that. She will not be harmed. No one will be harmed." I suppose he was trying to smile reassurance, but he managed only a devilish grin. "Do not worry. I am not stupid. I will take care of this."

With that, he marched like a pompous toy soldier out of the room. Apsley followed him and closed the door behind them.

"Lock it, please," I said.

"I must go," Mrs. Danley said. "Come along, Dorothy. Yes, lock it after us, child, and try to sleep. Try to have a good night. Stay with her, Clair. We will all be better in the morning."

After they had left, Clair locked the door, helped me out of my clothes, wrapped a clean piece of linen lightly around my neck to protect the cuts there, and helped me to bed.

I do not know if I slept. I probably dozed off, and perhaps I did sleep a little. But it was a long, painful night. I tried to think during those long hours. Why had this happened? Who had done it? The scar-faced man? Martin Shark's man? Was this the dire consequences referred to in the letter? Mr. Shark wanted something of me, and killing me wouldn't help him get it. But *did* he want something? He wasn't at Wattle —he never had been at the Red Lion Inn. Was he trying to lure me out into the open, then, to kill me in the woods? Had he tried to kill me tonight, or just frighten me? No, not just frighten: if Mrs. Danley hadn't come upstairs, I would be dead. I was quite sure of that. Could it have been someone not connected with Martin Shark? If so, who? All these questions kept going around and around in my brain, and the night kept getting longer and longer with them.

But at last the room lightened perceptibly, and then a pale yellow streak appeared opposite my bed. Presently, birds began their early morning chatter, and then all of a sudden, a brilliant gash of sunlight struck the wall: it was morning.

I fell into a deep sleep.

# ⚔️ Chapter Nineteen ⚔️

IT SEEMED ONLY a moment later that I opened my eyes and saw Clair sitting by the table in the alcove. The curtains behind her were still closed. She sat there not moving, looking down at her lap. How lucky I am to have her, I thought. Loyal, helpful, kind Clair—what would I do without her? How lost and alone I would feel without her, and without Mrs. Danley, too, the sweet, dear woman.

"I have got to find my way out of all this," I murmured aloud without meaning to.

"Oh, miss, you are awake," Clair said, getting up. Then she came over to the bed and sat down on the edge of it. "How do you feel? Here, let me fluff these. There, now lean back," she said, putting all the pillows behind me so I could sit up in comfort.

"I don't know yet—better, I think, Clair. I will tell you when I have had my tea. Would you ring for Dorothy? I would love something hot to drink."

"Did you sleep?" she asked, walking across the room to pull the bell pull.

"Not very much. What time is it?"

"It is after eleven, miss." She went to the alcove and pulled open the curtains, letting the sunshine in.

"Then I did sleep—from shortly after sunrise," I thought aloud. "Isn't it strange how safe the daylight makes one feel, when there is really nothing in the darkness to be afraid of—or not usually. What is that?" I asked, nodding to something Clair had been carrying.

She had carried it with her ever since I had first seen her sitting by the table. Now she walked back to my bed, holding it in her hand, and sat down.

"Dorothy said to ring as soon as you were ready for your tea," she said. "So she will be here in a few minutes—as soon as she has made it. This is the cord the man used last night. I have been examining it."

She handed it to me.

"Gold colored, with a loop tied in one end," I said, as I took the piece of cord and fingered it. "Ugh, take it away!" I handed it back to her. "It is just a piece of gold-colored cord from a costume or clothing of some kind, I suppose. Is it something special?"

"It is special enough to tell where it came from. It is from a costume, all right, but not from a woman's, you may be sure. It is the kind of gold cord worn on a military officer's uniform."

"On a military officer's uniform?" I repeated. "Are you sure? How on earth do you know that?"

"Lady Warburton's youngest son, David, was in the army—I don't know which regiment. He wore this same gold cord on the shoulder of his tunic. You see, for a long time I have had a fantasy of designing a dress in a military style and using this cord as trimming instead of shoulder bows. But of course it couldn't be done. What would people think? Did I say something wrong, miss?"

"Not at all. There is Dorothy with my tea. Let her in, Clair. Bless you, Dorothy," I said. "How I have needed this. Clair, put the cord in the box with my letters and things so we won't lose it.

"Dorothy, you are an angel. Put the tray here on my lap. Yes, I am feeling better. I am quite recovered and will be going down to luncheon. What do you think of that?"

"Stay here with the door locked, miss," said Dorothy.

"No, I can't. We have got to find out what is going on, and I am going to do just that," I said.

I wore my mauve barège to luncheon. It had a high neck, and Clair arranged a long piece of mauve pink material as a scarf, which covered my neck to the chin and fell in two long streamers down my back. She parted my hair and looped it over my forehead, but otherwise she pulled it tightly back in a bun. The effect, I thought, was exceedingly stylish.

I was rather pleased with myself as I walked into the dining room. Mother had already been seated at the table and had begun her soup. She sat alone—my stepfather was not there.

She looked up, mildly surprised to see me. "Good afternoon, my dear. Are you feeling better?"

"Yes, thank you, Mother," I replied.

"We are so happy that you are up and about and looking so well, miss," said Apsley, as Coventry helped me to be seated.

"Thank you, Apsley," I said.

But there was no further conversation during the meal—we ate in silence.

"Will there be anything else, my lady?" Apsley asked, during the custard. He was preparing to leave the dining room.

"Thank you, no, Apsley," Mother replied.

"And, miss," he said, "if there is anything that any of us can do to be of the slightest assistance—"

"Thank you Apsley," I said. "Were you in the staircase hall when my stepfather returned last night?"

"Indeed I was, miss," he replied.

"Did Colonel Lawson return with my stepfather?" I asked.

"Colonel Lawson did not return, miss, because he never left. Just before his lordship left the house to chase the poacher last night, he asked Colonel Lawson to guard the east front rooms and the east entrance from the gardens, in case the poacher tried to get into the house. Titus was to guard the north rooms and the north entrance, Coventry the south rooms and south entrance, and I the entrance front rooms and the staircase hall. Edward had the night off last night, miss, and I believe was not on the grounds."

"Then Colonel Lawson was in the house all the time," I said. "When did he leave for the rectory?"

"I don't know, miss. I did not see him after he went off toward the east front. Henderson, or perhaps John, could tell you when he set out in the gig. He came in a gig, miss."

While Apsley had been speaking, Titus had come tiptoeing into the dining room and was now whispering into his ear.

"As a matter of fact, miss, John is in the staircase hall at this very moment. He has asked to see you, miss."

"Ask him to wait, please, Titus," I replied.

"If there is nothing else, miss?" Apsley asked.

"No, thank you, Apsley," I said.

"I really don't see why you are asking all these questions about Mark," Mother said, after we had been left alone. "I could have told you he was helping guard the house. He left just before your stepfather returned. I was waiting in the hall chamber and saw him go, if that makes any difference."

"You seem very concerned about Mark, Mother. More than about your own daughter?" I asked. "It does make a difference, as it happens. I was choked last night with a length of gold cord—the kind that is worn on a military officer's uniform. Colonel Lawson was a military officer, and he was in the house at the time. Who is to say he was on the ground floor guarding the east front rooms and not wandering about elsewhere?"

Mother's face was blank with incomprehension for

a moment. Then her hand went to her temple. "Where is the cord?" she whispered.

"I really don't see why you want to know, Mother," I said. Then I got up from my chair and left the room.

"Yes, what is it, John?" I asked, approaching him in the entrance hall.

He had been walking nervously, I thought, back and forth—a few steps one way, a few steps the other way. His hands were clasped behind him, and he had been looking down at the marble squares of the floor.

"Good afternoon, miss," he said, looking me in the eyes. "I have something important to tell you concerning the accident last Friday afternoon." He spoke softly so that Titus could not hear.

"Yes, what is it, John?" I asked.

"If you would accompany me to the stables, I could show you," he said. "If you would, miss, there is something important."

"Very well, John," I agreed. "Titus, will you go find Clair for me, please? She is probably in the servants' hall. Tell her to bring a shawl and plan to accompany me for a walk in the park." When he had gone, I turned back to John and said, "Would you accompany us back to the house after you have shown me whatever this mysterious thing is, John?"

"Certainly, miss," he replied. "I do not wish to be mysterious, miss. Thunder did not throw you of his own accord, miss. He was made to throw you. But I would prefer to show you how, rather than tell you about it."

"Made to throw me? But that is impossible, John. There was no one anywhere about last Friday when Thunder threw me. We were completely alone." John gave me that obstinate look of his, which I could never help but admire. "Very well, then," I said, "I shall wait for you to show me."

We did not speak further. And after a while, Clair

came down the staircase with one of my shawls and put it around my shoulders. Titus held the door for us, and we walked out of the house and to the stable block.

"If you would come to the saddle room, miss," John said, after we had passed into the yard. "Perhaps Miss Clair could wait for us here."

"I would prefer—" I began.

"I will sit on the bench there, miss," Clair said. "I will be able to watch the saddle room door from there."

"Very well, John," I said, and he led the way.

The saddle room was dark after the brilliance of the sunshine, and it was a moment before I fully realized that John had taken my saddle off the wall and was carrying it to a wide workbench beneath the one window of the room. Then he flung it down on the bench among the odd bits of leather straps and buckles.

I walked over and stood in front of the bench beside him. "We do bits of repairs here sometimes," he said. "We clean the saddles on the rack outside, of course," he added as if to apologize for the dust and disorder on the workbench. "Now let me show you." He reached down and lifted back the flap of my saddle as far as it would go and held it there. "See those two holes in the leather high up above the girth guards? Now, watch." He reached up and took something from the window frame. "See these?"

"They look like nails with rather large flat heads," I said, still mystified.

"That's what they are, and they fit in these holes like that." He inserted two of the four nails in the two holes in the leather and let the flap fall back in place. "That's where they were when you went riding last Friday on Thunder. The holes didn't go through the lining then, and the nail heads stuck up a bit. Your weight in the saddle pressed them down and pushed the nail points through the lining and into Thunder's back. These other two nails were in the right side of the saddle in the same place. Sharp? Feel them."

I took one and felt the point. It was sharp as a needle.

"How would you feel with four of these pounded into your back?" he asked.

"Just the way Thunder felt," I said, looking up into John's eyes. "I would probably go mad with the pain, too."

John looked down at me seriously, intently.

"You know what this means?" I asked. "Someone wanted Thunder to throw me and trample me to death the way he killed Patrick Meagher."

"It looks that way, miss. I certainly couldn't have seen the nails when I saddled Thunder, and I wouldn't have noticed them when I took the saddle off him if I hadn't seen the blood on his back and the ragged holes in his flesh. I found him over near Fawsley that night and brought him back here, and he nearly went wild again with the pain when I was taking the saddle off him, but he quieted down as soon as it was done."

"But that was Friday night, John, and this is Tuesday afternoon. Why did you wait so long to tell me?" I asked. "Don't you realize that if you had told me before last night—"

"Yes, miss," he interrupted, "but I couldn't say anything because his lordship told me not to. You see, miss, my job is to obey orders, and I do that. When I got Thunder back here that night and got the saddle off him and got him into his box—which was not easy, and there wasn't anybody else around to help—I went to tell his lordship that Thunder was back. I told him about the nails, and he came to have a look. He knew what it meant, all right. But he said he knew what to do, and he'd take care of getting the one who done it, and not to tell you because it would only worry you—

and there was no point in your being worried. He said to keep Thunder, not let anyone ride him, and not say anything about it to anyone so there would not be a scandal about it, and that he'd take care of it. So I just cleaned up the saddle, cleaned up the blood on Thunder, and kept my mouth shut."

"But you told me about it today, John," I said.

"Yes, after last night—I thought you should know," he said. "We all heard about it, miss. Well, after last night, I knew his lordship hadn't got the one who did this." He pointed to the saddle, frowning. "Till he does, there's a murderer loose at Warton Hall, and it's more important to protect your life than to obey orders. Be careful, miss. We'll all be looking and watching, and if you need any help, you can count on all of us here at the stables."

"Thank you, John. I do appreciate being able to count on you—it means more than I can say," I replied. "Who could have done this? Do you have any idea?"

"No, miss, I don't. Nobody on the estate would do it, but a stranger could come in here any time. The door's never locked—there isn't any lock. Why should we lock it? He'd be taking a terrible chance, though. There are a dozen men always coming and going around here. It's a busy place, the stable block is."

"But it wouldn't have taken long to do, would it?" I asked.

"No, miss, not more than maybe eight or ten minutes. He'd have to hammer the nails down through the leather just the right distance, and that would make a noise. And at night he'd need a light. It would be a chancy thing to do, at best, miss. There's rooms in the tower just above where some of the grooms sleep, and there would be the chance that they might hear if he did it at night, miss. He must have been lucky, I guess."

Just then we heard a strange sound—not very loud.

It sounded as if it had come from the room next door, as if someone or something there had fallen against the wall or brushed hard against it. The walls were made of horizontal boards fitted closely together and were not, I was sure, more than one board thick. It was not surprising that we should hear something happening in there.

At the sound, John was gone in an instant, and almost immediately I heard his footsteps running across the floor of the room next door. They stopped, and then as quickly, he was back at my side.

"Feed room," he whispered. "Nothing, nobody."

"Do you think it was—oh, it is useless to speculate. One more question. Patrick Meagher's saddle?" I asked softly.

"I thought about that," he said in a low voice. He seemed surprised that I had thought of it so quickly. "I don't know which one he used that day, but it must have been one of these." He pointed to the wall. "I've looked them all over—no nail holes, miss. No, Thunder killed Meagher because he wanted to, and he didn't kill you because he didn't want to. I suppose you were right about him all along, miss."

"Thank you, John, and thank you again for telling me all about this," I said.

I turned from him, and walked out of the saddle room and back to where Clair was sitting. As I walked, I heard John hang up the saddle. After that he came out to join us, and we walked together back to the house.

As we rounded the corner of the entrance front, I saw Owen helping Mother mount Lady Jane. She was dressed in a black habit and top hat with a veil. It streamed behind her as she galloped past us without the slightest sign of recognition. Her face was flushed, I thought, and I sensed an unusual urgency about her as she sped in the direction of the rectory. Now Mark will know of my suspicions, I thought, which will probably be all to the good. Or will it? Will the knowledge make him bolder the next time? Have I made a mistake in telling Mother?

John left us at the entrance front steps, and I turned to Clair and said, "I can't bear to be locked up in my room all afternoon, and I have to think. Let us go to the bridge. It is in full view of the whole south front of the house. From there, we will be able to see anyone coming for a long way across the grass. We will be perfectly safe there."

We walked across the park, that golden afternoon, under a heady blue sky spotted with wandering white cloud puffs. And when we reached the bridge, we sat down on the marble bench built into the sunny side of it. The bench was warm from the sun, and from it we could look out over the sea of grass. Before us lay the long south front of the house and, to the right of it, the gardens, the orangery, and the glasshouses. To the left was the entire length of the drive and the distant gate houses.

"One can see what has become my whole world from here, Clair, my whole nightmare," I mused aloud. "I have got to *do* something. I cannot go on doing nothing. He will try to kill me again, I know he will. He has tried it twice, and he will try it again."

"Twice, miss?" Clair asked.

"Yes, that is what John wanted to show me at the stables. The murderer—I can't believe I am actually using that word in connection with myself. Someone is actually trying to kill me, and that makes him a murderer. I don't believe this is happening to me at all, Clair. Things like this don't happen to people, except in cheap novels, perhaps. But it *is* happening to me. I am being stalked by a murderer who craves my death, and I am frightened, Clair. Terribly frightened."

Then after a moment I gestured to everything in front of us, and said, "All this could be heaven on earth, but it was wrong from the start—sinister, some-how, evil.

"The murderer put sharp nails in Thunder's saddle so that when I rode him, the weight of my body would push the nails down into his back, and he would throw me and trample me to death the way he trampled a man named Patrick Meagher to death two years ago."

Clair looked back at me wide-eyed, but she did not speak.

"I must *do* something. I cannot stay locked up in my room forever. If only I could get away from here," I thought aloud.

Then I turned sideways and rested my arm on the back of the bench and laid my head on my arm. The sun beat warmly on it, on my face, and on my throat, which was still very sore. My head hurt—a pain had begun to stab behind my eyes. So I closed them to lis-ten to the swishing of the stream below me.

But my mind could not rest. I must get away, I thought. And then I thought back over all the things that had happened to me since I had come to Warton Hall: that first meeting with Martin Shark and seeing the scar-faced man; being followed and spied upon by him; and Dorothy's story about the murder of the sixth earl and the death of Patrick Meagher. I thought of the Wensleys and the Bishams and the ball. What had my mother said to my stepfather that night? Why had he struck her? And Mark Lawson—who *was* he? What is he doing for my stepfather? What kind of work is he doing in the mausoleum at night? Who is trying to kill me? I could no longer escape the fact that it might be Mark. Mark! Why?

"Why?" I murmured aloud. "Why, why, why?"

"Miss?" Clair asked.

She had realized that I wanted to be quiet, so she had remained silent until now.

"Why should anyone want to kill *me*, Clair? What have I done? That is what I cannot understand. I am nobody. I don't matter to anybody. I have done nothing. Why?

"Oh, I can't think any more," I said, getting up. "My head is aching, and I would like to lie down. We will go back to the house and lock ourselves in my room, and I will sleep awhile, and then I will think some more. I must do something. I must get away from here."

"What has been happening during the day?" I asked Dorothy when Clair had let her into my room that evening to turn down the bed and bring some fresh drinking water.

"Don't you want some more light in here, miss? It is so dark with just that one low lamp by the bed," Dorothy said.

"Yes, turn it up, please, and light the others. We were watching the moon rise. It is lovely, in spite of everything. Come and see it. Did you ever see a more orange moon?"

The beauty and the danger, I thought. Then I said to Dorothy, "And would you close the curtains, please?"

"Keep the door locked, miss. Don't go out at night. Stay locked in here, miss. There's evil in this house. I feel it," Dorothy said.

"I will. Now, tell me. Has anything happened that I should know about? Tell me about Lord and Lady Milne and the Clarksons."

"Lord and Lady Milne and Lady Eulalia and her brother, Lord Gorm, left before morning prayer and without even having breakfast, miss. Dolly Paget told Elsie Tate, and Elsie Tate told me. They was all packed and dressed for travel and waiting when she went in with their tea. All four of them were huddled together, like, in Lady Milne's room. Dolly was told to go tell their coachman and footmen that they must have their carriage ready to go at the entrance front in twenty minutes. *Twenty minutes,* can you imagine? All they wanted was to get away from here, and I can't say I blame them at all. Well, they barely took a sip of tea before they trooped down and out onto the drive. Without even a good-bye to anyone, they left."

"And the Clarksons?" I asked.

"Right after breakfast, miss. Henderson drove them to the early train."

"Anything else, Dorothy?"

"No, miss, except that his lordship has given orders to Mr. Apsley and the footmen and Mrs. Danley that he be informed of where you are at all times and who you're with. Henderson and John were in his office this afternoon, late, for a while. According to Mr. Apsley, they're to keep a watch on you if you should go riding or out in a carriage. Everyone will be looking out for you, miss, but that doesn't mean you're safe, not by a long shot."

"That is comforting in the extreme, Dorothy," I said.

"Oh, miss, I'm sorry," she said. There were tears in her eyes and her pitifully thin hands, clasped in front of her chest, were shaking. "I'm *frightened!*"

"There, there. We will find a way out of all this, I promise you. Now, please try and be calm. Were there any visitors? Did anyone come to see my stepfather from the outside world, so to speak?"

"Mr. Bisham came to call on you late this afternoon, but you had said you would not be at home. Lord Plummer was with your stepfather in his office for a half-hour earlier, but Lord Plummer and his son didn't come together. That is all I know, miss."

"I did not say I wouldn't be at home, not to Apsley nor anyone else," I said. "I would not have been, of course, but I wonder if my stepfather thinks I will be protected by having no contact with my friends? Oh, probably not. Apsley may have taken it upon himself to think I was not well enough, which was true, but he shouldn't have. Oh, it doesn't matter."

"Do you have everything you need, miss?" Dorothy asked. "If you want anything, ring. God bless you, miss, and lock up behind me."

She left, and Clair locked the door behind her and then wandered silently back to the alcove and stood near me holding aside one of the curtains and idly looking out the window.

"How quickly the moon gets smaller," she said. "Why it is only half the size it was just a little while ago. It doesn't get smaller, of course, but I wonder why it appears—how odd! There is a light at the mausoleum. Now it is out."

"Now you see a figure with a limp walking along, silhouetted against the sky," I said, without getting up from my chair. "Now it disappears below the hill, walking toward the abbey ruins."

"Yes!" said Clair, turning to look at me. "How do you know that? Can you see through walls?"

"I have seen him there before, three or four times. It is Colonel Lawson. He is doing something up there at night. I don't know what. I have been there during the day, and I have found his lantern hidden in the grass, but nothing seems disturbed. I don't know what he does, but if he has to do it late at night, there is something very strange—something very wrong about it."

Clair had turned back to the window and was looking out again. "How odd," she murmured. "Rather frightening, actually."

After that, we were silent for some time.

"Do you ride, Clair?" I asked, finally.

"No, miss," she replied.

"Then Henderson will drive us."

"Where, miss?"

"To the rectory. I want to talk to the rector. We will go tomorrow after luncheon. Now, help me to bed. It is getting late. I know I won't be able to sleep, but I can rest. Poor Clair—did you sleep at all last night on that hard couch?"

"Yes, I did, miss. I am one of those lucky people who can sleep anywhere at any time." She smiled.

"Well, don't wake me in the morning if I should sleep late," I said.

And that is exactly what I did. I slept until well after eleven, for I had not fallen asleep until after the sun had risen.

# Chapter Twenty

"DOROTHY, WOULD YOU ASK Titus to come up, please?" I asked. She was just leaving the room with her water cans.

As Clair locked the door, I glanced at the clock on the bedside table. It was ten minutes past noon. We had gotten off to a very late start that morning, but I didn't care. I hadn't even dressed yet. I still wore my dressing gown. But I was not concerned about these things, I was concerned about the weather. And for perhaps the fifth time, I walked to the alcove to look out. The clouds still hung dense and low above the gardens, and I prayed it would not rain. Inside, it was so dark that we had lit the lamps. Finally, after pacing back and forth for a time, I walked to the mirror over the washstand.

"Do you think it will ever heal?" I asked Clair, while I examined my neck in the glass. "Such a beastly, red-black color. And those cuts—my neck looks clawed by an animal, a big cat, perhaps. It is horrible. Will it leave a mark, do you think, Clair?"

"No, miss, most likely not," she said. "Give it time to heal. This is only the second day. It will gradually fade away, and you will never know it was there. You will see. Is it still as sore as it was?"

"A little less, I think." Then after a moment, I said, "I am too nervous to go down to luncheon. I couldn't bear sitting through it. There, that must be Titus. Let him in, will you please?"

"Yes, miss?" Titus asked.

"Titus, I will have luncheon here in my room, and Clair will have something here, too. Whatever the chef decides will be perfect. And would you ask Henderson to have a carriage at the entrance front at two-thirty, please? Clair and I will be going out for a drive; we will not be going very far."

After we had finished eating and Titus had cleared away the dishes, Clair helped me into my black velvet caraco and buttoned the front up to the high neck. Then, to hide the bruises on my throat, she wrapped a scarf about my neck and fastened it in place with the diamond and emerald brooch.

"How somber you look," she said. "Wait, wait!" She ran across the room to the bouquet on the table, picked two yellow rosebuds, and fastened them against the scarf with the brooch. "There, that's better," she said.

"I don't feel like wearing flowers today, Clair," I said, "but it doesn't matter. Bring my black bonnet for me and the black shawl-mantle with the fringe, and bring a shawl for yourself. You may need it. It will probably be chilly in the carriage. Hurry, it is almost two-thirty."

We descended the grand staircase to the hall just as a clock chimed the half-hour. Coventry opened the door for us. Henderson sat on the box of the carriage. I could see him through the open doorway. But as we walked toward it, the stubby little figure of my stepfather appeared from outside, blocking the way.

"Where are you going?" he demanded.

"For a drive," I retorted.

"Where?"

"If you must know, to the rectory to see the rector. I think, under the circumstances, that nothing could be more appropriate than that I seek the solace of God through a minister of his church. The way things are progressing, it may be my last chance to do so. Or do you intend to keep me a prisoner in this house?"

"I am trying to protect your life. You do not thank me for it. Do you hear that, Apsley? Do you hear how my daughter thanks me for protecting her life?

"Henderson," he called, "Drive her to the rectory in Fawsley and drive her back. Do not drive her anywhere else. When you have returned, come and see me in my office."

He stalked abruptly into the house and passed us without another word. Then we descended the steps with Coventry following, and he helped us into the carriage.

"That is all right, Coventry. We can manage. It will not be necessary for you to come," I said.

When we arrived, Clair ran to the door of the rectory for me. It was opened by Thompson. They spoke for a few moments, and then Clair glanced back apprehensively at me. Finally both she and Thompson hurried toward me.

"Mr. Ashley is not at home, miss," Clair said. "He has gone to the village to visit an old lady, a Mrs. Putkin, who is very ill, but Mr. Thompson said that the rector told him that if there was anything important, he might send the groom down and the rector would return at once."

"Thompson," I said, "it really is most important that I talk to the rector. I *must* see him this afternoon."

"Then I shall send Adam to fetch him, miss. Will you come into the rectory and wait, then? There is a fire in the drawing room, and I will show you in there. I know the rector would want you to be comfortable while you wait, miss."

"Thank you, Thompson," I said, as he helped me

down from the carriage. "I am sorry, Henderson, but I don't know how long I will be."

Then Clair and I followed Thompson into the house and down the hall into the drawing room.

"Please make yourself comfortable, Miss de Riocour, and I will dispatch Adam at once," Thompson said, as he walked back toward the entrance hall.

"Oh, Thompson," I called after him, "is Colonel Lawson at home?"

"No, miss. Colonel Lawson will not be back until sometime late in the afternoon, I believe."

When Thompson had gone, Clair helped me remove my mantle and I sat down on the edge of the sofa next to the fire. My hands were cold, and I held them out to the flames. But I could not sit still: I began pacing up and down, and then I crossed to the window, pulled the curtain aside, and looked out.

"That must be Adam," I said to Clair. "Yes, it is. He is going down the path toward the village. I hope we don't have to wait here very long. It shouldn't take him more than ten minutes to walk almost anywhere there. I wonder where the old woman lives? He should be back in a half-hour, don't you think?"

But we must have waited an hour. During that time, Mrs. Hobson had been in twice to look at the fire, but otherwise we had been undisturbed At last, I heard a door shut, then voices and footsteps in the hall. And then the rector burst into the room.

"I will wait in the hall," Clair whispered.

"My dear," the rector said, coming toward me.

I went to meet him and extended both hands. He took them in his and guided me to the sofa by the fire.

"Sit here by me," he said. "It is chill this afternoon, so we have a little fire to take away the cold and damp and bring a little cheer.

"There now," he said after I was seated. "I am so glad Adam came to fetch me. I thought I had been permanently neglected, that you would never visit me again, that—my dear, there is something wrong." He paused and looked at me intently. "I know you were thrown from your horse, but I heard you were not badly injured and were quite yourself on Monday. If you had been seriously hurt, I would have come to you, but now you have come to me. Something has happened. What is it?"

"Where is Mark Lawson?" I asked.

"I don't know. He has gone out on High Point. He said he would be back later in the afternoon."

"He hasn't told you what happened on Monday night?" I asked.

"That there was a poacher or—a stranger—wandering about the grounds? Yes. But he was evidently frightened away. Was he found, then? I only heard about it this morning. Lawson was in London on business all day yesterday, and we didn't have chance to talk until this morning. Suzanne! Tell me what is wrong!"

"You don't know?" I asked.

"No, I don't. How could I? And I won't know, it seems, if you don't tell me."

"Someone has tried to kill me two times, and I think it was Mark Lawson," I said.

"Kill you? No!" He looked at me in astonishment. "Do you know—? What makes you think so? You must be imagining this."

I held the scarf away from my neck so that he could see the bruise and the cuts. "Does this look like imagination?"

"My poor child! Oh, my dear—you had better tell me everything."

"Someone arranged sharp nails in my saddle so that when I rode Thunder my weight would push them through the leather lining into his back and make him throw me. I think Mark Lawson did it. He appeared out of nowhere after I was thrown. He must have been following me to see if I would be trampled to death.

"Then on Monday night, someone tried to strangle me in a dark corridor at about eleven o'clock with a piece of gold cord from a British army officer's uniform, and Mark Lawson was in the house at that time. He didn't leave the house until almost eleven-thirty and he had been wandering about alone since about ten-fifteen.

"Who is Mark Lawson, rector? He has no house in Durham. Wellfield House has been a burned-out shell for years and is owned by a friend of Lord Aldergate's. Why did he lie to us? What kind of work is he doing for my stepfather? Why does he want to kill me? I have never done anything to him."

"Suzanne, you are being hysterical," the rector said. He jumped up and rang for Mrs. Hobson. "Mark Lawson didn't try to kill you. He wouldn't try to kill anyone. I have known him all his life, and he is—" He stopped as Mrs. Hobson entered. "Mrs. Hobson, bring some brandy. Miss de Riocour is not feeling well."

"I am feeling perfectly well," I said, getting up from the sofa. "If you have known him all his life, perhaps you will tell me who he is, where he came from, and just what he is doing here."

"Suzanne, I can't, please believe me. Lawson will be back soon. Please sit down and wait—"

"You *can't?*" I interrupted. "Believe you? You know, and you won't tell me. Sit down and wait for the murderer? I thought you were a friend. I thought I could depend on you. But you are in league with him. You and he are working together in whatever is going on here, aren't you? *Aren't* you?

"I should never have come!" I flung the words back at him as I grabbed my cloak and ran from the room and down the corridor toward the entrance hall.

"Come along, Clair, quickly," I cried, running past her. Reaching the entrance door, I grabbed its handle and wrenched it open before a startled Thompson could open it for me. We ran out onto the drive and climbed into the carriage. Henderson had decided to wait for us on the drive and had turned the carriage around in the meantime.

"We can go now, Henderson," I said, and we began to move away from the house at once.

As we did, I glanced back and saw the rector standing beside Thompson in the doorway, with Mrs. Hobson peering out from between them. But I was no longer interested in the Reverend Ashley: I wanted to be locked in the safety of my room at Warton Hall.

"I should never have come," I said to Clair, as we turned from the rectory drive into the abbey road. "I thought the rector was a friend, but he won't help me. I have no friends."

"You have me and Dorothy and Mrs. Danley," Clair said.

"Yes, thank you." I patted her hand. "And I have myself—"

But I never finished the sentence because of what happened then. Ahead of us, a brougham stood by the side of the road, and as we approached, a man on horseback rode out from behind it and stood in the middle of the road, blocking our way. It was the scar-faced man.

"Hoa, hoa," cried Henderson, bringing the carriage to a halt. "What the bloody hell do you think you're doing? Get out of the way and let us pass."

The scar-faced man smiled a single-toothed smile. A metal object glinted from beneath his coat. A pistol? I wondered. But he did not move, and except for the pawing of the horses, there was not a sound. Then even the horses were still, and in the tension that followed, I knew Henderson was getting ready to explode.

But something attracted my eye to the brougham. From its open window, a pudgy hand, with several diamond rings on its fingers, hung limply. I could see nothing more of the occupant: he lay back out of sight.

"Just a moment, Henderson," I said.

"Good afternoon, Miss de Riocour," said a voice from inside the carriage. "This is not the most pleasant afternoon for a drive."

Then the man in the carriage leaned forward, and I could see his face. It was Martin Shark. His hairless eyebrows rose, opening his beady eyes wide, and he gave me a smile of exaggerated pleasure.

"How enchanting to see you again, mademoiselle," he said. "We hope you have had a pleasant visit at the rectory. We have been waiting here for you for almost an hour, but no matter. 'How poor are they that have not patience.' Shakespeare: *Othello.*

"We are so disappointed," he continued, "that our appointment of last Friday could not be kept, but another opportunity is at hand. May I extend a most cordial invitation to drive with me in my carriage?" As he said these words, he deftly unlatched his carriage door, and it swung open. "Your safe return to Warton Hall will be our most sacred pledge," he concluded, pressing his hand to his chest. He bent his head and shut his eyes for a moment. Then, looking at me from under his brows, he smiled broadly and extended his hand in courtly invitation.

Clair covered my hand with hers.

I shall be forced to go if I do not do so willingly, I thought. They will hardly allow us to say good-bye and proceed back to the Hall. Reluctance will accomplish nothing, and I must not appear nervous or afraid.

"We would be delighted, sir," I said. Then I opened the carriage door, stood, and began to gather my skirts. "Come along Clair."

"But surely, mademoiselle," Mr. Shark said, "we

can talk more freely and more—um—comfortably if we are alone. I would suggest that your maid and coachman return to Warton Hall. I will drive you safely home when our visit is at an end."

"Splendid," I replied, stepping down. "Henderson, you may drive Clair home."

Then I walked across to Mr. Shark's carriage and taking his extended hand, stepped up into the cab and swung the door closed behind me.

At once, we sped off, down the road toward Fawsley, and I settled myself in the tiny space beside Martin Shark.

"Miss de Riocour, his lordship expressly forbade. . . ." Henderson called after us.

I glanced back at him. He continued to shout in our direction, but I could no longer hear him above the noise of the horses and the squeaking of the carriage springs. Behind him, Clair sat stunned, her hand to her mouth, looking after us.

"What did you wish to speak to me about, Mr. Shark?" I asked, taking the initiative and trying to sound calm and authoritative.

"All in due course, good lady," Martin Shark replied, reaching across me to crank the window closed. "We have anticipated our little rendezvous for some time, each of us. Let us savor it and sip of its enchantments, leisurely. 'The wisdom of a learned man cometh by the opportunity of leisure; and he that hath little business shall become wise.' *Ecclesiasticus*."

As he spoke, he examined me closely from the corners of his eyes. Now he smiled, very much like a spider lying lazily in the center of his web might smile at the fly that was safely enmeshed nearby and would become his dinner. The air inside the cab did nothing to alleviate my discomfiture. It had become warm and stuffy already, and the mountainous man, who sat beside me huddled in his heavy woolen frock coat, smelled unpleasant.

"Pray excuse my manners if I say that you are looking lovely this afternoon," he continued. "My spirits soar with delight. Beautifully gowned, in the best of taste—his lordship has lavished every—um—attention."

"He has been very kind," I replied. "I have everything I could desire." Then, after a pause, "Mr. Shark, I must tell you that I wanted very much to keep our appointment at the Red Lion Inn last Friday, but my horse threw me as I rode to meet you, and I hit my head and was obliged to return to Warton Hall where I spent the rest of the day in bed. I was in no condition to ride out again that day."

"Ah, mademoiselle, we are distressed to hear it," he said, laying a dirty hand on my arm. "We can only rejoice that your indisposition was brief and that fortune has found you flourishing again: driving across the countryside for afternoon visits at the great houses of wealthy and titled new friends; delighting in dinner parties and at-homes; reveling at their balls; and enchanting wealthy, handsome, and eligible young men. All this enhanced by a princely dowry, destined to bring titles and joy forever. Such a pity that it all must end."

"End?" I asked.

"End," he replied, gazing out the window languidly, his hands folded contentedly in his lap.

By then, we had turned into an unfamiliar lane so narrow that tree branches brushed the windows of the carriage as we plodded along it, leaving drops of moisture behind to run down the glass and blur the world outside. A mist had risen from the ground, making us the center of its close, milky sphere.

"Wealth," Mr. Shark whispered, "clothes, titled friends, parties, balls, dowry—gone, all gone. This is the end. Pity, such a pity."

"What do you mean?" I cried, reaching for the door handle. "You promised to return me safely home."

Then he began to laugh. The great, fleshy mountain shook with laughter. "No, no, no," he said. "How excitable you are! How imaginative! Ho, ho, ho." He took a handkerchief from his breast pocket and wiped his forehead with it and then, still holding it, laid his finger on the side of his nose, as he had done the first night I saw him. He looked sideways and down at me. "Pray remain seated. I *will* keep my promise. You will be safely home tonight. Ho, ho, ho. Words—what fragile, capricious things they are. 'All words are no more to be taken in a literal sense at all times than a promise given to a miller.' Thomas Lamb." His tiny eyes popped at me. "Or was it a butcher?"

"Oh, you will be fine enough physically—still in the best of health, one would presume. But, alas, your house of good fortune, as with your stepfather's, will have fallen to ashes. A teaching job, I suppose, in a filthy, little girls' school somewhere. . . ." He trailed the last word off in a long murmur, as again, he directed his attention to the misty branches outside the window.

"Mr. Shark, I do not understand," I said. "Would you kindly explain whatever it is you wish to say in a way that I can understand."

"Your stepfather will soon be a poor man with no title, no house, no estates, without a penny to his name. You, too, will be poor, with no prospect of marriage."

I was so startled and mystified by this that I could only stare at him.

"I see that I speak—hm—plainly enough. It was my hand," he said, holding up his right hand in a dainty gesture for me to see, "the art of this very hand that placed his lordship in the mansion house with the estates and some two hundred thousand pounds per year at his disposal. And it is this very hand that must remove him.

"But so that you may fully understand the situation, I must confide, mademoiselle, the depths into which

302

*my own* personal fortunes have fallen," he continued. "I am prostrate, penniless, destitute. A great artist, one of the greatest talents the world has ever experienced. That will be evident forever. But I have no bread to feed me." He dabbed at the corners of his eyes with his handkerchief. "Consequently, I must journey to a far-off land. My only hope is to start anew. But before I leave my beloved country, I must put right a grievous wrong that I have done, or I shall not sleep on the high seas. A great man once said that a wise man can live *with* his iniquities, but that he cannot leave them behind."

"You interest me, Mr. Shark," I said, my pulse quickening. "What have you done concerning my stepfather that needs undoing?"

"It is difficult, most difficult to bare my sin," he answered. His hand lay theatrically on his chest. "You have heard, no doubt, of the trial to determine—um—legitimacy of your stepfather's claim to the Trevenbury title? The documents introduced at the trial were—um—to be quite blunt—forgeries. Ah! I see you are surprised. A clever scheme. A clever man, your stepfather, but alas, all too stupid at one and the same time. My art, and my art alone, brought it all to a successful conclusion." He gave me a long, shrewd look, assessing his effect upon me.

"Fitzjames's father was not George Osborne, the seventh earl of Trevenbury. Fitzjames's father was a man by the name of Jack Cobbe—a laborer in a brewery. He died the day Fitz was born, of a blow from a barrel that fell from a loft and struck him on the back of the neck.

"Fitz's mother, Mary Danley, could never have married the seventh earl. Indeed, he sacked her for stealing some of her dead mistress's jewelry. He could never prove it and never did get the jewels back, but he knew she had stolen them. That's where the emerald brooch—which Fitz used at the trial and which, incidentally, unless I am very much mistaken, you are wearing at this moment—came from. Fitz added a little engraving to the back of it, of course. Have you read the inscription? No? There was a little engraving done on the rings, too—quite ordinary work, actually.

"But the marriage register, the love letters, and the will were—um—all the product of the humble artist with whom you ride this afternoon." He smiled at me with enormous pride.

"Oh, but my stepfather knew his father," I said. "He visited him at Warton Hall and spent hours closeted with him. His father acknowledged him—"

"Not publicly! Forgive me for interrupting, mademoiselle. He did not acknowledge Fitzjames publicly, according to Fitz's story." His hand tapped my arm. "His lordship did not acknowledge Fitzjames to anyone but Fitzjames himself during his lifetime, not even to the servants, according to the story that Fitz told at the trial. The truth of the matter is that the seventh earl knew Fitz only as James Aberdeen, an author of books on architecture and the history of English country houses. But as Fitz explained it at the trial, he had taken the name of Aberdeen at his father's request— to spare his lordship the embarrassment of a son's sudden appearance out of nowhere.

"The seventh earl was very proud of his house and family history and was only too happy to tell Fitzjames Aberdeen, an author gathering material for a book, all about them during those long afternoons they spent together and in many letters. Very clever of Fitz, of course. These letters provided the crest for the engraver and, more importantly, provided me with all the material I needed for some of my masterpieces. I must tell you that I have been given the supreme gift of being able to recreate any hand to perfection— indistinguishable from the original.

"Parts of the old earl's bonafide letters to Fitz, I say *parts,* were exhibited at the trial. They were the pages dealing with unimportant discussions of the history of the house and family, but the important documents—the marriage register, the birth certificate, the love letters, and the will, as I have said, were my work. They should be in a museum along with my other works."

"Such as the diary of Nell Gwyn?" I asked.

"You amaze me, dear lady," Mr. Shark said, looking at me in surprise.

"Why did you employ Patrick Meagher—or should I say Patrick Meeker—to steal it for you?" I asked.

"To make certain pages of it read as they should," he replied, as if the answer should be obvious. "I was able to borrow the diary again later, and certain changes have been made. Meeker was rather a clod, I'm afraid, but no matter.

"We all know that many events in history," he continued, "not to mention our daily lives, have not happened the way they should have. There is no explanation for this—um—except that they have been mistakes—errors of destiny. I have been fortunate to be allowed, with my gifts, to correct many of history's corrigenda.

"For instance, mademoiselle, it will soon be known that Elizabeth was not excommunicated forever from the true church. That would have been most unfortunate, indeed. Letters will come to light revealing that the excommunication was recanted by the pope at her entreaty. And history tells us that the little princes died in the tower, but this would have been monstrous, don't you agree? Letters are about to be discovered in Richard's own hand telling of their safe spiriting away to Holland. Can you imagine how this revelation will enhance Richard's reputation? But these are only two examples.

"So you see, in many respects the history of our beloved England will now be more nearly what it should be, thanks to the genius of the hand and the

sensitive perceptions and enormous comprehension of
—um—yours truly." Again he deigned to smile upon
me.

"How extraordinary," I said, smiling back. "And so,
of course, you recommended Mr. Meagher to my stepfather when it was time for him to find someone to
murder the seventh earl so that he might claim his
inheritance."

"You find me speechless with wonder," he replied.
"How you learned of the—um—enforced demise of
his lordship would be fascinating indeed, but—um—
that shall wait until another time.

"The death of the seventh earl," he continued, "was
one of those accidents of destiny of which we
were speaking, though a relatively unimportant one.
You see, just at that time, I fell desperately, appall-
ingly in need of money to sustain myself while
I launched into a prolonged period of artistic pro-
ductivity. Some letters of Catherine of Aragon to
Ferdinand II had been—um—delivered into my hands.
She had expressed herself in, shall we say, a mis-
guided fashion, which, of course, had to be corrected.
Well, Fitz had agreed to pay me five thousand
pounds for my artistry on his behalf, but he could
not very well do that until he came into the inheritance." He might have been explaining to me how
to bake a loaf of bread, his tone was so matter-of-fact.
"The seventh earl was in excellent health and might
have lived on forever. I had already waited patiently
for his death for two whole years. Meeker merely
helped progress along for me.

"It was completely accidental that I needed the
money so desperately at that particular time and that
Meeker was available. But for all Fitz knows, the old
earl died a natural death of the heart—there is no
proof to the contrary, you know, and no one's the
worse for it. As a matter of fact, we are all the better.
These accidents are sometimes most fortunate." He

chuckled softly and folded his hands contentedly across his enormous lap.

"A fascinating story, Mr. Shark," I said, "but an intelligent man, such as you obviously are, would not expect me to believe a story simply because it was told to me."

Before answering, Mr. Shark rolled down the window and pulled himself far enough forward to lean out of it. "Turn about!" he called up to the driver. "Turn back to the Abbey Road." Then he fell back, breathless with the effort, and rolled up the window.

I had been grateful for the breath of fresh air and the brief chance to think uninterruptedly. He wants more money of course, I thought, and he wants it from me, but learn all you can before the negotiations begin, Suzanne, and when they do, play along with him.

"It is your intelligence that is to be commended with the greatest admiration," Mr. Shark said. " 'Honest, unaffected distrust of the powers of man is the surest sign of intelligence.' George Christoph Lichtenberg: *Reflections*."

"In your letter requesting a meeting at the Red Lion," I said, "you stated that you were staying there and that the landlord would have a private room set aside for us. Mr. Stallard, the proprietor of the Red Lion had never heard of Martin Shark. Martin Shark had never stayed at the inn. I believed what you told me in your letter, but I was misled. How can you expect me to believe this fascinating but, I am afraid, fantastically imaginative tale?"

"Ah, but I did not state that I was *staying* at the Red Lion; I merely implied it. There was a slight—um—deception there, to be sure, but deceptions are *necessary* at times. There is, perhaps, someone who would like to know if I journey here from London for a day or two and where I stay when I do—that must remain my secret.

"We were to talk that afternoon in this carriage, by

the side of the road leading to Wattle—in the same fashion as we do now, which I am sure you will agree is most satisfactory. But alas, though I waited, you did not come.

"But to get back to the—um—fanciful tale," he said with a chuckle. "You doubt me? Excellent! This, then, will interest you."

He reached into the inside pocket of his coat, drew out a folded piece of paper, and handed it to me. I unfolded it carefully and held it to the wan light at the window. It was a page taken from a church marriage register. As I examined it, Mr. Shark leaned close. I could feel his breath on my face as he pointed to the paper with a torn fingernail.

"You see, there, the name Mary Danley?" he said. Then his finger slid across the paper. "You see, there, the name of her husband? Jack Cobbe! He did not even have a middle name. This is the original page that Fitz removed, ever so carefully, from the marriage register of Berkley Church before inserting the —um—more advantageous one. It was easy enough to borrow the register. The rector was nearly blind and the church poor and neglected in an area of factories and breweries.

*"This* is the original page. It was agreed that it would be returned to Fitz when I received my payment in full. But I made him a copy instead." The expression on his face was that of a man who loves figs and has just bitten into a perfectly ripe one. "He thinks he is safe because he has the original page that could destroy him." He began to laugh softly, his great bulk quivering. "But he has only a copy. His ruin is here with us." He took the register page gently out of my hands, then folded it, and returned it to his pocket, patting it in place.

"But of course if you need more proof, ask Mary's sister, Ruth Danley, the housekeeper at Warton Hall. Now that you are one of the—um—conspirators, she'll tell you all about it, and no doubt she'll be glad to unburden herself to a sympathetic ear."

I did not reply at once, but decided to appear thoughtful: I gazed out the window for some moments as if deeply troubled.

"But surely there is no need to despair," I said at length. "Perhaps I can help you?"

"Help, good lady?" he asked, in make-believe bewilderment.

"Surely, if your fortunes improve, you would not find it necessary to leave England, and so, your conscience could be at rest with its secret."

"You are a most perceptive young woman, Mademoiselle de Riocour."

"Mr. Shark, I would be a fool not to seize an opportunity when it is, as you say, 'at hand.' " Make this believable, Suzanne, I thought. "My father is long since dead in France. My mother and I are strangers. I must rely upon myself, and myself alone, to create some kind of future security, and I do not mean teaching in a school or working for a living. No, Mr. Shark, I have greater ambitions." I looked at him and clenched my jaw and narrowed my eyes to correspond with his.

"What amount of money would keep you in England?" I asked, trying to keep all emotion out of my voice.

"I should think five thousand pounds," he replied. A trickle of spittle found its way from the corner of his mouth.

"Again as much as you were originally paid?" I asked. "I suppose my stepfather refuses to 'help you' any further? Was that the occasion of our first meeting? He is not afraid of your telling all? But, never mind, it will be worth it to me. Where can I reach you with the money? In London? I will have to sell some jewels, which may take time." I hoped I sounded convincingly calculating.

He drew a dirty card from his coat pocket and held it out to me. "The address is written on the back. I shall entertain you there with the greatest of pleasure within the month."

"Providing that you agree to give me, at that time, the original page from the marriage register," I said.

"But of course, mademoiselle. That is understood."

"Within the month, then," I agreed.

After driving along in silence for a while, I asked, "Your man does not speak?"

"Alas, no. An affliction from birth," he replied. "A devoted servant—um—of long standing."

"He has devoted a great deal of his time to spying upon me. I wonder that you could spare him to so great an extent."

"We have been concerned about your new environment and whether it would be—um—compatible."

"Surely you must have been certain of that by Monday evening."

"Monday evening?" Mr. Shark asked, still gazing out of his window.

"Yes. What did he expect to see at Warton Hall on Monday evening?"

"You must be mistaken. He was in London with me on Monday evening. It was someone else you saw. Why do you ask?"

"Mere curiosity. He has followed me so often that it is quite natural I should imagine I saw him," I said. "Ah, here we are passing the abbey. I suggest you drive to the rear of the stable block at the Hall, and I shall get out there. Tell your driver to take the left fork in the road when we come in sight of the stables. There is no need for my stepfather to know about our meeting."

"Quite so, mademoiselle," he said.

We did not speak again, even when I had opened the door and stepped out of the carriage. And when I

310

stood on the ground, the brougham began to move at once, turning around quietly on the grass. It rolled away and vanished in the direction we had come from.

# ⚔ Chapter Twenty-one ⚔

THE MIST HAD THICKENED into fog, and the fog had brought darkness with it long before its usual hour. I watched the dense mist swallow up Mr. Shark's carriage, and then I turned toward the house. Lamps had been lit in the summer parlor, the drawing room, the dining room, and all the rooms on the ground floor of the north front. Each distant window wore a gauzy, yellow halo—the only color in the gloomy, gray world before me. There in the dining room, Apsley and the footmen are arranging the table for dinner, I thought. How comforting it seems, somehow, to know that they are going about that ordinary task. Yet somewhere near, perhaps in that very house, someone waits to take my life.

I had felt safe from him in Mr. Shark's carriage, but now, alone in the gardens, I was frightened. Did the murderer wait for me behind that hedge or behind the rhododendron? I caught up my skirts and ran as fast as I could past the rhododendron to the cobbled lane and down it toward the kitchen-yard door. Twice I stopped running and walked a bit and then ran on again. With each step, the damp bottoms of my petticoats and skirt brushed against my ankles. My cloak was damp, too. My hands were moist from hugging myself as I ran.

It seemed to take forever to reach the house, but finally I brushed by Benjamin's wagon and bolted down the steps to the landing before the kitchen-yard door. I stopped to listen. Horses' hoofs pounded on the turf beyond the hedge, and then a voice cried, ". . . from where they saw her last." It was Mark Lawson's voice, and it set me in motion. I opened the door at once, stepped inside, shut it quietly behind me, and rested my back against it to catch my breath and think.

"First I must find Clair," I thought. But where would she be? Would she be waiting for me in my room, in the entrance hall, or in her own room? I couldn't go wandering about alone looking in all those places for her. Instead, the passage in front of me beckoned, and I crept silently down it. It led to the servants' hall where the spiral stair ascended to Mrs. Danley's rooms.

The servants' hall was empty—their supper was not until well after nine. A clatter of activity came from the kitchens beyond, but I didn't see a soul as I dashed across the room, around the end of the long dining table with its perpetual between-meal plate of bread and cheese, and up the stair to Mrs. Danley's sitting room. I knocked softly on her door, but there was no answer. Hesitating a moment, I opened it and stepped into the room.

It was almost dark: no lamp had been lit, but a fire burned low in the grate, casting an orange glow. The room was chilly in spite of the fire, so I did not remove my cloak. I sank into the chair by the fireside and pulled my cloak more closely about me.

I will be safe here, I thought, if I don't light a lamp. The table has been set, and I don't think anyone except Mrs. Danley will come in. She can summon Clair for me when she does. But why isn't she here now? There is nothing for her to see to at this hour.

"I will just have to wait and see," I thought aloud.

Though I sat quietly waiting for Mrs. Danley, my mind would not rest. Why? Why? I wondered. If I could only stop asking myself *why*. Why does someone want to harm me? My hand went involuntarily to the bruises on my throat, and I shivered. I mustn't catch a chill, I thought. This caused me to get up and throw a shovelful of coal, as quietly as I could, on the fire. The flames flared up, licking the new coals. I drew a little stool to the fire, sat down, and gazed into the flames.

"Why? Why?" I asked them.

Why doesn't Mrs. Danley come? I thought. I have spent half the day waiting, it seems. And someone else, nearby, is also waiting—waiting for another chance to take my life. It was someone who knows horses who tampered with my saddle. Mark Lawson was in the cavalry, and if anyone knows about horses, he does. He followed me that day to watch Thunder throw me. And it was someone connected with the army who would have had that gold cord. Mark Lawson was an officer in the army and wore that very cord on a uniform, I am sure of it. It had to be either Mark Lawson or the scar-faced man who tried to strangle me, but it couldn't have been Mr. Shark's man—he was in London on Monday night. So my stepfather couldn't have seen him from the window. Then was all that searching on horseback a pretense—a pretense to set Mark Lawson loose alone in the house to strangle me? If that was the case, my stepfather had helped him in this attempt to kill me. But that is absurd. Why should my stepfather want me dead? I am useful to him. I have fulfilled his plans: we have been accepted—welcomed—into society. My dowry and I can bring him social contacts all over England. I am no threat to him in any way. How could I be? Unless. . . .

At that moment I remembered that Mr. Shark had called my stepfather *Fitz*. They must have been old friends to have been on such familiar terms, and they must have worked together for some time to create all those forgeries for the trial. If so, my stepfather must have seen Scarface at least once, and probably many times, and must know who he was.

Then my stepfather must have known it was Scarface who broke into my room from the description Mrs. Danley gave him, and from that, he must have realized that I had some connection with Martin Shark. But even if he thought Mr. Shark and I were working together—even if he thought I knew about the forged papers—there would be no reason for him to think I would expose his hoax. Would I be likely to expose my stepfather as an impostor and thereby throw away wealth, position, a good marriage, my whole future? He would hardly think so. No, and he certainly wouldn't hire Mark Lawson to kill me: at worst, he would demand to know what Martin Shark and I were doing together.

But my thoughts were interrupted by footsteps and the door to the ground-floor corridor opening. Then Mrs. Danley stepped into the room. She gasped when she saw me.

"Miss de Riocour!" she cried. "How did you get here? We have been so worried about you." She closed the door and held it by the handle. "Go!" she whispered. "You must go! Go away from Warton Hall. Go anywhere, but leave. Go now—tonight! He's—there's danger—terrible danger."

She ran across the room to me, and knelt on the floor in front me, taking hold of my arm with both her hands and shaking it. "He's going to kill you," she said. "He's going to kill you *tonight!* He told me so." Then she burst into tears and covered her face with her hands. "God! Oh, my dear God," she wailed, "it's all my fault. It's all my fault."

"Mrs. Danley!" I said, reaching down and taking a firm hold of her shoulders. "Who?"

"If I hadn't agreed to do it—oh, God, why did I do it? If I hadn't, you would still be safe at school."

"Mrs. Danley, get up!" I cried. I stood and tried to

lift her dead weight into a chair. "Come sit here and try to control yourself." But I couldn't lift her. "You must help me. I need you, and you can't help me if you go on like this. Pull yourself together. *Please!*"

She looked up at me, pulled herself to her feet, and stumbled to a chair.

"If I hadn't lied—if I hadn't helped him—you would still be safe at school," she murmured. "It was wrong, and I knew it, and now we are paying for it. You have got to get away from here."

She twisted her handkerchief into a wad. Her eyes glazed with fright, and she tried to choke in the sobs that rocked her silently back and forth.

Brandy, I thought, and I rushed to the cupboard. But I needed a light to see what I was doing. Would it be safe to light a lamp? It would be, if only I could lock the door. I glanced at it again, but even before I did so, I knew there was no key. Nevertheless, I had to take care of Mrs. Danley, so I pulled the curtains across the window and then looked about for matches. Where? On the mantel? Yes, they were there. I lit the lamp on the table next to Mrs. Danley's chair, went back to the cupboard, and poured brandy into a glass.

"Drink this," I said, handing it to her. Then I sat down on the edge of the chair opposite her and said, "Now try to be calm and tell me what happened."

"It's all my fault," she said, after she had sipped her brandy. "Fitzjames isn't an earl. I lied in a court of law for him and helped him get the title. I didn't mean any harm, and Fitzjames said that I could stay right here and go on as if nothing had happened. 'You're happy here, aren't you?' he says. 'This is your whole life, isn't it? It's what you have worked your whole life for—being head of everything at Warton Hall,' he says. 'Well, you can go on just as if nothing had happened. All you have to do is be in London for a day and say what I tell you to say to the court.' And then he threatened me. He said horrible things would happen to me. And, in the end, I did it. I didn't mean any harm. Why, I wouldn't harm a hair on your head, my *dear* child," she sobbed. The tear paths on her cheeks glistened in the lamplight.

"I know all about that, now," I said. "I know you didn't mean any harm. Of course you didn't. I understand, Mrs. Danley. *I understand!* Please try to collect yourself. Now, tell me what happened."

"I was sitting here doing my mending," she began, "when I hear Clair coming down the hall screaming, 'Your lordship, your lordship, she's been kidnapped. She's been taken away.' And then Clair begins banging on Fitzjames's door. His office door, that is—it's the room next door, you know. So I drop my mending and rush out just as Fitzjames opens his office door and lets us in. Clair says that a man stopped your carriage and you went off with him.

"Your stepfather tells Clair to describe the man. She says the man on the horse had a scar on his face, and the man in the carriage was fat. And then Fitzjames says he knows who it is, that he will take care of it. He tells Clair to get out, get out of his office, and he slams the door shut after the poor thing.

"So I says to him, 'You have to do something. You have got to find her!'" she continued, as if acting it all out would somehow relieve her hysteria. "And he says, 'I will do something. *Tonight,* I will do something. Do you know who she is?' he screams. 'Do you know who her father was?'" She paused dramatically, looking at me, wide-eyed.

"Who?" I whispered.

"'John Osborne!' he screams at me. 'John Osborne! Do you know who John Osborne was?' he screams. 'He was the seventh earl's brother. And do you know what that makes her? That makes her the natural next of kin. Warton Hall is hers. The estates are hers. But it's mine, and it's going to stay mine.' I never saw him that crazed. I thought he would fly to pieces, what with his little arm waving up and down like it does."

Mrs. Danley was calmer now: the brandy was doing its work.

"How could he know that?" I asked.

"That's what I says to him. 'How do you know she's the heir?' I ask. 'John Osborne only had a son, and he was lost in the war. He never had a daughter,' I says.

" 'John Osborne had a daughter by my wife,' he says. 'How do I know? She told me so,' he says, but he isn't screaming now. He says it deadly soft like. 'She told me so,' he says, 'at the ball. You wonder why I struck her? Everyone wonders why I struck her. I ask her who the father was, and she says John Osborne, and she says she's got letters to prove it. She made the one who can take it away from me, my own wife. I should kill the—' I won't say the word, my dear."

"Then he says, 'She goes riding with Shark.' I am sure the name was Shark, like the fish. 'What do you think she's up to with him? I knew as soon as you told me about the man with the scar. My little step-daughter is plotting to take it away from me, that is what she is doing. That is what they are both doing. But it's mine, and it will stay mine. I will get rid of her, don't you worry. I will get rid of her tonight. Tomorrow there won't *be* anyone to take it away from me.'

"Then he tells me to get out and to keep my mouth shut, that I have always done so and that I have got as much to lose as he has. That if they ever find out what I have done, I will go to prison for it.

"I have been watching for you ever since from the long gallery windows. Clair was there, and we watched together, and then it got dark and the fog—

"You have got to *go,* my dear. Go anywhere. Get out of this house. Go tonight! Go to London. Oh, my dear, what are we going to do?" She sat silently, then, staring at me.

Out of the corner of my eye, I thought I saw the door begin to swing open. I turned and saw that it *was* opening, slowly, without a sound. And then my stepfather stood in the open doorway.

"You have got to *go*," he mimicked. "You turn against your own flesh and blood. You betray me. I cannot trust you," he shrieked at Mrs. Danley.

"And you!" he said to me. His voice was suddenly muted, controlled, vicious. "So here you are. That is convenient. Did you enjoy your drive with Martin Shark?" With every other word or so, he took a half step toward me. "You think I do not know where you have been? You think I do not know what you have planned? You plan to expose me. Martin Shark will write a confession to the forgeries. He will disappear for a while. Then he will return after you have exposed me—after you have taken possession of this house and the estates. You will pay him. *How much will you pay him?*" he screamed at me, his control lost. But he had stopped moving. He stood an arm's length in front of me. *"How much will you pay him?"*

"No! Stop it!" I shouted back at him. "That is not true. Martin Shark demanded money from me, yes. He said if I didn't pay him five thousand pounds *he* would expose you and that my future would be ruined. He needs money and was trying to frighten me into giving it to him, that is all. He was just trying to frighten me. But he can't do anything to you or to me because you have the original marriage register page. As long as you have that, no one can expose you. That is the only proof there is that you are not the son of Matthew Osborne."

My stepfather looked at me for a moment in surprise. Then his eyes narrowed, and his stunted arm quivered, flashing a glimpse of an object inside the little sleeve of his coat. He carried a cudgel or billy concealed there, holding it in place with his grotesque, three-fingered hand.

"Yes, that is true," he said, with a crafty smile. "As long as I have the register page, I am safe. As long as I have the register page, no one will believe you. No one will believe Shark, either. No one will believe that my father's name was Jack Cobbe. As long as I have the register page, we can go on as before, eh?

"But, my dear, I do not have the register page," he whispered, and his right arm shot out and his hand gripped my wrist. "Did you think I would not discover it was gone? Where is it? What have you done with it?"

I tried to wrench myself free of him, but I could not: my wrist might as well have been embedded in a wall. It was a shock to find such enormous physical strength from this little man.

"I don't know what you are talking about," I cried.

"You stole it. You will tell me where it is, my dear." He punctuated the last two words with a twist of my arm that made me gasp with pain.

"Let her go!" Mrs. Danley screamed. She stood, then, and flung herself upon him, pummeling his head with her fists. "Let her go! Let her go!" And as my stepfather released me to fend off her blows, she cried, "Run, run! He's going to. . . ."

But I had already darted around the table and was flying out the door toward the little landing and the spiral stairs. As I reached them, I heard the sound of a blow behind me. My stepfather must have struck Mrs. Danley. The sound was like an overripe tomato falling on a stone floor.

It had all happened so quickly, and I was so frightened that I couldn't think. But somehow I scrambled down the stairs, finding fingerholds between the stones in the wall to keep from falling, and then dashed across the servants' hall to the long passage to the kitchen-yard door. I stumbled down it, feeling my way in the darkness. At last, I felt the door to the yard under my hands, found the knob, and pulled. The door opened to a night that was lighter than the passage: I could distinguish wet steps and the faint, misty shape of the hedge.

Cold, wet air slapped my face.

This brought me to my senses. "Mrs. Danley," I thought aloud, "I can't leave her." I turned at once and, in the darkness, found the stairway to the summer parlor. I slipped up it to the third step. But then I stopped to consider. How could I get back to Mrs. Danley's room? My stepfather will be after me. Just then I heard him plunging headlong down the passage, toward me. I flattened myself against the wall of the stairwell, and he shot past me and out the open door. I had no idea he could move so fast. I could hear his boots drumming on the stone steps as he ran up them to the yard.

Now! I thought, as I scrambled down the stairs, but at that moment a figure appeared, silhouetted against the distant light from the end of the passage. It bounded toward me. I shrank back from it into the cover of the stairwell, and then Mark Lawson hurtled past me and out the door into the night.

Who else would come running down the passage in pursuit of me? I wondered. Apsley? The footmen? I peered cautiously around the corner of the stairwell, but the passage was empty and silent.

I ran back to the servants' hall, greatly aided by the square of light ahead of me. My luck, however, had run out. Just as I was about to enter the room, a short, plump, gray-haired woman in a white dress and apron, came out of a passage on the other side of the room, ambled over to the table, took a piece of cheese, and began to nibble at it daintily, while she leaned against the table and looked dreamily around the room.

"Go away. Go away!" I willed her with all my mind, and then as if propelled by my thoughts, she turned and sailed majestically back down the corridor toward the kitchens.

As soon as she was out of sight, I raced across the servants' hall, up the spiral stairs to Mrs. Danley's door and slipped into the room. A draft blew the door shut behind me.

The room was deserted. It had not been disturbed except that the lamp now sat on the floor behind the dining table. But no—I had made a fatal error. It was not deserted. I suppressed a gasp as the pint-sized figure straightened up, silhouetted by the light of the lamp he held in his hand. He must have been stooping to examine something on the floor behind the table, and he now stood, his back to me, still staring at it. His concentration was so great that he had not heard me come into the room or the door close.

In that instant of panic, I knew that my stepfather would turn around and see me. I could feel, again, that viselike grip as he held my wrist and the pain as he twisted my arm.

Something must have told him I was there because he turned around and said, "She's dead, miss. I ain't never seen a dead person before."

"Monk!" I cried. "Oh, Monk!" My heart was pounding as I ran to him.

Before us, Mrs. Danley lay on her back on the floor looking up at us with staring, sightless eyes. Her mouth hung open in a silent scream. A deep, red cavity indented her skull at the hairline. Blood had trickled from her nose to the corner of her mouth and then to her chin. One arm reached out from under her at an impossible angle—he must have broken it before she died.

"I ain't never seen a dead person before," Monk repeated, still staring down in fascination at the figure on the floor.

"No," I said.

"His lordship or the colonel did it. They was here. I heard it."

"Where were you?"

"Under the table in the servants' hall."

"What were you doing there?"

"I followed you from the stables. I didn't want you to be left alone."

I found myself kneeling with my arms around the little boy. "Oh, Monk, how did you know? How did you know?" I began to cry.

"You'll have to get hold of yourself, miss," he said proudly, putting both of his hands on my shoulders. "We have to get you away from here. We have to find a way."

"I am all right. I am all right," I said.

I stood up, smoothed my dress, wandered over to the table, paused, and picked up a spoon. I must have felt that handling an everyday object would help calm my nerves. I mustn't panic, I thought. Mrs. Danley is dead, and I can't help her. But I don't want to die, too.

"I must get away from here," I thought aloud.

"That's what I just said." Monk looked across at me.

"We must get out of this room. Suppose they come back? If I could only get to Thunder," I said.

"From one killer to another," Monk replied.

"You know Thunder is not a killer, don't you, Monk? He threw me and had a perfect chance to stomp me to death, but he didn't."

"Yes, miss. I suppose so, miss—if you say so. Well, we'll have to get you on Thunder, then."

"How?" I asked. "My stepfather and Colonel Lawson are out there looking for me, and maybe Apsley and the footmen and everybody else as well. How do I know? I could never get to the stables, let alone saddle Thunder, and you couldn't saddle him either because you could never reach high enough."

"No, miss."

If I could ride Thunder to the railway station at Taunton, I thought, I could hide myself nearby and wait for the first train in the morning. Then I fingered my brooch. This would take care of me until I decided what to do.

"I'll pull you there," Monk said. "I'll pull you there in the wagon." He looked up at me with an expression of exaggerated cunning.

"Monk, this is no time—"

"I mean it, miss. It'll work. I help you into Benjamin's wagon. It's right outside the door like it always is. Then I cover you up with the sacking," he made a circular movement with his arm, "and pull you right through the enemy lines, see? They won't think anything of it."

I looked down at him in amazement. "Yes! Yes, Monk. Yes!" I said. But what about getting Thunder saddled?"

"John'll do that," he said. "You hide in the wagon covered up—no one will look for you there—and I'll run and get John and tell him you says to saddle Thunder. Then, while he does that, I'll run back and pull you to the stables, slow and easy, as if I got all the time in the world and don't care a thing."

"Yes," I replied.

"On second thought, I'm not sure, miss."

"Why not?"

"His lordship has Bourton saddled and ready to go, miss. He sent word by Henderson about five o'clock, and then he comes hisself about six o'clock to see that he's ready. He says he might need to chase the poacher or something, miss. So there Bourton stands, in his box, all saddled and ready to go."

"But I think Thunder can outrun Bourton. I know Bourton won the Grand National," I said, putting out my hand to silence Monk, "but that was two years ago, and he had been in training for it. I know Thunder, and anyway, I will have a head start. Let us do it, Monk. It is my only chance."

"I got two pounds. You can have it."

"Thank you. I will need it for the train fare, and I will pay you back, I promise. We must go! Someone may come in, or they may come back."

We left the room, stepped out onto the landing, and crept down the stairs. Monk went first and I followed, but only to a point where I could watch him descend the rest of the way to the servants' hall. At the bottom step, Monk held up his hand, signaling that someone was there and that I should wait. So I stood still—hardly daring to breathe.

"He, he, he. Oh, Monk!" a girl's voice cried. "Oh, you little terror. He, he. Ha, ha, ha. Monk! Stop that! Oh, look out. Go away! No! This way, Alice. Look out! You'll pay for this, 'tiger.' I pity the girl you take a fancy to. I'll tell Mrs. Danley, I will. You should be ashamed!" Then the voice, which had become more and more distant, was cut off by a door slamming shut.

In a moment, Monk reappeared and proudly motioned me to follow him as he tiptoed exaggeratedly toward the kitchen-yard passage. And in half a minute, we stood peeking out the open door into the yard. Then Monk stepped outside, again motioning me to remain behind, ran up the steps, stood beside Benjamin's wagon, looked about, and then beckoned me to follow. As I ran up the steps to him, he cupped his hands to make a foothold for me. I stepped on them, he hoisted me up, and I swung myself over the sides of the wagon and let myself down to the floor of it, pulling the sacking over me at the same time. After that, Monk must have climbed the side of the wagon to check on me because I felt him arrange my cover. Then I heard his footsteps as he moved away, and all was quiet.

It was dry in there under the burlap, but it was also stuffy and dusty, and I began to feel how uncomfortable it is to lie on bare boards. To make myself as inconspicuous as possible, I lay doubled up on my right side, with only a small space between my knees and my chest, my arms bent with both fists under my chin.

This is foolish, I thought, as I lay there. I should never have paid any attention to Monk. He is only a child. What does he know about danger? Why, this is only a game to him. It will never work, I know it.

Lying in the darkness, completely covered up, I could tell what was happening only by sounds—each one seemed very loud and very important. Each drop of moisture falling on a paving stone, each distant rustle of the hedge or a bush, each footstep might help to answer the question: would I get out of this alive?

So I listened. I heard a birdcall from quite near. It called again—a strange cry, too loud and, somehow, too strong for a bird. No, it wasn't a bird: it was a man imitating a bird. It sounded for the third time, and then all was still.

Then without warning, a voice whispered, "Suzanne! Suzanne! I won't hurt you." The voice came nearer. I heard a brushing and snapping of branches and then four footsteps on the paving stones in front of me. Silence. "Suzanne, where are you? Suzanne? Answer me. I won't hurt you."

I hardly breathed.

But I listened intently. I heard the footsteps recede toward the stables. Then silence. Mark Lawson had stopped, or was it that he was no longer walking on the stones? Was he standing there looking back at the wagon? I wondered.

I heard horses approaching at a walk, probably on the other side of the hedge. They stopped, and two voices spoke softly to each other, but I couldn't distinguish enough to guess whose voices they might be.

Lying not very far away from them, out in the open, I felt terribly vulnerable. Especially since I couldn't see if danger approached. My ribs and head were beginning to ache from lying on the hard, wooden floor.

Then my heart lurched. Something heavy landed on my left shoulder and walked down my arm and crossed to my hip and then slipped silently down into the valley between my knees and chest. It began to paw the sacking. It pawed and purred and pawed and purred and then, paying no attention to a couple of swift jabs from my elbow, flung itself down and with little movements curled itself into a ball. The purring soon stopped; perhaps it slept.

For a long time after that, I heard nothing except occasional splashes as drops of moisture struck the cobbles. Between them, the silence sounded heavy and loud, like the constant droning of some enormous phantom insect. It continued. The cat did not move. Monk did not return.

I sensed rather than heard stealthy footsteps, and I held my breath. Was that breathing? Yes, someone was breathing. And then I felt the side of the wagon tremble for an instant. Someone leaned against it— only the inch-thick wooden siding separated us.

He would certainly look into the wagon.

His breathing continued, but I did not feel him move again. It was the cat that attracted his attention. It moved—just a quiver at first, and then it must have sat up or stood or perhaps stretched. I heard a low grunt. The side of the wagon shook as he rubbed hard against it, and I felt the cat hurled against my leg to the sound of a blow. It screamed like a tortured baby and leapt to my foot and then away, crying as it went.

For a moment the breathing continued louder than before, and then a voice said, "So there you are." It was my stepfather. "Did you think I would not find you? Did you think you could get away from me?"

I could not move or breathe, let alone answer him: I was too terrified. I knew that it was all over, but I was too frightened to get up, and somehow there seemed no point in doing so. He was going to kill me.

"Come here," he ordered.

"Sir?" a girl's voice answered.

"Ah," my stepfather groaned.

If an actor could put that intense a feeling of disappointment into one word, his fortune would be made.

"What is your name?" my stepfather demanded.

"Nelly Tettle, my lord. I wasn't going nowhere, my lord. I just come back from the farm where I seen my old mum. I wasn't doing nothing wrong, my lord."

"Go into the house!" my stepfather shouted at the poor girl. "Tell Apsley I want him here. Tell him to bring the footmen. Tell him to come at once. Do you understand?"

"Yes, my lord."

"Well, go. Go fast. *Now!*"

I heard her run down the steps to the kitchen-yard door, and then my stepfather began to pace up and down. His footsteps would become soft, and then he would return to the wagon with a loud clatter. He was making no attempt to be quiet any longer.

". . . find her. Just let me find her," I heard him whisper.

When my stepfather was some distance away, the wagon began to move. I heard my stepfather's footsteps just before the wagon's metal-rimmed wheels ground on the stones of the lane, but I had not heard Monk approach or lift the wagon handle. In a moment of panic, I thought that it might not be Monk. It might be someone else.

"You," my stepfather cried. I heard him run toward me. "You! What are you *doing?*"

"Taking the wagon, my lord," Monk replied.

"Taking the wagon? Where? Why?"

"It's Wednesday night, my lord," Monk said.

"Well, what of it?"

"It's the night of the servants' dance, my lord."

"What has that to do with the wagon? Why are you taking the wagon? Answer me!"

"I'm taking the wagon to the farm, my lord, for old Benjamin. He wants to bring his missus to the dance, and old Mrs. Twiddle can't walk a step, my lord; so he brings her in the wagon and takes her back in it every Wednesday night so she can watch the dancing."

"All right, all right, *all right!* Go. Go!" My stepfather screamed.

That was superb, Monk, I thought, as we began to move again. What a wonderful little boy you are. You were right—this will work. It will work after all. Now, all I have to do is mount Thunder and ride away. And I shall never look back.

"Tiger," my stepfather shouted at us from behind. "Stop. *Stop!*"

We stopped moving.

"Yes, my lord?" Monk asked.

My stepfather ran toward us and stopped beside the wagon. "Have you seen Miss de Riocour?"

"No, my lord," Monk replied.

"If you do, come and tell me where. Do you understand?"

"Yes, my lord," Monk said.

We began to roll forward again after that, and in four minutes we arrived at the rear entrance to the stable yard.

Then Monk pulled the sacking aside. "It's all right. We're here, and you can come down now, miss."

# ✥ Chapter Twenty-two ✥

"WHERE IS THUNDER?" I asked Monk, as he helped me down from the wagon. "We must hurry. I will need every minute's start I can get. My stepfather is sure to hear me ride out and come after me."

"In his box, miss. John wouldn't saddle him," Monk said.

"Wouldn't saddle him? Why?"

"Too soon after the nails in his back, miss. He didn't say so, but that's why, miss. I know John. Maybe you could take Queen Bess—she's a fast one. At any rate you better talk to John."

"You knew about the nails?" I asked.

"I heard you and John talking through the wall from the feed room yesterday."

"So it was you. Yes! Where *is* John? I certainly do want to talk to him."

I was furious at having gotten this far, only to be thwarted by John. If he had saddled Thunder, as I had ordered, I could be away from here in a moment, I thought. Now, I can go nowhere, and my stepfather and the servants are searching the gardens between the stables and the house now. They will certainly search the buildings here, and soon.

"John's sitting on the bench by the saddle room door, smoking his pipe. You can just see him from here," Monk replied, pointing diagonally across the yard. "See him, miss? I'll just push the wagon in here out of sight—"

I did not wait to hear the rest of what Monk said, but strode across the pebbled yard toward John. He rose and took the pipe out of his mouth as I approached him.

"You refuse to saddle Thunder?" I demanded.

"Yes, miss," he said.

"May I know why?"

"He's not fit, miss."

As I looked into John's obstinate face, my anger vanished, spent, leaving behind despair. I could not fight this man; it was the wrong way to handle him. And I could not fight my stepfather with only a small boy to help me. I couldn't fight at all, any more. So I turned from John and looked out into the foggy night, and my tears blurred the surroundings into splashes of light and darkness.

"You said you would help me. You said I could count on you." I whispered.

"And you can," John replied. "I'll take you to your stepfather. You'll be safe with him."

"No!"

"You've been listening to too many wild tales from that one." He pointed to Monk, who by then was standing by my side. "Why, if he had his way, American Indians would be coming through the gateway ready to take our scalps off our heads."

"My stepfather wants to kill me, John," I said, turning back to him.

"That's what this young one was telling me a while ago. Now, miss, you know that's not so—"

"Listen to me, John," I interrupted. I spoke urgently now. "Mrs. Danley is dead. I was in her room when my stepfather came in. She was alive then. My stepfather carried a small metal club. I ran out the door, and as I left, I heard him strike her. I returned as quickly as I could, but by the time I got back, she was dead. Her head has been smashed in. My stepfather did it, and he hired Colonel Lawson to put the nails in my saddle and to strangle me. I know it is unbelievable, but it is *true*, John—I swear it. My stepfather is not an Osborne at all—he is an impostor. I must get away from him. I must get away from Warton Hill. Saddle Thunder for me, John, and quickly, please."

"I don't believe it," he said.

"It's true," cried Monk. "I saw her laying there dead, like I was telling you."

"John," I said, putting my hand on his arm, "if you deliver me to my stepfather and find that I am dead in the morning, you will wish you had saddled Thunder for me. Is it worth taking the *chance?*"

"But we don't know how Thunder will behave," John replied. "He's not had a saddle on him since that day, and he's not nearly healed. Queen Bess—"

Men shouted to each other from the direction of the house.

"Do you hear that?" I cried. "He has Joseph and the footmen and I don't know who else, searching for me. They will be here soon. Queen Bess couldn't outrun Bourton, but I think Thunder could. Please, John, and hurry."

"Monk, come with me and bring out the saddle," John ordered. "I'll get the bridle and then bring out Thunder." He spoke softly, decisively, now that he had made up his mind.

He hurried into the saddle room with Monk at his heels, and it seemed only a moment until he emerged from the stable leading Thunder. Monk staggered toward us, lugging the saddle. I held Thunder while John saddled him.

"Beautiful Thunder," I whispered. "Help me now, beautiful fellow. It is all right, Thunder. It is all right."

I crooned to him and stroked his neck. He was nervous, cautious. His ears pricked, the muscles of his neck tensed, and his eyes rolled warily. John put a pad on him. I held my breath as John lowered the saddle gently onto Thunder's back. "Easy Thunder, easy boy." It was all right: Thunder didn't seem to mind the saddle at all, though it might be quite another matter when my weight was added to it. We would have to take that chance.

But something moved under the lamp at the rear entrance to the yard. When I turned to look, however, it was gone. Had it been my imagination?

Would John never get the girth buckled?

"Stop! Stop her. Don't let her get away." It was my stepfather.

He had seen me and was flying toward us. His little arm flapped, his legs moved in a blur, and his feet hardly seemed to touch the ground.

Calmly, John ran his hand down the bottom of Thunder's belly, testing the girth, and then he nodded to me.

My stepfather was almost upon us.

John cupped his hands. I stepped on them, he lifted me into the saddle, and I flicked an adjustment to the stirrup.

"Stop!" my stepfather shrieked. He lunged at us and grabbed at Thunder's reins.

But he missed them because, at that moment, the startled animal reared. Then Thunder came crashing down with a scream upon the spot where my stepfather had stood. He had jumped aside just in time, but, in doing so, had lost his balance and fallen to the ground.

Before he could get up, we were off at a trot.

"Here," shouted Monk, running toward us from one of the buildings and waving something in the air.

I reached down and took the notes from Monk's hand as we sped past him. Then we shot out of the rear gateway, scattering a group of men as we passed through them. Titus was one of them. He called something, but I could not hear what it was.

A little farther on, Mark Lawson stood in our path

with his arms flung apart, but he jumped aside when we did not slacken our pace.

We came to the Abbey Road. And suddenly I could see all about me. The fog was gone! A breeze had come up from the sea and blown it away.

Now that we were in the clear air, I urged Thunder into a canter and then into a full gallop. He had been edgy at first, but now he seemed to be enjoying his ride.

A million stars lit our way, and we were free.

We galloped down the road toward the abbey, but though I looked for the ruins, I could not see them. It was a moment before I realized what had happened: the road and the meadow on either side of us ended in an opaque wall of fog that hid the buildings from view.

Damn the fog, I thought. I should have known the air might not be clear all the way. The breeze had blown the fog into long swaths, leaving clear spaces between the swaths. I had seen fog like this many times on the Normandy coast where Nana and I had sometimes spent our summers when I was a child.

There was no telling how wide this band of fog ahead of us would be. It might be a hundred yards or it might be a mile wide. There might be another valley of clear air beyond and there might not be.

I glanced back across the stretch of clear air that we rode through, as if that would, somehow, help me to forecast what lay ahead. Behind me, Warton Hall, the stable block, and the woods lay hidden behind their fog curtain. But there, passing through folds where the fog swept the ground, rode a lone horse and rider. It was my stepfather on Bourton. As soon as he was in the clear air, he whipped Bourton into a fast gallop. I have never seen a man and beast fly through space so fast. I was their target.

Terror folded its icy wings about me.

"Faster, Thunder! Faster!" I urged, and we flung ourselves into the fog wall ahead and blessed it for hiding us.

After the clear, starlit air outside, the mist inside the fog bank pressed heavily down upon us, and it was much darker. If one could ride through a black pearl, I thought it would be like this. It was impossible to see more than a few feet in any direction, so I slowed Thunder to a trot. For a short distance, we were able to see the phantom shapes of bushes and small trees growing on either side of the road, marking the way. But soon only short-cropped grass grew there, and it was lost in the mist. So we slowed to a walk, straining our eyes to stay on the road.

As we groped our way, I wondered how long it had been after I had ridden out of the stable yard before my stepfather had left it. How long would it have taken him to get up from the ground, run to Bourton's box, open the door, jump on his back, and ride out after me? He must have done it in two minutes—three at the most. I had a possible lead, then, of three minutes. Unfortunately, however, time was not distance.

How far behind me was he now? I brought Thunder to a halt and listened. Bourton's hoofs pounded on the road at full gallop. Then I heard Bourton slow to a trot and I knew they were entering the fog bank with me. They had had a few seconds more light than I had had, though, since the fog was moving in my direction.

We dared not pause for more than a moment. We began walking again almost at once. I could not see far enough ahead to go faster. To do so would be to risk losing the road and becoming lost in the fields and woods. That would be madness. If only I could find the ruins, I thought, I might hide from him there, but I couldn't see them. It was all I could do to keep us on the narrow strip of road that vanished a few feet ahead of us in the fog.

Then, out of the fog just ahead of us, the fork in the road appeared. Straight ahead the road led to Fawsley and Taunton, to the left to Wattle. I knew, then, exactly where the abbey ruins lay even though I couldn't see them. Instantly, Thunder and I stepped off the road and began walking softly, blindly in the direction of the ruined church, and in a moment the wall of it loomed before us, and we stopped to listen.

I heard my stepfather riding down the road. He was just opposite me. Only that narrow strip of grass separated us, and he was riding at a slow trot. How could he go so fast in the fog and still see the road? How close, how terribly close he was. I had gotten off the road just in time.

But what if the fog should lift? I wouldn't think about that. It was still as thick as ever: my stepfather was only ten yards away, but I couldn't see him. By then, he had seen the Wattle fork and had passed on. He knew the Wattle Road would be a cul-de-sac and that I would not go that way. He was leaving me behind. I breathed deeply with relief and reached forward and stroked Thunder's neck.

"Good boy," I whispered.

But then I sensed that something was wrong, and I knew at once what it was—there was no sound. My stepfather had stopped. He was listening. I held Thunder still, held my breath, and listened, too.

Thunder was listening also, and then as if feeling the tension, he laid back his ears, tossed his head, and lurched backward a step. I felt the reins to quiet him but he was restless. Then my heart stopped: he pawed the turf, threw back his head, and whinnied.

In the silence his cry was deafening.

My stepfather knew we were here now, yet he remained motionless. I would have heard Bourton's footsteps if he had begun to walk toward us.

Then I realized why he had not moved: horses were approaching. They rode down the Abbey Road toward us from the direction of the Hall. Mark Lawson and someone else from the stables, no doubt, were coming to help search for me.

I stroked Thunder's neck to quiet him and listened to them approach. They came nearer. They rode abreast of me. Soon they would halt, and I would hear whispered directions from my stepfather. Or would he make no attempt at secrecy, and send them upon me, shouting his orders? I could not go fast enough in this fog to get away from him, and I would not be able to hide indefinitely from three people, even in these ruins.

But the riders did not stop. They continued down the road toward Fawsley: the sound of their horses' hoofs grew softer and softer, and then I couldn't hear them at all. My stepfather hadn't intercepted them. Instead, he must have slipped off the road and let them pass him by. He didn't want their help. Why not? And why did he now remain still?

The silence lasted for only a moment: then Bourton began walking. I heard the clip-clop as he retraced his steps to the Wattle Road, and then the relentless soft thuds on the grass as he walked toward me.

Behind me gaped the doorway to the transept of the ruined church. As quickly and as quietly as I could, I walked Thunder through it into the church and backed him against the wall just to the right of the doorway, where I could look out to see if my stepfather passed by.

I felt the reins, held my breath, and listened. He was coming. The sound of Bourton's footsteps grew louder. He was just on the other side of the wall from me.

Then I saw Bourton's head, then his neck, and then the whole misty-black silhouette of horse and rider. My stepfather strained forward—his mouth open, his eyes staring into the darkness ahead. They passed the

337

doorway within three yards of me and slowly disappeared into the mist.

But then again he stopped. He was listening.

I waited.

Shortly Bourton began to walk on. I heard his footsteps in the grass. Just a moment more and they would be—

Suddenly, to my horror, I found myself looking into my stepfather's face. He had turned Bourton around and retraced his steps. There he sat, staring directly into my eyes. His body strained toward me, his little arm jerked up and down, thudding against his chest. He bared his teeth. He did not move.

Could he see me in the shade of the wall? I could not wait to find out: I had to move. I turned Thunder, and we bolted toward the nave.

I knew that if I could get to the nave, I could gallop down it and out the door at its end. The grassy floor was unobstructed, and the columns of the aisles on either side would guide me. Once in the open, I would gallop in the direction of the Abbey Road. If I could follow it at a gallop, I would. If not, I would at least get away from that monster.

Whether or not he had seen me before I moved, I shall never know: but as soon as I had done so, he leapt after me. Bourton's hoofs thundered on the turf behind me, and my stepfather let out a shout—a high, piercing cry of triumph. We fled from it, flying through the air, but after a moment I glanced over my shoulder to see that he was moving rapidly to overtake us on my left side. My heart sank when I saw the look of determination on his face. He was going to catch me—he had willed it so.

The column, I thought. I must find the last column of the aisle. It would indicate the beginning of the nave. Immediately, as if summoned, the column appeared out of the mist on my right, and I led my forehand around, swinging Thunder into an abrupt right turn. His shoes dug into the turf, and we angled away down the body of the church at a full gallop.

"Bitch," my stepfather screamed, as he skidded Bourton around and hurtled after me.

I heard his shouts above the pounding of hoofs. I strained my eyes to find the lighter square of the doorway at the end of the building. My stepfather was at our heels. He was almost upon us. There was the doorway! If only I could make it through before he caught up to us. I glanced to my left, and my blood froze. Bourton lunged forward, and my stepfather rode beside me—no more than two feet away. He raised his arm into the air, and shrieking, he struck me. The blow lashed my face like fire and threw me off balance. I let go of Thunder's reins, but my leg was firmly under the horn, and I managed to keep my seat. Thunder slowed. The little monster shot ahead of us and pivoted, forcing Thunder into a tight half turn, and then he sprang back to my right side, grabbed my arm near the shoulder, tore me out of the saddle, and flung me to the ground.

I had to get up. I had to get up from the ground, but my body wouldn't obey. If I could raise myself on one elbow. . . .

As I tried, they came at me with a deafening roar of hoofs, and then the hoofs fell silent. Bourton screamed, and the great horse reared high in the air above me.

I remember nothing more.

# ❧ Chapter Twenty-three ❧

WHEN I WOKE, I lay on a bed, and it was dark. I felt for the covers. There were none. I felt the buttons of my jacket instead. I was fully dressed. But though dressed, I was cold, and my head ached. Something pounded inside it, sending waves of pain and nausea through my body. I slid my fingers to my eyelids, hoping to ease the pain, and winced as I brushed my right cheek. My skin was stiff and dry and sore there, and as I explored gently, I found a sticky place in front of my right ear. Above that, my forehead was untouchable. And then I realized that my fingers were wet and slippery. I knew it was blood.

But where was I? The air in the room smelled musty and stale: it had not been aired. And it was pitch black, without the faintest suggestion of light. Perhaps there was a bedside table with a lamp on it. I reached out to see, but my hand struck the wall. It would be on the other side, then. But my hand struck a wall there, too. Walls abutted the bed on both sides of me. Then I reached up and touched the ceiling—only a few inches above my head. Surely the ceiling couldn't be that low, I thought. The walls and low ceiling, I discovered, were padded. This was a box that I was in—a large, cloth-lined box. I was in a—

"Oh, God!" I murmured. "No!"

I lay still, my eyes tightly closed, telling myself that it couldn't be real, that this was a thing that could not happen. I told myself that I lay in a loft or attic having a low ceiling. That was the explanation. It was all perfectly ordinary.

But I knew that I was rationalizing, and my hands began to feel all over the quilted sides and roof of the coffin. The lining was old and fell to powder at a touch, and the air quickly filled with dust from my explorations. But I continued, desperately trying to find something to disprove what I knew to be true. And as I became more and more frantic, I began to tremble and couldn't stop. Then I lost control of myself completely and clawed at the sides of my prison, tearing the lining to shreds and breaking my fingernails and burning my fingertips as I scraped them against the siding underneath. It is not possible to describe the terror.

I must have fainted. Whether I fainted once or several times as I lay there, I don't know. It was a time of panic and vivid dreams. I remember two of them perfectly: floating through endless tunnels where strange musical sounds echoed, and flying slowly through the night among a flock of languid white birds.

Later I regained consciousness, and my mind was reasonably clear. My head ached terribly; I was cold; my clothes were damp; and terror swept through me again. I came very close, in those minutes, to wanting to be dead—to wanting to be spared the torment and pain that I knew waited for me.

But then, something took control, and I knew that I had to get out of there. At least I had to try.

I tried to lift the lid of the coffin with my hands and arms and then with my shoulder, but I could not. I could feel the crack all around where it began: a breath of air blew on my fingertips from it. It was heartbreaking to know that the lid opened but that I could not make it do so. Would there be catches on the outside to hold it closed? I couldn't remember. But even if there were none, I was probably too weak to lift it, and my head hurt too badly to move very much.

Should I cry for help? Help from whom? From the caretaker! I was quite sure that I was in the mausoleum: the draft of air from the crack told me that this was probably so. Then the caretaker must come sometime. I could call. No, that would make me breathless and then the dust would make me choke, and I would use up what little strength I had left. But I had to signal somehow. I could make a noise. I could strike the side of the coffin. I scraped away the lining with my foot until I had exposed the wood underneath and began to tap it with my shoe. This will take little energy, I thought, and the thud will surely be heard outside. So I tapped slowly with my foot, conserving my strength, and fainted or slept and dreamed intermittently.

Sometimes, between fantasies, I was able to think. Now I knew what Mark Lawson had been doing in the mausoleum. He had been preparing this place for me. Who had originally lain here? Whose resting place had I usurped? Were there other intruders, like me, in the mausoleum? Were any still alive? Would anyone come?

I remember fingering the limp, broken roses still pinned to my scarf and whispering aloud, "For me, the Reaper didn't ride a carriage; he rode a horse. And I can smell the roses."

I have no idea how long I had lain there—how many terrible hours I had endured. But when I had almost given up hope, it happened. All of a sudden the coffin jerked, slid briefly, and then hinges shrieked. The roof above me was thrown open, and I stared into a blinding light.

"Thank you, God," I prayed silently.

But then the lantern was lowered, and I cried out in despair. I looked into the face of Mark Lawson, and I knew he had come to be sure that I was dead.

# ⟨⟨ Chapter Twenty-four ⟩⟩

I DREAMED that a kindly, white-haired man held me in his arms and gave me hot, sweet tea to drink. I dreamed that I lay in a fairy tale room; that my bed was draped in gossamer white muslin; that the walls were covered in white paper splashed with tiny red rosebuds; that directly across from the foot of my bed was a dormer with a pointed Gothic window in it; that outside, the roof was edged in white wooden lace; and that below it, centered in the window, the moon shone. But it was not the moon because it was daylight. It was the sun, a pale white disk glowing through a thin morning fog. It looked as though it had been cut from paper and pasted in the sky.

I slept.

"Who is that?" It was Clair's voice. "Get out! What do you think you are doing here? Rector! Rector!"

Someone ran upstairs. "What are you doing? How did you get into the house?" Mr. Ashley's voice demanded.

"I ain't doing no harm, sir. She can't be left alone. I'm staying right here and seeing that no one gets in there. No one's going to get to her if I'm here." It was Monk's voice.

"We will take good care of her. You had better go back to the Hall," said the rector.

"No, I'm staying here," Monk said.

"Let him stay!" I cried. "Let Monk stay!"

"All right, he will stay," Clair said. "Everything is all right. There is nothing to worry about now."

I turned my face toward her voice and saw her shut a door quietly and tiptoe quickly across the room to me. She poured something from a cozied pot into a cup.

"Can you take some of this?" she asked, lifting me up a bit. It was hot, sweet tea.

"It is so much nicer from you," I remember saying.

"There now," she said, "go to sleep. Just sleep, and I will be right here by you."

I closed my eyes and slept.

The paper sun had gone, but the rosebuds and the wooden lace outside the window were real. And so were the muslin hangings on the bed where I lay. Across the room from me, Clair sat in a chair before the Gothic window in a little dormer, her head turned away from me: she was gazing out of the window.

And as I looked about, I saw that a fire blazed in the fireplace, making the room very warm. No, I had never been in this room before. Clair and I were alone in it, and the door was shut.

"Is there any more tea?" I asked.

"Oh, you are awake. Yes, I just made some," Clair said. She got up, walked across the room to my bed, bent over me, and placed her fingers on my forehead for a moment. "No fever—that is good. Would you like to sit up? Here, let me help you."

She lifted me up, fluffed the pillows, and took two more from the bed beside me and placed them behind my back. I leaned back into them, gratefully. I felt weak, and my limbs felt heavy and tired. Then Clair wrapped a woolen shawl snugly around me and gave me my tea. The cup and saucer seemed to weigh a pound in my hand, but the tea was hot and delicious.

"I am at the rectory?" I asked.

"Yes. How do you feel?"

"I don't know. My head—it is sore." I tried to feel it but touched a bandage. My whole head was bandaged. I felt for my hair: it was still there. "How did I get here? I am so warm!"

"The doctor said you were to be kept warm. They have been heating bricks all night for your bed. We will just keep you comfortable—"

"You can't go in there. Miss de Riocour is not to be disturbed." It was Monk's voice.

"Monk?" I asked. I couldn't help smiling.

Then someone knocked on the door.

"Yes," Clair said, smiling back at me as she hurried toward the door. "Yes?" she asked, opening it a crack.

"Chief Constable Pritchard and Constable Williams. We'd like to speak to Miss de Riocour for a few minutes if she's awake."

"She's not to be disturbed," Monk declared.

"I am afraid Miss de Riocour is not in any condition to talk to anyone, constable," Clair said.

"It's important, miss, or I wouldn't ask."

"Clair, ask them to come in," I called. "I must talk to them. It is terribly important."

Two huge men entered the room, bowing their heads as they came through the low doorway. Clair closed the door behind them.

"Miss de Riocour?" asked the first man, who was slightly taller than the second.

"Yes," I answered.

"Chief Constable Pritchard, miss, and this is Constable Williams."

"My stepfather murdered Mrs. Danley at Warton Hall, constable, and he almost succeeded in killing me," I began. "He is dangerous and—"

"Excuse me, miss. All in good time, miss," Constable Pritchard interrupted. "I was told that you were not to be excited. Could we go a bit easy, like? Now, if we could sit down. Bring that chair here, constable, and you sit over there in that one. That's right."

"Would you pour me more tea, please, Clair," I said, as Constable Pritchard sat down in the chair beside my bed. "I think it would help steady me."

I sipped it while the constable studied me. He had taken a notebook and a pencil from his pocket, and now he flipped the pages of the little book until he found a clean one. I waited for him to begin.

"Lord Trevenbury is your stepfather, Miss de Riocour?" Constable Pritchard asked after a moment.

"Yes," I answered.

"Mrs. Danley was the housekeeper at Warton Hall?"

"Yes."

"You say your stepfather murdered her. When did this happen, miss?" he asked.

"On—Wednesday evening. What day is this?"

"It is Thursday, miss," Clair said.

"We'll hear from Miss de Riocour, if you don't mind," Constable Pritchard said to Clair. "We will save time that way."

"Last night, constable," I said.

"Would you tell me, please, everything you know about Mrs. Danley's death?"

I told him everything that had happened from the time Mrs. Danley had come into her room the day before until I returned and found her dead.

"You did not see your stepfather strike Mrs. Danley, then?" Constable Pritchard asked. It was clear that the chief constable would handle this. Constable Williams did not say a word.

"No, but I heard him do so," I replied.

"Would there have been time for anyone else to have entered the room and struck Mrs. Danley?" he asked.

"No, I am certain there would not have been."

"Now, you say that your stepfather attempted to murder you yesterday?"

"Yes."

"Had he made any attempts on your life before yesterday?"

"Have you been talking to other people about all this?" I asked.

"Naturally, but please let me ask the questions," he said, and he smiled.

I like him, I thought. "Of course," I replied. "My stepfather did not make any other attempts on my life, but he hired Colonel Lawson to kill me. Colonel Lawson made two attempts on my life."

"Will you tell me, please, everything you know about those two attempts on your life?"

I told him about the nails in the saddle, being thrown by Thunder, Mark Lawson's sudden appearance, the attempt to strangle me, and the cord.

"I am afraid Miss de Riocour cannot be subjected to any more of this, constable," Clair said when I had finished. "Miss de Riocour has been through a terrible ordeal and has suffered seriously from shock. She is very weak and should rest now."

"Thank you, Clair," I said, "but I can continue. The constable should know what has happened. I will sleep when we have finished."

"There was a fire the night before you were thrown from your horse," the constable asked. "Do you know anything about how that fire could have started?"

"No," I replied.

"His lordship set it," Monk called from the doorway. "I saw him do it."

"I'll talk to you later, young man," Constable Pritchard said. "Meanwhile, you will remain outside with the door closed, please." Then he turned to me. "Do you recognize this?" He handed me the piece of cord that was used to choke me.

"Where did you get—" I began, but then I thought better of asking. It was an effort for me to take the cord from him. "Yes, I recognize it. This is the cord that Colonel Lawson used in his attempt to strangle me. It is the kind of cord used for decoration on British army officers' uniforms. I recognize this particular length of cord because of the way the loop is tied in the end of of it." I gave it back to him.

"To whom did you show this length of cord after the attempt on your life?" he asked.

"Why, to no one, I think." I was surprised at the question. "The first time I really saw it was when Clair showed it to me the next morning. Clair told me where it came from, and just as Dorothy, the chambermaid, came in that morning, I asked Clair to put it in the box where I kept my jewelry and letters. It has not been taken out since."

"Miss Clair, did anyone beside Miss de Riocour and yourself see this cord between the time the attempt was made to strangle her and the time you put it in the box the following morning?"

"No, sir, I don't think so," Clair said. "As soon as I knelt to help Miss de Riocour in the corridor after she had been attacked, I removed the cord, which was still around her neck. I kept it. When we got her to her room, I slipped it under the couch where she was lying. It remained there until we had been left alone for the night, and she was asleep. I wanted to examine it at my leisure. Why do you ask?"

Constable Pritchard sat deep in thought for a few moments looking at the cord and fingering it. "Would you show us how the cord was arranged around her neck when you found her in the hall, please?" he asked, handing the cord to Clair.

Clair took the cord and fed one end of it through the loop in the other end to form a noose. Slipping the noose over her head, she pulled the end of the cord until it was snug around her neck. Then she removed it and handed it back to the constable.

"Thank you," he said. "Now, Miss de Riocour, can you answer a few more questions for me? Good! You

348

went riding with a heavy-set man in his carriage yesterday. Would you tell me about that, please?"

I told him about Martin Shark—how he had hired Patrick Meagher to murder the seventh earl and why. I told him about the forgeries, how my stepfather had used them to secure the inheritance, and my stepfather's real name and history. I related the entire conversation I had had with Martin Shark.

"I see," he said, falling into deep thought again. "Did you believe him? I don't suppose this Mr. Shark thought to bring any kind of proof of all this with him?" he asked, almost as if he were thinking aloud.

"Yes, as a matter of fact, he did. He showed me the original register page, which had been taken out of the marriage register of Berkley Church in London. He had it in his pocket. It showed the names of my stepfather's parents: Mary Danley and Jack Cobbe. Don't underestimate Martin Shark, constable. I am afraid he is a very clever man."

"Well, well, well," he said, looking out of the corner of his eye at Constable Williams. Then after a pause, he continued, "The housekeeper at Warton Hall was —ah—his lordship's aunt?"

"Yes," I answered.

"We are almost finished, Miss de Riocour," the constable said. "I'm sorry to tire you, but the murderer should be dealt with, if possible, at once. You understand that, I'm sure. Would you please tell me all you remember about what happened after you left Mrs. Danley's room last night?"

I told him about being pursued by my stepfather. I told him about hiding in the wagon, riding out on Thunder, and finally being caught in the abbey ruins, and regaining consciousness in the mausoleum.

"It is not necessary," he said, interrupting me, "to go into detail about that last part of your ordeal. That would be too painful. You remember seeing Colonel Lawson in the mausoleum?"

"I—the last thing I remember was seeing Colonel Lawson's face. I am sure he had come to be certain that I was dead."

"Just one more question. You claim your stepfather wanted you dead because he was afraid you and Mr. Shark were about to expose him. Was there any other reason?"

"Yes—"

"Don't be afraid. What you tell us will be held in strict confidence."

"You see, constable, my father was John Osborne, the late seventh earl of Trevenbury's brother. He and my mother—were never married. My stepfather knows this and is under the impression that I am the legal heir to the estates, there being no other living kindred. Of course this is a fallacy. I know that a natural child has no right of inheritance under English law."

"I *see!*" he replied. "Yes, ordinarily that is true, but when there is no other living kindred, a plea is presented to the Lords of the Treasury recommending that Her Majesty grant the property to the natural child. This is usually done—it is almost a certainty. One would need to furnish the proper proof of paternity, of course.

"Well! This clears things up considerably, I think." He stood and put the gold cord in his pocket. "Thank you, Miss de Riocour. You have been most helpful. I want you to be absolutely certain of one thing—you are perfectly safe here. Be assured of that, and I hope you will soon be fully recovered." He started for the door. "Come along Williams," he said.

"We'll have our little talk now, young man," I heard him say to Monk as Constable Williams closed the door behind them.

"How did I get to the rectory, Clair?" I asked, sinking down into the bed. "He said that I am perfectly safe here."

"I don't know, miss. . . ." Clair said.
But I don't remember any more. I was asleep.

A knock on the door woke me, and I turned my head to see it open slowly. I was frightened.

"How is everything?" It was Mr. Ashley. "I just wanted to be sure that our patient was comfortable." He walked over to my bedside. "Did I startle you? I *am* sorry. You realize that you are safe here and among friends? You have had a terrible fright and have suffered from shock and exposure, but you are well on your way to recovery and will be up and about, as good as new, in a day or two. Rest. All is well.

"I shan't stay and tire you now. We will have plenty of time to talk later. Mrs. Hobson is preparing a tray for you, Miss Clair, and will bring it up in a few minutes. Should our patient have something to eat, do you suppose?" he asked Clair.

"I think so, if she is hungry," Clair said, looking at me. "Perhaps some soup and a slice of toast?"

"That would be delicious," I said.

"So be it," said the rector. "I will see that it is done. Rest this afternoon, my dear, and we will talk later." He smiled down at me, laid his hand lightly on mine for an instant, and then went out of the room closing the door silently behind him.

"Mrs. Hobson has some luncheon for you in the kitchen," I heard him say to Monk. He said something more, but I couldn't hear what it was. Then I heard two pair of footsteps descend the stairs.

A moment later, horses trotted by outside the window.

"Who is that, can you see, Clair?" I asked.

"It is Chief Constable Pritchard, Constable Williams, and Colonel Lawson," Clair said. "Constable Pritchard is carrying a bundle wrapped in heavy paper. Colonel Lawson is riding between the other two." She turned from the window and came to sit in the chair that was still next to the bed, where Constable Williams had placed it. "They all looked very grim. I suppose they are taking Colonel Lawson to the jail. I am not surprised—why, he might have been in the house all morning, right here with us."

"Constable Pritchard said we are safe," I said, "and I believe him. I can't help but feel sorry for Mark Lawson, somehow. You know, I liked him very much at first." Memory tugged me back to that afternoon in the pagoda, but then I struck the feeling away.

"What happened to you after I got into Mr. Shark's carriage, Clair?" I asked. "What happened when you got back to the Hall yesterday? Were you worried about me? You were. I am so sorry to have upset you like that, but I had to talk to Martin Shark. I had to! And I was reasonably sure he would not harm me."

"There now, don't excite yourself, miss," Clair said. "Yes, I *was* worried. When we got back to the Hall, I went at once to his lordship and told him what had happened. I didn't know then that he wanted to harm you. Mrs. Danley was with me. He listened and then told me to get out of his office. He can be beastly rude when he is excited, as you know. Well, I decided to watch for you from the long gallery windows. In a little while, Mrs. Danley found me there, and we watched together. She had stayed behind with your stepfather after I left. Whatever they talked about left her very excited, but I could tell she didn't want to talk to me about it.

"At about six o'clock, Colonel Lawson and the rector came to ask your mother where you were. I heard them talking in the staircase hall and ran down the stairs and told them what had happened and then went back up to the long gallery to continue looking for you. Then I saw the rector and Colonel Lawson ride away toward Fawsley. After a while, when it was dark, Mrs. Danley left me, and I watched alone for about an hour. During that time, I saw Colonel Lawson return to the Hall, but I didn't see him leave it again.

"I was very worried and finally went down to Mrs. Danley's room to ask if there wasn't something we could do. When I got there, I found her lying on the floor—it was horrible."

"Yes," I said. "The dear, sweet soul. I can't believe she is dead. I would give anything in the world if she were still alive. I keep wondering what I could have done differently. We always do, after—but it doesn't do any good, does it?"

"I am sorry. Go on, Clair."

"Well, I ran to get Mr. Apsley, but I couldn't find him anywhere, nor any of the footmen, for that matter. It was positively weird. Finally, I found Dorothy and told her what had happened, and we went back to Mrs. Danley's room. Poor Dorothy. I should never have told her, but I needed to tell *somebody*. Eventually, we went back to the staircase hall, thinking that Mr. Apsley or Titus or somebody would be there soon, and there we found her ladyship wanting to know where everybody was.

"Just about then, we heard the men in Mrs. Danley's room, and we went to join them. Your mother came with us. Mr. Apsley and John and Monk were there when we arrived, and we all began talking at once. Monk was saying his lordship did it, but we weren't paying much attention to him. I wondered at the time how he could say a thing like that, and now *you* say his lordship tried to kill you. I simply can't believe it. Well, anyway, then John left to get Constable Williams—"

"Did you see my stepfather later last night?" I interrupted.

"The next time I saw him was about nine o'clock. He came down the grand staircase just as Colonel Lawson and the rector came into the house again.

Dorothy and I were sitting in the hall chamber, not knowing what to do——"

A knock on the door interrupted Clair, and then Mrs. Hobson entered the room carrying a tray.

"Here we are," she said. "My, you're looking better. Got yourself some color. White as a sheet you were when they brought you in last night—skin all dry and blood all over everything. A proper sight you were. We was up all night with you, but it was worth it just to see you come back to life like this." She set the tray on the bed. "There now, I'll be right back with yours, Miss Clair." And she vanished.

A dish of thick soup steamed, and thin slices of bread and butter lay on a plate next to a little pot of jam. Clair helped me to sit up, arranged the tray in my lap, and then poured my tea.

Mrs. Hobson brought Clair's tray, and then she left us, saying that there was a young wolf-boy in the kitchen eating her out of house and home and that she couldn't risk leaving him down there alone for a minute.

"Tell me what happened then, Clair," I asked when Mrs. Hobson had gone and Clair was settled in front of her luncheon. "Umm, this soup is ambrosia. Nothing ever tasted so good. Colonel Lawson and my stepfather?"

"His lordship and Colonel Lawson seemed to be having a terrible quarrel right there in the hall, but I couldn't hear what it was all about. Then Colonel Lawson turns and runs out of the house. The rector follows him, and I hear two horses riding off into the night.

"Then about nine-thirty, John arrived with Constable Williams. The constable went to see Mrs. Danley, and I understand he locked her body in her room and kept the keys. Then he questioned each of us alone in the hall chamber.

"I stayed up for hours, hoping you would come

home. Finally I went to my room and to bed, but I couldn't sleep. I was too frightened for you.

"Well, this morning, the rector's groom, Adam, came to the kitchen-yard door asking for me. He said that Mr. Ashley would like to see me in regard to you and that it was most urgent and confidential and could I come at once. I ran and got my shawl, without saying a word to anybody, and came straight away with him. The rector showed me up here and told me what the doctor said and asked if I would stay and take care of you. I was just so happy to see you—I was so worried last night."

"Thank you, Clair," I said. "Somehow I feel that everything will be all right now. I have the feeling that it is all out of my hands. Actually, it has been that way ever since I arrived here, hasn't it? I have been the center of a maelstrom: I have just stood still, and all these terrible things have been whirling around me, coming closer and closer. You know, so often it is not what *we* do, but what is done to us by people and circumstances.

"What will Chief Constable Pritchard do now? I wonder. I am so glad he came. We will simply have to wait and see, I suppose. And then when I am stronger —but that will have to wait.

"And Monk?" I asked. "What about Monk?"

"He appeared out of nowhere all of a sudden," Clair said. "He must have followed Adam and me this morning, and then you asked for him to stay. Do you remember?"

"Yes, vaguely," I answered. "Take the tray now, Clair, please. I don't know what it all adds up to, and I don't care. I am too tired. I think I will sleep a little more now."

So Clair helped me lie back comfortably, and in a moment I was asleep again.

At about the time in the late afternoon when one

wonders if it is too early to light a lamp, I heard a horse approach the rectory. I had slept all afternoon. Clair sat fast asleep in her chair—her chin rested on her chest, and her hands were folded in her lap. I hated to wake her, but her eyes opened at the sound of hoofs.

"Oh, I am so sorry," she said. "I must have dozed off. I wonder what time it is."

"You deserve a nap, Clair. You must be exhausted after not sleeping last night."

"How do you feel?" she asked.

"Oh, very much better, really much better—much stronger. I needed that sleep. Is there any tea left?"

"Yes. Here, let me help you, miss."

She walked across to me, and as she helped me to sit up, I heard footsteps on the stairs and then a knock at my door. It opened a few inches, and the rector peered into the room.

"Is she awake?" he asked softly. "Ah, yes. May we come in?" The door swung wide. "Lawson has just returned and has some extremely important news that he insists on telling us both as soon as possible."

Mr. Ashley entered the room and stood just inside the door. Mark Lawson stood behind him. I was frightened when I saw Mark. My ordeal of the night before had left my nerves more frayed than I realized. I pulled the covers up to my neck and stared at him. I couldn't move or speak.

The rector must have seen how frightened I was because he came over to the bedside and said, "Now don't be afraid, my dear. I am sorry to burst in on you like this, but I believe what Lawson has to tell us *is* important. He has assured me that you must hear it at the first possible moment, or I would have insisted that it wait until morning. Miss Clair is here, and so am I, and your little watchman is just outside the door. Lawson does not mean you any harm. He never has meant you any harm."

"I understand," I managed to say. "Yes, come in. Clair, please get a shawl for me, and will you light the lamp?"

Clair put her shawl around me while I watched Mark's shadowy figure walk quietly across the floor and sit in the chair beside my bed. I imagined him whispering through the fog, as he had the night before, "Suzanne, where are you? I won't hurt you." I shivered.

But when Clair had lit the lamp and I looked into Mark's face, I hardly recognized him. The sadness, the desperate, hopeless gloom had gone. His gray eyes sparkled warmly—the ice in them had melted—and he was smiling. There was joy and triumph there, and something almost of happiness. This was quite another Mark Lawson.

I was not afraid, then. "What is it, Mark?" I asked. "What is it you have to tell me?"

"I had better start at the beginning," he said, "and tell it to you just as it happened.

"After luncheon, today, Chief Constable Pritchard asked me to accompany him and Constable Williams to Warton Hall. He said that he had talked to Lord Trevenbury at length this morning, but that there were a few more questions that he would like to put to him and that he would be glad if I was there in case he needed to ask anything further of me.

"We arrived at the Hall," Mark continued, "shortly after two o'clock and were shown into the hall chamber where we waited a few minutes. Your stepfather and your mother were still at luncheon. They would see us, Apsley said, when they had finished.

"Very shortly, they arrived. Your mother sat in the chair next to the chimney piece, but your stepfather remained standing. He paced nervously back and forth, but he waited for Constable Pritchard to speak.

" 'Just a few more questions, my lord,' the constable said, 'if I may.'

" 'Certainly,' your stepfather replied.

"I will tell you the exact words as nearly as I can remember them," Mark said.

" 'Now, my lord,' said Constable Pritchard, 'you say that you saw Colonel Lawson, here, set fire to the hay barn on the'—he took his notebook out of his pocket and riffled through the pages until he had found what he was looking for—'night of Thursday, September the eleventh. And you allege that Colonel Lawson did this so as to distract attention away from himself while he hammered nails part of the way into Miss de Riocour's saddle. Is that correct?'

" 'Correct,' your stepfather said.

" 'But Colonel Lawson was at a dinner party that evening, all evening, at the rectory. There were five people present. The dinner party, I understand, was arranged at the last minute, without notice.

" 'Lady Trevenbury,' the chief constable asked your mother, 'do you have any idea who tried to strangle your daughter?'

" 'No,' she answered.

" 'Or what he might have used to do it with?' he asked.

" 'No.'

"Then the chief constable took a piece of gold cord from his pocket, and he turned to your stepfather and said, 'Now, Lord Trevenbury, you say that this is the length of cord that you claim Colonel Lawson used in his attempt to strangle your stepdaughter. You gave me this length of cord this morning. Would you mind telling me where you got it?'

" 'I found it in Suzanne's room,' your stepfather answered. 'It was in a box where she kept her jewels and letters. She stole some papers from me. I have been searching for them.'

" 'How do you know that this is the length of cord that was used, my lord?' Constable Pritchard asked.

" 'Because my daughter showed it to me. She told me about it.'

" 'When did she do this?'

" 'The night she was strangled.'

" 'Of course we shall have to verify that statement with Miss Clair, who was with your daughter all that evening after the attack,' the constable said.

" 'You think I am not telling the truth?' your stepfather shouted at Constable Pritchard.

" 'I am merely acquainting you with our procedure, my lord. To continue, you recognize the loop tied in the end of the cord?'

" 'Yes,' your stepfather answered.

" 'If the end of the cord was put through the loop in this fashion,'—the constable demonstrated as he spoke—'it would form a noose. Now, if the noose was slipped over a person's head and the end pulled, a person could be choked or strangled to death. This could be done with *one* arm and hand. Do you agree?'

"Your stepfather did not answer—he just glared at the constable. His little arm began to jerk up and down, and he tried to hold it still with his hand. He had stopped pacing and stood glowering at Constable Pritchard.

" 'Now, my lord,' the constable continued, 'yesterday afternoon Miss de Riocour rode off in a carriage with an extraordinarily fat man who was accompanied by a thin man with a scar on his face that stretched from his left eye to his mouth. Is that correct?'

" 'Correct,' your stepfather said.

" 'You say you have no idea who these men are?'

" 'Correct.'

" 'But *we* know who they are. The fat man's name is Martin Shark, and the other man is his servant and accomplice. We have word from the London police that he has been apprehended in connection with certain forgeries. Your name was mentioned in relation to some of Mr. Shark's activities. Isn't that strange?'

" 'Finally—Williams, hand me that package, please,' the constable said. He untied the string of the package he had brought with him and took a coat out of the paper wrapping. It had one regular size sleeve and one very small sleeve. The large sleeve and part of the front of the coat were covered with dry blood. 'This coat was found with Miss de Riocour's body. Do you have any idea to whom it belongs?'

"Your stepfather stared at the chief constable. He was stunned! Then he gathered himself together and said, 'This is a mistake! This is all a mistake. I have something to show you that will prove it. I will get it. It is in my office.'

"Before we knew what was happening, he had run out of the room in the direction of his office. The chief constable motioned Williams to go after him. We waited in silence for perhaps thirty seconds, and then we heard a pistol shot.

"We raced to your stepfather's office. He lay on the carpet with a bullet hole in his head. His desk drawer was open. The gun was still in his hand.

"Williams said that he had caught up with your father in the hallway outside his office and that your stepfather had asked him to stay outside, saying that he would only be a moment and then they would go back to the chief constable. Williams stayed outside.

"Your stepfather was dead of course," Mark concluded.

"I see—I can hardly believe it," I said. The pieces were rapidly falling together for me. And after I had thought a moment, I continued, "My stepfather could never have suffered the humiliation of losing his wealth and position and possibly facing trial and being hanged. He would not have been afraid of being hanged, but he could never have borne people watching. I am hardly surprised that he killed himself. In fact, I would have expected it.

"And you?" I asked, after another moment or two.

"This happened early in the afternoon, and now it is dark. What have you been doing since then?"

"I have been talking to my mother, and after that, I have been thinking," Mark said.

"Your mother? Near here? Where?" I asked.

"In the mausoleum. Her name was Cecilia Osborne."

"It was the funeral of your mother?" I asked. "Then you are—oh, Mark!" I closed my eyes. I couldn't look at him anymore.

"Stephen," he said. "My real name is Stephen James Osborne."

"You went to see her there, sometimes, in the night."

"Yes," he said.

"If you will excuse us, *my lord,*" the rector said, with a grin, "I believe that Miss Clair and I have some things to discuss." He turned to me. "That is, if you can get along without us for a little while, my dear."

"Yes," I said.

He got up and hurried out of the room, and Clair followed him. After that, Stephen and I sat silently looking at each other—neither of us wishing to speak.

"You must despise me," I said at last.

"No," he said.

After another silence, he came and sat down on the bed beside me and took my hand in his and held it to his cheek.

"It can't be this way," I said. I grasped his hand in both of mine and placed it on the blanket between us. "You see, your father was John Osborne. He was my father, too."

I will never forget the look on Stephen's face, then. The shocked disbelief that I saw there wrung my heart.

"That is what my mother told my stepfather at the ball," I explained. "That is why he struck her. That is partly why he wanted to get rid of me."

He had been looking deep into my eyes trying not to believe me. As I watched, he became the Mark I had known before. The veil of despair spread over his face again, his eyes froze, and his mouth lost its curve. For a long time he looked down at my hands, and then he disengaged himself gently and walked out of the room.

# Chapter Twenty-five

THE NEXT MORNING, Mrs. Hobson brought my breakfast on a tray and suggested that Clair might like to have hers at the table in the kitchen. So when I had finished eating, Clair took the tray, saying that she would be back after she had had her breakfast.

"Is Monk still out there?" I asked, as she went out the door.

"Goodness, no!" Clair said, turning toward me. "He went back to the Hall. He was overjoyed that Colonel Lawson—I mean Colonel Osborne was to be the earl of Trevenbury. I suppose, since your stepfather was an impostor, Colonel Osborne will be the eighth earl. It is all so hard to believe. Well, his new lordship told Monk that he would have a place at Warton Hall as long as he wanted it. Monk was a very happy little boy. You know, your stepfather had sacked Monk the night before last. I think he rather worships Colonel Osborne. I won't be long," she said, stepping out into the hallway.

"How is she this morning?" I heard the rector ask.

"Oh, she is much better—almost her old self again," Clair answered.

"Good morning. May I come in?" Mr. Ashley asked from the partly open doorway. "How does our patient feel this morning?"

He brought the chair and placed it beside the bed where it had been the day before.

"Like a fool," I answered.

The rector's eyebrows rose, but he said nothing. He sat down, crossed his legs, folded his hands in his lap, looked at me, and smiled.

"I don't know how I could have suspected Mark— Stephen—of being such a terrible person," I said, "and you of working with him. It was all—just—there, all of a sudden. I don't know when. I was sure that Stephen was working for my stepfather and that he had been employed to kill me, among other things. And I believed that you were helping him or at least were on his side. I know it sounds ridiculous now. You saved my life, and you have been so kind to me. I feel like such a stupid, ungrateful fool."

"Nonsense," the rector said. "What did make you suspect Osborne? I am curious."

"Well, I suppose it began the morning he had the meeting with my stepfather. I remember that I was surprised when he came out of my stepfather's office because my stepfather had told me he was going to Weymouth that day."

"You are sure that your stepfather was *in* his office and that there *was* a meeting?" he asked, his eyes twinkling.

"Oh, dear! You mean Stephen was in there alone? Searching through my stepfather's papers, I suppose. And he didn't want me to know. I hadn't thought of that. Well, anyway, then there were the mysterious visits to the mausoleum. Of course he had to go secretly, and it *was* his mother."

"Some people find great solace in being near a loved one that they have lost," the rector said.

"Then there was the lie about the house in Durham. Why did he say that?" I asked.

"Wellfield House was once owned by the Osbornes —two hundred years ago. I suppose it was the first place that came to mind that day. After all, he had to make up some story about his past."

"Yes. Then there was my stepfather's dinner party

on the night he tried to strangle me. How my step-father bragged about Mark, I mean Stephen. I can't get used to calling him Stephen. He bragged about me, too—how necessary I was to him. It was all to throw suspicion on Stephen and away from himself, of course. I see that now. Actually, a great deal of my suspicion came from my resentment of his always being at the Hall—that is, his affair with my mother. He was her lover. She told me so. I was jealous, truthfully, and hurt, and it was easy to believe the worst.

"But you must admit that my stepfather was very clever in throwing suspicion on Stephen. It was my stepfather who set fire to the barn so that he could drive the nails into my saddle undisturbed and undetected while everyone else was fighting the fire. He must have thought he could blame it on Stephen if necessary. And it was my stepfather who tried to strangle me—we know that now. How easy it must have been to leave his horse tied to a tree somewhere that night, creep up the back stairs, and wait in the dark for me to walk by. No wonder Mrs. Danley said it was a tall man—he stood on one of the steps leading to the corridor. Then, when it was over, all he had to do was run down and out of the house, get on Bourton, and ride back to the front of the house later. He had been out hunting the poacher all the time—or so it appeared.

"There is probably a military tailor somewhere in the vicinity where he could have gotten the gold cord."

"There is one in Exeter, I believe," said the rector. "And there are others nearby, I am sure. That would present no problem. What a truly vicious man. I don't believe anyone is *all* bad, but perhaps he came close to it. I am sorry, my dear."

"Don't be. I hated him. I shouldn't say it, but I can't be a hypocrite."

"Tell me about his coat," I asked. "Was it really in the—"

"Yes, it was there," the rector said. "We recognized it at once, of course. You see, you must have been bleeding a great deal from that gash on your head, and the blood had gotten all over your stepfather's coat. He must have thought that, since no one was going to find you, no one would find the coat either if he left it there. He had to get rid of it, naturally.

"He must have been a very strong man. His coat wasn't the only thing he left behind. There was a rope, also. Do you remember it?"

"No."

"It was tied around your waist when we found you. I suppose that was how he hoisted you upon his horse to take you to the mausoleum."

"But how did you find me?" I asked. "How did you know I was there?"

"It was Osborne who knew it," the rector said. "He returned to the rectory just after you left here the day before yesterday. Your mother had told him that she was afraid your stepfather wanted to kill you and put the blame on him, and she told him what you had told her about the gold cord. She said she couldn't imagine why her husband wanted to do such a thing and that she was very worried about it."

"I knew she would tell him about the cord," I said.

"Yes, well—then I told Osborne about the *two* attempts on your life, just as you told me, and we set out at once for Warton Hall to find you and bring you back here. I should never have let you leave that afternoon, but I couldn't think how to keep you here without telling you about Osborne. I should have told you at once, of course, but it all happened so quickly, and your story was such a shock to me. I wanted to talk to Osborne before I did anything. I knew you had Miss Clair with you, and it was still daylight, and I thought you would be safe for an hour or two.

"The first time we went to the Hall, Miss Clair told us about your going off in the fat man's carriage, and we went out to look for you. Then we went back to the Hall a second time to see if you had returned. Osborne went in, and when Apsley said you had not returned, he made some excuse and headed for your stepfather's office, looking for him. I waited outside with the horses. Then Osborne heard your voice in Mrs. Danley's room, but by the time he had gotten over the surprise and made up his mind to rush in, you had run out of the room, and your stepfather had run out after you, having just killed Mrs. Danley. As a matter of fact, Osborne saw your stepfather go out the other door to the spiral stair as he entered the room.

"Later, about an hour after we had lost you in the fog on the Abbey Road—"

"Oh, it *was* you," I interrupted. "I thought it might be Stephen, but I had no idea that you would be with him."

"Yes. Well, after we lost you, we returned to the Hall a third time. Osborne accused your stepfather of killing you as he had killed Mrs. Danley. Your stepfather accused Osborne of killing Mrs. Danley and said that she was alive when he left her and that he had lost you in the fog. He said he was sure you had run away, that you had disappeared, and that we could be certain that we would never see you again. He was practically bragging about it to our faces. You know how he loved to bask in his achievements."

"Yes, I certainly do." I said.

"Osborne had been to the mausoleum the night before," the rector continued, "and had found a tooth, of all grisly things, on the floor near the wall, together with wisps of rotten, torn cloth and some bits of dusty debris. He wondered what had been going on. He knew it was something strange, but it was late, and he didn't investigate. But then when your stepfather said 'disappear,' Osborne thought he knew. He reasoned that the way to make a person disappear would be to put him where no one would ever think of looking for him. No one would ever think of looking for a body where a body would already logically be. The perfect place to dispose of a body, then, would be in a coffin in a mausoleum. So we rode straight to the mausoleum, and when we got inside it, we heard your tapping. Thank God you were still alive. Osborne carried you here on High Point. You don't remember that?"

"No," I said.

"You know, if your stepfather hadn't been so positively evil, you might not still be alive. Have you thought of that?"

"I don't understand," I said.

"He didn't kill you. No, much worse—he left you to die slowly. How long you would have remained conscious is anybody's guess.

"But we must not think about that any more. It is all over, and all is well." Then after a pause, he said, "Tell me about this man Martin Shark."

I told him about our conversation in the carriage. "I wonder if the London police have really apprehended him, or if that was a clever bluff on Chief Constable Pritchard's part. I know one thing—as soon as I get well, I am going to London and to the police there, and if they haven't caught up with Mr. Shark, I shall go see him with some money, and the police will go with me. That man is a menace and should be in prison. I am sorry he can't be hanged for the murder of the seventh earl."

"It is all too incredible," the rector said. "You know, I was completely taken in by Fitzjames. Everyone was —the courts, the press, everybody. So when Osborne arrived and told me he was going to prove that your stepfather was an impostor, I told him he was wasting his time—that one can't prove what is right and true to be wrong and false. But he would try, and he concentrated on your mother. It was information he was after—I doubt that he was ever her lover. I felt the investigations could do him no harm, though I never ceased trying to discourage him.

"You see, his father died while he was in the Crimea, and his mother died the night he arrived home in London. So I was especially pleased to have him here to rest and recuperate from the shock of her death and the war.

"It is strange how things work out, isn't it? It rather strengthens one's belief in God, don't you agree?"

We sat silently for a few minutes, each absorbed in his own thoughts, and then the rector looked at me and said, "What has happened to Osborne? Yesterday when I left you here together, he was full of joy—happy, almost triumphant. But when I returned last evening, he was his old gloomy self. And you don't seem very happy, either. Did something happen between you two?"

"Yes," I said, returning his gaze. "Stephen told me who he really is, and I told him that his father was my father, too."

"What?" the rector asked.

"Stephen's father was also my father—that makes us half-brother and sister."

"But that is preposterous."

"That is what my mother told my stepfather at the ball. That was one of the reasons he wanted to kill me. You see, he must have become something of an expert in the laws of succession and inheritance while he plotted his hoax. He must have realized immediately that I could come into the estates by petition, and if I were to prove him a fraud, with Mr. Shark's help, well. . . . Of course he had no idea that Stephen Osborne was still alive."

"I see," the rector said.

"And now I wonder what is going to happen to me?" I said. "I suppose I could teach, but that seems a bleak future. And I certainly cannot afford to keep Clair with me. Where will she go?"

"Let it wait a bit until you are fully recovered. Sometimes things take care of themselves. We never know what the future will hold, so don't worry about it. And you must know that I will always help you."

Shortly after the rector left me, he rode out toward Warton Hall. Clair left me soon after that. She meant to fetch a nightgown and robe from Warton Hall for me, one or two things for herself, and some of our toilet things. And I asked her to bring the little box that contained my jewels and letters.

She returned shortly after I had finished the luncheon that Mrs. Hobson had brought on a tray.

"Adam drove me," Clair said, as she entered the room. "The servants were at their dinner, so I was able to go through the kitchen-yard door without being seen. The servants' hall door was closed, thank goodness. I used one of your bags and brought these two nightgowns for you and your wine-colored robe. Will you want to change into one of these now, miss? Which will it be? The pink one?"

"Yes, thank you, Clair."

She laid the pink gown across the bottom of the bed, went to the armoire, and hung up the yellow one and the robe.

Then she said, "Let me hang these in my room, and I will come right back."

She reached into the bag and took out her comb, brushes, and toilet things and ran into the room next to mine, carrying her nightgown and a dress.

"There now, I will help you into this," she said, when she returned.

I sat on the edge of the bed, then stood up, and Clair helped me change nightgowns.

And as she did so, she said, "Your room at the Hall was a *sight!* Your dresses were all tossed about, and everything was thrown out of your drawers onto the floor. I brought your box. It had been broken open, and the jewels had been tossed aside and the letters rifled, but I collected everything I could find and put it all back. It looked like a burglary, but nothing was missing."

"It must have been my stepfather," I said. "That is how he got the piece of gold cord, but he was really looking for Mr. Shark's copy of the marriage register page. I wonder where it is? The day before yesterday in Mrs. Danley's room, he accused me of having stolen it. He tried to force me to tell him what I had done with it. He was a little mad—I am sure of it. I will never forget the vicious look in his eyes when he twisted my arm. Thank God I got away. How could I tell him what I didn't know?"

"It is best not to think of it, miss," Clair said.

"Yes, it is all over. Help me into the robe now, please. I would like to walk a few steps and sit up for a while. Oh, and you brought my slippers. Whatever am I going to do without you?" I said. She helped me into the robe, and I stepped into the slippers. "I won't be able to keep you with me, now. I won't have the money."

"Do you think you should be out of bed so soon?" she said, walking beside me to the chair by the window.

"I am really feeling very strong— Oh, a bit unsteady on my feet, but lying in bed won't help that."

"Don't you worry about me, miss. I know you will give me a good character, and I will find another place easily enough. But what about you? What will you do?"

"I don't know, Clair. I haven't really given it much thought—teach, I suppose."

Just then I heard a horse approaching. I looked out of the window and saw my mother riding up the drive on Lady Jane.

"What is she doing here?" I wondered aloud. "I

371

don't want to see her. I don't think I want to see her again, ever. That is a terrible thing to say, isn't it? Close the door, Clair, please."

Clair closed the door, and we sat in silence. After a few moments, we heard the distant drone of voices. Then someone climbed the stairs and knocked on the door.

"May I come in?" the rector asked.

"Yes," I called.

"Ah, you are up and dressed," he said. "I am so glad." Then he paused a little awkwardly. "Your mother is downstairs. Do you think you could come down for a few minutes if I help you? I believe she has something to tell you."

"Yes, I could come down, but I don't wish to, rector. I do not wish to see her."

"I think you should, my child," he said. "Will you trust me in this, and let me help you down the stairs? It will only be for a few minutes."

I thought how much I owed him. "Very well," I said, standing up, and I began walking slowly toward the door. "I shan't be long, Clair."

We walked to the stairs and slowly down them. The rector put his arm around my waist, and I put my hand on his shoulder to steady myself. I realized, then, that I was still very weak.

"You don't seem very happy to see me, Mark," Mother said.

I could hear her distinctly. Her velvety voice carried perfectly to us as we made our way down the corridor to the drawing room.

"Stephen," Stephen said.

"Stephen, then. I am *so* happy for you, but why didn't you tell me, dear? I would have *helped* you. One does help the one she loves, you know."

"Does she?" Stephen said.

"You know she does, but you were quite right—I

wouldn't have believed a word of it if you had told me. I could never have lived with Fitz if I had known he was a fraud, you must realize that. It has all been such a complete surprise and a terrible shock. That man Shark—was that his name? A common criminal forger and my husband—I feel so cheap and humiliated, and it will be such a tiresome scandal when it all comes out. These last days have been so dreadful," she murmured, and I could imagine the helpless-doll expression on her face and her hand going to her temple as she spoke.

"But we have the future, darling—you and I," she continued. "This might interest you, my sweet. I found it among my husband's things. You should have it, of course."

By then the rector and I had reached the drawing room doorway, and I saw my mother standing with her back to me, facing Stephen. He held a folded piece of paper in his hand. He unfolded it, but sensing that someone had entered the room, he looked up at me.

Mother turned around to follow his gaze. When she saw me, her eyes opened wide, her right hand grasped her forehead, and she opened her mouth to scream. But no sound came. She stood, frozen still, staring at me.

We walked toward her across the room, and even when Mother and I stood facing each other, she seemed unable to move.

"Did you think I was dead, Mother?" I asked. "Didn't they tell you I was alive?"

I walked past her to the chair by the fire and, with Stephen's help, sank into it. Mother continued to stare at me.

"You had better sit down, Lillian," the rector said. "Won't you sit here?"

After we had sat looking at each other for some time, she said, "Yes, I thought you were dead."

"This is very interesting," Stephen said. He had

been examining the paper that Mother had given him. "Do you recognize this, Suzanne?" he asked.

He handed me Martin Shark's copy of the marriage register page from Berkley Church.

"How much that would have meant to me, Lillian," he continued, pointing at it, "if you had given it to me a month ago. How grateful I would have been then, but now I find it only mildly interesting. Thank you, none the less."

"But it is the proof that my husband had no claim—" Mother began.

"I know that, Lillian," Stephen interrupted, "but it should be obvious to you that, even if his claim to the title had been legal, the inheritance would have become mine at your husband's death. I am the next of kin." He took the paper that I handed back to him, and he shook it at my mother. "This is proof that you forfeit your dower rights as an impostor's wife, that you are not, and never were Lady Trevenbury— merely Mrs. Cobbe."

"But darling, I only want to help. Now we can look forward to the future, our future together. Give it back, and I will put it with Fitz's things for—"

"It is only a copy, Stephen," I said.

"I know that," he said, "but I am sure it is indistinguishable from the original and so, equally useful." He folded it and put it in his pocket. "Who could prove it a copy? Only Martin Shark. How? Only by producing the original, which I wish he would do, though I doubt that he will."

"I suppose you kept the letters with that document," I said to Mother, as I gestured to Stephen's pocket.

"Letters?" she said.

"The letters that prove my father was John Osborne. I should think my stepfather would have wanted the letters as well as the copy of the register page. You say the copy was with his things? But if that were so, why was he searching so frantically for it? Was he also searching for the letters?"

"Letters," Mother said, rising from her chair. "Where did you find the document? Why was he doing this, that, or the other? I don't see that it could possibly matter now. I must be going."

"There are no letters," the rector said. "Please sit down, Lillian. We are not finished."

"Paul!" she said, surprised at his tone.

"Sit *down,* Lillian," he said.

Mother sat down as a peevish little girl would.

"These two young people," the rector said, "are under the impression that Suzanne's father was John Osborne. I suggest you tell them who he really is. Tell them now."

"Very well, Paul," Mother replied, looking casually at me. "His name is Paul Ashley. Reverend Paul Ashley is your father, Suzanne. You may thank him for being responsible, financially and otherwise, for your education all these years both here and in France. This can easily be verified by checking with the schools if you don't believe me—not that it makes any difference, really. Are you satisfied, Paul? May I go now?"

"Why didn't you tell me?" I asked my father.

"Would you have believed me, my dear?" he answered. "Yes? Well, I thought it best that your mother tell you herself."

Then I turned back to my mother. "But you told my stepfather that my father's name was John Osborne. You told him that at the ball. And you told him there were letters to prove it. Why?"

"I lied, obviously," Mother said. "Surely you must know why, Suzanne. Please don't be tiresome. I have a headache."

"You wanted him to—"

"My dear, I warned you in the carriage that night on the way home from Mendley House. You really should have taken my advice."

"I suppose you thought a natural child could inherit under English law."

"Of course," she said.

"And you told my stepfather that I had stolen the marriage register page and the letters?"

"Yes. That is really quite brilliant of you," she said, leaning her head on the back of her chair and closing her eyes. Two fingers of her right hand touched her temple.

"I see," I said. "If you will excuse me—father, Stephen, I think I shall go back upstairs now."

"May I help you?" Stephen asked.

"Thank you, but there is no need. Clair will help me if you call her."

"Ashley," Stephen said, "Suzanne and I are going to be married—that is, if she will have me. I know we have your blessing. Suzanne, a wife must learn to obey her husband. I am going to ask you a question, and you will answer, 'Yes, Stephen.'"

"May I help you upstairs, Suzanne?"

"Yes, Stephen—darling," I replied.